"What do I
he

"The golden ribbon from your left sleeve, to — the others I have already won," Kat replied with a smile.

"If we continue, all my clothes will fall to your feet." Untying the satin ribbon, he held it out to her. "You would not wish to see me so...at one with nature, would you?" he murmured as he drew closer still.

The idea of him standing stark naked before her both startled and fascinated Kat. Their fingers touched, and a dizzying current raced through her as if her blood had suddenly begun to boil.

"Perish the thought, sire! Our weather here is most unpredictable. You might find you'd catch a sudden chill."

He took the ribbon from her shaking fingers, tied it in a love knot over her pulse point, then sealed the knot with a feather-light kiss. "Then perchance you might find it in your heart to keep me warm?" he whispered, the gleam in his eye turning to blue flames.

Dear Reader,

It's June, so start thinking about your summer reading! Whether you're going to the beach or simply going to relax on the porch, don't forget to bring along a Harlequin Historical® novel. And speaking of summer, we are thrilled to present *Midsummer's Knight* from award-winning author Tori Phillips. Critics have described Tori's books as "superb," "electrifying" and "not to be missed!" In this delightfully mischievous sequel to *Silent Knight,* which earned 4¹/₂★ from *Affaire de Coeur,* a confirmed bachelor and a reluctant widow betrothed against their will switch identities with their friends to spy on the other, and fall in love in the process!

When a young woman kills her stepfather in self-defense, she flees, only to be discovered by a kind cowboy who takes her back to his parents' Missouri home as his "wife," in *Runaway* by the popular Carolyn Davidson. And in *Widow Woman,* a compelling Western by longtime Silhouette author Patricia McLinn, a beautiful rancher must win back the heart of her ex-foreman—the man she once refused to marry and the unknowing father of her child.

Laurel Ames returns with *Infamous,* her eighth book for us. In this fun and frothy Regency, a dashing nobleman and spy, having put up with a very silly and snobbish mother and sister all his life, finally meets a woman he feels is worth pursuing—much to his family's chagrin!

Whatever your tastes in reading, you'll be sure to find a romantic journey back to the past between the covers of a Harlequin Historical® novel.

Sincerely,

Tracy Farrell
Senior Editor

Please address questions and book requests to:
Silhouette Reader Service
U.S.: 3010 Walden Ave., P.O. Box 1325, Buffalo, NY 14269
Canadian: P.O. Box 609, Fort Erie, Ont. L2A 5X3

Midsummer's Knight

Tori Phillips

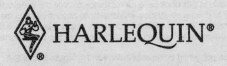

HARLEQUIN®

TORONTO • NEW YORK • LONDON
AMSTERDAM • PARIS • SYDNEY • HAMBURG
STOCKHOLM • ATHENS • TOKYO • MILAN • MADRID
PRAGUE • WARSAW • BUDAPEST • AUCKLAND

ISBN 0-373-29015-2

MIDSUMMER'S KNIGHT

Copyright © 1998 by Mary W. Schaller

This edition published by arrangement with Harlequin Books S.A.

® and TM are trademarks of the publisher. Trademarks indicated with ® are registered in the United States Patent and Trademark Office, the Canadian Trade Marks Office and in other countries.

Printed in U.S.A.

Books by Tori Phillips

Harlequin Historicals

Fool's Paradise #307
Silent Knight #343
Midsummer's Knight #415

TORI PHILLIPS

After receiving her degree in theater arts from the University of San Diego, Tori worked at MGM Studios, acted in numerous summer stock musicals and appeared in Paramount Pictures' *The Great Gatsby*. Her plays, published by Dramatic Publishing Co., have been produced in the U.S. and Canada, and her poetry is included in several anthologies. She has directed over forty plays, including twenty-one Shakespearean productions. Currently she is a first-person, Living History actress at the Folger Shakespeare Library in Washington, D.C. She lives with her husband in Burke, Virginia.

"There was a star danced, and under that was I born."
—*Much Ado About Nothing*

This book is dedicated with a great deal of love to our first grandchild, Konrad Martin Schaller, born March 22, 1997. He rode to earth on the tail of a comet and decided to stay.

Chapter One

Why, this is very midsummer madness.
—*Twelfth Night*

Hampton Court, England
May 1530

"Ma...marriage?" Sir Brandon Cavendish, gentleman of the king's bedchamber, stammered out the loathsome word. His stomach twisted into a hard knot.

Even though he was winning the set, Brandon lowered his racket. A tennis ball whipped by him, missing his ear by inches. He barely noticed its passing. "Me, your grace?"

His opponent, Henry, the eighth of that name and king of England, roared with glee. "My point, Cavendish! Ha! Have I ruffled your fine feathers at last?"

Brandon flexed his broad shoulders. "Nay, sire! I see you are jesting to put me off my game." At least, Brandon hoped that was the king's only motive for introducing such a vile subject on such a lovely day.

Henry's answering laughter reverberated around the dark green wooden walls of Hampton Court's tennis hall.

"Aye, I would put you off your game, my lord, but we do not speak of tennis. Look you, second service!" With that barked warning, the king drew back and fired another buff-colored ball at his victim.

This time Brandon managed to return the serve, but without his usual strength. God's nightshirt! What piece of deviltry was the king up to now? His Grace seemed to be in unusually good spirits, even if he was down by two sets. Brandon mopped the perspiration out of his eyes with the loose, frilled sleeve of his shirt, then ran his fingers through his damp blond hair.

"This game is mine, sire, though I warrant you took that last point most unfairly."

"How so, Cavendish?" The king crossed to the side gallery where a page waited with silver goblets and a pitcher of chilled wine. "I think you are growing fat with old age."

Brandon bit the tip of his tongue lest he point out that the king was both older and more stout than he. Brandon knew just how far he dared to go when speaking to the large, perspiring man next to him. Great Harry played the part of the bluff and hearty sportsman, but underneath that smiling exterior, there lurked a vain and vicious temper. What was the loss of a game or two of tennis to the loss of one's place in court—or worse?

Brandon drank deeply from his goblet. The crisp white wine cleared his throat of dust, and of the sour taste that the mere thought of marriage always left in his mouth. He knew he was poor husband material; his interest in wooing a woman never lasted longer than a fortnight. He wiped his lips with the back of his hand. "'Tis unfair to speak of wedded bliss to a man when he is at serious play, your grace," he remarked mildly.

The king's gray eyes twinkled behind the narrow folds of his lids. "Aye, but in this matter, I am serious, Cavendish."

Taking a deep breath, Brandon tried to clear the humming in his ears. "If you speak to me of marriage, sire, I fear you toss your words into the wind." *I would tire of a wife in a month's time.*

The king's thin lips pursed under his red mustache. "Ha! This bachelor state does not please your father."

Brandon groaned inwardly. What had his sire done now?

"Last week, Sir Thomas sent me a long letter, begging my assistance in a grave family matter." Henry signaled the page to pour another round. "It seems that you have turned a deaf ear to all his entreaties concerning your future."

A very unfilial thought crossed Brandon's mind. Why couldn't his well-meaning father have left him alone? "My future is to serve your pleasure here at court, your grace," he replied, picking his words with care.

"Aye, and so you shall—but not at court." With a roar of laughter, the king whacked Brandon between the shoulder blades.

Brandon nearly slopped his drink on the king's brown suede shoes. He licked his dry lips. "May I know what boon my father has asked of you, your grace?" *Do not saddle me with a wife, I pray.*

"Aha! Now you have hit upon the subject of my speech, you wily rogue!" He gave Brandon another bone-crunching whack. "The good Earl of Thornbury has grown tired of waiting for his firstborn to choose a bride and settle down. He has grown weary of requesting you to do so. In his wisdom, he has turned to me, his king and liege lord." Henry's brow furrowed and his countenance grew dark. "How well I know the yearning for an heir!"

The nearby spectators in the gallery went deathly still. Not even Brandon dared to respond to such a dangerous statement. The king's frantic desire for a son to succeed him had sent the saintly but sonless Queen Catherine to a distant manor in the midlands. In her place, Viscount Rochford's younger daughter, Lady Anne Boleyn, kept Henry and his court dancing to her tune with her promise to give the man she married a house full of sons. The subjects of marriage and heirs constantly played a raucous tune in the king's besotted mind. Henry's Great Matter, as he called it, obsessed him.

Now, thanks to the prompting of Sir Thomas Cavendish, that obsession had turned outward, and Brandon did not like the direction in which it was aimed.

"The choosing of a wife is not a thing to be taken lightly," Brandon murmured, not daring to look the king in the eye. He twirled the handle of his racket in his hand. "And certainly not when there is still one more game to be played." He prayed that Henry would drop the uncomfortable subject.

"You speak the truth, Cavendish." The king's mood brightened again. "And your last game draws apace."

Licking his lips again, Brandon wished for a third cup of wine. The wicked gleam in Great Harry's eyes unnerved him. "A game of tennis, your grace?" he bantered.

The courtiers in the gallery, including many of the ladies with whom Brandon had flirted over the years, leaned forward to hear the king's reply. Lady Anne Boleyn and her companion, Lady Olivia Bardolph, smiled openly at Cavendish's discomfort.

"A pox on tennis, you clodpate!" roared the king, his voice shaking the rafters of the tennis hall. A wide grin spread across his thin lips. "I speak of the marriage game—for you, my fine friend. Since you have danced out of Cupid's way for many years now—" the king swept a glance over the colorful, bejeweled company in the gallery "—much to the disappointment of many a fair lady here, we have taken it upon ourselves to arrange a match."

Brandon gritted his teeth as he heard a breeze of female tittering behind him. "A wife for me, sire?" His heart thudded within his chest. "You have so many affairs of state, your grace. My father's request will take up too much of your most valuable time."

"Let your fears take flight, Cavendish! 'Tis done!"

"The match is already arranged?" The humming sound grew louder in his mind.

The king's laughter drowned out everyone else's. "Aye! And to a fine lady with a fat estate in Sussex. Lady Katherine Fitzhugh of Bodiam Castle! By my command, Cavendish, you shall wed her on Midsummer's Day. The banns were proclaimed this morning at Lambeth Palace by the Archbishop of Canterbury himself. This week, you will ride into Sussex to woo your betrothed."

The laughter, which filled the cavernous tennis hall, could not drown out the hammering of Brandon's heart. Marriage to an unknown lady in less than a month? An end to his freedom? Why had his father decided that he needed another heir? Several children already scampered around the family home at Wolf Hall in Northumberland. Brandon saw no reason to take a wife. He had enough domestic responsibilities as it was.

Belle, his daughter, would turn the household into a merry hell if Brandon brought home a new mother. And what of Francis Bardolph, his page? Brandon cast a quick glance at the boy's self-absorbed mother who sat in the gallery. Francis didn't suspect his true parentage as yet, but daily he grew to look more and more like a Cavendish. How could Brandon present an unsuspecting bride with two love children?

"What ho!" cried the king to his amused court. "Regard my Lord Cavendish! He looks like a great, goggle-eyed turbot caught in a net. Perchance you have won this tennis game, knave of hearts—but methinks, I have won the match! Ha!"

"Sweet angels! What have I done to deserve this fate?" Lady Katherine Fitzhugh sank to the cold comfort of one of the stone benches in her rose garden at Bodiam Castle. She fanned herself with the parchment she held in her hand. The letter dripped with the thick, red wax seal of the king himself.

Miranda Paige, Kat's gentle cousin and companion, abandoned her trug basket on the newly turned flower bed. "Sweet Kat, is it ill news from court? What has that peevish nephew done now?"

"Marriage," Kat managed to gasp when she got her breath back. The bodice laces of her green gown had suddenly become too tight.

"Fenton has married without your knowledge?" Taking out her handkerchief, Miranda began to flap it in front of Kat's face.

"Nay, nay, worse than that!" Kat reread the king's missive, in the vain hope that she had misunderstood his message. Alas, she had not. "God shield me, Miranda, I am doomed."

"Shall I call Montjoy to help you to your bed, coz?" Miranda stopped waving her handkerchief, much to Kat's relief. "Do you require a cordial for a headache? Shall I call—"

Kat cut her off. "Call down thunderbolts and hail to rain on Hampton Court, Miranda! Send a storm of fiery arrows into every bleating idiot who utters the word 'marriage' to me!" Remembering her two disastrous forays into matrimony, she shuddered.

"Who is to be married?" Miranda asked, taking Kat's hand in hers and giving it a squeeze. "Is it me?"

Despite her distress engendered by the king's command, Kat smiled into her cousin's hopeful eyes. Poor Miranda! Ignoring the unhappy examples of Kat's late husbands, she had always harbored a childish romantic fantasy of true love.

"Am I to have a husband at last?" Miranda prodded,

craning her neck so that she could read the letter in Kat's hand.

"I wish that were so! Nay, 'tis I the king commands."

"To marry him?" Miranda's jaw all but dropped. "But he is already wed to good Queen Catherine these past twenty years—and they say he has a paramour besides."

"Nay, Miranda! 'Tis to some popinjay of the court named..." Kat consulted the letter again. "Sir Brandon Cavendish, eldest son of the Earl of Thornbury—whomever *that* might be. After the good Lord saw fit to take Fitzhugh to his eternal reward—"

"May God have mercy upon his soul," Miranda murmured at the name of Kat's second husband.

"Save your breath! That man is roasting his backside upon the devil's spit!" Kat closed her eyes in the effort to blot out her last memory of Edward Fitzhugh's face, mottled with insane rage.

Miranda quickly made a sign of the cross. "'Tis bad luck to speak ill of the dead, Kat. Say a prayer!"

"Say one for me," Kat retorted. "Fitzhugh heard enough of my prayers and pleading during his lifetime. I shall not taint my mouth any further for his sake." She shook the king's letter, causing the red seal to bounce merrily on its white satin ribbon. "These past two years have been a paradise for me. After surviving two such husbands as mine, I had hoped to spend the rest of my life in gardening, and caring for my people. I did not expect to be saddled with yet another piece of vermin such as this...Cavendish! I will never be any man's property again!"

"Perchance he will be different," Miranda suggested, a faraway look glazing her green eyes.

"Perchance the piglets in yonder sty shall sprout feathered wings and fly! Bah! I am sick to death of husbands!"

"You could write to the king and beg him to change his mind," Miranda suggested in a soothing tone.

Kat snorted. "Ha! An angel from heaven would be unable to dissuade His Grace once he has made his decision. Alack, I am undone, Miranda!"

Miranda picked up the parchment from the bench where Kat had dropped it. She ran her finger across the name of the suitor. "I wish you could give him to me. I am willing to take a chance."

"You are moonstruck, dear coz. Marriage is heaven for a man, but hell for the woman. All husbands want are housekeepers and broodmares." Kat chewed her lower lip as she thought of her barren womb. "Our good king has got marriage on the brain. He should settle his own affairs. Let him marry the Boleyn woman, and leave me in peaceful widowhood."

"Hush, sweet coz!" Miranda glanced over her shoulder. "'Tis not wise to speak of the king in such a disrespectful manner, even here."

Kat sighed. "Aye, gentle coz, you give me good counsel. But what am I going to do with this horse's backside who claims me?"

"When does the letter say he arrives?"

"'Twas written a week ago Monday. The king states that I should expect to receive this Lord Cavendish very soon. Sweet angels! For all I know, the man could be here by supper time today!" Kat rose and began to pace up and down the crushed shell path of the rose garden. She must find a way out of this marriage, or else her hard-won happiness would soon vanish like snowflakes in July.

"Mayhap he will get lost along the way here," her cousin suggested with a grin.

"Peace, Miranda. This marriage is no laughing matter. I wish I could spy out this proffered husband, then I would know better how to deal with him." She could not face a loveless marriage again.

Returning to her task of pulling weeds, Miranda sang a child's silly tune. "'A Cavendish came a-hunting in the wood, to-woo, but the white-tailed doe was not at home, to-woo. The Cavendish came a-hunting in the wood, and though his aim was true and good, he shot a rabbit and not the doe, to-woo.' ''

Pausing at the end of the path, Kat cocked her head, as Miranda repeated the nonsense song under her breath. An outlandish idea bubbled up in Kat's mind. Her grin deepened into trilling laughter. The sound startled Miranda out of her song.

"Sweet lark, you have hit it! I have the very plan when this Cavendish comes a-wooing!" Grabbing her cousin's hand, Kat pulled her out of the flower bed. "Come, we squander the precious daylight with our idle chatter. There is much work to be done."

"What did I say?" Miranda asked as Kat hurried them back to the castle. "What are we going to do?"

"To exchange a doe for a rabbit!" she answered with a mischievous grin.

"They have gone, my lord." Tod Wormsley tweaked his master's bedsheet. "'Tis safe to come out."

Poking forth his head from under the covers, Sir Fenton Scantling glowered at the door of his small chamber. God's teeth! How dare those London merchants send their hirelings into the king's palace here at Hampton Court to seek Fenton and loudly demand payment of his bills! Fenton hoped that no one of importance had heard the ruckus. How dare those minions call him such disgraceful things through the keyhole!

Fenton kicked away the rest of the covers, then swung his legs over the side of the bed. He studied his reflection in the glass that hung on the wall opposite him. He brushed the wrinkles out of his sleeveless doublet made of a rich mulberry brocade and straightened the slim gold chain that hung around his neck. His sniveling body servant, Wormsley, stood behind Fenton and fluffed out his white silken puff sleeves that had become crushed under the bedclothes.

"This color suits me, does it not, Wormsley?" Fenton mused as he leaned closer to the glass to inspect his teeth. Good. No unsightly remnant of food clung there from the noonday dinner.

"Right well," Wormsley murmured, holding out Fenton's flat hat fashioned in a matching shade of velvet mulberry. He curled the cream-colored feather through his fingers. "And costly, if those tailors who came to call are to be believed."

Wheeling on his servant, Fenton raised his hand to strike him for his impudent tongue. Then he thought better of it, as the youth regarded him with a smug expression. *One day, churl, you shall push me too far.* "By that gleam in your eye, Worm, there is something in the wind. Out with it!"

Wormsley blew on the feather, causing it to flutter. "Since you stayed in London until late last night, you have not heard the news."

"Has the king finally gotten his bloody divorce? Or has Mistress Anne Boleyn announced that she is with child? Ha! That would set the whole court in an uproar!"

"Neither, my lord. The news I speak of pales next to the king's Great Matter, but it touches upon you personally." Wormsley flicked an invisible speck of dust off the cap.

Fenton itched to wipe the hint of a smile from the rogue's mouth. "Out with it, varlet! I have no patience today to play the fool with you."

Wormsley ran his tongue around his lips before replying. "There is to be a marriage, my lord. The groom is none other than Sir Brandon Cavendish—"

Fenton burst out laughing at this surprise. "So the knave of hearts has been trapped at last! Did he get some poor damsel with child? Has her father threatened to kill him?

Ha! I cannot wait to rub this in his face. I warrant, he does not go to the altar willingly. This is news, indeed!''

Wormsley cleared his throat. ''It is an arranged match requested by Sir Brandon's father and commanded by Great Harry himself. The bride is no maiden, though she is quite wealthy. We speak of your aunt, Lady Katherine Fitzhugh, and the wedding date is in four weeks—on the twenty-fourth of June, Midsummer's Day.''

Fenton's tiny ruffled collar suddenly choked him. He couldn't breathe. He opened his mouth but no sound emerged. He pointed to the half-empty flagon of wine on the side table. Wormsley filled one of the gray-and-blue salt-glazed cups to the brim with the deep red burgundy. Fenton drank it down in one gulp, though its slightly sour taste curdled the back of his tongue.

What had Fenton ever done to deserve these ill tidings? Hadn't he been a dutiful, though often absent, nephew to Kat? Hadn't he always been polite enough to that mewling cousin of hers, Miranda? Didn't he always bring them a little present or two whenever he had to visit Bodiam— when his funds had run low again? How he had danced the galliard when his late, unlamented Uncle Edward had worked himself into a fatal stroke two years ago! In due time, all those prosperous estates and rents of Bodiam Castle should be his as Kat's only heir. Marriage to a healthy—and lusty—stallion like Cavendish would ruin his hopes of a wealthy future.

''My lord, are you well?'' Wormsley asked, pouring another cup of the vile drink.

''Are you brainsick?'' Fenton roared back at him. He quaffed the wine. ''Of course, I am not well. Nor should you be, for where my fortune and fate go, yours will follow. Where is Cavendish now? Has he left Hampton Court yet?''

''Nay. He tarries, hoping that the king will change his mind.''

Fenton paused in his fuming. A slow smile cracked his lips. "Then the match does not sit well upon the bridegroom's shoulders?"

"I hear that he all but fainted on the tennis court when the king informed him of his future happiness."

Chuckling, Fenton rubbed his palms together. "I can well imagine, considering his amorous reputation with the ladies. This is better than I first thought." He snatched up his cap and set it at a jaunty angle on his head. "I shall seek out Sir Brandon and have a little talk with him pertaining to family matters. Look for me after supper, though I may tarry awhile at the gaming tables. God's breath, suddenly I feel that fortune smiles upon me this day."

Locating Cavendish was not difficult, despite the maze of galleries at Hampton. Every tongue at court wagged of Sir Brandon's romantic downfall. The closer Fenton drew to his quarry, the more tales he heard whispered behind lace fans and perfumed handkerchiefs. Fenton found his man deep in conversation with Sir John Stafford, his boon companion. The two lounged under one of the arches in the palace's cobbled courtyard.

The knights were as alike as most brothers. As tall as the king himself, both men boasted the blond hair, broad shoulders and slim hips that made the women of Hampton Court, from countess to scullery maid, hungry to gaze upon them. When the king's golden duo strode by, other men straightened their own postures. Before confronting the pair, Fenton pulled back his shoulders and lifted his chin a notch. Though they spoke in low tones, he caught the tail end of their discussion.

"Take good heed, my friend," Stafford counseled Brandon. "Though your father might be swayed to forget this marriage, you know the king will not. Nothing annoys our sovereign lord more than the idea of not getting his own way. Be wise. The anger of our most noble prince means death.'' The speaker caught sight of Fenton. ''Here comes a flattering rascal.''

Stifling his contempt at that description, Fenton executed a flourishing bow. ''Good day, my Lord Stafford, my Lord Cavendish—or should I call you my uncle Brandon, since we are soon to be related?''

A thunderous expression crossed Cavendish's face as both men returned Fenton's bow.

Good. My unwilling uncle-to-be is as unhappy over this match as I am—perhaps even more so.

''What ill wind blew you here, Scantling?'' Cavendish rumbled.

Fenton took a small, prudent step backward.

''Judging from the odor that hangs about him, I would say he came directly from the haunts of the London stews.'' Stafford's clear blue eyes sparkled with merriment at Fenton's displeasure.

Fenton forced a wide smile across his trembling lips. ''Gentlemen, gentlemen, I do protest your unwarranted remarks. Especially as I have made it my urgent business to forewarn you, my Lord Cavendish, before you seek my aunt's favor.''

''What are you prattling about, Scantling?'' Brandon growled. His chiseled features furrowed with barely concealed impatience.

Drawing closer to the men, Fenton lowered his voice. '''Tis Lady Katherine, Sir Brandon. I feel it best you know about her before—''

Gripping Fenton's shoulder, Cavendish shook him like a wet rag. His fingers bit painfully through the thickness of Fenton's padded brocade. The young man chewed his lower lip to keep from swearing a loud oath in Cavendish's face. Best not to annoy a wounded bear.

''Out with it, man! Is she poxed?'' Brandon shook him again.

"Nay!" Fenton winced. "As far as I know, she is pure as snow. 'Tis her age I speak of."

Brandon released his grip on Fenton's shoulder. "You babble riddles to me, and I am not in the mood for games." He lowered his face to Fenton's. "I am more in mind to stab something—soft. Be plain and quick. My dagger itches to be free of its sheath."

Fenton swallowed. Cavendish's forthcoming marriage had certainly soured his usual good humor. "'Tis this, my lord. My Aunt Katherine is…er…quite old. Indeed, I am much surprised that the king chose her for you. She is past the time of childbearing. And she has always been barren—at least, with her first two husbands."

"How old?" Brandon exploded the words out of his mouth.

Fenton allowed himself a small laugh. "Ah, you of all people should know the ladies, Sir Brandon. They are forever changing the dates of their births to suit their purposes. I cannot say my aunt's exact age. But I think she is closer to your lady mother than to you." He coughed behind his hand to hide his grin.

Cavendish said nothing, but stared out across the courtyard at the chapel windows gleaming in the midafternoon sunlight.

"*Two* husbands, you say?" Lord Stafford whistled through his teeth. "Pray, what happened to them?"

Fenton controlled his glee. Like massive trout, these mighty lords were rising to his colorful bait. "I am surprised! Did no one tell you that my aunt had been married before?"

Brandon threaded his fingers through Fenton's chain. He tightened his hold on it, pulling the younger man closer. Fenton prayed the golden links would not break. The chain had cost him several months' allowance.

Icy danger lurked within the depths of Cavendish's startling blue eyes. "Tell me now," Brandon murmured in a warning tone.

Fenton inhaled a deep breath. "Aunt Kat was first married to my Lord Thomas Lewknor. They say he took sick on their wedding night, and then spent eighteen painful months in bed. Nursed, of course, by my good aunt. He died finally—foaming at the mouth," Fenton added for good measure.

A look of horror crossed Cavendish's face.

"And her second husband?" prompted Stafford.

"'Twas Sir Edward Fitzhugh."

"I knew of him." Brandon narrowed his eyes. "He was a brawler of the first order, as I recall, and had a temper like wildfire. I knew he often beat his servants. I felt sorry for the lady who was married to him."

The softened tone in Brandon's voice did not suit Fenton's purpose at all. "Aye, you speak the truth. My step-uncle was the devil's own spawn. 'Tis no wonder that my aunt grew weary of him. Even an angel would have lost patience with Fitzhugh the Furious." Fenton lowered his voice. "They say he died of a sudden stroke in his brain."

He allowed the implied accusation to hang unspoken in the air before he continued. "I had just come up to court at the time, so I cannot speak from personal knowledge as to the exact manner of his death. Fitzhugh was buried under the chapel stones by the time I had returned to Bodiam Castle." He did not mention that it was six months after Fitzhugh's death before he had found time to visit his widowed aunt. No need to muddle the tale with petty details.

"I see." Cavendish's blue eyes took on a cloudy aspect. Fenton had no idea if this change boded good or bad for his intent. Licking his lips again, he plunged on. "I thought to warn you, my lord. After all, two husbands have met with dubious endings while in Aunt Katherine's care."

Brandon turned his full attention back to Fenton. "You

have done well to speak to me. I am in your debt, my lord.''

''Once the king understands your concerns of marriage with my aunt, I am sure he will change his mind, and match you with another, more agreeable lady,'' Fenton suggested smoothly.

''Who knows what the king will do, save God and the Lady Anne Boleyn? But I shall pursue the matter.'' Brandon bowed. ''Your servant, sir.''

Fenton returned the courtesy. ''God give you a pleasant day, my lords.'' He left the two golden giants with the thoughts he had planted. Now to pen a loving note to dear Aunt Kat, and warn her of the lecherous fortune hunter coming her way. If Sir Brandon failed to move the king against this marriage, Lady Katherine Fitzhugh would surely do the task.

Brandon watched Scantling's thin figure retreat down the colonnade. He curled his lips with distaste.

Stafford whistled again. ''An old crone who is a husband killer? Zounds, Brandon! You have landed in a fine pickle barrel this time.''

Brandon rubbed his chin. ''Perchance, but consider the source of this news.'' He hated to admit that Scantling's wasp tongue had stung him.

Jack met Brandon's gaze. ''I heard that Scantling's creditors grow daily in number, especially since your forthcoming marriage has been broadcast.''

''Aye.'' Brandon nodded. ''Scantling's resources are very slender, and his waste is great. Methinks the devoted nephew speaks with his own interest in mind.''

''The boy has a peacock's air about him,'' Jack agreed. '''Twould be no surprise to find the print of his lips upon his own looking glass.''

Brandon merely grunted in reply. If only there was a way he could meet this elderly widow without her knowing who he was. A good soldier always scouted the lay of the land before engaging in battle.

Jack grinned. ''As to his aunt, if I were you, I'd hie down to Sussex and see this lady for myself. If she is withered, or a witch stirring a poisonous brew, then I'd—''

Brandon's laughter cut off Jack's further speech. Good old Jack! Brandon clapped him around the shoulders.

''You have struck the bull's-eye, my friend! Aye, let us be off for Bodiam Castle at first light tomorrow. 'Tis time you went a-courting.''

Jack's eyes widened, and his skin took on a paler hue. ''I, a-courting? What do you mean?''

Brandon laughed again as the intriguing idea continued to take shape in his mind. '''Tis called a midsummer's madness, Jackanapes. And we have much work to do twixt now and then.''

''Methinks you have already been touched by the moon,'' Jack muttered, shaking his head.

Chapter Two

Miranda looked up from her embroidery hoop as Kat entered their chambers on the second floor of the central square tower. Sunlight streamed pleasantly through the open casement window, and a light breeze carried the scent of fresh-mown hay and hot mint into the room. Kat waved another letter in her hand.

"More news, coz?" Miranda tried to keep the note of disappointment from her voice. She had been looking forward to enacting Kat's bold masque, especially since she had the starring role. She prayed the letter's contents wouldn't scotch the plan. "Has...has the king changed his mind?"

"Nay, no such luck as that!" Kat settled herself amid the plump woolen cushions on the window seat. She slit the wax seal with her fingernail. "'Tis from Fenton."

"Ah, I should have guessed." Probably another plea for more money, Miranda thought as Kat unfolded the thick paper. "What does he say now?" She paused, then changed her voice to mimic Fenton's whine. "'Dearest Aunt Katherine, how I miss you, and I pray daily for your continued good health!'"

Kat smiled over the top of the paper. "His opening

words are something like that. Go on, soothsayer. Tell me what else does my loving nephew write?''

Miranda threaded her needle with buttercup yellow silk. ''Let me think. Ah! 'The court is ever busy here, and all turn upon the king's fancy. We are to enact a new masque, and the costumes are quite elaborate. I am to take the part of...''' Miranda considered a moment as she knotted one end of the floss, then she continued, '''Of Apollo, a high honor indeed. But, dearest Aunt, the costume requires a great deal of golden thread and cloth-of-gold material. Alas, I fear my allowance, generous as it is from you, cannot cover this unforeseen expenditure...' And so on, and so on. How much does the little beggar want now?''

Kat shook her head. ''Not this time!''

Miranda rolled her eyes. ''May the clouds rain cats and dogs!''

Kat frowned as she perused the letter. ''He writes of my marriage, and wishes me joy in it.''

''Ha! There is something else between the lines. I can feel it.''

Kat arched one eyebrow at her cousin. ''Only too true, I fear. He then goes on to say that he knows Sir Brandon Cavendish well.''

''I do not like the sound of that!'' Miranda jabbed her needle into the collar of the night shift she worked upon.

''Sweet Saint Anne!'' Kat erupted. ''Oh, Miranda, I must be the most unfortunate of women on this green earth!''

Miranda put down her sewing and regarded Kat more intently. ''How now?''

Kat rattled the offending paper. ''Fenton warns me that this Cavendish toad is far too young for me. 'Barely dry behind his ears,' he says. This...boy has only just won his spurs, and he is much given to...God shield me!''

''What?''

Kat read, '''Cavendish is a ruffian who will swear,

drink, dance and revel the night away. He commits the oldest sins in the newest fashion. In short, dear Aunt, Sir Brandon is as lecherous as a monkey. He will top anything in skirts between the ages of seven and seventy.'" Balling up the paper, she hurled it toward the fireplace. "Alack! I am undone by the king's whimsy. First, I nursed an old man on death's door, and then tried to tame a devil, and now I am offered to a half-grown rooster to school! 'Tis enough to make me consider taking the veil!"

Miranda watched Kat pace the newly waxed floorboards for a few minutes, then she quietly asked, "Do you believe Fenton?"

Kat stopped in midstride. "Not as far as I can throw him. We both know from experience that Fenton says and does nothing that is not to his own advantage. 'Tis not my happiness he is concerned for, but my purse strings. With me married to a husband, no matter how young, Fenton will experience more of a money problem than he already has. And if, perchance, this…whoring, lusting fledgling manages to get me with child, Fenton will stand to lose a great deal more—in fact, my whole estate." Kat stroked her chin with her forefinger.

Miranda sighed. "A babe would be sweet to have in the house. Do you think it is possible?"

"How do I know?" Kat snapped. "My first husband was too ill to breach me, and my second…" She shuddered at the thought. "Let us not dwell upon the second at all. A babe." She considered the idea. "Hmm. I fear I am past my ripe years. A babe would be a gift from God that I would bear willingly even if I had to raise its father alongside of it."

"Do we still go forward with our plan?" Miranda asked. She sent a silent prayer to heaven. 'Twould be such fun to be wooed, even if the bridegroom was just a few years out of leading strings. A lusty youth! Perhaps he still had all his teeth, unlike Kat's first two husbands.

Kat smiled grimly. "Of course we will."

"Do you truly think it will work?"

Taking Miranda by the hand, Kat led her to the gold-framed glass near the bed. "Look you, dearest coz. We are as much alike as sisters, which is not surprising considering that our dear mothers were exactly that. Even though you are a few years younger than I, we are of like stature, of like figure—though, I do confess with envy that your waist is an inch or two narrower. Our hair is the same shade of auburn, our eyes the same green." Kat turned Miranda toward her and cradled her face between her hands. "Best of all, no one at court, other than Fenton, has ever seen Lady Katherine Fitzhugh. No one will know that we have exchanged places."

"I will know," announced a dirgelike masculine voice from the doorway. "And I like it not."

Kat laughed, this time with a happier note. "Ah, Montjoy! You never like anything at all, but only delight in pointing out the dark side."

Montjoy sniffed as if his nose ran with a cold. "What you propose is a lie, my lady." Wagging his forefinger like a schoolmaster, the castle steward shuffled into the room. He regarded both women with a doleful mien. "Mark my words, Lady Katherine, a relationship begun with deceit will end in misery." He dragged out the last word in three long syllables.

Laughing all the more, Kat draped herself around the old man's shoulders. "Montjoy, my good conscience, what would we ever do without your joyful presence to gladden our days?"

Montjoy took out a large stained handkerchief, and blew his nose loudly before answering. "You'd be gone to the devil, my lady, and there is the beginning and end of it." He sighed deeply.

"How now, Montjoy," Miranda said, taking his hand

in hers. "Have you told everyone in the household of Kat's plan? Will they all play this game with us?"

Blowing his nose even louder, Montjoy managed to look sadder than before. "Aye, mistress, I have told them, much against my will. Even down to the potboys and stable lads. Scamps, every last one of them! They love you too much, my lady. They have all agreed to this...this folly of yours. When the king's man comes to court you, we are all to call Mistress Miranda by Lady Katherine's name, and Lady Katherine will become Mistress Miranda. What will the poor man do when he learns the truth? How long do you intend to keep him hoodwinked? 'Tis against nature. I am sure 'tis a sin."

Kat tickled him behind his ear. "No doubt, Montjoy, so storm heaven with your prayers for us. In the meantime, we shall make merry sport with this youthful bridegroom of mine. Only for a day or two, until I can spy out his true nature. He will not put on a false front with the poor cousin of Lady Katherine."

"Only a day or two?" Miranda asked a little too brightly. She had hoped for a week, at least. A week of sweet love words whispered in her ear, of flowers and poetry, and perhaps even a song sung just for her.

Kat crossed around Montjoy's spare form and hugged Miranda. "Mayhap a week then, if 'twill please you, Miranda. I am in no hurry. Midsummer's Day lies three weeks away."

"It does not please me—not one hour of it!" Montjoy moaned.

"But you *will* play the part, won't you, dearest, sweet Montjoy?" Kat wheedled with a smile.

The older man sighed as if he balanced the weight of the world on his shoulders. "Aye, my lady. You know that I will, as long as I do not have to tell the lie direct."

"We will pray most earnestly that the occasion will

never arise,'' Kat soothed him, with a wink to Miranda over the steward's gray head.

Miranda managed to smother her giggle. She would never offend Montjoy's dignity for all the world, but he was such fun to gently tease.

Outside, the blare of a hunting horn trembled through the warm forenoon. For a moment, maid, mistress and man gaped at one another with wordless wonderment. Then all three rushed to the window and stared out across the moat toward the fields beyond.

''By our larkin! 'Tis the lusty youth come to woo at last, or else, I am much mistaken. That was Granger's horn. I stationed him in the high meadow to give us fair warning.''

Miranda crumpled her embroidery in her hands. Her mouth went dry and her heart began to beat faster. Despite the sweet breeze coming through the open window she felt very light-headed. ''Now? This minute?'' Leaping trout! She was about to become the lady of the manor and she had yet to decide what to wear.

'''Tis the knell that summons us down the primrose path of perdition,'' Montjoy predicted in an ominous tone.

Kat smiled, though Miranda saw the corners of her mouth tremble. *Good! I am glad that Kat is as nervous as I.*

''I am filled with much good cheer that you are so happy, Montjoy.'' Kat clapped her hands. ''Quickly! Let us be about our preparations. Montjoy, receive our guest, and conduct him to the hall. Have Columbine take her place in the minstrel's box, and tell her to play something soft on her lute. Miranda, do not stand there like a goose— hurry! Put on my pale green silk at once!''

Miranda blinked. ''Why *your* green? Mine is of the same material.''

''Aye, but mine is richer trimmed as befits a lady of my station. 'Tis only right and proper for the Lady Katherine to receive her betrothed in one of her best gowns. So be about it! Montjoy, send us Laurel to help my cousin dress. Oh, do hurry, everyone! They shall be upon us at any moment." Kat shooed the reluctant steward out of the room, then started to unlace Miranda's brown woolen day gown.

"M...my betrothed." Miranda's hand fluttered to her throat. Even if this masque lasted only a day, she would remember it for the rest of her life. All her dreams were coming true—a silken gown with gold lace and seed pearls—and a real live suitor to charm.

The horn sounded again. Miranda swallowed hard. Kat swore under her breath when she tore a nail on one of Miranda's points. Laurel, a short, dimpled girl of sixteen, rushed into the room.

"My lady, they come! I saw them from the battlements. What a grand sight, to be sure! They are still far-off, but you can just spy their banners waving near the crest of the hill," she informed her mistress with a great deal of giggling. She relieved Kat of Miranda's knotted laces. "Aye, and a right colorful display they are, too. Mistress Miranda, how did you get yourself into such a tangle?"

Kat paused in smoothing the wrinkles out of her dove gray woolen gown. "Not Mistress Miranda this day, Laurel. She is now my Lady Katherine—and don't you forget it."

Laurel giggled again. "Oh, aye, my mind mistook. What a piece of tomfoolery this will be! Miss...your pardon, my Lady Katherine, would you kindly not wiggle so much? How can I dress you properly if you must dance a galliard while I do it?"

Standing on her tiptoes, Miranda tried to see out the window. "Are they in sight yet? What does *he* look like?"

Adjusting her plain gray coif, Kat glanced out the window again. "Stars! He has brought half the king's army with him."

"Goodly men?" Laurel's voice sparkled with interest.

"Where?" Miranda asked at the same time. Both women joined Kat at the window. All three leaned far out over the stone ledge and fixed their gaze upon the opposite hill where a large, colorful group of men paused on their horses. "Great wailing wolves, coz! We are about to be invaded!"

"Is all our company drawn near?" Brandon's gaze swept over the group: two squires, his master huntsman, his falcon, several panting greyhounds, three grooms, a dozen men-at-arms and a grinning co-conspirator, Jack Stafford.

"Aye, my lord," replied Jess, the huntsman. "Is that the lady's home?"

Brandon swallowed down the knot that had formed in the base of his throat. Ridiculous! Ten years jousting in the lists of England and fighting on the fields of France had not made him feel half as nervous as he did at this moment.

"Bodiam Castle," he snapped.

"A pleasant place to look upon," Jack observed.

"Aye, I have seen worse prisons," Brandon remarked, his brows furrowed above his eyes.

The men behind him guffawed. Brandon twisted the reins between his fingers. God's death! Why did his stomach play havoc with his breakfast? 'Twas only an old woman. At least, her castle looked welcoming, he thought as he studied his new estate-to-be.

Situated comfortably in a gently rolling valley on the banks of the river Rother, Bodiam's white limestone walls reflected the bright sunlight. Brandon guessed that the square fortress had been built several hundred years ago, but he could see it was well maintained. Stout barrel towers guarded each corner with square towers at the center of the north and south curtain walls. Above each tower, a colorful banner waved in the breeze.

The bright sun glinted off the diamond panes of glass that filled the wide arched windows on the second and third floors—as curious to the eye as lacy-cut paperwork. The open drawbridge lay snug against the near bank of the moat, and a bevy of white swans glided leisurely across the still green water. Above the open portcullis, a flag, larger than the others, snapped against its pole. A silver unicorn lay on a green silken field—the Lady Katherine's personal device, Brandon presumed.

"Well?" Jack poked Brandon with his crop. "Do we ride to yon castle, or do we turn tail?"

Brandon glared at his best friend. Jack winked back at him. With a sigh of exasperation, Brandon turned his horse and faced his party. If only his men would stop grinning like monkeys! Thank all the saints that his brother Guy was safely five hundred miles away with his French wife and baby daughter! Guy would be hooting at him by now.

"Men," Brandon began, then cleared his throat to banish the high-pitched frog that lurked therein. "From now on, you will render the service due me to Sir John. Until further notice, he is Lord Brandon Cavendish, and I am Jack Stafford. That goes double to you varlets." Brandon glared at the squires, Mark and Christopher.

The two seventeen-year-olds nodded with wide smirks on their faces.

"One word of our disguising from any of you, and I will personally take a whip to your backs." Brandon tried to sound as if he meant it. The trouble was, he didn't— and the whole company knew it. "On the other hand, if this farce plays out well, there will be a golden angel in each of your pockets come Midsummer's Day."

"You can rely upon us, my Lord…ah…Stafford," Jess answered for the company.

Jack adjusted his new blue velvet hat and straightened

the red felt traveling cloak about his shoulders. "Do I look like the high-and-mighty Sir Brandon Cavendish, eldest son of the Earl of Thornbury, my Lord Stafford?" he asked with a merry gleam in his eye. "Do I look the part of the panting bridegroom?"

"You look like the very devil," Brandon muttered. He glared at the castle again, then threw back his shoulders and took a deep breath. "Sound your horn, Jess. They know we are here. Let us make a brave charge and engage the enemy in her lair."

Brandon urged Windchaser into a gallop down the hill, followed closely by Jack and the others. The greyhounds gave tongue, while Jess blew his horn like the angel Gabriel announcing the final judgment day. The halloo of the men and hounds, and the thudding of the great horses' hooves on the soft greensward did much to relieve the tension of Brandon's coiled nerves. If this was to be a battle of wits and hearts, he would attack bravely.

The two lords reined their horses into a sedate walk as they approached the drawbridge. A clear girlish giggle sang over their heads. Brandon and Jack glanced up just in time to see three women, two with reddish brown hair, and the other one with hair the color of ripe wheat, duck back from the tower window. The entire south battlements appeared to be filled with many smiling maidens and a few stern-looking men-at-arms.

"Methinks the enemy has spied us, and has appraised our strength," Jack remarked with a chuckle. "Comely wenches. This little holiday in the country may prove quite diverting for me."

"Your eyes are only for the Lady Katherine, until I say otherwise," Brandon growled as he walked his horse across the wooden planks of the drawbridge. "Best remember that, my friend."

Jack feigned a sigh. "I shall woo up storms of tears and swoons. I shall give my very best performance to date.

Too bad 'twill be wasted on a lady of advanced years,"
he added, arching his eyebrow. "And one reputed to be a
witch."

"Bite your tongue, Stafford," Brandon rumbled under
his breath. He did not like to be reminded of that uncomfortable possibility. Having to marry her was bad enough.

With a grin, Jack shook his head. "Nay, not so. I am
Sir Brandon, and *you* are his boon companion, Jack Stafford." They passed through the double gateways into the
castle courtyard. "And now, let our play begin."

Chapter Three

Running her fingers along the round, whitewashed wall of the tower's stairwell, Kat descended the spiral stone steps that led into the hall. The cool stone under her fingertips gave her a welcome reassurance. The dulcet tones of Columbine's music told Kat that everything was proceeding according to plan—so far. At the base of the steps, she straightened her coif, fluffed out its white veil over her shoulders, then took a deep breath. *Let us see what manner of schoolboy has come to call.* Lifting the trailing hem of her skirts, she swept into the lofty central chamber.

At the sound of her entrance, two blond giants turned in her direction. Halting abruptly, Kat nearly fell over a small footstool. Sweet angels! Who were these men, and where was Sir Brandon?

"Good day, fair lady," said the first. Doffing his blue cap, he swept her a low courtly bow. His mellow baritone voice sang pleasantly in her ears. "Do I have the honor of addressing Lady Katherine Fitzhugh?"

"I...that is..." To cover her confusion, as well as to give her time to think, Kat dipped into a graceful curtsy. Her knees wobbled under her skirts. Had she mistaken the identity of her visitors? Were these gentlemen emissaries from the king, and not her betrothed at all? If that was the case, she should reveal herself immediately. And yet...

Rising slowly, Kat smiled with a false brightness. "Pray, forgive me, my lords. We do not often entertain such noble gentlemen as yourselves here at Bodiam. I fear you must think me a ninny."

She advanced closer to them, praying that one or the other might introduce himself. Kat caught her breath. What a handsome pair! The one in the velvet hat easily stood six feet in height. His blue eyes reminded her of a summer sky reflected in a pool of clear spring water. He held his lean body gracefully, perhaps a little too gracefully for her taste.

The second man cleared his throat, then bowed in turn, though he did not sweep so low to the floor as the first. "Forgive us, my lady. Methought your usher had announced our arrival. In truth, it seems your whole castle saw us ride in. Permit me to introduce Sir Brandon Cavendish of Wolf Hall." He pointed to his companion.

Kat blinked at the smiling man, then dropped into another curtsy. Cavendish? This was no beardless youth— though his handsome face was clean shaven—but a man in his full prime. *This* was the bridegroom whom the king had chosen for her? *Miranda will swoon on the spot when she claps an eye on him.*

"And I am Sir John Stafford, come to bear witness of your joy to the king." Stafford cleared his throat again.

Kat looked up fully into the second man's face. This time her traitorous knees deserted her. She swayed. Moving swiftly, Stafford caught her before Kat collapsed into an undignified heap of petticoats and gowns. With a hint of a smile playing about the corners of his lips, he guided her to one of the high-backed armchairs.

"Are you well, my lady? Shall I call for your usher?"

"Nay," Kat gasped. "My thanks, good sir. I slipped upon the floor. I...er...we take pride in keeping the floor tiles polished with beeswax. How very clumsy of me!" *I sound like a complete fool!*

Kat's cheeks flamed. If Sir Brandon presented a picture of a Greek god come down to her hearth, he paled in comparison to Sir John. Slightly taller than his friend, Stafford's shoulders filled—nay, strained—the seams of his forest green doublet, as if he would burst out of them at any moment. While Sir Brandon's voice reminded her of warm honey dripping from the comb, Sir John's deeper tones promised something more dangerous and exciting.

The room wavered before her eyes. Kat gripped the arms of the chair. She must get hold of herself. She was no giddy maiden on a May morning, but a woman of nearly thirty years. 'Twas almost the dinner hour. No doubt her dizziness stemmed from hunger.

Stafford knelt by her chair and took one of her ice-cold hands in his. "Clumsy is not a word I would use to describe you, my lady." Stafford's brilliant blue eyes twinkled with open amusement. He brushed his lips lightly across the back of her hand.

Angels in heaven! What magic is this stranger working upon me? And in full view of my betrothed—no, not my betrothed. Not yet. I am not Kat.

"I fear I am no lady…" she began, then stopped, realizing how scandalous that must sound.

Sir John's smile widened as he continued to hold her clammy hand within his large warm ones. "No lady?" His gaze roved from her eyes, to her shoulders to the outline of her breasts under the plain bodice of her gown. "Your beauty gives the lie to that."

Kat's pulse skittered alarmingly. *This man is seducing me in my own hall—before dinner, or even before proper introductions.*

Kat sat up straighter. "I am Mistress Miranda Paige, cousin to the lady of the house."

"My loss," Sir John whispered under his breath.

Not sure what he meant by that, Kat plunged on with her part. "My Lady Katherine begs your patience, my lords. The suddenness of your arrival has put us all in a whirl. She is above, preparing herself to receive you, Sir Brandon."

Poor Miranda! What a shock this handsome gallant was going to be to her! Kat prayed that her cousin would keep her wits about her upon first introduction.

"A masterpiece of perfection takes time to prepare. 'Tis made all the more desirable by the wait," Sir Brandon replied, shooting a quick glance to his companion.

"Just so," Sir John murmured. After pressing his lips on the sensitive skin of her palm, he released Kat's hand.

Like a lark caught in a snare, her heart fluttered wildly within her breast. An uneasy silence settled over them. Kat thanked her foresight for having Columbine play her lute. The girl's sweet music filled the gap in the conversation. Biting the inside of her lips, Kat struggled to think of something clever to say. Neither Lewknor nor Fitzhugh had bothered to pay her court. She had never set eyes on either of her husbands until they had met at the church door to take their wedding vows. During thirteen years of loveless marriages, the opportunity for witty conversation and harmless flirtation had never presented itself—until now. *Sweet Saint Anne, help me!*

"I must confess, Mistress Paige, I did not expect to find so agreeable an interior to your lady's castle when we first rode through its gate." Sir Brandon surveyed the room with approval in his expression. "A fortress on the outside, and a pleasant bower within."

Kat released a pent-up breath. At least, the man—her betrothed, she had to remind herself—had given her a blessed opening. "Yes, I am...*we* are quite pleased with the result of the plaster and paint over the rough walls. The linen-fold carving on the paneling is my...cousin's especial pride. Much work has been done since my...my lady's husband died." *Careful—watch every word. Miranda! How long does it take to change your gown?*

"Ah, yes, I had heard that the Lady Katherine was married before," Sir John remarked with the suddenness of a duck snapping at a water beetle.

Kat wrinkled her nose. "Twice," she answered shortly. *Why spoil her appetite for dinner, or the good company of these worthy gentlemen, with wretched thoughts of Fitzhugh?*

"And were they happy matches?" Sir John persisted.

"Nay, my lord, they were not. I pray you, for my lady's sake, do not mention her past husbands." *Have done with them for once and all!*

"Good day, my lords, and welcome to my...oh, squealing piglets!" Miranda stood transfixed in the doorway, staring at the guests. She flushed a charming rosy hue.

Miranda looks ten years younger!

Kat hastened to her side. She clasped her cousin's cold hand. "My lords, I present to you the Lady Katherine Fitzhugh."

A startled look passed between the men, then, as one, they swept off their caps and bowed low.

"Leaping trout!" Miranda moaned softly. She gripped Kat's hand like grim death.

"Does heaven weep for loneliness since you flew down to earth, sweet lady?" Sir Brandon gushed.

"Your servant, my lady," his companion added in a brisk tone.

"Say something!" Kat hissed at her cousin.

"Welcome to Bodiam," Miranda chirruped.

"You have said that already," Kat whispered, guiding her transfixed cousin closer to the men. *Don't bolt, Miranda,* she silently begged. *Please do not give the game away just yet.*

"Wa-was your journey long?" Miranda looked from

one man to the other. "Which one is Sir Brandon?" she whispered to Kat out of the side of her mouth.

Kat spied a ghostly smile flit across Sir John's lips. He must have heard Miranda's question.

Sir John poked Sir Brandon's rib cage with his elbow.

"I—I...fair lady, I have the honor of being the eldest son of Sir Thomas Cavendish, Earl of Thornbury. I am Sir Brandon Cavendish. I bring you the greetings and good wishes of my family and of our great king, Henry, who has made my present happiness possible." Sir Brandon bowed low for a fourth time.

Kat winced inwardly as she watched Cavendish dive toward the floor again. *Hang it all, my betrothed is full of foppery!*

"Oh!" Miranda squeaked. She turned a little pale.

"Do him courtesies," Kat prompted in Miranda's ear. "And for the love of all that is holy, don't faint."

"'Tis I who am honored, Sir Brandon." Miranda sank into a full curtsy. She remained frozen in that position.

Sir Brandon dropped to one knee before her and took her hand in his. "The honor of your fair hand is a gift I shall cherish all my days. Believe me, sweetest lady, when I tell you that I shall ever remember this moment in my heart and in my dreams." He kissed each of Miranda's fingers in turn.

Kat happened to glance at Sir John and caught him rolling his eyes toward the vaulted ceiling. Aye, Sir Brandon's greeting was a bit thick—like butter oozing on a slice of hot bread—but his words certainly had quite an effect upon Miranda. Kat wondered if the two of them were going to remain kneeling in the middle of the floor for the rest of the day. Kat shot another glance at Sir John.

He acknowledged her look with a slight lowering of his eyelids. Then he cleared his throat again. Kat wondered if he was coming down with a cough. Perhaps Sondra could prepare an elixir for his sore throat.

"Permit me to introduce myself, my Lady Katherine."
Sir John arched one golden brow at the couple before him.
"I am Sir John Stafford, gentleman groom of the king's
bedchamber."

"Aye," Miranda replied, not glancing at the speaker.
She seemed to have lost herself in the depths of Sir Brandon's blue eyes.

*Get up, coz, and behave yourself. That is supposed to
be my husband.* Kat looked across the couple to Sir John.
He shrugged his shoulders in reply. Though his motion
seemed outwardly simple, he radiated a vitality that drew
her like a dancing moth to a candle flame. Her heart
bounced. That one was a rogue, she decided. Such an at-
traction would be perilous. Why couldn't her betrothed
have been Sir John? At least he didn't talk in sugared
subtleties.

"The lady may find the floor—polished though 'tis to
an enviable shine—to be a bit chill," Sir John suggested.
His golden eyebrows arched with meaning.

Kat caught herself admiring Sir John's clean, straight
jawline. She swallowed with difficulty.

"Your pardon, my lady." Sir Brandon rose in one fluid
motion, bringing Miranda up with him. "I was enrap-
tured."

"Has my...my cousin offered you some refreshment after your journey?" Miranda gripped Sir Brandon's hand.

"Nay." Sir John gazed boldly at Kat, which made her
feel hot and cold at the same time. "But I am willing to
take whatever refreshment she may offer."

The very air crackled around Kat like lightning come to
earth. The implication of his softly spoken words sent tingling waves of forbidden excitement crashing through her.
Sir John's eyes appeared to turn bluer as his gaze caressed
her. Though the day was warm for May, a cluster of goose
bumps sprouted along her arms. Angels in heaven! What
was this churl insinuating? What an utterly improper, ut-

terly rude, utterly…delicious idea! Impossible! *I am fast losing my wits!*

"I need no other refreshment, now that I am bathed in my lady's eyes," Sir Brandon murmured, drawing closer to Miranda, who, for her part, stood rooted to the floor tiles.

Kat tittered—something she had not done for almost two decades—and twisted a knot within the folds of her gown. "We do not often hear such goodly speech, as we live so far from the court."

"I fear my friend may have overstepped his bounds at this first meeting, Mistress Miranda." Sir John glared daggers at Sir Brandon's back, as if to remind him of his manners. "Jack…jackanapes, Brandon! Mayhap the Lady Katherine would like to see the gift you have brought her?"

Sir Brandon dropped Miranda's hand. "Forgive me, I pray you. I find myself most marvelously at sixes and sevens." He drew out a red velvet pouch from inside his gold-embroidered doublet. With a brilliant smile, he held out the gift to Miranda. "For you, sweet lady, as a pledge of our betrothal."

"You are too kind," Miranda murmured. She almost let the bag slip between her trembling fingers. Glancing at Kat, she raised her eyebrow in question.

"Pray seat yourself, coz." Kat pushed her toward the chair.

Clutching the bag to her breast, Miranda melted into the safety between the chair's carved wooden arms.

"'Tis all the excitement of meeting such noble gentlemen," Kat babbled to their guests. "It has quite overcome my lady."

"That feeling is shared by one who desires to draw closer to her heart," Sir Brandon replied with a flourish.

"God's teeth!" muttered Sir John.

With shaking fingers, Miranda managed to untie the red

tasseled cord and spread open the pouch. She lifted out a golden chain made up of dainty rose-shaped links. A swan, fashioned from a large freshwater pearl, its wings tipped with square-cut diamonds, dangled from a gold-and-pearl clasp at the center.

"Crickets!" Miranda gasped, holding up the jewel to catch a sunbeam.

"Sweet Saint Anne!" Kat exclaimed at the same time.

In the minstrels' gallery, Columbine missed a note. The lute clattered to the floor, then lapsed into silence.

"But I cannot accept such a gift as this!" Miranda's green eyes glistened with a watery sheen as she glanced from Kat to Sir Brandon, then back to Kat.

"The necklace does not please you?" Sir Brandon shot a puzzled expression to his friend, then looked at Miranda once again. "You do not care for pearls—or swans?"

"Oh, aye, I love them both, but I…"

Kat gave Miranda's shoulder a hard squeeze. "'Tis such a costly gift, my lord. We lead a very simple life here in the country. We do not often see the jeweler's art at Bodiam. Indeed, I cannot recall when we last did see such a thing of beauty as your gift, Sir Brandon."

Miranda ran a finger lightly over the pearl which made up the swan's body. "Never," she echoed.

"'Tis obvious. You have quite taken my lady's breath— and her good sense—away." Kat squeezed Miranda again.

Miranda gazed up at Sir Brandon. A warm glow bathed her face. "Trust me, my lord, when I tell you, that never before in my life has anyone given me such a gift as this. I thank you for it, and bless you for your kind thoughts. Truly, I will remember this day forever."

"May I be so bold as to fasten it around your neck, my lady?" Sir Brandon drew near to the chair. "Such a jewel requires the proper setting, which only you can give it."

Miranda shot a quick glance at Kat.

Say aye, Miranda, but pray, do not faint now. I do not

think it wise that my betrothed should carry you up to our bedchamber.

"Do so, Sir Brandon," Kat gushed. "I long to see it upon her."

Sir Brandon made a great show of brushing back Miranda's hair. Kat noticed that his fingers played across the back of Miranda's neck as if he were strumming a lyre. Closing her eyes, Miranda sighed deeply. By the book! Her cousin was besotted already! Kat promised herself to have a lengthy and very specific talk with Miranda later on about the hazards of letting nature take its course.

"The bauble looks well upon her," Sir John said loudly, very loudly. "Stand back, Brandon, my good friend, so that we may all enjoy the view. By my troth, my lady, I think your little musician will come near to falling over the gallery rail."

Kat looked up to see Columbine leaning far over the side. "Columbine, attend to what you are about!"

"Your pardon, my lady," the girl apologized, before disappearing from view once again. The lute resumed play. Kat noticed that Columbine now strummed a ballad of love.

"My thanks, Sir John. As you can see, a few pearls and a diamond or two are enough to make our world spin a giddy turn."

Eyeing Miranda, Kat wondered if she was going to say anything more. Her cousin's stunned silence didn't seem to alarm Sir Brandon. He gazed upon Miranda with the most idiotic look on his face. Kat didn't notice that Sir John had moved to her side until he spoke.

"I apologize to you, Mistress Miranda." His voice washed over her like cooling waters on a hot day.

"Whatever for, my lord?" Kat stared very hard at the tip of her black satin slipper.

"We did not expect to find that two women of beauty

and charm graced the hall of Bodiam Castle, or we would have thought to bring two such swans.''

Kat laughed nervously. She did not dare to look up into those searing blue eyes again. Sir John stood so close she could feel the heat from his body. His presence befuddled all her senses. ''I...I have no need for such a fine gift as that, my Lord Stafford. As you can see, I dress plainly, and I know my station in life.'' *Please God, forgive me for all these lies.*

''As I know mine, mistress. Permit me to speak plainly. I have a brooch that I wear upon my cloak.'' He opened his large hand and held out the ornament for her inspection. A flat golden rose of the familiar Tudor design nestled in his palm. ''I would deem it a singular honor, if you would let it adorn your gown—in a place near to your heart.''

''Oh, Sir John!'' Kat gazed up at him. He towered a full head taller than she. His teeth flashed a brilliant white, as he successfully disarmed her objections with his smile.

''Do not reject my request, Mistress Miranda. I am in no position to offer you more, though not for lack of desire,'' he added, his voice dropping to a honey-warm whisper in her ear.

Her toes curled inside her slippers.

''Then I will accept your offering, my lord, and I shall wear it—as long as my name is Miranda Paige.'' Kat smiled at him brightly. Unfamiliar tears pricked behind her eyelids. It must be the dust in the wainscoting.

''I fear the pin is sharp, and the clasp bent from wear,'' he continued, caressing her with his seductive voice. ''Shall I pin it on for you?''

Kat experienced a rushing of wind in her ears. She took a small step backward. ''My thanks, Sir John, but I think I can manage the clasp myself. Perchance, one day you may do me that service—if ever I learn to know you better.'' Stars above! How did that wanton suggestion pop out of her mouth? Kat bit her tongue, before it could utter anything else of a scandalous nature.

"My lady?" droned Montjoy, who had been standing at the doorway for who knew how long. "'Tis past the dinner hour, and Philippe swears that his soup will be ruined. May I have your leave to set the tables, and lay the cloth?"

"Aye!" chorused all four of the ladies and gentlemen in the hall. Afterward, each one looked at the others with astonishment. Then they burst into a wild, relieving round of laughter.

Sweet saints! Kat lamented. 'Twas only the first hour of this game, and already she was fast losing herself—to the wrong man!

Chapter Four

"Fenton lied!" With a cry that mixed together anger, surprise and despair, Miranda fell backward onto the thick mattress of the ornate canopied bed she shared with Kat.

"That is old news, indeed." Seating herself on the window seat, Kat watched the lengthening purple shadows of twilight steal across Sondra's herb garden below. "Fenton would gag on his own tongue if he ever told a complete truth." She traced the golden petals of the rose brooch still pinned to her bodice.

"Sir Brandon is a far cry from a schoolboy." Miranda sighed.

"His maturity was obvious from the first moment," Kat replied, musing upon Sir Brandon's companion.

What a bold look Sir John Stafford had! Never in all her days had any man gazed at Kat in quite that way. The memory of his dark blue eyes and the manner in which they had appraised her all during dinner sent prickles of a nameless desire dancing up her thighs. She squeezed her legs together. Kat couldn't decide if she should feel complimented or insulted. As Lady Katherine Fitzhugh, she would have chided Sir John for his lack of manners. After all, she was going to be married in three weeks to Sir Brandon.

Sir Brandon Cavendish. Aye, he was another breed all together, and one Kat did not find pleasing. Too much bowing and scraping. Too many flowery speeches. She mistrusted a man who sounded as if he both dined and supped upon almond sweetmeats. A honeyed tongue might well conceal a vicious temperament. Closing her eyes, Kat rested her head against the cool plastered wall behind her. No thank you! She had had her share—and more—of that sort of husband. May Fitzhugh the Furious rot in hell!

On the other hand, as Lady Katherine's shy "cousin," Kat had been thrilled by Lord Stafford's obvious attentions. What woman would not? So tall, so fine looking, and what a delightful voice—especially when he chanced to murmur something softly into her ear, such as "Please pass the salt." Kat sighed. How was that bold piece of brass to know that all during the savory course he was mentally undressing the wrong woman?

Kat ducked her head lest Miranda see the smile that played about her lips. Really! John Stafford was too deliciously wicked by half! Kat must be on her guard around him. Oh, yes! She would watch every move he made. Kat sighed again with pleasure at the thought.

"Kat! You have not heard one word that I have said!" Miranda hurled one of the stuffed bolsters at her cousin.

Kat pulled herself back to reality and caught the pillow before it sailed out the open window. "How now, coz?"

"Aye, that is the question indeed!" Miranda pulled off her headdress, then shook out her hair. "While you were woolgathering, I asked you—several times, in fact—what are we going to do now?"

Kat knotted her brows. "Aye, a good question."

"'Tis no point in pursuing this counterfeit any longer, Kat." Miranda carefully lifted off the swan necklace from around her neck. The last ray of the departing sun caught itself within one of the square-cut diamonds. The jewel flashed a rare light about the room. "Tomorrow, you must confess our little game to those fine lords, and pray that they see the mirthful side of it. Here.'' She held out the costly betrothal gift to Kat.

Kat blinked. So soon? But she knew nothing of Sir Brandon, save that he had a somewhat handsome face, if only he didn't look like a sick sheep about the eyes! She must have more time in which to judge the true measure of her husband-to-be. A few hours between the late dinner and the cold supper had not been sufficient. In fact, Kat could not remember a single sensible thing that Sir Brandon had said.

Sir John, on the other hand, had praised her well-laid table, the quality of her ale, the good manners of her servants, the furnishings and appointments of the hall, the cleanliness of the stables, the size of her tilled fields, and he spiced the conversation with a few well-chosen compliments to her person—that is, to ''Miranda.'' One would almost believe it was Sir John Stafford who had come to claim her manor and herself.

''Heigh-ho, Kat!'' Miranda swung the necklace back and forth on her fingers. ''A penny for your thoughts, or would a pearly swan suffice?''

Kat shook herself, then stood up. ''Keep the bauble,'' she tossed over her shoulder to her cousin. She withdrew a stick of waxed candlewick from a jug on the mantel, lighted one end from the low fire on the hearth, then applied the flame to several candles around the room. A warm, golden glow pushed back the night shadows creeping into the far corners of the chamber. ''Sir Brandon gave the necklace to you. He would take it amiss if I appeared wearing it.''

''But he gave it to me only because he thinks I am the Lady Katherine.'' Miranda fingered the delicate links of the gold chain. '''Tis truly a beautiful gift,'' she breathed.

Kat touched Sir John's rose brooch. ''Aye, you speak the truth,'' she murmured. *I would have you wear this close to your heart,* he had said. And surely her heart nearly burst from its accustomed cage to answer aye! Kat drew in a steadying breath. What devilment had gotten into her this evening?

"Aye, 'tis beautiful, and it looks far better upon your bosom than on mine. Keep it, I say, Miranda, and let the matter rest."

"But, Kat…"

"But me no buts, sweet coz. My mind is made up."

Miranda cocked her head. "To what end?"

Throwing back her head, Kat laughed her first easy laugh of the day. "As to the end, I cannot say, for our game is not over yet."

"Kat! How could you do this to Sir Brandon? He is the most handsome, kindest, sweetest-spoken man that ever has graced this castle. He will make you as fine a husband as any woman could hope for. And you make a…a mockery of his good intentions?"

Kat lifted her brows in surprise. Never before had she heard Miranda raise her gentle voice—and certainly never to her. How now? What goblin had stolen her cousin's normal good wits? Could it be that piece of mischief who wore a blue bonnet and a red cloak? When Sir Brandon had brushed his lips across Miranda's in a good night's wish, what imp had he breathed into her? Miranda had all the marks of a first love about her. Kat swallowed back a small pang of envy. *I wish I could feel that way about Sir Brandon myself. I need more time to grow used to him— like an eternity.*

"Peace, coz." Kat smiled at Miranda. "I mean no disrespect to my Lord Cavendish. He may be all that you say he is—and more," she added quickly, when she saw that Miranda was about to protest again. "But let us not act in haste. Midsummer's Day is still a few weeks away. Let us continue as we are. I must find out if there is any grain of truth to Fenton's report of Sir Brandon's drinking, gambling and dallying with all manner of women.''

"Fenton is a braying jackass," Miranda stated as a matter of uncontested fact. She replaced the swan jewel around her neck, then regarded herself in the looking glass. "And you are right, Kat. This sweet bird nestles well upon me." She sighed.

Miranda is besotted—or bewitched. I really must find her a husband—and quickly. Would that she could have mine!

"The devil take you, Jack! Wherever did you learn such sweet-toothed speeches as the ones you spouted like a water pump all afternoon?" Brandon poured himself a full goblet from the jug of burgundy that a serving wench had laid out for them in their chamber. The knights had been quartered at the top of the northeast tower overlooking the stagnant moat. Its foul odors wafted up on the evening breeze.

Brandon tossed down the tart ruby wine in one gulp. "All that treacle in one sitting went near to making me puke into my trencher."

"Your Lady Katherine is an angel fair." Jack threw himself into the large chair before the fire and dangled one leg over its thick wooden arm. "You should pay her more mind, instead of her cousin. After all, Lady Katherine is the one you are going to marry, you prowling tomcat. You had better not forget that fact. And pour me a cup of that before you drain the whole pitcher."

"So my betrothed lady pleased you?" Brandon cocked one eyebrow as he handed his friend a brimming cup. "Tell me, if you can clear your palate of all that clinging honey, what is your honest opinion of my intended bride?" Brandon drank off another half cup, to wash down the unsettling word "bride."

"As sweet a lady as ever walked upon the earth," Jack murmured into his wine.

"Ha!" Brandon barked. "Does the devil speak the truth? Is this Sir John Stafford who instructs me in love? He, whom the whole court calls the Jack of Hearts? He that has wooed three times the number of maidens that I have ever met, and who has tumbled more women than even the great Royal Bull himself?"

Jack glared at Brandon. "You should know, my friend. We have shared a wench or two in our time."

"Aye, but in my youth." Brandon push aside those memories. Ever since the results of his indiscretions had come home to roost, he had been as celibate as a monk—almost. "Lay all posturing aside, Jack. What do you think of the lady?" He could not bring himself to call Katherine "wife" as yet. It stuck in the craw of his throat.

Jack regarded his companion with a serious expression. "I swear upon God's holy book, Lady Katherine Fitzhugh is beyond peer. In a word, she is…adorable…sweet…virtuous…beguiling."

"Those are four words, not one," Brandon remarked. God's teeth! What ailed the legendary Jack of Hearts? He meant what he was saying. Katherine's relative youth had been a pleasant surprise, but "adorable" or "sweet"?

Jack ignored the interruption. "And she is far younger than we were led to believe. In faith, we need to hang Scantling up by his heels when we return to court. He has played the fool with you."

"Aye, he did, indeed." Brandon stared moodily into the fire. "Methinks he wears a dagger in his words."

Jack's eyes softened. "Looking at the Lady Katherine, 'tis hard to believe that she has ever been bedded, let alone by two husbands. You are a lucky dog, Brandon, and that is no mistake."

"Am I?" Brandon lifted one brow slowly. He didn't feel particularly lucky. More like trapped.

"What do you mean?"

"The Lady Katherine. She is fair, she is fine, she is reasonably young." He gave Jack a piercing look. "She may also be a witch."

"Go, hang! If you were not nose deep in a crock of wine, I might take you seriously, and be forced to challenge you to combat for the lady's honor," Jack growled in a low, dangerous tone.

Brandon leveled his gaze at his friend. "Think, not with your lusting fancy, but with that brain God saw fit to give you, man. How do we know that who we saw today was the true lady?"

"You are horn-mad," Jack observed. "And you speak with a voice soused in wine."

Brandon leaned toward him. "Listen to me, clodpate. Perhaps Lady Katherine has conjured up an apparition, and she puts on this pleasing look of youth and innocence, as a woman would don a gown for a feast. Perhaps she fed you a love charm in your quince sauce, and thereby hangs the tale. In truth, I have known you to take many a woman merrily, but never have you taken one seriously."

Jack stared at him for a moment, then grinned and shrugged. "Methinks *you* are the one who is charmed—by too much ale at supper, and too much wine in your cup now. On the morrow, all will be well when you reveal your true identity."

Brandon cocked his head. "How now?"

Jack snorted. "Are you deaf, as well as thickheaded, my friend? Tomorrow, at the earliest convenience, we shall beg that sweet lady's forgiveness for the foul trick we have played upon her. You will tell her the truth of your parentage. The game is up. 'Tis too cruel by half to deceive her any further."

Brandon poured himself another cup, but this time he merely sipped the contents. Jack was right about one thing. By tomorrow morning, Brandon's head would be thick and pounding from too much imbibing. But fall upon his knees in front of that whey-faced milksop who could barely stammer out two sentences together? Never! At least, not until he knew her better.

Fenton was a lying cur—of that, there was no doubt. But the flap-eared knave may have woven a warp of truth amid the woof of lies. Better to marry a dishcloth than a witch, if one had to get married at all. The devil take King Henry and his damnable matchmaking! The winsome face of Katherine's fair cousin broke through the dark clouds of his musings. Ah, Miranda! Now there was a woman to cheer a man's soul, and body. The Lady Katherine was watered-down ale compared to the zest of the strong brew he spied beneath Miranda's plain garb. He had caught her secret appraisals behind her thick, lowered lashes. Thick enough to fan a man's desires into a bonfire. 'Twas a shame Miranda was not his promised bride. He would not grow bored with her to warm him.

Getting up, Brandon stretched to his fullest height. "To-morrow, you will still be Sir Brandon, and I shall attempt to do my best at aping the manners of his good friend, Jack Stafford."

"But…what of the ladies?" Jack gabbled.

"'Tis the ladies I think upon every waking moment. Aye, they shall probably haunt me in my sleep, as well." *Especially the one who wears my poor cloak pin upon her creamy breast.* Brandon shook himself. "Cheer up, Jack. I do not pronounce a sentence of execution, but one of merriment. You delight in talking gibberish to the Lady Katherine, who—God only knows why—takes pleasure in your ramblings. And I…" Brandon grinned widely. "I shall pursue good Mistress Miranda."

Jack punched his friend in the arm. "Oh, aye? And play a double false face upon your wife before you've even married her?"

Brandon massaged his arm. "Nay, not that. But to seek

out what truth lies behind Kat's smile. Do not look so strange at me, Jackanapes. While at supper, I heard her serving wenches call her that name under their breath.''

"Mind how you call the fair lady to her face, or you'll have me to answer for her," Jack rumbled.

Brandon took pleasure in returning his friend's ham-fisted punch in his sword arm. "I shall record that warning in my book of memory, Jack-of-all-trades. And I shall study that page every day for sweet friendship's sake. My word upon it.''

Jack tottered toward the bed. "How long do you plan to continue this mummery?''

"No more than three weeks," Brandon answered in a soft undertone. "I mean to enjoy my last moments of freedom until my wedding day. After that, my fate will be sealed, come rack or ruin.''

"And a sweet good-night to you, too," Jack replied, just before he fell face first amid the bedclothes.

Chapter Five

The arrow flew across the green velvety lawn and embedded its shaft in the red heart of the straw-filled target. Its fletching of gold and red feathers vibrated with the shock of impact.

"Bull's-eye, Sir John! I win yet again!" Kat regarded her missile with supreme satisfaction. "I am most amazed that Sir Brandon boasted of your skill at archery, my lord, for you have yet to come within an inch of me."

A devilish look of some secret amusement stole into the depths of Sir John's brilliant blue eyes. Kat's heart turned over in response.

"I fear my prowess has been much overrated, Mistress Miranda," he murmured, a sly smile curving his lips. "Methinks I have forgotten the wager. What do I owe you this time?"

"The golden ribbon from your left sleeve, Sir John, to match the others I have already won." Kat smiled, though her lips trembled as he drew nearer to her.

"Faith, mistress, if we continue to shoot at yon target, I shall not have a lacing left to hold my apparel together. By the rood, all my clothes will fall to your feet." Untying the satin ribbon, he held it out to her. "You would not wish to see me so…at one with nature, would you?'' he murmured as he drew closer still.

His steady gaze bore into her, daring her to answer his scandalous suggestion. The idea of him standing stark naked before her both startled and fascinated Kat. She blinked her eyes, to banish the wanton thought, then she tugged the ribbon from his hold. As their fingers touched, a dizzying current raced through her as if her blood had suddenly begun to boil. She laughed to cover her nervousness as she fumbled to tie her latest prize around her wrist.

''Perish the thought, Sir John. Our weather here is most unpredictable. You might find you'd catch a sudden chill, if you were thus exposed to our varying winds.''

Sir John took the ribbon from her shaking fingers. He tied it in a love knot over her pulse point, then bent his head and sealed the knot with a featherlight kiss. ''Perchance you might find it in your heart to keep me warm?'' he whispered, the gleam in his eye turning to blue flames.

Kat's heart danced a lively galliard as his lips softly grazed her tender flesh. A hot flush stole into her cheeks. She must not faint!

''Larks and sparks, Sir John!'' Kat flicked a nonexistent piece of fluff from her peach-colored sleeve. ''I am not used to such fine speech as yours. Please tell me, at King Henry's court, what do the ladies wager, if not for some article of clothing?''

Sir John chuckled as he straightened up. ''His Grace is most generous with all the ladies, Mistress Miranda. In the evening after the supper has been cleared away, he gives each lady a small bag of silver coins for gaming at cards.''

Kat's eyes widened. ''His Grace is very generous. And you? Do you also wager with the king's bounty?''

Laughing, Sir John adjusted his green velvet cap over his sleek blond hair. ''Nay, innocent Miranda, I must provide my own coins.''

"Ah," Kat said thoughtfully. This turn of the conversation offered her the opportunity to test another part of her nephew's vivid description of her betrothed.

"And my Lord Cavendish?" She glanced over her shoulder at the other couple farther down the archery range. Her eyes narrowed. Surely Sir Brandon need not hover so close behind Miranda, as he helped her draw back her bowstring! And why was her cousin giggling in such a wanton manner? What jest had the man whispered into her ear? Or was it more than a jest? *Remember, coz, he is supposed to be marrying me.* The thought did not cheer Kat.

"What about my Lord Cavendish?" echoed Sir John, who also regarded the pair. His eyes darkened to a deeper blue. "He seems to find your cousin…most entertaining."

"Aye," Kat snapped. She turned away from the loving scene before she said or did anything to betray their ruse. *I really must have that serious talk with Miranda tonight, ere she finds herself bedded before I am wedded!*

"We were speaking of Sir Brandon," Sir John reminded her, clipping his words, like the gardeners clipped the hedge of yew trees.

"Aye. Sir Brandon." Kat ran her tongue across her lips. "Tell me, does he gamble much?"

Sir John lifted one brow as he smiled down at her. "Define 'much,' Mistress Miranda."

Playing with the ribbons that she had so recently won, Kat twined the satin streamers through her fingers. "Does my Lord Cavendish wager large amounts of money when he is at the card table? Forgive my boldness, Sir John, but as Katherine's cousin, I must be concerned with her welfare. Therefore I ask you plainly. Does Sir Brandon lose much in gambling?"

Behind them, Miranda's giggle rose half an octave, accompanied by the richer tones of Sir Brandon's laugh. Sir John glared over Kat's head at the two. "*Sir Brandon may* lose his shirt and the skin under it, if he does not take more care in the future,'' he muttered, more to himself than to Kat. His darker mood passed when he glanced down at her again. ''But in answer to your question, Sir Brandon is an excellent player of all manner of games.'' He leaned closer to her. ''And, Mistress Miranda, I speak from very close association.''

His warm breath, mint scented, fanned her face. Another wave of giddiness swept over Kat. It must be the weather. Perchance the wind bore some strange pollen to make one feel giddy in the middle of the afternoon.

''Just so,'' she murmured. Mayhap she needed a tonic. She must speak to Sondra about that later. ''And you swear that my cousin need not fear that Sir Brandon will spend her fortune at cards and other wagers?''

Sir John placed his hand over his breast. ''Upon my heart and soul, I do swear…for him, that is. My…friend comes from a wealthy family in Northumberland, and he is well provided. Cards do not hold him in their thrall, as they do many others—such as your cousin's knavish nephew.''

Kat cocked her head. ''How now? I…and my cousin have not heard this tale before. Pray, enlighten me, Sir John.''

Another giggle pierced the warm afternoon. Sir John curled his lips in disgust. ''Let us walk the garden paths, Mistress Miranda. I fear that so much billing and cooing between yon lovebirds is very distracting to my thoughts.'' He offered her his arm.

''Gladly, Sir John.'' Kat slipped her hand around his elbow. Under his green velvet sleeve, she felt the strength of his muscles. For a moment, she imagined herself enfolded in his strong embrace. Her mouth went suddenly dry.

They passed through an opening of the yew hedge into the intricate knot garden. The crushed shells of the path-

ways crunched under their feet as they paced out the geo-
metric design of the trimmed boxwood plantings.

"You spoke of Fen...young Sir Scantling, my lord?"
Kat prompted, after the archery range was out of sight and
sound.

"Aye, mistress. Pardon my bluntness, but he is an ass-
head."

Sir John's muscles tightened a little under Kat's fingertips. She wondered what the young fool had done to incur
the wrath of so noble a lord as Sir John.

"You may speak plainly with me, my lord. I am not
being wooed for my wedding day." *Not yet, thank God!*

"You should be," Sir John muttered under his breath.
Then he cleared his throat and continued in a louder tone.
"Scantling plays nightly at cards, dice or any other wager
the courtiers might devise. Once he even bet upon the outcome of a louse race!"

Kat missed a step. Sir John's hand steadied her. "By
the book! Do you speak of a race between bugs?" she
gasped.

Sir John's lips twitched, and his eyes twinkled azure fire.
"Aye, I do. And he lost even that one! He has the most
rotten luck, and poorest judgment in the entire court. Your
cousin is obviously not aware of it, Mistress Miranda, but
she has been taken out of pocket for a great deal of money
by that king of shreds and patches. Gambling is a sickness
with him, and one that he will not throw off. He will beggar Lady Katherine's entire estate within a twelvemonth,
unless I can..." Sir John pressed his lips into a thin, hard
line.

Kat gripped his sleeve, bunching the rich material between her fingers. She found it extremely difficult to make
disinterested conversation. God shield her! What a dithering fool she had been! How Fenton must have laughed
each time she sent him yet another letter of credit to her
goldsmith on London Bridge!

"Mistress Miranda?" Sir John murmured in her ear. "You have turned quite pale. Forgive me for being the bearer of bad tidings."

Kat shook her head. "Nay, Sir John, have no fear on my account. You do not know it, but you have done me a good service. I am in your debt. 'Tis better that you tell *me* of Fenton's perfidy, than to tell my cousin. She is a gentle creature, and would likely faint at the news." Kat looked up into Sir John's eyes, warmed by the depths of concern she saw there. "I am made of sterner stuff."

"So I perceive, sweet Miranda." He leaned over her, blotting out the late afternoon sun. "And I salute you for it."

Brushing his lips against hers, he took her wholly by surprise. His kiss imparted a velvet warmth that left her mouth burning and her body quivering for more.

"Sir John," she murmured, standing on tiptoe.

"Aye," he growled. His lips nibbled her earlobe. "'Tis a name I wear like a hat on a holiday, but 'twill suffice for now. Let me drink from you again, and we'll take tomorrow when it comes."

"Aye." She sighed as his large hand cupped her face, holding it gently. His touch was almost unbearable in its tenderness. Not once in thirteen years of marriage had she ever been caressed like this. Closing her eyes and parting her lips, she rose to meet him.

His mouth recaptured hers, his kiss more demanding this time. His tongue traced the soft fullness of her lips, then grew bolder as it explored the recesses of her mouth. Gathering her in his arms, he held her close, gently rocking her back and forth as he deepened his kiss. Kat drank in the sweetness of his mouth with a reckless abandon she had never known before. Bright colored stars danced behind her closed eyelids. She tried to remember to breathe.

Brushing her lower lip, Sir John slowly released his hold upon her. Kat shivered as his warmth left her.

"I am fortune's biggest fool, sweet Miranda. Pray, pardon me." Turning on his heel, he left her standing in the middle of the path.

Squinting into the lowering sun, Kat watched his tall figure striding toward the stables. She touched the place his teeth had grazed her skin. By our larkin! What folly had she done? Her breathing slowly returned to normal, though she did not yet trust her knees to carry her back to her chambers. The memory of his kiss burned on her lips.

"Nay, Sir John, you are not the greatest fool in Bodiam today," she whispered. "I claim that title for myself alone."

Let tomorrow come! My betrothed may kiss like a candied carrot, but this moment with Sir John will remain mine forever.

"On such an evening as this, one might spy Cupid disguised as a firefly, flitting among your flowers, fair Katherine." Sir Brandon gave his lady's hand a little squeeze as he helped her settle herself on one of the stone benches in the far corner of the garden.

Miranda trembled at the sound of his rich, mellow voice. He smelled of mint, wood smoke and some other scent that was his alone. The combination made her feel quite giddy. "Perchance Cupid will attend the wedding day." Placing her hand over her breast, she closed her fingers around the swan pendant. She clutched it as if it were a talisman.

"I...I thank you again for this lovely gift, Sir Brandon. Ka...that is, my cousin teases me much, and says that she thinks I even sleep with it at night."

"Would that I could sleep with you at night." Sir Brandon's lips hovered dangerously close.

Miranda licked her own lips, which felt as parched and cracked as empty wineskins. "In due time, my lord, in due time. I am an honest woman, and would wait until after the wedding vows are spoken before any bedding is done.''

Sir Brandon pulled himself upright, though his arm still held her waist. ''You speak the truth, dear lady, and remind me of my manners. I fear I have become too lax at court. Pray forgive me.''

''There is nothing to forgive, my lord. I am glad to see that the bridegroom is so eager for the wedding day.''

''He'd better be,'' Sir Brandon growled under his breath.

His changed tone jarred Miranda. ''My lord?''

''Nothing, my love. 'Tis but a vow I have made. On your wedding day, your bridegroom will be all that you deserve—and more.'' He caressed her cheek with his forefinger, then brushed a stray tendril of her hair from her forehead.

A light crunching sound on the shell path interrupted further conversation and action. Violet, one of the chambermaids, dashed up to them, and bobbed a curtsy.

''Mistress...my Lady Kat,'' she babbled. ''My...your cousin suggests that the air has grown too cold for dallying in the garden, and she prays that you join her and my Lord Stafford by the fire in the hall.'' The girl paused for breath. ''*Are* you dallying, mistress?''

Sir Brandon stood up and stretched. His height towered over the young maid. ''Not anymore.'' His teeth flashed white in the rising moon's light. He offered Miranda his arm. ''Shall we join your vigilant cousin, my lady?''

Standing, Miranda brushed down her lavender skirts. ''Aye, methinks 'twould be a good idea. Thank you, Violet. Tell my cousin that we are coming.''

The girl curtsied again, winked at Miranda, then ran off into the shadows giggling like a magpie.

Sir Brandon's lips twitched. ''Sweet Katherine, is there some malady that affects your servants?''

Miranda slipped her arm within his. ''How so, my

lord?'' Together they strolled slowly down the path in Violet's scampering wake.

Sir Brandon rubbed his chin before answering. ''Ever since our arrival at your home, all your maids have taken to winking, giggling and giving each other sly looks and elbow prods. Tell me, are my face and form worthy of their mirth?''

Night's welcome darkness hid Miranda's grin. ''Nay, my lord. I suspect 'tis because we have so few men around here. When you and my Lord Stafford arrived, accompanied by such a handsome army of retainers, our maids did not know what to do. Please forgive their behavior. They are simple country girls at heart.''

Sir Brandon unlatched the wicket gate in the yew hedge and held it open for Miranda to pass through. ''That brings me to another question, sweet lady. I have noticed that all your maidservants have the names of flowers. Daisy, Pansy, Rosemary, and now, this one is Violet. Pray how is this so? Were all their mothers gardeners?''

Miranda couldn't control her sudden burst of laughter. ''I am sure you must find it puzzling, my lord. Nay, originally they were called Mary, Anne or Margaret. 'Tis understandable when you know that the three parishes hereabouts are Saint Mary, Saint Anne and Saint Margaret.''

''I see,'' Sir Brandon said, but in such a manner that Miranda realized he was as confused as before.

''When Fitzhugh died, my cousin dismissed all his retainers. Instead, she took in as servants many daughters of the poor farmers in the area.''

Pausing midstep, Sir Brandon looked down at her. ''You say your cousin did this? Not you?''

''I...'' Miranda could have bitten her tongue in two. ''My cousin has acted as my housekeeper for many years, Sir Brandon. She knows much better than I how to run the estate, so I am pleased to let her do it. 'Twas her idea to rename the girls for all the flowers of the garden, instead of calling them Mary One or Mary Two. Much less confusing.''

Sir Brandon resumed their stroll. Miranda breathed a small prayer of thanksgiving. How could she keep her wits about her, when every time the handsome lord looked at her, she wanted to melt into a puddle at his feet?

He coughed, then cleared his throat. ''I do not mean to distress you, especially on such a sweet evening as this, my love, but since you mentioned it, how did your late husband expire? I am told 'twas sudden.''

Miranda gritted her teeth at the loathsome memory of Fitzhugh the Furious and his last moments on earth. ''The doctor said 'twas a stroke in his brain that caused it, my lord. He died in the midst of beating my cousin.''

Sir Brandon stopped so suddenly that Miranda bumped into him. He caught her around the waist, then drew her closer. ''He *struck* your gentle cousin?'' His voice rose with a fury she had not heard before.

Squaring her shoulders, Miranda looked him straight in the eye. Kat hated to recall Fitzhugh, and with good reason, but Sir Brandon should know what a hell her life had been during her second marriage. Perhaps he would treat Kat with the loving kindness she deserved.

''Aye, 'twas his custom. Sometimes he used a belt, sometimes a small whip of leather thongs, sometimes merely his hand. It pleased him in some devilish perverse way to hear her cry, and to see her bleed.''

''God have mercy,'' Sir Brandon whispered. ''Why didn't you stop him? You were his wife!''

Miranda hung her head. The memory of her hiding in the stable loft or under beds was a shameful one. She answered in a barely audible voice. ''Fitzhugh treated his wife as shamefully as he did his servants. No one dared to interfere with the master of the house. 'Twas a sweet relief when he went to court for a month or two. 'Twas paradise on earth when he died. I fear no tears were shed at his funeral.''

Enfolding Miranda in his embrace, Sir Brandon hugged her with a fierce possessiveness. "Sweet Jesu!"

She reveled in the moment of such overpowering love, then she placed her palms against his chest and looked up at him. "There is one boon that I beg you, Sir Brandon.''

"Name it. 'Tis yours for the asking," he replied in a husky tone.

"When you are married, I beg you to promise me that you will never raise your hand to your wife, and to treat her kindly every day. Please. Swear to me this vow.''

Sir Brandon took one of her hands in his. "Upon my soul's hope for eternal salvation, I swear to you that Sir Brandon Cavendish will never touch his most precious wife except with gentle love.''

Closing her eyes, Miranda sighed with relief. "I am in your debt, my lord. You do not know how happy you have made me.''

"And I would make you happier, if it were in my power.''

He bent his head to kiss her, but Miranda perceived his intent and stepped out of his embrace. If she let him kiss her now, she might not be able to hold back.

Hugging her arms, she shivered. "The night grows colder, my lord. Let us hurry indoors.''

Sir Brandon nodded, then tucked her arm around his again. "You speak with great wisdom, my lady," he muttered.

As they mounted the low steps to the garden door of the castle, Miranda turned to him. "One final request, Sir Brandon. I beg you not to speak of this matter to my cousin. Even now, the memory of that terrible time grieves her.''

Cavendish placed his hand over hers. "You have my bond and my oath upon that, my lady. I shall not speak a word of it—to her.''

Chapter Six

"He beat Miranda?" Brandon slammed his fist against the chimney flue in the guest chamber. The rough stone scored his flesh, but Brandon barely noticed the pain.

"Aye, both of them, and often. Lady Katherine was loath to speak of it." Jack poured his friend a cup of wine. "Drink some of this. 'Twill take the taste of gall from your tongue."

"That vile, creeping, venomous viper dared to lay his hand on that sweet lady?" Brandon snatched the cup, then tossed back the contents in a single loud gulp. The roughness of the unwatered wine made tears spring to the corners of his eyes.

"On both ladies, my friend," Jack reminded him in a chiding tone. He poured Brandon another drink.

"I remember that villainous toad at court." Brandon's lips curled like a snarling dog's.

"And I, as well. A barrel-chested bruiser—blustery, shouting the rafters down, and always red in the face." Jack yanked off one boot, then the other in preparation for bed.

"A poor sport in the tiltyard, and hard on his squires." Brandon rubbed his forefinger across his upper lip.

And while her husband sported at court, his poor Kath-

erine and sweet Miranda cowered within the cold walls of
Bodiam, waiting in terror for the master's return. The
thought of them under the hands of that barbarous brute
made Brandon shake with anger.

"Did no one try to protect them?" Turning away from
the fire, Brandon stared at Jack.

Meeting Brandon's look, Jack returned its intensity.
"Who could? That laughable chamberlain, Montjoy? Too
old. The paltry men-at-arms? Too cowardly. The cook?
The maids? The potboy? Who would dare challenge their
lord in his own household?"

"What about Lady's Katherine's most loving nephew,
Fenton?" Brandon sneered. He already knew the answer
to that one.

"Katherine told me he was Fitzhugh's willing pupil.
That sniveling malt worm knew where his future lay, and
'twas not with his aunt." Jack flung his other boot against
the far wall. "Of course, things changed the moment Fitzhugh dropped dead."

Brandon released a long breath. "At least, we know that
Lady Katherine didn't poison her last husband. God's
teeth, Jack! I wouldn't have blamed her one whit if she
had!"

Jack untied his sleeves. "That slandered lady is blame-
less of the first one's death, as well. I asked her chambermaid. Lewknor was in his eighties when he married
Katherine. She was but fifteen at the time."

"A pox of wrinkles! What was her father thinking to
shackle her to a dithering graybeard?" For the first time
in nine days, Brandon gave a caring thought toward his
intended bride.

"Lewknor's fortune." Jack peeled off his brown velvet
jacket, then tossed it onto the nearby chest. "Bodiam was
originally Lewknor's castle. The old man didn't want a
bride, he wanted a nursemaid. It took him eighteen months
to finally cough his last."

"Leaving a rich, young widow." Brandon resumed his contemplation of the fire.

"Aye, and an avaricious father. Katherine was wed again before the turning of the year. For all his monstrous ways, Fitzhugh had a vast fortune in land and tenants in this shire. My congratulations, Cavendish. You are marrying a beautiful lady, who owns most of Sussex. 'Tis time you gave some thought to her."

Brandon glared over his shoulder at Jack. "What do you mean by that last remark?" he growled.

Jack narrowed his eyes. "'Tis high time you pay court to your future wife. In the past week you have barely spoken to her save for courtesy."

Brandon tightened his fingers around his wine cup. "'Tis because I cannot get a word in edgewise with you singing, jabbering or composing rhymes to her," he muttered.

Jack hurled one of his stockings at Brandon. The smelly article hit him on the back of the neck. "I have been speaking and singing for you, you hedgepig. Remember? I have been wooing that innocent lady in your stead, while you go prancing off behind hedges with her comely cousin. 'Tis time to bring this charade to an end."

"Before you fall in love with Lady Katherine yourself?" Brandon asked softly, not looking at Jack. He didn't need to.

The fire crackled in the silence.

"How I feel is mine own affair," Jack finally replied. He climbed into the wide, canopied bed they shared and slipped between the sheets. "Look to yourself, Brandon. Katherine has been sorely used by her first two husbands. She does not deserve that fate a third time. In fact, I gave her my oath, in your name, that you would not."

Brandon spun around. "The devil take you, Stafford! I would never hurt her, no matter what. You should know that!"

"Not with your hands, no, but what about your heart?" he asked from the depths of the bed. "And what about your children? When do you plan to surprise her with them? Think on that."

"Aye, I will." Brandon set the cup down on a stool, then pulled his heavy wool cloak from the peg.

Jack hitched himself up on his elbows. "How now, man? You need not go wake her, and tell her your secrets this minute. Tomorrow will suffice. She'll need a good night's sleep, before you reveal who you really are, then spring two nine-year-olds upon her."

"I will tell her about Belle and Francis in my own good time, and 'twill not be at breakfast—on that you may lay a winning wager." Brandon fumbled for his golden brooch that held the cloak together, then swore under his breath when he recalled where it had gone.

Jack's frown penetrated the chamber's semidarkness. "Where are you going? 'Tis near midnight."

"To the devil, for I am in hell already." He flung open the door.

Jack flopped back against the pillows. "Give him my regards, and don't fall off the wall walk. 'Twould be a nasty swim in that stinking moat. I bid you a pleasant evening's stroll."

"You were begot between two fishmongers!"

"And shut the door behind you. The draft is bone chilling."

Brandon slammed it with a resounding thud.

The night guard on the northern battlements gave a startled nod as Brandon stalked past him. The half-moon hung in the dark bowl of the night, and an errant cloud teased about the diamond points of a thousand sparkling stars. Brandon drew to a halt at the center of the walkway, directly over the giant winches that raised and lowered the portcullis. Resting his arms on the chest-high wall, he stared unseeing at the black silhouette of the home park forest.

I am a very knave and my lying tongue will double back upon itself, and choke me. Aye, and a good riddance too! Brandon gnawed his inner cheek. What a hell broth he had brewed by this simple-seeming deceit! Hadn't his good mother told him that liars are always trapped within the web of their own making? Now he strangled in it.

What was he going to do? Jack was not the only one who had lost his heart where he least expected. Jack still had an ounce of his wit about him. For himself, Brandon had refused to mark each passing day as one closer to his wedding. Instead, he pretended he was on a straw-hatted holiday in the company of too-fair a maiden.

Kinswoman to my new wife! What a lack-witted dolt I am! I do not have half as much brains as earwax! And what will I do after I am married to Katherine, when I must face each new day with Miranda's shining presence on my left hand? Come, hot tongs and cruel spikes, sear me for I am on the rack now.

Miranda! Her image swam up in his mind's eye. Just today he noted how the early June sunlight caught the many different shades of red and gold in her hair, creating a vision most pleasing to the eye. How could he bed the shyer cousin, and not dream that it was Miranda he held in his arms in the dark of night? His marriage vows would be a lie, even worse than the one he was living now.

Nay, for the sake of his soul, and for the loyalty his honor compelled him to give to Katherine, he must send away the tempting cousin as soon as the wedding feast was over. Jack could take her back to Henry's court. Miranda would have no dearth of suitors there within a fortnight. Brandon gritted his teeth. The court—where far too many hot-blooded men had far too much time on their hands. Where Miranda's good virtue would not last a month. The bored nobles needed a good war to occupy their lusty minds.

Send Miranda to a nunnery? Brandon grimaced in the dark. God help the abbess who had her for a novice! Nay, the lady was as unlikely for the nunnery as his brother was to become a monk—which, thanks to a French angel named Celeste, he hadn't. But the nut and core of the argument still remained. Miranda must go. As her new kinsman, the most honorable thing he could do would be to set her up at court with a goodly dowry. 'Twould be for the best that she marry.

Bowing his head, Brandon dug his knuckles into his closed eyelids. He didn't want to think of anyone touching her except himself! Miranda had gotten under his skin, into his dreams, invaded his heart and befuddled what was left of his wits. 'Twas true what the wise old folk said: love turns scholars into madmen.

Love! Brandon swallowed down the knot in his throat. Aye, he did love Miranda, and she must never, ever know it. 'Twas one truth he would never tell, come rack or ruin.

Jack was right. Brandon needed to clean his slate of all falsehood. The wedding was a fortnight away. So be it, but let him be Jack Stafford for two more days to ease himself gently out of Miranda's good graces. Then, with his honor frayed but intact, he would spend his last two weeks of freedom wooing the poor, hoodwinked Lady Katherine. Jack would have to take Miranda out of the castle daily to go hunting, or whatever, while Brandon mended his marital fences. Brandon knew he could never pay court to Katherine under Miranda's beautiful, watchful eyes.

Belle! The face of his love child rose in his mind. Great Jove! What would Katherine say when he told her she was going to be a mother as well as a wife? He prayed she would not succumb to an attack of the vapors. She would need all her strength once she had met Brandon's little sprite. He shuddered at the thought. Perhaps it might be better to wait before revealing Francis's true relationship. He hoped Katherine would not notice the resemblance— at least, not at first. One child at a time.

Great Harry! You may be my king and liege lord, but, by Jove, 'tis well you are not within the reach of my fist this moment!

"Wormsley! Where are you hiding that poxed carcass of yours?" Sir Fenton Scantling's voice echoed throughout the servants' hall in the cellars of Hampton Court Palace.

Hastily wiping his mouth free of clinging drops of ale, Tod Wormsley detached himself from a cluster of his fellow servants and hurried toward his fuming master. He tried to ignore the giggling of the maids behind him. It was an embarrassment for a master to have to search out his man below stairs. A good servant should always be wherever his master expected him to be. Tod cursed the swaggering braggart under his breath, as he took the stairs two at a time. He prayed Sir Fenton wouldn't box his ears in front of everyone.

Tod's hopes proved short-lived, as Scantling roundly dealt him a stinging blow.

"Ass-head! I have been seeking you this past quarter hour!" Fenton kicked Tod out the door into the passageway.

Tod stumbled but managed not to fall onto the dank paving stones. He bit back the stream of words that bubbled to his lips. Instead, he murmured, "Pray excuse me, my lord. Methought you had gone to London, and—"

"Aye, and now I have returned again, as you can plainly see!" Sir Fenton shouted into Tod's ear.

By his high color and the smartness of his blows, Tod guessed that something had gone foully awry. "Pray you, sir, what's amiss?" He jumped back to avoid another kick.

"I have been ill-used by that whore!" Scantling

screeched. Clasping Tod's elbow in a painful grip, Sir Fenton pulled his manservant down the corridors to his small bedchamber.

"Which whore is that, my lord?" Tod asked, between gasps of breath. Hang it all! Had his master contracted the pox from his latest jade?

"The bitch that holds my purse strings!" Scantling rounded a corner sharply.

Tod clipped his shoulder against a low stone corbel and sucked air through his teeth as much in surprise as in pain. "Do you speak of the Lady Katherine?"

"Aye, that she-devil!" Flinging open his door, Sir Fenton pushed Tod inside. "Pack!"

Tod massaged the pain in his arm and shoulder. "Where do we go? For how long, my lord?" He fought to keep the anger out of his voice. When Scantling got into one of his tearing rages, he became like a maddened dog, and equally dangerous.

"Pack it all! Thanks to Aunt Kat's pending nuptials, I am now the most sought-after man in London." Scantling snatched up the ever-present jug of wine and poured himself a large cup.

Scrambling under the bed, Tod tugged at the two large saddlebags stored behind the trundle. He cracked the back of his head on the bed board. Cursing the pain, he succeeded in hauling the thick leather packs out to the middle of the room. Scantling flopped onto the only chair and stared moodily out the window. Tod breathed a small prayer. Perhaps the violent fit had passed. Tod opened the chest and began stuffing his master's linen into one of the large side pockets.

Sir Fenton took a deep drink of his wine. "Ill-used, Worm, that's what I am. Not more than ten minutes after I had left the barge at the foot of London Bridge I was accosted by tradesmen."

"Very distressing, I am sure," Tod remarked. He folded

Scantling's gold satin doublet, before wedging it on top of the shirts. Casting an appraising look into the chest, the young servant calculated that he would need either a third saddlebag or a canvas roll to carry his master's enlarged wardrobe in its entirety.

Sir Fenton snorted. "Damnable ass-licking curs! When I gave them my custom, they were happy enough to extend my credit twice over. The name Fitzhugh was well-known among the tailors and jewelers of London Bridge. My business was their boundless pleasure." He poured himself more wine.

Tod stuffed handfuls of gold chains into the toes of Scantling's white satin dancing slippers. Just one of those chains would have fed Tod's brothers and sisters for a year or more. "You have always had good taste in fashion, my lord," he murmured.

"Aye, and now, thanks to the news of my aunt's marriage flying about the city, I shall be reduced to rags and tatters."

When hell freezes over. Tod ground his teeth as he rolled up one silken pair of hose after another. The spoiled son of Lady Kat's dead sister had never known a minute of want, thanks to the good lady's tender heart for taking in the sniveling boy.

"Did my lady stop your line of credit at the goldsmith's?" Tod ventured to ask. He knew he might get another cuff on the head for the impertinence of the question, but the words were out of his mouth before he could stop them.

"Not yet, but my creditors have decided not to wait. They want payment in full now, before Cavendish wraps his grasping hands around Kat's estate, and stops all my payments cold as coffin nails." Scantling sipped his wine as he drummed his fingers on his knee. "One of the fat-lipped churls even insinuated that my days of spending have come to an end."

And then there will be the devil to pay. Tod shuddered inwardly at the thought. He piled Scantling's velvet bonnets one on top of the other, expertly curling the feathers of one inside the crown of the next in the stack.

Sir Fenton pulled on his lower lip—a habit that indicated deep thought. "It appears that my plan to sour this pernicious nuptial between the bride and groom has missed its intended mark. I had hoped one or the other of the couple would have taken my advice to heart, and would have persuaded the king to change his mind. Instead, I have news from Bodiam that both parties find each other pleasing." Leaning forward, he skewered Tod with the pinpoints of his hard dark eyes. "'Tis not pleasing at all to me. God rot Kat's soul! Aye, and Cavendish's too! I will not be made a fool's hat stand by either of them. Nor do I intend to be dealt out of my uncle's inheritance. 'Tis mine!"

Tod hunched over the saddlebags and whispered a quick prayer to mend the terrible curse of his master. Lady Kat was too kind. If Tod possessed half her spark and fiber, he would leave this monster's service immediately. But Tod knew himself to be a coward. As vile as Sir Fenton could be on occasion, he still gave Tod a far better living than the boy would have had as the third son of a pig farmer.

"You have a plan, my lord?" he asked, struggling to buckle up the bulging pack.

"Aye. We will steal out this night, and ride for Bodiam. Don't turn your mouth down at me, boy, or I'll do you a turn that will leave you more thankful to walk instead of ride. There are only a few hours of darkness these nights, and I know the way well. Once there, I will speak with honey words to my aunt, expressing my desire for her happiness and my concern about the tedious management of her estate.

"On my way back to the barge, I stopped at the Inns

of Court, and had one of those watery-eyed students draw me up a paper of guardianship. 'Tis a bastard piece of composition, but 'twill suffice. If Kat is as besotted as my sources tell me she is, she will sign the paper in a twink, then return to the arms of her lover. After that, I care not a fig if she swells up with a bellyful of brats. The estate, the lands and the rents will be in my care. Cavendish can whistle up the chimney!''

Hoisting the first pack over his shoulder, Tod sagged under its weight. He dropped it in the corner, then returned to fill the second.

Sir Fenton rose from his seat, then paused to admire himself in the looking glass. He straightened his bonnet and adjusted the fall of his latest gold chain. ''I will take my supper with the king in the hall. I expect our horses to be saddled and ready by eight of the clock.'' He turned to go.

''My lord?'' Tod licked his lips. He rarely interfered with Scantling's plans, but the Lady Kat had been good to the boy and he wanted to give her some warning. ''If we are discovered gone in the night, your creditors will assume that you have fled straightway to Bodiam, and they will pursue you there. Methinks you would not want your debts and your aunt brought face-to-face.''

Scantling paused. ''For once, you speak with a grain of sense. Go on.''

''If, instead, we leave openly on the morrow, with many words in many ears that you have gone north to visit friends at Oxford, then your creditors will hie themselves in the wrong direction.''

Sir Fenton grinned like a tickled cat. ''I like this pretty plan. And then?''

''Meanwhile, we shall ride westward as far as Bath, before turning south and from there to Bodiam. That way we shall elude those who seek you.'' *And I shall try to send warning to my lady.*

Fenton ran his fingers down the jaunty white plume in his bonnet. "Finish packing, then take yourself back to your hall and enjoy your supper. Dally with a maid. Drink with your scurvy fellows and spread the word of my trip to Oxford. You have done well, Worm." Turning on his heel, Fenton went out the door, banging it behind him.

Sinking down on the floor next to the bed, Tod drew in one or two deep breaths. His master's changeable moods always unnerved him. He knew that Sir Fenton was most dangerous when he seemed the calmest. Glancing at the table, he spied writing materials there, beckoning to be used. The boy swore against the Fates that had left him unlettered. He prayed he could find someone in the servants' hall who was Sussex-bound.

The new day dawned as bright as the seven before it. Kat hurried through her dressing and barely tasted the bread and butter that Laurel had brought to break her fast. Miranda hummed as she prepared for the day, as well. All in all, this past week had flown most agreeably. Thank heavens, Miranda had ceased to ask when Kat planned to end the game! Just another week in Sir John's company, then...

"Well met, ladies, and a joyous good morrow to you both!" Sir John bowed as Kat and Miranda joined the handsome knights in the hall.

"Well spoken, Sir John," Kat returned. "Have you been taking lessons from my Lord Cavendish?"

Sir John wobbled a smile. "Aye, mistress, I fear he has bent my ear of late for my lack of good manners." He glared at Sir Brandon, who merely smiled in return.

"Then permit me to order some lemon juice for your dinner, in case the honey of your speech sticks to the roof of your mouth and renders you useless for the rest of the day," Kat replied with a grin.

"What shall we do betwixt now and dinner?" Miranda,

as the lady of the house, asked her guests. "What is your pleasure?"

Sir Brandon opened his mouth, then shut it and glanced at Sir John. Stafford cleared his throat.

"Perchance you will accompany me on a ride in the forest, my Lady Katherine?" he mumbled, not looking at the real Katherine.

Kat looked at him with amazement. *How now? Did Sir John get up on the wrong side of his bed this morning? Have my teeth turned green? And why is he looking at Miranda in such a sickly fashion?*

Before Kat could speak, the housekeeper, Sondra Owens, hurried into the hall. Daisy and Violet followed close behind her, their arms laden with bolts of colorful fabric.

Sondra bobbed a quick curtsy. "Your pardon, Mistress Miranda, but I have much need of you."

Kat raised her brows. "Now? This minute?"

Sondra's eyes took on a merry look. In fact, she seemed to radiate excitement. Kat could not imagine why.

"Aye, mistress." Sondra pointed to the serving girls and their burdens. "'Tis near a fortnight to the wedding, and we have yet to begin Lady Katherine's gown."

"My wedding gown?" Miranda squeaked, looking at Kat like a frightened doe in a trap.

Sondra laughed. "Aye, bless you, my lady. 'Tis a great day when the mistress of Bodiam takes her true love for a husband. I'll not stand by and see you do it in a made-over gown from a year ago. I've brought up bolts of cloth from the storeroom," she continued, including both gentlemen in her conversation. "And I need the good offices of Mistress Miranda. She and my lady are much alike in form and figure, as I am sure you've noticed by now, my lords. I will set the pattern to Mistress Miranda, and cut out the gown to her, so as to save my lady's time. Lady Katherine, you can entertain the gentlemen as free in mind as a bird in the air. Mistress Miranda and I will do you a gown to make the sun blush for shame.''

Kat frowned at her. *By the rood! Sondra has danced too long in the moonlight, and has now a touch of the madness that comes from it! Using me as a dress form! Ha!*

Kat forced a smile while she answered in sweet tones. ''Sondra, a word in your ear. My lady, my lords, pray excuse us.''

''We shall count the moments of your leaving as tears, mistress.'' Sir Brandon grinned at her, showing an alarming number of white teeth.

God shield me! I shall go screaming mad if I have to marry that…that prattling honeycomb.

Kat led Sondra to the nearby alcove. Once away from prying ears and eyes, the mistress turned on her housekeeper. ''What do you mean by this, Sondra? Have you lost your wits? You know my size and shape better than I do, and can make up a dress for me in your sleep.''

''Tis true,'' Sondra agreed. Her purple eyes sparkled, and her lips could barely contain her smile.

Kat put her hands to her hips. ''And I do not intend to waste good cloth on a special gown for my wedding to that babbling peacock. My blue silk with the lace will do well enough. After all, I am no virginal maiden, but a woman who is facing her third husband, God help me.''

''Tis true—if that were true, my lady,'' Sondra replied with a wink. Her laughter bubbled like a waterfall on a spring day.

Kat cocked her head. ''How now? I spy some great mischief. What mean you by 'tis true if true? What has happened?''

Leaning toward her, Sondra whispered, ''Send the noble lords to the woods with Miranda. We must confer in utmost secrecy. I have news that will make your heart sing like a thousand larks. Trust me, my lady.''

Kat regarded Sondra for a long moment. The woman

was more than a mere housekeeper, but a friend and confidante since Kat had come to Bodiam. Some folk in the nearby village called Sondra a white witch because of her healing arts and herbal knowledge. Kat knew this to be false, yet Sondra possessed an intuitive power that had no explanation. Perchance she really could read souls. In any event, Kat trusted her implicitly.

"My lady? Will you give me an hour of your time, and both your ears? You will not rue it."

Kat sighed then nodded. "Aye, Sondra. You knew I would. Go to my chamber, and I'll attend you there in a moment. As for the cloth, tell the girls to bide with it awhile."

Sondra laughed and clapped her hands. She quickly hustled the maids with the fabric from the hall as Kat rejoined the others.

"I trust that you did not weep too many tears for me in my short absence, Sir Brandon," she remarked as she joined them.

"Nay, mistress, he was afraid the torrent might wash off his smile," Sir John muttered.

"M...Miranda?" The real Miranda lifted one delicate brow in question. "How now?"

"Sondra has given me good reason to tarry here. I am sure the talk of patterns, pins, laces and stitches would bore you to even more tears, Sir Brandon, than my mere departure did just now. Pray, all of you, ride out as you planned. Meanwhile, I will be trussed up like a gilded swan. We shall meet at dinner. Enjoy the morning, Sir John. Perchance the clean air will clear away the sugar from your palate."

"Perchance, mistress." He glowered, not at her, but at Sir Brandon. "I regret that my speech offends you. At dinner, I promise to amend that, for I will not speak at all." Nodding to Miranda, he continued. "My Lady Katherine, if my speech does not offend *you*, will you ride with me—and Sir Brandon?''

Miranda, clearly surprised by Sir John's sudden attention, flushed, then nodded. He offered her his arm, while Sir Brandon took the other. The trio went out into the bright sunshine of the day, leaving Kat harboring thunderstorms in her heart.

'Tis for the best, I suppose. I was growing too fond of Sir John. I must turn my mind to the other one. By my heel! That foppish bore is enough to make stones weep!

Chapter Seven

Kat closed the door to her chamber, then leaned against it. Sondra sat on the window seat, contented as a dairy cat enjoying the morning sun. Folding her arms across her chest, Kat tilted her head to one side. "How now, Sondra? What is this marvelous news you have for me?"

Sondra patted the cushion next to her. "Do you want the long or the short of it, Lady Kat?"

"Tell me the short first, then the longer version." She settled herself next to her housekeeper.

"What was sauce for the goose is now sauce for the gander." Sondra's smile deepened into laughter.

Confused, Kat shook her head. "Riddle me no riddles, Sondra, but speak plain."

Sondra chuckled. "'Tis this—he, who calls himself Sir Brandon, is not that worthy lord at all. He is, in fact, Sir John Stafford. And he, that calls himself Sir John—and playing the fool of love with you—is none other than the real Sir Brandon Cavendish—and your intended husband by royal command."

Kat fell back against the deep frame of the window. Her cheeks flushed while her hands grew icy. She had difficulty drawing a deep breath. She didn't know whether to laugh or cry.

"How did you come by this information?" Kat managed to gasp. Her mind whirled like a weather vane in a storm. The most handsome, fascinating man she had ever met couldn't possibly be the very one who was to marry her in two weeks. "Why the deceit?"

Sondra tapped the side of her nose. "You will find the answer to the second question in yourself, my lady. 'Tis the same reason as your own counterfeit—to spy you out. As to the answer to the first…" She broke off with another laugh.

"Peace, peace, good Sondra. Tell me all, before I fly out this window with distraction."

Sondra leaned closer. "Do you know which one of the Lord Cavendish's men is the master huntsman—Jess, by name?"

Kat considered the several dozen men who had taken up lodgings over the stables. "The tallest one?"

Sondra nodded with a secret twinkle in her eye. "The very same, and a fine specimen of manhood he is, too."

"*He* told you?" Kat wondered if the huntsman had merely spun an amusing tale to entertain an interested admirer.

"Aye, though he didn't know it."

Kat cocked her head. "How now? What did you do to the poor man, Sondra?"

Sondra rolled her eyes before answering. "What I did, and what he did, is not important, except to the two of us. But before we did anything together, I…I filled his tankard with a goodly portion of our best brew."

Kat began to understand. "You befuddled his mind."

Sondra dimpled. "He's a very big man, my lady, so I did not water down the ale, but gave it to him full strength. By the turn of the night, that great long man was set afire with desire—and more than a little drunk."

"Sweet angels, Sondra! You could have killed him!"

"Nay, but it did loosen him up a little more than I had

planned. The night was well spent, indeed." Sondra
grinned at the recollection. "In truth, I am stiff and sore
this morning."

Kat chose to ignore the nature of Sondra's ailments.
"And the huntsman told you of his master's switch in
identities?"

"Aye, afterward...as he hovered on the brink betwixt
wakefulness and deep sleep, Jess murmured that he was
the most satisfied man in Bodiam." Pausing, Sondra
blushed. "He said he was happier to lie with me in his
arms, and be content, than to go to bed alone with only a
false name for comfort like his master did."

"But did Jess say exactly what he meant by that?"
Kat's thoughts ran ahead of Sondra's story.

If John was indeed Brandon, that would explain his odd
behavior this morning. With a fortnight before Midsummer's Day, his conscience must have pricked him. Kat
snorted as she recalled John's...nay, Brandon's kisses in
the garden. The devil take the rogue! What did the churl
mean by wooing *her*—his betrothed's spinster cousin? Or
was he merely toying with an innocent maid's affections
to amuse himself before he lost his bachelorhood? Biting
her lower lip, Kat banished the unpleasant idea.

"Did Jess name the lords by their proper titles?"

"Aye, he did—with a little prodding from me."

"Good heavens, Sondra! Your huntsman is even now
riding with his master and Miranda. He is sure to confess
to them that he has spilled the secret."

Sondra shook her head. "Not so. As I said, the drink
was more than he needed. In fact, he does not remember
what was said, or done, this past night. He was most surprised to awaken at the cock's crow this morning to find
me a-lying in his arms."

Kat grinned. "I can well imagine."

Sondra winked. "Jess is a fine piece of work, my lady.
He apologized for not remembering how I got there in the

first place, but he made sure we'd both have something to remember before I left his side.''

Kat's ears warmed under her veil. She tried not to imagine Sondra and Jess sporting in her stable loft.

Sondra turned more serious. ''But the heart of the matter is still the same. All this time, you've been dallying with your bridegroom, and he has been dallying with a lady whom he thinks is not his bride.''

''What a perfidious slug!'' Kat rose and began to pace across the square patch of sunlight. ''And once again, I will be wed unto a man with a false heart. God rot him!''

''Peace, my lady. I think not.''

Kat stared at her friend and wondered if the wise woman had read Brandon's soul. Kat was half-afraid to know.

''How now, Sondra?''

''I think my Lord Cavendish is gone full over his head in love with you—not with Lady Katherine Fitzhugh, mistress of Bodiam, nor even with her quiet cousin, Miranda Paige. He is in love with yourself, by whatever name you choose to be called.''

Sitting again beside Sondra, Kat took one of her friend's hands in hers. ''Tell me the truth. Are you certain of this?''

''Aye, I am. 'Tis as plain as the sun a-shining out there this minute. You only have to see the man a-looking after you to read the love in his face. Now your poor lord finds himself tied up in knots tighter than a rabbit in a poacher's poke. He knows he is in love with one lady, while he thinks he must marry the other. All the while, 'tis one and the same woman that he loves. Sir Brandon has been caught in his own trap.''

''How wonderful, Sondra!'' A satisfying laugh welled up from deep inside Kat. She could not hold it back, nor did she want to. ''This plan of mine has worked out even better than I expected! 'Tis too rich a dish to be gobbled all at once!'' She leaned back against the wall, laughing even harder. Sondra joined her.

After a few minutes, their merriment subsided into a few giggles and a hiccup or two.

"Would you be in the market for a piece of advice or two?" Sondra asked with a knowing gleam in her eye.

"Aye, you know I would. What do you suggest? A love potion to make my Lord Cavendish reveal the truth?"

Sondra cocked her head in thought. "I could devise something of that nature, but methinks there is a better way."

"What?"

"By letting Sir Brandon's dilemma take its own course."

A plan began to form in Kat's mind. "Meanwhile, I shall remain Mistress Miranda, and wait until Brandon makes his move."

"And Miranda herself? By our larkin, my lady! I have not seen her so happy in many a year."

"Neither have I." Kat considered the future, her thoughts leaping on top of each other as frogs on the same lily pad. "We will not tell Miranda this new information. If she knew that she was being wooed by a reasonably handsome, somewhat intelligent and eminently available man, she would retreat inside her shell and so throw away this sudden chance at love. Nay, let her be me awhile longer, and so ensnare John Stafford, until he begins to woo her for himself, and not for my Lord Cavendish. Indeed, I do believe Stafford has already fallen under Miranda's spell. When Midsummer's Day comes, and all truths are revealed, I will provide a generous dowry for her. My Lord Stafford will fall to the marriage yoke as if he had been poleaxed."

"And me, my lady? What if I bring my great hunter to heel?"

Kat hugged Sondra. "Then you shall have a goodly dowry, as well, and a new gown to be wed in."

"All will come out pat in time, mark my words, my

lady." Sondra drew out her measuring string from her deep apron pocket. "Speaking of wedding gowns, Lady Kat, what of yours? Surely you do not want to go to the altar in your old blue dress now, do you? Not when you'll be a-marrying for love."

"Do you really think so, Sondra?" Kat feared to hope for such a happiness. "Does he love me truly?"

"Aye, my lady. They say the third time is the charm, and pays for all. Now as to your gown. What about that white damask brocade and golden lace you bought at the Whitsuntide fair for next Christmas? 'Tis a fine cloth, and all the maids are a-perishing to make a hundred love knots to adorn it."

Kat wrinkled her nose. "The damask would be heavy for this season of the year."

Sondra winked at her. "Mayhap, but you could wear fewer petticoats underneath it. I am sure your noble lord would not mind having less to peel away."

Kat swallowed. The vision of Sir John—no, Sir Brandon—untying the laces of her shimmering gold and white gown swam through her imagination. "Is there enough material for two gowns, exactly alike?"

"Aye. What new mischief do you plot now, Lady Kat?"

"And have we veiling thick enough to hide my features, if I wore it over my face?"

"We do." Sondra arched one brow.

"Then here is my device. Come my wedding day, both Miranda and I will be garbed and veiled exactly alike, so that none can tell the difference. We shall not unveil, until after the vows have been exchanged."

"Even if the noble lords have confessed all?"

Kat nodded with a smug expression. "Aye. Miranda and I will play our parts to the very end, and my cunning, crafty, double-dealing Lord Cavendish will not know whom he has married, until the sticking point. That should teach him that I can play his game as well as he—and beat him at it.''

''And Miranda?''

''She will never confess our disguising on her own, for she is tried and true to me. She will play my part, willingly or not. But, let us hope, Sondra, that, for good Miranda's sake, my Lord Cavendish does not sound the retreat too soon. I think I shall much enjoy watching him spin around in this whirlwind of his own creation.''

Stretching his feet out under the table, Brandon tried to concentrate on the chessboard before him. His mind was hardly on the game. He took a long swallow of his warm spiced wine. Considering the past twelve hours, he was forced to admit that this was one of the worst days of his life.

Despite his honorable intentions to do right by his bride-to-be, things had gone wrong from the start—beginning with the hurt expression on sweet Miranda's face, when he had offered his arm to Katherine and had escorted her out of the hall. He knew that Miranda's look of reproach would rise up and haunt him in the dark of night for years to come. All for the sake of honor. Honor be damned!

And what had he gained for his sacrifice and Miranda's pain? Absolutely nothing.

Brandon cast a sideways glance at Jack and Katherine, who sat on the cushioned seat below the huge triple-light window of the great hall. Outside, a summer tempest raged, casting jagged streaks of lightning to the earth. Thunder rolled across the soaking fields like cannon fire. The fury of the weather went unnoticed by the pair, who enjoyed a private game of cards. Katherine's laughter floated over the slash of the rain against the diamond-cut panes of window glass. Jack—the churl—whispered yet another compliment to her, judging from the blush on her cheeks.

This morning, when Brandon had offered his assistance at the mounting block, Katherine had turned to Jack and had given him her hand to help her into her saddle. During that tiresome ride, Katherine insisted on staying by Jack instead of riding next to Brandon, no matter how often Jack obligingly dropped back. When they dismounted to look across a field of ripening hops, 'twas Jack she asked to help her down. And Jack helped her up again, when 'twas time to return for dinner. Brandon could have been out alone with his falcon for all the good it had done him.

Who was Katherine to be so choosy of her companion? A simpering, giggling, pale-faced ninny, who had not more than an ounce of sense in her brain. When she opened her mouth, which was not often, her speech was that of a girl-ish maiden and not of a woman brought twice to the marriage bed. No wonder she relied on Miranda so much! Without her steady, intelligent cousin to oversee the running of the household, Bodiam would have been in a state of complete shambles by now. How would Katherine survive without Miranda to help her? How would he?

"'Tis your move, my lord, and has been this past quarter hour." Miranda nudged his foot with her toe. "Have you gone to sleep, or are you merely trying to find a way of saving your bishop's pawn?"

Brandon blinked, then pulled himself up straighter in the chair. "Your pardon, mistress. I was woolgathering."

He avoided looking into the green eyes that sparkled a challenge to him from the other side of the chessboard. He knew, if he gazed into those orbs of flashing fire, he would be lost—all his fine intentions blown out the window. He must maintain his control and his honor. Be courteous but not familiar with Miranda.

Brandon shot another glance at the pair on the window seat. Blast Katherine! She had turned him down as flat as a griddle cake, when he had suggested a game of chess after supper. She had even acted insulted at his offer of his company. She preferred Jack, the grinning ape, who merely shrugged at Brandon, then engaged the lady with his own wit and wiles. *What does she think I am—a squawking crow?*

"By the stars, Sir John!" Miranda blew a wisp of her auburn hair out of her eyes as she bent over the board. "You have already lost three pawns and a knight to me. What's one pawn more?"

Brandon sent her a quick glance from under his hooded lids. He drew in a small breath. How utterly delectable she looked with the candlelight playing the wanton with her hair, turning it into a riot of reds and golds. Gritting his teeth, he moved his bishop one place on the diagonal.

Miranda's eyes widened. "By the book! You've opened your queen to my attack! In faith, I will not let you take your move back, Sir John. I mean to win this game." She swooped her castle deep into his side of the board.

'Tis no matter. I am lost to you already, sweet minx. Take my queen, my bishop, my heart. I am a condemned man.

"My mind dwells upon other things," Brandon murmured. He hardened his voice with a deliberate ruthlessness, then pointedly stared at Katherine.

Miranda followed the direction of his look. "Oh? The wind blows in that direction now, does it?" She smiled with a perverse pleasure. "Does my cousin please you, Sir John? Do you think she will make Sir Brandon a good wife?"

"She will make him—" Brandon caught himself before his true thoughts slipped out "—a wealthy man," he finished. He sought solace in his wine cup.

"Indeed?" Miranda regarded him with a smug expression playing about her full, luscious lips. "Methought my Lord Cavendish was heir to a large estate in the north."

"He is," Brandon snapped, staring at the bottom of his empty cup. "But a man can never be too rich." *Weep, my good mother, for the lies I must weave for blasted honor's sake.*

Miranda lifted the jug beside her, and poured them both more of the sweetened drink. ''And do you think my cousin will make Sir Brandon a happy man?''

She will render me stark, staring mad within twelve months. Aloud, Brandon replied, ''I am no soothsayer, mistress. I have no idea what their marriage will be like. Only time will tell.''

''Just so, my lord.'' Removing her coif, Miranda shook her head. A tumbling waterfall of red-gold cascaded over her shoulders. ''Your pardon, Sir John, but this coif pinches, and I am beginning to get a headache. Your move, I believe.'' Her eyes glittered.

Knotting his hand into a fist under the table, Brandon dug his nails deep into his palms. His move? *Don't ask me what I would move to do, delectable chit. 'Tis a wonder I don't sweep this table clear of the pieces, and lay you down right here.* Why couldn't she keep her hair covered like every other respectable spinster? His fingers itched to comb through those tresses that dangled so enticingly near.

With a low groan, Brandon pushed back his chair and rose abruptly. ''Pray excuse me, Mistress Miranda. I must attend an urgent call of nature.''

She smiled up at him. ''Then you have my leave. But hurry back, my lord, before your strategy grows cold.''

''Never fear on that score, mistress,'' he growled. ''My thoughts are always hot. Indeed, they burn me up.'' Turning quickly, he strode out of the hall toward the nearest garderobe. Her laughter followed him, echoing down the corridor.

Wrapped in his own dark brooding, Brandon failed to see Montjoy until he bumped headlong into him. The old man stumbled backward, and would have fallen, had not Brandon caught him in time.

"Your pardon, steward," Brandon apologized. "I was lost in my thoughts."

Montjoy drew himself up to the top of his frail height. "The passage is dark, my lord."

"Aye, but not enough to warrant my blindness. Are you well?"

Montjoy sniffed. "I am never fully well in my joints, my lord, especially on such a vile night as this." He sighed deeply. "'Tis a cross I must bear alone."

Brandon hid his grin behind his hand. The castle servants called the poor man, Melancholy Montjoy, and, unfortunately, the name was most appropriate.

"To save your steps, and the pain in your joints, is there some office I can perform for you?" Once he was lord of Bodiam, Brandon decided he would settle Montjoy in dignified retirement.

The steward bowed gravely. "I am unworthy of your kind attention, my lord. However, if it is not too much trouble, would you inform my mistress that Sir Fenton Scantling has arrived?"

The shock of Montjoy's announcement hit Brandon with the force of a mailed fist in his gut. "Scantling? Here? Now?"

Montjoy's heavy lids flickered. "You know my Lord Scantling?"

"Aye, at court." Brandon glanced over his shoulder into the hall. No one seemed to have heard Montjoy. "Where is Fenton now?"

"In the antechamber, my lord. He is much covered with mud and the filth of the road, and..."

At that moment, the subject in question appeared at the top of the entry stairs. Scantling's long cloak ran with rainwater, creating a series of puddles as he advanced.

"There you are, you malmsey-nosed knave!" Scantling strode up to Montjoy. "The devil and his dam take you for leaving me in that bunghole to shiver myself into a chill.''

''I thought to inform your aunt—''

''I will tell my aunt what she needs to know. *You* attend to my needs this minute, old man.'' Fenton snapped his fingers. ''A bath, fresh dry garments, a hot supper and—''

Stepping between the pair, Brandon glared down at his nephew-to-be. The rain had plastered Fenton's hat to his head, giving the young man the unappealing appearance of a drowned rat.

''A good master is known by the way he treats his servants, Scantling,'' Brandon remarked with cold contempt in his voice. To Montjoy, he added, ''Prepare my lord's room, Montjoy, and he shall be there presently, after his aunt has put a flea or two in his ear.''

''You overstep your bounds, my lord,'' Fenton bristled. Brandon gripped his arm and flung him against the wall. Scantling gasped. ''Does my aunt know of your roughshod ways?''

''I ought to tear out your lying tongue and give it to the dogs for their breakfast, you sniveling vermin! Why did you tell me that your aunt was an old crone and a witch? Look you!'' He stepped aside, so that Fenton could see into the lighted hall. ''Does that good lady look like either one to you now?''

Scantling narrowed his eyes at Brandon. ''Nay, she looks more like a wanton jade, with her hair all in her face like that.''

About to defend Katherine against Fenton's slander, Brandon halted before he spoke. He stared again into the hall. Katherine and Jack still played at their card game. Though she leaned her head closer to Jack's, Brandon could see that her headdress was still firmly in place. On the other hand, Miranda sat back in her chair with her eyes closed, idly running her fingers through her bare, loosened tresses.

"Though why Aunt Kat is wearing one of Miranda's dresses, I can't begin to guess," Scantling continued with a sneer. "Perchance, she hopes you will think she is a poor widow. Be advised, my lord. My aunt is truly a conniving shrew."

A small nerve jangled in Brandon's temple. He licked his dry lips. "Your aunt looks pleasing in her cousin's dress. It becomes her figure right well. I asked that she wear it especially for me." God's nightshirt! Had Brandon been served up in his own juices? Who had hoodwinked whom?

Fenton's lips curled. "You are much besotted then, my lord. You do not know my aunt's true colors."

"For once you speak the truth, Scantling. Fear not, for I will unmask her ere I wed her. On that, you have my promise." Brandon stared at Miranda—or was it Katherine—basking in the firelight.

"And take a hellcat into your bed?"

Closing his hand around Scantling's throat, Brandon banged the varlet's head against the stone wall of the passageway. "Be mindful of that tongue of yours, Scantling. The dogs are hungry. Now get to your chamber, for your greensick face offends my eyes. I will tell the lady of your arrival. I am sure the news will bring her much good cheer."

Brandon released Scantling. The youth pulled away from him, as if Brandon harbored the plague. Without another word to either the knight or the hovering Montjoy, Fenton stamped up the stairs to the bedchambers. His wide-eyed servant scampered close behind with a bulging saddlebag over each arm.

Brandon spied Montjoy easing down the hallway toward the kitchen. "Worthy steward, a word with you."

Montjoy's eyelids blinked several times in rapid succession. "My...my lord?"

Brandon dropped an arm around the old man's thin shoulders. "Montjoy, I know you are an honest man."

"As God in heaven is my witness, my lord."

"Falsehood is your sworn enemy, no doubt?"

"A-aye, my lord." Montjoy's lips trembled.

Brandon tightened his grip. "So tell me the truth, as God in his heaven is your witness, Montjoy. Is yon lady in the plain green gown and without her headdress—the lady who is beating me in chess—is she, in sworn truth—your mistress, Lady Katherine Fitzhugh?"

Montjoy wavered for an instant, then drawing himself up, he stared squarely at Brandon. "She has always been so, my lord. Do you require anything else?"

Chapter Eight

"My Lord Scantling has arrived, my lady," Columbine whispered into Kat's ear.

Kat bolted upright in her chair. Fenton would give the game away, unless he thought it would be worth his while to keep quiet. Thank heavens, John—nay, Brandon—was still out of the hall. "He's here? At Bodiam?"

Columbine's head bobbed. "Aye, he's in his chamber now, screaming for food and hot water." Leaning closer, the maid whispered in Kat's ear. "There's more, my lady. Tod Wormsley took me aside. Methought he was trying to steal a kiss, but instead he asked me to warn you. Sir Fenton is overwhelmed by debts. Tod said they left the court to escape his lord's creditors. Now your nephew has come to make you sign over the guardianship of the estate to him before your wedding day. Tod says Sir Fenton carries a paper in his pocket drawn up by a lawyer."

"By the rood! We must do something quickly."

"'Tis what I thought, my lady. But what?"

Blast Fenton! Creditors and coercion? The ungrateful little wretch! As if Kat didn't already have enough on her hands, and an approaching marriage that she still preferred not to ponder.

"Give my regards to my Lord Cav...Sir John when he

returns from the privy. Tell him I'm…I've been taken with a sick headache, and I have gone to bed.'' Kat cast a quick glance at Miranda. Still playing their game of cards, she and Stafford appeared lost in their own world. ''Make no mention of this to Miranda—not yet.''

Slipping out of the hall, Kat headed for the stairs to the kitchens. ''And tell my noble partner that I concede the chess match to him this time,'' she tossed back over her shoulder.

''Aye.'' Columbine bobbed her head.

Kat sighed with relief when she found Sondra sipping a mug of warm ale and spinning ghost stories by the kitchen fire. As the summer thunderstorm battered the castle walls, the housekeeper held spellbound a dozen of the younger servants with her tales of sprites and supernatural creatures.

''Sondra! A word in your ear! Make haste!''

A dozen pairs of bright eyes looked up at Kat.

Sondra put down her mug and clapped her hands, scattering the group like a wind among autumn leaves. ''Away with you, my poppets! Our lady desires private conference with me. And Pansy, stay out of the sugared nuts, if you please. They are put by for the wedding feast.''

Wedding feast! Kat gulped. She couldn't think of that now. She sank down on a low stool next to Sondra. ''Fenton has returned and is up to no good. He plans to force me to sign over Bodiam to him! Sondra, give me good counsel. What am I to do?''

Sondra raised her brows to a point in the middle of her forehead. ''Aye? That explains why the potboys scampered away so fast. Montjoy asked for hot water for a bath. Methought 'twas for you or Mistress Miranda.''

''My mind is at sixes and sevens, Sondra. I cannot think, save to wring Fenton's mangy neck. Tell me. Is there any of your potions or elixirs that could make him sleep for a week or two?'' *Then let my Lord Cavendish deal with the boy. There may be yet one or two saving graces to this match.*

"Nay, my lady, but you have put your finger on the problem. He must be gotten rid of."

Kat nodded. "Aye, before he can wave his silly paper about, or speak with either of the knights, and tell them who I really am. Hang it all! He might even seize upon this gentle game as proof that my mind is unhinged. I would not put such a ploy past him. Where Fenton goes, trouble skulks close behind."

Sondra eyed a huge cauldron on the fire with a critical squint. She snapped her fingers. "I have it, Lady Kat! Yonder is my lord's bathwater. I will steep nettles and the leaves of crowfoot in it. The mixture will render your fine nephew with such an onerous rash that he will think the castle is suffering from a plague of fleas. Furthermore, 'twill give a devilish burning to those private parts that all men cherish most dear."

Kat tried to suppress a giggle but failed miserably. "Oh, admirable Sondra! I like that very much."

"Meanwhile, I will insist that fresh sheets be put on my lord's bed—sheets that I will rub with rue and more nettles. I promise you, my lady. He will have the worst night's sleep of his life."

Catching Sondra's enthusiasm, Kat added, "And do you have a way to make him sneeze his head off?"

"Aye, we'll stuff his pillows with black pepper and ground hellebore."

Kat's smile broadened with approval. "And we will instruct everyone to tell Fenton that a rare malady lurks about Bodiam, one that we have all suffered this spring. Fenton has such a childish horror of any illness, he will take himself back to court in a wink." Kat shook her head. "Poor Tod! I fear we must treat the lad as badly as we do his master. Slip a packet of Philippe's special spiced toast into Wormsley's bag before they go. Perchance the treat will help sweeten Tod's itchy spirits.''

''Aye, that, and a bright silver shilling will cure Tod of any discomfort,'' Sondra suggested.

''You speak wisely, as always, my dear friend. Above all, let no one else, save you and me, know of this trick.'' Sighing, Kat rolled her eyes. ''Sweet angels! There are so many plots thickening under this old roof! Pray we do not find ourselves in our own hot soup!''

Sondra winked at Kat. ''Just so long as there is none of my pepper and nettles in that pot with us, my lady.''

''Methinks your game has run its course long enough, Brandon.'' Jack observed as they tended to their horses before retiring.

Brandon merely grunted in reply. Murmuring soothing words in his horse's ear, he brushed his huge chestnut charger with long, smooth strokes. Windchaser was a noble steed in the tiltyard, but thunderstorms made him skittish. Meanwhile, Brandon's thoughts were far from the realm of clean straw and leather tack. Scantling's revelation had so confounded him that he had barely spoken a word to anyone since the young lord's unheralded arrival.

Jack continued. ''By morning's light, that peevish whipster will have sniffed out our secret. Then there will be hell to pay. And pay, and pay, if I know anything about Scantling.''

''Aye,'' Brandon answered, barely listening to Jack.

God's teeth! For the past two weeks Brandon had been dancing court to his intended bride, instead of her poor cousin! And Jack...Brandon glanced over Windchaser's withers at his friend's back. And Jack—the most notorious heartbreaker in Henry's court—had tripped over his own feet and fallen for a shy country maiden.

Brandon grinned in the darkness. What an infinite jest! All the sophisticated wiles, all the rich gowns, elaborate coifs, dazzling jewels, enticing perfumes and artful cosmetics employed by the court beauties had merely entertained Jack, never ensnared him. Yet one unadorned spinster, past her bloom of youth, had him bending to her whims. High time Jack felt the sting of Cupid's arrows!

"What do you think?" Jack asked over his shoulder.

Brandon shook his head. Think about what?

"Your pardon, Jack. My mind wanders amid the whirl of recent events." He ran his hand over his horse's sleek flank. Windchaser nickered with pleasure.

Jack snorted. "Your mind has been a bubbling stew pot ever since we left Hampton Court. Indeed, it grows thicker daily. I said, why don't we abduct Fenton and his man in the dark hours of the night, truss them up in sacks like a couple of roosters and leave them on a roadside far away from here?"

Brandon walked around to Windchaser's near side. "'Tis a tempting thought, but one that will do us no lasting good. Like an unwanted cat, Scantling will return within a day, and he will know where to lay his grievance."

"Then I repeat, the jig is up. Our little piece of mummery is over. Draw the curtain. Put out the light and—"

"Peace, Jack! Your chatter makes my head pound."

"Nay. 'Tis the spiced wine that does that."

Spiced wine...and the cunning minx who poured it. In his mind, he heard her ask him again, 'Do you think Lady Katherine will make him a happy man?' *Aye, if she doesn't drive me to distraction first.*

Brandon massaged the bridge of his nose. Kat must be taught a lesson—one that she would never forget once they were married. She needed to learn the importance of honesty and truth. Brandon gnawed on his lower lip as he thought of how this might be accomplished. As for Scantling, let the devil take the morrow, and the knave with it.

Jack returned his brush and currycomb to the shelf above the stall. "What do you think Lady Katherine will say when she learns 'tis you, and not I, she is to wed?'' He tried to sound noncommittal but failed in the attempt.

Methinks she'll be relieved, if I have read her mind correctly. Brandon cleared his throat. "Methinks we start at shadows before we know the substance behind them. Let us see why Scantling has abandoned the pleasures of court, and come in the middle of the night to visit his aunt. Patience, my friend. My good mother used to tell me that all things come to them that wait.''

Jack pulled on his jacket. "Aye, but your good mother is not here, Cavendish, and waiting was never a virtue of mine.''

Brandon clapped his friend on the shoulder. "Tomorrow, if the weather proves fair, methinks you and I should go hunting at sunrise, and stay out of Scantling's eye until the evening. If he doesn't see us, he will not tip our hand.''

Glancing at his friend, Jack pursed his lips. "So you mean to persist in this subterfuge?''

"Aye, I do.''

"Till when?''

Brandon twitched his lips with silent amusement. "Does Lady Katherine grow tiresome to you, Jack of Hearts? Are you so anxious to be rid of her?''

Jack gripped his companion by his sleeve. "By my troth! The lady is new-made every morning, and she grows in beauty as the day lengthens. You, you dolt, have not the wit to see it! If you were not my friend...'' Jack cursed under his breath.

Brandon cupped his hand around his ear. "How now? I did not hear that. What would you do to me if we were not pledged to each other by friendship?''

"I'd beat the devil out of you," Jack growled. "Then, perchance, some good sense might find room in that pulp you call your brains.''

Throwing back his head, Brandon laughed. The deep, rich sound filled the stable. "Then I accept your physic,

Jackanapes. At dawn, instead of hunting, we will ride to a convenient spot beyond the prying eyes of ladies, servants and surly nephew. There you may have at me—if you can.'' Stretching his arms over his head, he cracked his knuckles. ''Methinks I have grown soft and fat this past fortnight. I need some good exercise.''

''And I,'' muttered Jack.

''Mark you, dawn comes early.'' Brandon cuffed Jack lightly on the back of his head, then danced out of range.

''Not early enough,'' Jack replied, his teeth glowing blue-white in a flash of lightning.

''Wormsley! You whoreson villain! Do something!'' Another head-exploding sneeze ripped through Fenton. He wiped both his nose and his streaming eyes on the sleeve of his nightshirt. ''Death and damnation! What plague has visited us?''

He scratched the back of his neck with one hand, while massaging his tender manhood with the other. Devil's tongs and pitchforks! His balls burned and itched.

Wormsley's sneeze answered him. ''I do not know, my lord,'' he replied. Two more sneezes followed in quick succession.

'''Tis fleas, I vow,'' Fenton growled, as he heaved one of the pillows across the room in Wormsley's general direction. ''Methought you said the maid had changed the sheets.''

''Aye, she did,'' Wormsley gasped. ''I watched her.''

Fenton heaved another pillow. ''Wart-nose! You watched her little ass a-twitching, and not what she was doing. I have been cursed with foul linen.'' He sneezed again. ''When I find her, I shall beat the wench black and blue!'' Another sneeze.

Tod gulped. ''Not so, my lord. My pallet was untouched, yet I—'' He sneezed and coughed at the same time.

"Cease your tittle-tattle, slug. Get you below stairs, and find the healer, Sondra Owens. Don't come back until you have that blond witch in tow. God's death!" Fenton sneezed again. "The first thing I will do when I have mastery of Bodiam is burn that chit. Fetch her, before all my skin peels off!"

Fenton hurled the chamber pot after the lackwit to speed him on his way. It hit the door as Wormsley shut it behind him.

"My lady?" Leaning over Kat, Laurel held up a lighted candle.

Kat sat up in bed. "Aye, Laurel, I am already awake. Who is it at the door?"

"Tod, my lady. He looks awful, and he says his master is sore afflicted with flea bites and sneezing."

Kat grinned. *Bless you, Sondra!* "I come, but quietly. Let us not wake Miranda." After sliding out of the covers, Kat hastily donned a long, quilted dressing gown.

Standing just outside the door, poor Tod presented a pitiful sight. Laurel's candlelight made his reddened eyes, swollen nose and blistered skin look all the more grotesque.

"How now, Tod? Your face has swollen up like a ripe strawberry." Poor lad!

"Aye," Tod replied with a mournful groan. "'Tis a plague for sure."

Despite his stricken appearance and obvious discomfiture, Kat had to bite the inside of her cheek to keep from bursting into laughter. The poor boy looked ten times worse than she had expected. Perhaps Sondra had been a bit overzealous with the ground pepper and nettles.

"What ails you, Tod?" she asked, trying to keep a straight face.

He rolled his watery eyes, sneezed again and scratched his thighs as the same time. "If I knew the answer, my lady, I'd be a scholar of renown,'' he gasped. ''I itch and sneeze. My throat is like a raw wind in January.'' He sneezed once more.

Kat assumed a concerned expression. ''Then we must brew you up some chamomile and coltsfoot tea with honey.''

Tod shook his head and sneezed. ''Nay, mistress, not for me. 'Tis Sir Fenton. He has not slept a wink since he lay down. Indeed, he has not lain much abed. He has tossed and turned, and even hopped up and down in the middle of the mattress, as if he had a devil on his back.''

Kat pretended to ponder Tod's description. ''This illness sounds more serious than I first thought. Have you spoken to Mistress Owens?''

''Your pardon, my lady,'' Tod muttered in between sneezes. ''I looked for her in the maids' dormitory, but they said…that is, I could not find her.''

Kat glanced at Tod out of the corner of her eye. He looked redder in the face than before.

''How now, Tod?'' she asked with a small chuckle. ''Where did the maids say she was?''

He cleared his throat. ''With Sir Brandon's huntsman, and no one knows where they have gone to ground.'' The youth coughed, though not with a surfeit of ground pepper.

Kat grinned as she followed him down the corridor. Handsome enough boy, she reckoned, once he had filled out. One of these fine days, someone like Columbine or Laurel will take notice of Tod, and then he'll be the one seeking cover.

Kat heard Fenton long before she got to his chamber. Squaring her shoulders, she drew in a deep breath. *Beard the lion in his den.*

''About time!'' Fenton bellowed when she entered the room. ''What does a man have to do to get your attention, mistress?''

Kat set the candle down on the bed table, then cast him

a stern look. "A sweet voice and pleasant speech go far in catching a woman's ear, nephew."

Fenton paled slightly when he saw her clearly. "I mistook. Methought you were Mistress Owens." A bout of furious sneezing cut off Fenton's further remarks. He clutched at the rumpled bedclothes. "The devil take all. Do something! My skin feels like it is being chewed in a thousand places. Don't just stand there, Aunt Katherine. Oh, most delicate fiend!"

Putting her hands on her hips, Kat drew herself up. "Did you get me from out my warm bed to curse me, Fenton? Is that your recipe to make yourself well?" Picking up the candlestick, Kat turned to go.

Fenton flew out of the bed and fell to his knees on the bare floor. "Cure me, if you have any pity in your heart!"

The room erupted with more sneezing as both Tod and Fenton gave in to their distress. Even Kat's nose twitched. She noticed that Fenton had thrown his sheets and pillows into total disarray. The closed air of the chamber must be swarming with the finely ground pepper and hellebore. After replacing the candlestick on the table, Kat shook out her camphor-scented handkerchief and breathed into it.

Now to add a bit of spice to this brew. "I confess, I am much amazed. I did not think the malady would strike you so soon, Fenton," she said in a surprised voice. "It caught you and Tod much faster than the others."

Fenton paused in the midst of clawing his shoulder blades. "What damnable pestilence are you talking about?"

Kat lifted her shoulders with an air of helplessness. "I did not want to worry you about it, my boy, seeing how you were so busy attending on His Majesty. I know how much the king dislikes any news of illness. 'Tis why I did not write you of it. This strange malady came upon us on May Day. All the castle began sneezing, wheezing and scratching fit to die." Her handkerchief hid her grin.

Fenton trembled all over like a dog come in out of a rainstorm. "Aye? And what did you call this sickness?"

Kat shook her head slowly from side to side. "No one had ever seen the like before, not even Sondra," she intoned in a solemn voice. "Not even the priest," she added. Kat crossed her fingers behind her back and sent a quick prayer to heaven. *Lord bless me! I promise to confess this lie come Advent.* "For want of a better name, I called it Queen Mab's Revenge."

Fenton fell into a coughing fit. "Never heard of it!" He blew his nose with a wet-trumpet sound. "What quackery did you practice to rid yourself of this tomfoolery?"

"'Tis no sham, as you can experience for yourself, nephew. Sondra believed that one of the maids must have insulted the faerie queen—all unknowing, of course. You know how goose-brained our girls can be sometimes."

Fenton scratched his head with both hands. "Fie upon it! I care not what is the name nor the cause. Give me the remedy!"

"Ah!" Putting her finger to her lips, Kat pretended to think deeply. "As to the remedy..."

"Aye?" Fenton practically sat up and begged.

Wrapping her arms around her sides, Kat pinched herself to squelch her mirth. "I cannot say."

"What?" Fenton all but shot straight up in the air. "Bitch! You speak with malice."

Kat narrowed her eyes. Her nephew had gone too far. "You have no right to insult me, Fenton." She picked up her candlestick again. "Remember who took you in when my sister and her husband were killed in that carriage accident. Be advised, Bodiam is not your house, but mine. And soon, 'twill belong to my...my husband, Sir Brandon Cavendish." Her lips trembled slightly as she thought of Midsummer's Day. She drew herself up. "I doubt that my lord will take kindly to his wife being name-called and abused by one who should know better."

"'Tis true," Tod muttered from his corner, where he had been sneezing and scratching in miserable silence.

Kat started for the chamber door. "And so, my lordling, if there is nothing else upon your mind, I bid you a pleasant good night."

Fenton crawled after her on his knees.

Oh, what sublime justice is this! I wish Miranda and Sondra could see this sight! 'Tis a shame I play this role in the dark with only poor Tod for an audience.

"One moment! You cannot leave me like this!" Fenton burbled. "For sweet charity's sake, tell me. What did you do to get rid of this Mab's Revenge?"

Kat pretended to think. "As I recall, we bathed in a tub full of vinegar. God save us! It hurt enough to make a strong man sing for his sins. Then, of course, we burned all our clothes."

"All?" Fenton gulped. "Everything?"

"Every last lacing and codpiece, Fenton." *He's thinking of his expensive wardrobe now. I can hear the cogs in his brain whir around.* Kat stifled a giggle, then continued. "Then we ate a diet of lettuce leaves, chervil, cress, mustard—and water. No wine or ale, for fear of bringing the rash back."

Fenton sneezed several more times during this recitation. Kat racked her brain to think of what other hideous thing she could add to the so-called remedy.

"Oh, aye, and no bed sport—in bed or otherwise. For fear of further inflaming a man's…ah…private parts, you understand."

Fenton's only rejoinder was a strangled gargle.

"But the very best remedy of all…" Pausing, Kat gazed down at the twitching heap at her feet. Her lips curled up with smug satisfaction.

"What?" gasped the prostrate wretch.

"Why, is to leave Bodiam altogether, as quick as you can, my dear, before the infection takes root and grows."

"Does that work?" He quivered.

Kat inhaled the camphor from her handkerchief. Please Lord, she couldn't sneeze now! "Aye, Fenton. We found that was the best remedy of all. When we returned after a fortnight, we had no more ill effects. Methought the sickness had moved on, but alas, alack! I was mistaken!"

"Wormsley! Pack! Now!" Fenton coughed, then scratched even more furiously.

Kat pretended to be taken by surprise. "What? In the middle of the night. The storm has made the roads treacherous."

Hopping about, Fenton jammed one of his legs into his hose. "This very minute! I will write to you soon, when I am well enough to hold my pen. Have the guard wake up those slugs in the stable and have them saddle our horses. We will not stay another hour in this perfidious pesthole. Not one more minute!"

"Aye, I think you take the wisest course." Kat backed toward the door. "You were always a clever boy. Remember, it takes a fortnight for the cure to work."

In his corner, Tod sneezed continuously as he struggled to unbuckle the saddlebag. Taking pity on the lad, Kat bent over him. "There'll be a little packet for your trip on the chopping table, Tod. Here." She held up her handkerchief to his nose. "Breathe in deeply," she whispered.

Tod blinked several times as the camphor assailed his nostrils. His eyes widened with mute surprise.

Kat put her finger to her lips, smiled warmly at Tod and then winked. "God keep you on your journey, Fenton," she said in a louder tone.

"Go to the devil," he retorted, before collapsing into more sneezing and coughing.

Kat hummed to herself as she made her way back to her bedchamber. This past half hour was well spent. She drew in several deep breaths of clean air, then yawned. To bed, and a good night's sleep. Kat knew she needed all the rest she could get, the better to match wits with such a crafty, handsome devil as Sir Brandon on the morrow.

I have not had so much fun in a month of Sundays, she thought, just before she blew out her light.

In the morning, the sun rose with welcoming rays above the new-washed world. No one at Bodiam rued Sir Fenton Scantling's mysterious midnight departure. On the other hand, cleaning up his bedchamber took the combined efforts of six poor maids, all a-sneezing.

Chapter Nine

Brandon mopped the sweat from his forehead with the back of his torn sleeve. His tongue probed the split on his lower lip. His shoulders ached. The skin on his knuckles had already begun to swell.

"The devil take you, Jackanapes! Fall down, for sweet Jesu's sake."

Lumbering across the flattened grass opposite him, Jack blinked his blackening eye and shook his head. "Nay, Cavendish! My lady's honor is not yet satisfied." He slurred the last word, then spat out some blood.

"*Whose* lady, again? Methought we were fighting over my wife." Zounds! Brandon had forgotten how stubborn Jack could be when he put his nose into the wind.

"Not yet," Jack gasped. He lunged at Brandon, hurling them both to the damp ground.

They spent the next few minutes rolling over and over, as first one, then the other combatant fought to get a good hold. A few grunts, an oath or two, and a great deal of wheezing accompanied the struggle. Finally Brandon managed to flip Jack over his head. His friend landed on his back with a loud "oof" as the air flew out of his lungs. Brandon fell on top of him.

"Do you yield to my superior force?" Brandon asked,

straddling Jack's chest. He felt far from superior at that moment.

Still fighting to get his breath back, Jack could only nod. With a grateful sigh, Brandon rolled off his friend and lay on the ground beside him.

"By my troth, Jack, I am not…as young…as I thought," Brandon panted.

Jack groaned in answer.

"Ten years ago…in France…remember? King Henry's visit to King Francis…Field of Cloth of Gold?"

"Aye," Jack managed to reply.

"I used to wrestle all comers in the morning, and never be winded at dinner. Good sooth, Jack! You have a nasty right fist." Brandon massaged his belly gently. Perhaps he would have only soup and some custard for dinner today.

"You haven't lost too much of your cunning, either," Jack responded, breathing easier now. "Though, methinks you have put on more weight since we last met in this fashion. 'Tis your weight that bested me."

Brandon didn't even have the energy to deliver a half-hearted punch. "'Tis not fat. Merely muscle."

"Ha! I pity your poor wife, when she has to bear your load!"

Brandon allowed his gaze to wander to the leafy roof above them. A light breeze played amid the tree branches. His wife! Katherine Fitzhugh—she, whom he had called Miranda. A small smile flitted across his lips. Thank the stars, Jack was in no position to see it.

"Methinks my wife will not protest as much as you, clodpate," Brandon murmured, envisioning the first time he would bed the delectable lady with the cinnamon and gold hair.

Pale ivory skin, green flashing eyes, a rippling laugh that started deep in her throat and bubbled out like pure spring-water. Slim and supple like a willow tree, bending to his will. Velvet and silk under his exploring fingers.… Bran-

don's body reacted with typical anticipation. Oh, heaven!
His balls ached.

He flopped over onto his stomach. "Tell me, Jack, as
one man to another, what do you think of Katherine?"

Jack squinted at him with his good eye. "Man to man?
No holding back?"

"Aye. The plain truth. We are friends here."

"I think the Lady Katherine must be the model for some
master craftsman in church glass." Jack sighed. "Her face
is delicately carved in ivory tones, faint musk roses bloom
upon each cheek. Her nose is exquisitely dainty. And her
lips! Perdition take me, Brandon, I would long to drink
the honey from those lush portals."

Brandon arched his brows. Jack had the lovesickness
worse than he first thought. "Go on. Tell me more. What
about her body?"

Jack groaned. "I am winded and sore, and in no shape
to save my skin, Brandon. If I continue in this vein, you
must, in good conscience, flay me to the bone. Your bride
has made me desire pleasures that are not mine to have,
much less to describe them to the bridegroom."

Brandon plucked a piece of grass and drew it between
his teeth. He welcomed the bittersweet tang of its juice.

"I'll grant you, Lady Katherine has been richly en-
dowed with beauty, for a spinster of her years," he added,
watching Jack's face through half-shut eyes.

Jack snorted. "She is a woman who knows no bound-
aries of age. Indeed, methinks she has grown better in wit
and witticisms with each passing season."

Brandon chewed the blade. Witticisms? He racked his
brain to remember if he had heard Miranda say something
clever.

"But once you are back at court, you'll soon forget
Katherine."

Jack's fist knotted at his side. "Do not speak to me of
court. 'Tis garish, full of false faces and double-dealing.

Your lady is true, virtuous womanhood. She is the one woman in the world that I value most. I envy you your happiness.''

Brandon hid his grin behind his hand. ''Oh, I understand. You find her wealth just compensation for her country ways and simple interests. You had ever a nose for a good thing, Jack of Hearts.''

With another groan, Jack rolled over so that he could face his inquisitor, who lay less than a hand's span away. ''If my eyes did not see two of you just now, I would challenge you all over again for that last remark. You wound my pride, Brandon.''

Brandon licked his lips as Jack fell deeper into his trap. ''Then, if it were possible, you would marry Katherine, even if she hadn't a groat to her name?''

Jack stared at Brandon as best he could with one eye swollen shut. ''Aye,'' he answered hoarsely. ''If that sweet lady came to the church door to be married in only her shift, I would honor her. But what of you? You throw pearls to pigs!''

Brandon whistled through his teeth. ''Truly, you speak of marriage? I thought you had torn that word from your vocabulary.''

Jack's gaze never wavered. ''I seem to have found it again in a rose garden.'' He rolled onto his back. ''But you talk nonsense—toys of the mind. Lady Katherine is yours by the hand and will of Great Harry. Methinks, not even God would dare to change that fact.''

Brandon pursed his puffy lips, then picked his words carefully. Once said, he could never retrieve them again. ''What if I told you that the lady you so admire is yours for the asking?''

Jack lay very still. Brandon saw him swallow several times.

He continued. ''What, if I told you, that the Lady Katherine is not that lady at all?''

Jack slowly turned his head so that his good eye could read Brandon's face.

Brandon tilted a golden brow. "What if I told you that the lady you want to marry is, in truth, Mistress Miranda Paige? What, if I told you, that the real Lady Katherine has been playing cat and mouse with me?"

Jack hauled himself into a sitting position. Pain etched across his face with the effort. "How did you come by this intelligence—if such foolish fancy could be called intelligent?"

Brandon's face split into a wide grin. "Fenton Scantling."

Jack's burnished brows shot up. "Does one drop of truth ever fall from that whining rascal's lips?"

"Aye, when he doesn't realize it."

"Do you believe him?" Jack's fingers coiled and uncoiled as he spoke.

"Aye, especially when old Montjoy confirmed it." Brandon chuckled. "By the book, my friend, you've gone pale as an eggshell. Feeling light-headed from my blows?"

Jack took a deep breath. "Not the blows of your fists, but of your words. Speak plain, for my head is ringing like a church bell on New Year's Day. You mean to tell me, that the lady I have been wooing—in your name—is truly Mistress Miranda?"

"Aye."

"And, all unknowing, you have been playing at hearts with your true-intended bride?"

Brandon quirked his mouth into a rueful grin. "Aye."

Jack started to laugh but broke into a rasping cough instead. "'Tis too comical. We've been justly served up on a platter at a fool's feast. A recipe of our own making! Ods bodkins, Brandon, I cannot laugh, my ribs are too sore!"

Brandon hoisted himself to sit opposite Jack. "And now, my friend, what do you mean to do?"

Jack knitted his brows together. "Upon our return to the castle? Why, throw myself at Miranda's feet, beg her forgiveness at my double-dealing, and ask her to marry me."

"Just like that?" Brandon snapped his fingers then wished he hadn't. The joints were stiffening.

"Aye! I have no father from whom I must seek permission. I am my own man to chart my course. We'll wed as soon as the banns have been proclaimed if the lady...that is...Mistress Miranda will have me."

Brandon took a long look at the bloody, bruised, swollen, disheveled knight in front of him. "Well, I wouldn't ask her immediately, for you look like a dog's breakfast at the moment."

Jack inclined his head. "Aye, my thanks, and I return the compliment a hundredfold."

Brandon touched his nose gently. Hang it all! 'Twas as large as a turnip. He cleared his throat. "Be that as it may, Jack. Hear my device. Let us tarry in our borrowed feathers for a while longer—until the ladies themselves decide to call the game to a halt. 'Twill be good sport. *Now* you may woo in earnest without frightening your newfound mistress. Methinks Miranda is a skittish filly where marriage is concerned."

Closing both his eyes for a moment, Jack tilted his head back to bask in the sun's healing warmth. "Aye. 'Twould be only fair—seeing how our ladies have hoodwinked us thus far. By my aching head! I long to kiss Miranda's sweet lips in earnest."

"After yours have healed, I hope," Brandon observed, his tongue again touching the salty-tasting split on his own lip.

"Sweet Miranda," Jack said, and sighed.

Brandon grabbed a handful of Jack's grass-stained cambric shirt and pulled Stafford toward him like a fish reeled in on a line. "Nay, not Miranda. She is still Lady Katherine to you, jolt-head. Do not forget that!"

* * *

When Brandon and Jack appeared at dinner, both Kat and Miranda gasped. The knights were dressed in clean hose, snowy shirts, bright-colored doublets and jaunty bonnets. Their combed hair shone clean, their nails pared, and their teeth polished bright. On the other hand, their faces bore unmistakable signs of a recent disaster, and their movements, usually so lithe and graceful, reminded Kat of Montjoy on one of his "misery" days.

"Oh, poor Brandon!" Miranda escorted her lord to his place next to her. With tender care, she tucked his napkin into his collar before seating herself on his right. "Leaping trout! You look as if your horse tossed you into a bramble hedge."

Jack attempted to smile. With half his face still swollen and one eye shut, the result looked more like a grimace than a grin. "'Tis nothing, I assure you, my lady. A few scratches."

Kat eyed Brandon—the real knave of that name—as he gingerly sat down on the bench next to her. She covered her mouth with her napkin lest he see her grin.

"Good day, Miranda," he murmured, helping himself liberally to his wine cup. "I trust you had a pleasant morning?"

"Oh, aye." The concealing cloth muffled her answer. "Though I do not think mine was half as interesting as yours and Sir Brandon's."

"Does it hurt much, Brandon?" Miranda fluttered at Jack's side, patting his shoulder, stroking his wounded cheek and uttering a number of cooing noises.

He tried to smile again, with even less success than before. "Nay, my lady. I feel no pain when you hold my hand as you do now. In truth, I am transported from the agonies of purgatory to the joys of heaven. You are the angel of my delight."

"Pig's rot!" Brandon muttered under his breath.

Kat leaned closer to him. "And are you also in the agonies of purgatory, Sir John?"

He flexed his scratched, swollen hand stiffly. "I am not sure about purgatory, mistress, but I have been in hell for most of the morning." He grunted as he shifted on his seat.

"Did your horse throw a shoe, or run away with you?" Miranda asked Jack, her voice dripping with concern. "Pray tell me you were not attacked by a wild boar! I have heard from the woodcutters that there are several lurking within our district." She spooned a large portion of the creamed turnip soup, sprinkled with parsley. "Allow me to assist you, sweet Brandon. Open wide." She held up the brimming spoon.

Jack grimaced again. "I'll gladly open for you, my lady, but I cannot manage very wide."

"Poor Sir Brandon!" Miranda crooned as she shoved the spoon into his mouth.

Kat threw down her napkin. What was the point of hiding her amusement when neither man seemed particularly ashamed of his appearance? Indeed, Stafford lapped up not only the savory soup but Miranda's attentions, as well.

"Save your pity, coz," Kat told her. "'Tis as plain as a sunny day. Our guests have not suffered a riding accident. They have been fighting!" Kat flashed a challenging look at her dinner partner.

Brandon lifted his cup in a silent toast.

Miranda's green eyes grew rounder. "Oh, Brandon, who were you fighting?"

Jack looked down at his trencher, reminding Kat of a little boy who expects a scolding for dessert. His ears turned pink.

Kat rolled her eyes to the vaulted ceiling of the hall. "Hang it all, cousin! They have been fighting each other!"

Miranda nearly spilled the next helping of turnip soup on Jack's silver doublet. "Crickets!" she squeaked.

Jack took the spoon from her fingers, then kissed her hand. "'Twas for a good cause, my lady," he whispered.

"How now?" Kat tapped Brandon on the wrist—one of the few parts of his anatomy that did not appear to be injured. "Can you enlighten us, my Lord Stafford?"

Arching his back, Brandon winced. "My Lord Cavendish remarked that I was getting too fat, and that I needed some exercise."

Kat glared down the table at Jack. "Your pardon, my Lord Cavendish, but I beg to disagree with your observation." Kat regarded the man at her side. She was acutely conscious of Brandon's athletic physique. Her pulse accelerated. "I find my lord's form and figure to be...pleasing to the eye."

Dipping his blond head slightly, Brandon replied, "My thanks, mistress, but the...exercise was invigorating—and necessary."

Jack nodded, then blinked his good eye. "Cleared the air."

"We were growing too sluggish," added Brandon.

"Good for the blood," Jack explained to Miranda.

"Aye, my lord. I can see that. You made it flow," Kat snapped. She found herself wondering who had won the fray.

"Healthful," Brandon continued, giving her a lopsided grin, which she found most endearing.

"Relaxing." Jack swallowed another spoonful of soup with a satisfied purr.

Kat snorted. "Just so? And did *you* find this barbaric activity also relaxing, Sir..Sir John?" Kat tried to keep a stern tone in her voice, but found herself weakening toward the end.

Brandon turned his full gaze upon her. A faint light twinkled in the depths of his bright blue eyes. Featherlike laugh lines crinkled and deepened. "Aye, sweet Miranda. Afterward, I lay on my back a full two hours, snoring like a beached whale.'' Leaning closer, he whispered in her ear, ''You don't mind that I snore, do you, mistress?''

Kat had just bitten into a piece of saffron chicken. At the unexpected question, and the intimacy it suggested, her mouth went dry. She fought the overwhelming desire to kiss the injured lips that hovered so near. She managed to swallow the chicken with a gulp.

Her hand shook as she reached for her wine cup. ''Nay, my lord, why should I mind what you do in bed?''

Under the table, he closed his hand over hers. His mere touch sent a warming shiver through her. His thumb traced a lazy circle across her knuckles, causing her skin to tingle.

''You have relieved my mind a great deal, sweet Miranda.'' Lifting her hand, he brushed his bruised lips across her fingertips.

Kat mewed in the back of her throat.

Giving her hand a parting squeeze, Brandon turned his attention to the platter of ginger carp that his grinning squire had placed before him.

Somewhere deep within the most private part of Kat's heart, an unfamiliar response awakened and stretched, flooding her whole being with a deep sense of longing. Casting a sidelong glance at her dinner partner, she caught him watching her with the intensity of a kitten at a mouse hole. He slowly winked at her.

Kat jumped, knocking over her wine cup.

Angels in heaven! What is happening to me?

Chapter Ten

Curling herself up into a tight ball on her side of the mattress, Miranda wished she were dead. Sighing deeply, she tried to banish the tears that threatened to slip out from under her closed eyelids.

Great wailing wolves! Why had she ever agreed to Kat's mad scheme of exchanging places? After resigning herself to a lifetime of quiet spinsterhood, Miranda realized that she had fallen head over heels in love—with dearest Katherine's betrothed.

On that first day, Miranda had expected to greet some lean-shanked stripling. But both their guests had quickly put the lie to that assumption. Miranda couldn't believe her good fortune to be introduced to the handsomer of the pair as her "husband-to-be." After her initial shock at Brandon's unexpected maturity, it was easy to play the game—too easy. She must never allow Brandon to kiss her again as he had done after supper this very evening. He had tasted of honey mead and fresh mint. Her mouth quivered under his tender assault. Miranda had clung to him, her body demanding more.

Fie upon you! her conscience chided from a distant part of her brain. *This man is not yours, but your cousin's. Shame on you for desiring what is not yours to have!*

Once she was back inside the hall, Miranda had pleaded a headache, and all but flew up the stairs to her chamber. Later, when Kat had tiptoed in, Miranda pretended to be asleep.

Sleep? How could she, when a thousand little darts of guilt and envy pricked Miranda's soul?

If only Sir Brandon Cavendish were not bound to Kat! And by the king, no less! Miranda pursed her lips. Henry VIII was a great, meddling old fool, just because he himself was besotted with a woman who was not his wife. Miranda's anger at her sovereign outweighed any guilt she might have had for such treasonous thoughts. *Let His Grace play Cupid within his own court, but leave us alone at Bodiam!*

Miranda ran her tongue over her lips, tasting the memory of Brandon's kiss. But what of Kat? That kiss was meant for her. And what was my lady fair doing while Miranda wrestled with her conscience in the arms of the most wonderful man in the world? Teasing Sir John about his swollen nose!

Kat had totally taken leave of her good sense. Anyone could see that Sir Brandon was a far better man than Sir John. True, the two were much alike in color and form, but they were a world apart in their speech and manner. While Sir Brandon breathed poetry, Sir John muttered lists of castle improvements. What could Kat possibly see in the man? Why was she paying any attention to Stafford at all? She was supposed to be "finding out" Sir Brandon. Miranda sniffed. Two weeks, and Kat had not spent any more time in Sir Brandon's presence than she absolutely had to.

Which left Miranda in a ticklish predicament. Very ticklish. She squeezed her thighs together and tried not to dwell on Brandon's touch upon her cheeks, his arm about her waist, his long body pressed scandalously close to hers, and his...his manroot! Miranda gulped.

Tonight, when he had held her so tightly in his arms, Miranda felt, for the first time, the hard evidence of a man's passion. The brief contact both alarmed and intrigued her. These warring emotions still plagued her and banished sleep from her eyes. She sighed a third time.

"What ails you, coz?" Kat suddenly asked from the other side of the bed.

Miranda jumped. "Forgive me for waking you, Kat."

"I was already awake, and have listened to you sigh and weep. Come, tell me. Methinks 'tis not a headache that plagues you so."

Miranda rolled onto her back, and stared up at the dark, wine red canopy above the bed. "Oh, Kat, I am at sixes and sevens, and know not what to do."

Kat chuckled. "Ah, 'tis Brandon who banishes your sleep."

Miranda's cheeks flamed. "Never! Why on earth should I think upon your bridegroom?"

"Because you have been in his company night and day for over a fortnight. Because I have never heard you laugh so much, nor seen so many of your smiles and blushes as I have in recent times. Because you sing at dawn when you've spied on him. Because—"

"Peace, Kat! You prattle like a child," Miranda snapped.

"Oh, aye?" Kat sat up, pulling the covers with her. "Then let us have a serious conference, Miranda, for I am much concerned with your welfare."

Miranda closed her eyes, wishing she could close her ears as well. Kat had always had Miranda's welfare at heart. Throughout the horrible years of Fitzhugh's domination, Kat had protected Miranda, fed her, clothed her, schooled her and was Miranda's best friend in the world. How dare she return such devotion by desiring her cousin's handsome husband-to-be? Kat deserved the chance for a good marriage. But why did it have to be to this man?

'Tis not fair! a niggling voice whined in the recesses of her mind. Miranda squeezed her eyelids tighter to hold back a hovering tear of self-pity.

Kat gently shook her. "Miranda? Let us talk. I promise you, all will be well in time. What is it about Brandon Cavendish that particularly distresses you?"

With yet another sigh, Miranda pulled herself upright. "Nothing distresses me about him. He is peerless among men. 'Tis you who give me no rest at night."

"Aye? How so?"

"You have not spent one private moment in his company. You barely look upon him, let alone engage him in conversation. How long do you intend to keep up this deceit?"

"Till Midsummer's Day," Kat replied in a cheerful tone.

Miranda gasped. "The poor man! What is he to think when you present yourself to him at the church door?"

Kat laughed lightly. "They do say that midsummer brings a certain madness with it."

"'Tis not the magic of midsummer that infects Bodiam with lunacy, but you, Kat! This false face you have made me wear will cause me to loose my wits long before the wedding day ever comes." Miranda gave a small sob despite her efforts to stifle it. "And I am too young to go mad."

Putting her arm around Miranda's shoulders, Kat pulled her closer. "Have no fear, gentle cousin. You will not rue this time, I swear it to you. All will be well that ends well."

"How?" Miranda sniffed.

"What do you think of Sir John?" Kat asked, after a pause.

Miranda stiffened. "Is this your device? To marry me off to that...that bluff rascal? I'd rather retire to a nunnery!"

Kat laughed softly. "So, my Lord Stafford does not stand high in your estimation?"

Emboldened by Kat's apparent lack of anger, Miranda continued. "Nay. He does not sing well, nor write poetry. Granted, he is a handsome brute to look at, but methinks Sir John lacks a certain grace that Sir Brandon is blessed with in abundance."

"And you think these attributes are important in a good husband?"

Miranda sighed deeply. "Aye, I do!"

Kat hugged her. "Well, harken to this, dearest coz. I do not like the man who courts you, for all his pretty ways. If, by magic, mystery or mayhem, I could leave him to you on Midsummer's Day, would you take him?"

Miranda could scarcely believe her ears! Was Kat planning to run away and become a nun? How ludicrous! Of all the women Miranda had known in her twenty-eight years, Katherine Fitzhugh was the least likely person to yearn for a cloistered life.

"But how is this possible?" Miranda sucked on her lower lip with forbidden hope.

Kat laughed. "The moon will be full."

Miranda shook her head. Poor sweet Katherine! She was the one who had gone mad!

"Would you take him?" Kat prodded her.

Miranda swallowed at the thought. "Aye, in a heartbeat."

Kat hugged her again, then sang, "'Jack shall have Jill, naught shall go ill, and all shall be well.' Good night, coz, and sweet dreams attend you!" With a loud yawn, Kat slid beneath the covers.

Miranda stared at the dying embers in the fireplace. *I will speak to Sondra first thing in the morning. Perhaps Kat is in desperate need of a purge to clear her addled wits.*

* * *

Pacing behind the stables, Jess cursed himself for the twentieth time. Sir Brandon would have his hide when he found out what Jess had done. Actually, Jess had not meant to do it; 'twas Sondra's fault. Hang the pretty wench! If he hadn't fallen under her spell...

Jess licked his lips. Not that he minded being in Sondra's thrall. Aye, she was bonny and buxom, and she pleased him more than any other woman had ever pleased him. In or out of bed. She could make him laugh with her tales and her jests; she brewed a good ale; she had banished that troublesome wart on the back of his hand. At night, she warmed both his heart and his loins. Each morning, she left him with a kiss lingering on his lips, like a drop of honey. But, somehow, she had conned him into betraying his master. Now there would be hell to pay when Lord Cavendish learned of Jess's perfidy.

Was he a man, or a runny-nosed apprentice afraid of his master's ire? Jess drew up to his fullest height and expanded his chest to give himself courage. With a resolution stuck firm in his heart, Jess strode into the stables where he knew the knights were giving their horses their morning's oats.

"Good morrow, Jess." Brandon grinned at him over the back of Windchaser. "How fares the day? Will the weather hold?"

Jess blinked to accustom his eyes to the dimness of the stable's interior. "Aye, my lord. Not a cloud to be seen. Just now, I spied a kestrel winging high in the sky. 'Tis a good omen." He shifted his feet on the straw-strewn floor.

Brandon chuckled, then called to Jack, who was in the act of inspecting one of Thunder's shoes. "Do you mark that, Jack? Jess predicts 'twill be a fine day. A good day for hunting."

Jess looked up from studying the toe of his boot. "Hunting, my lord? Do you have in mind a hart, or some rabbits, mayhap a boar?"

Brandon flashed him a wicked grin. "Nay, we will not need your services this day, Jess, save to give Windchaser and Thunder a good run in the fields. I speak of a heart of a different sort. And our hunting grounds will be a picnic, eh, Jack?"

Jack's chuckle answered him.

Jess licked his lips. "Aye, 'twill be a fine day for that, my lord." *Tell him now,* his conscience prodded him, while Sir Brandon was in a good mood.

Jess cleared his throat. "My lord…" he faltered, trying to decide exactly how to begin.

Brandon patted Windchaser's rump as he crossed behind the horse. "Aye, Jess?"

"My lord…" he started again. God's nightshirt! What was he going to say?

Brandon regarded him with a thoughtful air. "Methinks you are much troubled, Jess. Has the delightful house-keeper thrown you out of her affections?"

Jess's eyes widened. "You know of her, my lord?"

Grinning, Brandon nodded. "Aye, with two large-eyed squires such as Mark and Christopher, there are scant go-ings-on in this place that we haven't heard about."

"Save for the personal activities of Mark and Christo-pher," added Jack, wiping his hands clean with a piece of old felt. "Come, Jess, you can tell me your sad tale, for am I not the acknowledged Jack of Hearts? I am at your disposal to advise you how to win back the good woman's interest."

"Nay, my lords. Sondra and me…" He shuffled the straw some more. "We do right well. That is not what I've come to tell you."

Brandon clapped him on the shoulder. "Well, then, out with it, man! My stomach rumbles for some bread and a bit of last night's roast duck. What is on your mind?"

Jess hung his head. "Your pardon, my lord. I beg your forgiveness, for I've gone and betrayed you."

Brandon shook his head slowly. "How now? Take me with you, huntsman. Just what have you betrayed?"

"'Twas not all my fault, my lord."

"It never is," Brandon muttered under his breath.

Jess felt a warmth crawl up the back of his neck at that remark. "But I'll take the blame for all."

"I'll wager two shillings the matter has a woman behind it," Jack remarked, leaning against the stall.

Brandon pointed to a bale of hay. "Sit down, Jess, and tell us this interesting tale."

Jess plopped onto the hay, took a deep breath and embarked with his story. "This morning Sondra left me as usual—"

Jack snapped his fingers. "Ha! The wager is mine!"

Brandon shot Jack a dark look. "Go on," he urged Jess.

"And as it was still some time afore I was to rise, I lay back and thought upon what we did—Sondra and myself—"

Brandon held up his hand. "We do not need to hear the details of that, Jess."

"Why not?" Jack grinned.

Jess plunged on, afraid that, if he was stopped again, he would lose his nerve. "And I got to remembering the first night we…ah, met, and the most peculiar thing of it was, that I didn't remember when Sondra came to me."

"How now? Forget taking that buxom wench?" Jack arched his eyebrow. "How much ale did you drink that night, Jess?"

"Jack!" Brandon growled.

Jess nodded. "Just so, my lord. 'Twas more than my usual. And as I lay there, twixt waking and sleep, it came to me in bits and pieces. And 'twas right pleasurable in the remembering." Jess grinned in spite of the situation.

"I am all ears." Brandon upended a wooden bucket, then sat down on it. "Pray, tell us more."

"Then, as I was remembering the things we said and

did, I recalled saying something like I was fortunate to be a-sleeping true, when my lord was a-sleeping false.''

Brandon whistled under his breath but said nothing. Jess relaxed a little. At least his master wasn't bellowing—not that bellowing was his lord's usual practice—but Jess wasn't too sure how Sir Brandon was going to react, when he finally got to the meat of the problem.

"And then Sondra tickled me in…well, in a private place of mine, and she asked what did I mean. And I, feeling drowsy and content, said something like that my lord was a-playing at being Sir John, and Sir John was a-wooing up a storm to Lady Katherine as Sir Brandon.''

"Hoy-day!" Jack slapped his leg. "The horse is out of the stable now!"

"And what did Sondra say?" Brandon asked in a calm tone.

Jess cut a quick glance in his direction and was relieved to see that Lord Cavendish had not changed color. This boded much better than Jess had hoped. "She did nothing but laugh and tickle me some more. And she asked me to repeat what I said. I confess that my mind was on my nether parts, and not on what I was a-saying. But the more I thought on it this morning, the more clear the vision got. And now, I swear to you, I believe I did tell her of your disguising, my lord. But I never did it intentionally, by God's holy word, I swear.''

Brandon patted the huntsman on his shoulder, which cheered Jess considerably. "Peace, my friend. 'Twas not your fault. It appears we are surrounded by a flock of scheming women.''

"Pretty ones, though," interjected Jack. "You have to give them that. I have never seen such a sweet bunch of posies in my life—chambermaids, housekeepers, musicians, companions—and the fair lady, who rules over them all.''

Jess blinked at Jack. "Aye, my lord. They are right handsome."

Just then Brandon laughed, the sound floating up from his throat and filling the stable. A few of the grooms looked out from the stall boxes where they were sweeping.

"And we three are a right handsome trio of pantaloons!" Brandon continued to laugh so hard he had to drape himself over Windchaser's back to support himself.

"Then you'll forgive me, sir?" Jess asked, looking from one lord to the other.

Jack shrugged. "Methinks he does—when he can get his breath back."

Brandon finally ceased, with a chuckle or two, then wiped his eyes with the back of his hand. "Gentlemen, had I a pitcher of Mistress Owens's beer, I would bid you join me in a toast to the fair ladies who have bedeviled our lives. Since I have neither beer nor cups, think on it when next you drink."

"Aye." Jess nodded. He could do with a cup of cool beer right about now. Confession took a lot out of a man.

Brandon fished in his poke and drew out a sixpence, which he handed to Jess. "Take that for your pains, Jess, and be gone. I am right glad to hear that Mistress Owens has not yet grown tired of you, even after she got what she looked for in the first place."

"Thank you, sir." Jess wasn't too sure what his lord meant by all that, but a sixpence in the hand was a far better punishment than a lick or two on his back.

"I take it you are not dismayed by this turn of events?" Jack asked.

Brandon smiled with a smug, cat-in-the-cream look. "Nay, 'tis better than I had hoped for, Jack."

"How so?"

"Why now, I have no qualms against seducing the sweet mistress of this fine abode. If I know who she is, and she knows who I am, then I have no fear of cuckolding myself—in her eyes.''

"But does the lady know that you know that she knows?'' Jack asked.

"Jackanapes! You quibble like a lawyer!'' Brandon rubbed his hands together. "What a picnic we will have this day! I have set my mind upon a most particular dessert—of a private nature—and I mean to enjoy it fully!''

Both the gentlemen burst out laughing. Jess scratched his head. Hang it all if he could understand the nobility! Nodding to the knights, who continued to bray at each other, Jess left the stable a satisfied man. A clear conscience, and a sixpence to go with it—not a bad day's work, and 'twas only seven of the clock in the morning.

"Queen Mab's Malady? Ha! A pox upon it! I have been made the fool of all fools, Wormsley!'' Fenton glowered through the red haze of his anger at his servant. "And by that bitch of an aunt!''

Wormsley returned Fenton's look with a complete lack of concern. Fenton curled his lip. Idiot! Kat had played her wicked deed on the boy, as well as the master. Didn't the slug care that he had great itching hives, or that his nose had run green snot and pepper for two days? Fenton gnashed his teeth. Hell wasn't hot coals and dancing devils. It was being cooped up in a rank Dover inn with a mewling idiot for company, and a tender skin racked with nettle stings and peeling blisters!

Wormsley snuffled. "Your aunt is a most loving lady, and has always shown you kindness, my lord. Pray, sir, hold still, so that I can apply this ointment upon the proper spots.''

The cooling medicine did very little to soothe Fenton's festering anger. "Loving and kind? Your head has been ass-kicked. She is a shrew, and a cunning woman—two traits I abhor in a female.''

"Perchance 'twas some of the maids who put the nettles in our beds, and pepper everywhere else." Wormsley's fingers swirled more ointment on the angry red welts down Fenton's back.

Fenton snorted. "If I believed that, I would beat every one of them within an inch of their miserable lives, then throw the little sluts out onto the road. Aye, methinks I will do just that, once I have Bodiam in my control."

"How can that be, my lord? Lady Katherine will be married in ten days. My advice is that you make peace with my Lord Cavendish, since he will hold the purse strings then."

"That great blond ape?" Fenton glared over his shoulder at Wormsley. What a puking moon-face the boy had! *When I can afford it, I will heave this bit of vermin back into the pigsty from whence he came, and find myself another servant, one whose thoughts will be the brothers of mine.*

"Sir Brandon would sooner see me locked in the clink for indebtedness than lift one finger on my behalf. He wants Kat's fortune all for himself. But I swear to you, he will not have that pleasure. Furthermore, I'll thank you to keep your advice to yourself."

Fenton smiled grimly to himself. He needed no one's help. Last night, a brilliant plan had sprung full-blown from his brain. As soon as he could sit upon his horse in comfort, they would return to Bodiam.

The problem had now come to a head. No more time to sweet-talk Aunt Kat into assigning over to him his proper rights. Besides, after the treatment he had suffered at her hands, Fenton was not inclined to be sweet to her about anything. Uncle Edward Fitzhugh had had the right idea— keep a woman in her place by a good swat or two. Never let them get the upper hand. Yes, 'twould be a pleasure to turn the tables on her—to make Kat beg and grovel for her sustenance. And the husband the king had sent her? This time next week, he'll be dead and in the ground.

"Dead," Fenton muttered aloud, savoring the very sound of the word.

Wormsley stopped his ministrations. "My...my lord?"

Fenton smiled at him. It pleased him to see the boy take a step backward. "Dead, Worm. Do you hear? Colder than a gravestone!"

The whey-faced servant licked his lips. "Who, my lord?"

"You will see anon. Aye, before Midsummer's Day. My double-dealing aunt will go to the church, not for a wedding, but for a funeral." Fenton removed his dagger from its sheath. He pointed it at the boy. "And I trust that you will say nothing, or 'twill be the worse for you. Mark me, you scurvy knave?"

Wormsley's eyelids blinked rapidly. "Aye, my Lord Scantling. I mark you well."

Fenton fingered the blade. Perchance, when he tossed Wormsley back into his father's sty, 'twould be in the manner of a corpse. Fenton needed no tale-teller in his shadow. In less than ten days, Lord Scantling would become a very rich man.

Chapter Eleven

"Do not twitch so, my lady," Sondra muttered through a mouthful of pins. "If you want the skirt's hem even, you must stand still."

Kat released a deep breath. "Aye."

For the past hour, Sondra had fussed over the fitting of Kat's wedding gown. First she worried about the hang of the outer sleeves, trying to make sure they were even. Now she knelt on the floor of Kat's chamber working on the hem of the chapel train.

Kat looked down at the dress she wore. The white brocade gleamed in the sunlight streaming through the window. Sondra had done an excellent job fitting the bodice; it accented the rise of Kat's breasts without revealing too much. Gold lace and pearls edged the square neckline. The underskirt, revealed by a split that ran from waist to hem, was made of sumptuous gold satin. The same material lined the gown's outer sleeves, while gold lace, sprinkled with pearls, made up the puffed inner sleeves. Truly, the wedding gown was a masterpiece fit for Queen Catherine herself.

A cold lump settled itself in the pit of Kat's stomach. Stars! This wedding was really going to happen! The past several weeks had been a pleasant diversion—almost like a dream, and one Kat had thoroughly enjoyed. Now the reckoning was due. In eight days—unless the world came to an abrupt end—Kat would wed for a third time. The game would be over. Reality would return to stay. Her fingers plucked at the lacy cuffs; a pearl bounced across the floor.

"My lady!" Sondra chided, a note of exasperation in her voice.

"Your pardon, Sondra."

The housekeeper retrieved the jewel, then she returned to her hemming. Meanwhile Kat's thoughts continued to race.

Sir Brandon seemed honorable enough, even though he still persisted in calling himself Lord Stafford. From the first moment of their meeting, his arresting good looks had totally captured her attention despite her resolve to the contrary. She found that she approved of his attitude of self-command, and, at the same time, his teasing, relaxed manner with everyone at Bodiam, whatever their station.

Kat thought of his firm mouth, curled as if always on the edge of laughter. She tried to ignore the memory of the kiss they had shared, but her body refused to forget it. Treacherously it yearned for more. Kat tossed her head. No doubt all the women of the court found Brandon deliciously appealing.

"Pray you, Lady Kat, hold still." Sondra sat back on her haunches to regard her work. Her eyes sparkled with pleasure. "Your new husband will take one look at you in that fine gown and he'll think he's died and taken flight with an angel. But, methinks that angels do not have such pensive looks, my lady."

"This wedding day comes too soon, Sondra."

Sondra cocked her head. "Aye?"

"I had not the mind to marry again." The dress felt suddenly confining. "And if I considered marriage at all,

I wanted to be free to make my vows as my heart dictated.''

"From what I've seen, you like the man well enough," Sondra observed. Shaking out the hem, she allowed it to swirl into graceful lines at Kat's feet. "'Tis not as if you haven't been bedded before.''

Aye, there's the rub. Kat swallowed. "'Tis that part that worries me.'' What if Brandon wanted children?

Sondra grinned. "I could brew you up a potion, my lady.''

Kat shook her head. "Nay, good Sondra. I need to be in full command of my wits when I encounter my Lord Cavendish in the marriage bed.''

There was a knock at the door, then Violet popped her head around it. The girl seemed out of breath.

"My lady, a word with you, I pray!'' she gasped.

Pray God Montjoy has not had heart palpitations. The old steward had looked a little pale and drawn in the days since Fenton's visit. Aloud, Kat asked, "What's amiss, Violet?''

After closing the door softly behind her, the girl tiptoed over to them. "I have a most marvelous secret, my lady!'' she whispered, her large brown eyes growing even more enormous.

Kat gave her a reproving look. "No tittle-tattle, I pray?'' Her maids tended to make mountains out of pimples.

The girl shook her head. "Nay, my lady. 'Tis gospel true.''

Rising from her position on the floor, Sondra put her hands on her hips. "Aye? So, do not take until Saint Michael's Day to tell us this great secret. Out with it. We are alone, as you can see. Miranda is off listening to Lord Cavendish sing more songs to her.''

Violet wrinkled her nose. "Not so, neither!''

Kat placed her hand over her heart; her fingers clutched the rose brooch. What had happened to Miranda? If that smiling rascal had taken any improprieties with her, he'd have the devil to pay with Kat! "What is it, Violet?"

"My Lord Cavendish, Lady Kat. He is not Sir Brandon at all."

Kat's shoulders relaxed. "Aye, this is old news to me."

Violet lowered her voice. "But there is more. I overheard their conversation with Jess in the stable this very morn."

Sondra's brow went up. "Oh, aye? And what was a chambermaid like you a-doing in the stable at the crack of dawn?"

Violet blushed a strawberry hue. "I was...talking with Patrick, one of Lord Stafford's grooms. He's Irish, methinks, but quite civilized. And ever so fine to look at." She giggled.

Kat rolled her eyes. While she had been occupied with entertaining her guests, her guests' handsome servants had been busy entertaining her susceptible maids. "We will discuss your stable activities later, Violet, but for the present, is there anything else you overheard?"

"Aye, what did Jess say?" Sondra wanted to know.

"That is the nut and core of it, mistress. Jess said that you, Mistress Sondra, had wheedled out the truth of his master's identity."

"Sweet Saint Anne!"

"Bestrew me! Jess is a stronger man than methought!"

Kat ran her hand through her hair. "What did Sir Brandon say when Jess told him of this? Was he very angry?"

"Nay, my lady. My Lord Cavendish—the real one—laughed so hard he could barely stand." Violet licked her lips. "Then he said something about trying to seduce the mistress of the house, and cuckolding himself. At least, methinks he said that."

Sondra put her hand over her mouth to hide her grin. "What a roguish knave!"

Kat played with an auburn curl between her fingers as

she considered the implications of this new twist. "That means that Sir Brandon, who is pretending to be Sir John, knows that I am really Katherine, even though I call myself Miranda."

"Aye, my lady. 'Tis why I thought it was important to tell you straightway."

A slow smile grew on Kat's lips. "But he doesn't know that I know that he knows!"

Violet's dark brows met in the middle of her forehead. "Your pardon, my lady? I don't understand."

"But I do!" Sondra clapped her hands. "Oh, Lady Kat! How the game turns, and turns again in a widening circle! Like the ripples in a pond when you toss in a stone."

"Aye, so long as I do not get caught in the snares of my own making." Kat tapped her cheek with her forefinger. "And now this smiling knave means to test my virtue—and my honor, as well."

"I know just the thing!" Sondra suggested. "This afternoon I will fix you a basket for your picnic with the noble gentlemen that will please every appetite."

A little warning bell sounded in Kat's mind. "No love potions, Sondra! Mark what I say. My Lord Cavendish does not need any additional urging. He has too much vigor already."

Sondra ignored her. "'Twill be a feast for lovers."

Kat tried to move but found herself hampered by her unpinned hem. "Sondra!"

Sondra unlaced Kat's gown. "Never fear, Lady Kat. You will enjoy what I fix for you. And what may happen after that?" She lifted one shoulder with a dismissive air. "Who can say?"

By the book! Her whole household had turned into Cupid's minions! At least, they had better be silent ones. "Sondra, Violet, say nothing—absolutely nothing—to anyone about this. Especially not to Miranda. Violet, I mean that particularly to you. If I hear one whispered remark out of little Pansy's mouth, I shall know where to lay my grievance.''

Violet drew herself up with an important air. ''My lips are sealed, my lady.''

''And I give you my pledge, Lady Kat,'' Sondra added. She scooped up the half-finished gown in her arms. ''Now, Violet, you can clean out all the fireplaces, which might take your mind off a certain wicked-eyed Irishman for the day. I am going to the kitchens. You, Lady Kat, deck yourself in your buttercup cambric. And prepare for battle.'' She pulled open the door. ''They say, 'All's fair in love and war.' You decide which it will be this afternoon.''

Taking Violet with her, the housekeeper skipped out, silvery laughter following in her wake. Kat stared after her, while her brain spun like a child's top.

Very well, my clever Lord Cavendish. Prepare yourself, for this afternoon you will meet your match. Seduce me, indeed! What does he think I am? An empty-headed maid whom he can toss on the ground for his pleasure? Nay, Sir Brandon! After this day, you will think twice before you change your stripes again.

Brandon released a contented sigh, stretched out his long legs, cradled his wine cup in his hand and leaned back against the trunk of a wide willow tree, under which the two couples had passed the afternoon pleasantly filled with wine, music and food. After many nudges and winks from Brandon, Jack had finally taken his fair lady on a walk. Within ten minutes, they had disappeared around the bend of the riverbank.

Now to begin his assault of this delectable fortress.

''By my troth, Mistress Miranda, methinks your cook must be in league with the goddess Venus,'' Brandon remarked, his gaze skimming over the remains of the picnic dinner.

Kat glanced up from the pile of daisies, cornflowers,

poppies and buttercups that she wove into colorful chains.
"How so, Sir John? Philippe is French, and not classically
inclined."

Brandon chuckled. "Worse and worse. The French are
the very votaries of love and all its ploys. Observe." He
pointed to the numerous dishes and bowls. "To begin, we
had plover's eggs stuffed with cinnamon, as well as mushrooms marinated in oil and vinegar."

"Aye?" Kat split the stem of a daisy, then tied a buttercup through it. "Did they not sit well in your stomach,
my lord? Methought the eggs were particularly tasty. They
are a rare treat."

*As you are a rare treat for me, Lady Kat. You look like
a tender yellow chick in your summer's day gown.* The
gold of his rose brooch gleamed in the late afternoon's
sunlight. It pleased him inordinately that Kat had worn his
poor gift every day. Moving his gaze upward, he approved
of the warm creamy color of her slender throat above the
provocative cut of her tight bodice. Her long, sensitive
fingers worked skillfully at her self-appointed task. What
those fingers could do, if she would entwine them around
him!

Crossing one leg over the other, Brandon fought to ignore the warmth in his loins. "Why, Miranda, did you
know that eggs are reputed to enhance fertility in women
and vigor in men?"

A faint blush stole into her cheeks. She bent her head
closer to her work.

Brandon grinned behind his hand. "Great Jove! The
eggs of a plover are especially noted for rendering a person
irresistible to amorous assaults. And to stuff them with
cinnamon, a spice well known to induce lively desire? I
am amazed that you are not panting with lovesickness this
instant." He moistened his dry throat with a sip of wine.

Kat peeked at him from under the wide brim of her
straw hat. Her eyes took on a deeper shade of green. "If

I am panting at all, my lord, 'tis with the heat of this June afternoon. You spoke of the mushrooms. Are they equally dangerous to consume?''

Brandon ran his forefinger around the wet rim of his wine cup. ''Aye, so I have been told. They say that if one shares a dish of mushrooms with a lover, it leads directly to the bedchamber.''

''Indeed?'' Kat pursed her lips. ''I suppose 'twould be true, if the mushrooms were poisonous.'' She added a cornflower to her chain.

Brandon took another swallow of the rich sugared burgundy. Kat was no one's fool. 'Twould make his conquest all the sweeter.

''The next dish was dove pie, if I recall,'' he continued.

''I believe so, Sir John, though you and Sir Brandon ate it up so quickly, I cannot be sure. Pray, what properties have the poor doves? Or is it the pastry you remark upon?''

''Doves, from the earliest times, have been considered the birds of love, for they do nothing but bill and coo. Do you feel inclined to coo, Miranda?'' He winked at her.

Pausing in her occupation, she appeared to give the matter some thought. ''I fancy that I coo to babes and small children, as well as to puppies, kittens and other assorted young creatures.'' She swept him an appraising glance. ''But since neither you nor I nor the river that babbles at our feet could be considered young, I am not moved to coo—nor to bill, for that matter.''

She is playing hard to get. Excellent! I like a challenge.

''Our main course was a goodly crock of hare stewed in a wine sauce,'' Brandon continued. ''My compliments to your cook for that inspiration.''

Kat threaded two more buttercups together. ''How so? Rabbit stew is a common enough dish.''

''Have you never been warned of the dangers of eating hares, especially in the springtime?''

"'Tis summer, my lord, and I've eaten rabbits all my life." She held up her chain to measure its length. "Pray enlighten me."

Leaning forward, Brandon lowered his voice to a conspiratorial whisper. "Hares have a universal reputation for exciting unbridled desire. Consider the vast number of offspring they produce." He winked at her again.

Kat yawned, covering her mouth in a languid motion. "And I suppose that the salad of cress, mustard greens, radishes and onions also has amorous qualities?"

"Just so, mistress mine. They stimulate vigor and hot desire."

"And you will no doubt tell me that the spiced cakes and peaches stewed in honey are also unsafe to eat in mixed company?"

Brandon nodded with mock seriousness. "Particularly the peaches, I fear. Why, I am amazed that mother church has not banned the eating of peaches by all except old married couples past their prime."

Kat bent closer to her dwindling pile of meadow flowers. Her hat hid her face. "'Tis very strange. I feel satisfied by the choice of foods and their manner of preparation. But lusty? Full of heated desire? Ready to leap into bed? Nay, my good lord. Far from it. Besides..." She flashed him a beguiling smile from under her brim. "You have forgotten. I am but a spinster maid, and know nothing of bed sport."

"Aye." Brandon inclined his head in tribute. "I had forgotten that point, for the moment." He poured himself more wine and wondered where to go to from there.

Kat's golden voice interrupted his scheming. "Tell me, my lord, how is it you know so much about the foods of love? Is it something they teach you when you live at court?"

Brandon allowed a small smile. "Our good king is most

interested in pleasing all the appetites. Food and love go hand in hand with Great Harry."

"Ah!" She furrowed her copper brows. "Methinks 'twould make a frightful mess to combine the two in close proximity."

Brandon's wine went down his windpipe. He choked. Dropping her flower chain, Kat scrambled over to his side.

"Sweet angels! My good lord, are you all right?" She thumped him on the back several times.

"Aye," he gasped, sputtering to draw a breath.

Kat struck him again between the shoulder blades for good measure. Zounds, the woman had a strong arm! He must remember that for future reference. Forsooth! If he had known 'twould take him half choking to death to get the cunning Kat within his grasp, he would have done that in the beginning.

"Sniff through your nose," she instructed, her lovely face very close to his. "Sondra always tells us that, and it works."

Brandon drew in air through his nostrils as commanded. Remarkably the raw, tickling sensation in his throat eased.

"Your Sondra is a wonder," he gasped, mopping his eyes with one of the picnic napkins.

Kat's lips twitched. "Aye, she is, indeed. Are you quite recovered, Sir John?"

He placed his hand over hers. "Only if you stay by my side like this, in case I am besieged by another attack of my windpipe."

She cast him a saucy glance. "If you did not guzzle your wine like a dog in the slops, you would not be prone to these uncomfortable outbursts."

Brandon coughed again. "I thank you for your advice, good mistress. I shall endeavor to remember it."

Kat smoothed out the skirts of her gown, then leaned against the tree beside him. Their shoulders lightly touched. Brandon itched to take her in his arms, but her cool demeanor counseled that he bide his time. The evening had barely suggested itself. The sun would not disappear for several more hours. Time enough. Taking her hand and lacing his fingers between hers, he marveled at the delicacy of her skin. She did not pull away. They sat in companionable silence within the bower of the overhanging willow branches for a few minutes.

Kat released a small sigh. "Tell me, my lord, do you know Sir Brandon well?"

Brandon rested the back of his head against the willow's rough bark. What was the minx up to now? "Aye, Miranda, as well as I know myself. Why?"

She cast her gaze down to their joined hands, then answered in a voice that reminded Brandon of the sound made by a butterfly on the wing. "The wedding day draws near, my lord, and I would have Lady Katherine take joy in its coming."

"And I desire the same thing, sweetheart," he replied with a tightness in his throat.

"As Katherine's closest friend, there are some things I must ask you—concerning my Lord Cavendish."

Brandon squeezed her hand. "And as Brandon's closest companion, I will try to answer your questions."

Kat caught him directly in her gaze. "First, why does your good friend drink so much?"

Brandon had been in the act of lifting his cup to his mouth. At her question, he put it down at his side. "You think he takes too much wine?"

"Mayhap, especially when he is angry or doesn't get his own way. Is this true, my lord, in your close observation?"

Brandon chewed his lower lip. "I had not noticed it before, sweetheart, but I will keep an eye on the problem in the future."

She smiled at him, her twin pools of green melting into soft mist. "That greatly eases my mind, my lord." Then she furrowed her dainty brows. "Fitzhugh drank far too much, and it made a monster out of him."

Slipping his arm around her shoulders, Brandon drew her closer to him. The spicy scent of potpourri filled his nostrils. "Tell me about Fitzhugh, if you can bear it," he suggested.

She trembled. "He was false of heart, light of ear and bloody of hand. No dog was more mad than he, no wolf matched him in greediness. Like a lion after prey, he took what he wanted, whenever he wanted. Had he been inclined to cannibalism, he would have boiled and eaten those who opposed him. God forgive me for saying this, but he is the one man I hate above all others."

Brandon squeezed her shoulder. "I heard that he beat you, and your cousin."

Kat closed her eyes. "Aye, and the less said of those times the better. I have spoken too much as it is."

"Do not think of him that was, but of him that is to come," Brandon murmured. "I swear upon my honor, that Sir Brandon Cavendish is a far better man, and will make his lady very happy."

She glanced at him from under the dark fringe of her lashes. "Then your friend must be a miracle worker, for Lady Katherine has had nothing but harsh words and ill treatment from every man she has ever known, beginning with her father."

"'Tis a wonder that the lady is so sweet tempered." Brandon lifted her hand to his lips. He lightly caressed her fingers. "Tell me of Lady Katherine's early days—so that I may tell Brandon."

She swallowed. "There is not much to tell. Her father, Sir Robert Addison, had two daughters, no sons. Grace was the eldest by nearly twelve years. Their mother died giving birth to m…my cousin. I believe her father never forgave Katherine for that. Grace married the second son of the Earl of Fairfax. They died in a carriage accident when her son, Fenton, was ten. Kat, then married to her second husband, took the boy in.''

Brandon gritted his teeth. "Fenton! A subtle, slippery knave, if you don't mind me saying so."

Kat shook her head slightly. "Nay, 'tis the truth. The boy was much taken with his Uncle Edward—Fitzhugh, that is—and aped him in all his ways. I fear he will grow worse as he grows older."

"He needs the firm hand of a new uncle," Brandon growled.

"Aye. Do you suppose that Sir Brandon can control him?"

Brandon returned a tight smile to her. "My oath upon it!"

"Good! For Fenton is a dreadful liar." Kat grinned, banishing the knot of worry and sadness that had clouded her face. "Do you know what he told us of Sir Brandon?"

Brandon gritted his teeth. "I can only imagine."

"He told us that Lord Cavendish was young, barely out of the schoolroom! We were most surprised when you...and Sir Brandon, appeared in the hall."

Brandon mused that it was no wonder both women had looked thunderstruck and gabbled like geese on that first meeting! Aloud, he remarked, "Your surprise was no less than ours. Fenton told us that you...ah, Lady Katherine was—" He stopped himself. Jolt-head! Women were very sensitive about their ages.

Kat stroked the fingers of the hand she held. Her feather-light touch threatened to shatter his self-control. Damn the stewed hare and honeyed peaches!

"Pray, what did that rogue say about us?"

Brandon licked his lips. "That Lady Katherine was quite elderly, and that she practiced witchcraft."

Kat's eyes widened, then she burst into a peal of rippling laughter. "And what have you learned since meeting me...my cousin?"

Brandon drew her closer still, so that her face was only a kiss away. His heart drummed against his rib cage. "I have learned that she is light of form and figure. That her eyes brim with kindness. And that her only witchcraft is to charm the hearts of all who meet her."

Kat sighed, her breath sweetened with the peaches. "You are beginning to talk like Sir Brandon."

"Believe me truly when I say that I speak with his heart and his tongue."

She moistened her lush lips. "And what else does his tongue say?"

"This," Brandon replied as he claimed her lips with his own.

Without quite knowing how, Kat found herself in Brandon's lap. She didn't care as she returned his kiss with a hunger that belied her determination to remain unmoved. How could she stay calm when his tongue sent shivers of desire racing through her?

Raising his mouth from hers for a moment, Brandon gazed into her eyes. "There is poetry on your lips, sweet mistress. I desire to study more of it."

She wove her fingers through his thick blond hair at the nape of his neck. "Teach me this poetry, for I have never tasted its sweetness before."

Reclaiming her lips, he crushed her to him. Her soul sang in joyful response. *If this is paradise, let me stay here forever!*

Brandon moved his mouth over hers, as if he would devour her. Then his lips left hers to nibble at her earlobe.

"Sweet," he murmured as he kissed the pulsing hollow at the base of her throat. His lips continued to explore her soft ivory flesh as they seared a path down her neck to explore the bared expanse of her bosom.

Kat's nipples tingled, then tightened with unaccustomed expectation. Her breath came in short gasps, shocking her at her eager response to his touch. Her mouth quivered with an aching desire to taste his again. Parting her lips, she raised her head to meet him.

Brandon's grip tightened around her. Kat relaxed, sinking into his cushioning embrace. She felt transported on a soft, wispy cloud, far away from fear, pain and humiliation. *I am home, at last.*

A loud shriek shattered the moment into a thousand jagged fragments. Another scream, calling for help, was followed by a tremendous splash of water.

Brandon tore his mouth from hers. "God's death, what has happened?"

Kat flicked her tongue over her burning lips. "Methinks 'tis Mir—my cousin."

A man's voice cried out, then a second splash followed.

Bunching her skirts in her hands, Kat struggled to rise. "Saints preserve us! They have fallen into the river!"

Chapter Twelve

Jack couldn't imagine how the disaster had happened. One minute, he had been whispering sweet nothings into Miranda's ear, and the next minute she was floundering in the river.

"Help me, ere I sink!" she cried as her skirts and petticoats ballooned out around her, making her look like a living water lily. Then the current caught her, and her clothing collapsed as it became waterlogged. Miranda's head dipped under.

"Sweet Jesu!" Jack cried, ripping off his doublet. He flung himself into the water after her.

He swam a few strokes, then saw her red hair floating just under the surface. With an icy knot in his stomach, Jack dived. The material of Miranda's flowing gown wrapped around him. For a split second, panic gripped him, then his foot scraped the bottom. Jack grabbed a handful of her clothing. Digging his feet deep into the muck and wrapping his arms around her waist, he pulled Miranda to the surface. Her arm, flailing in her desperation, struck his head smartly, but he hung on.

With a mighty effort to keep his footing, he maneuvered Miranda into the shallows just as Brandon and Kat appeared on the shore. Jack heard them both shouting something, but he was too intent on getting Miranda to safety. Her eyes were closed, and her face had gone chalk white. She couldn't die! Not now.

Splashing into the water, Brandon grabbed her. "I have got her, Jack," he shouted. "You can let go."

Dazed, Jack relaxed his hold. Brandon carried the unconscious woman up the slippery bank where Kat waited, anxiety etched on her face. A creeping heaviness stole into Jack's limbs as he saw Brandon lay Miranda on the grass. Jack could hardly pull himself out of the water. He didn't care. He should have died with her. To have held happiness in his hands for such a brief moment, and now to have lost her in a blink of an eye? He stumbled up the bank, his soaked boots slipping sideways in the slick mud.

He fell to his knees at Miranda's side. "'Tis my fault, villain that I am," he gasped. "I must have frightened her."

Brandon didn't reply, but rolled Miranda onto her stomach, and began to knead her back, forcing the water out of her mouth.

"If only she had known me by my real name."

"Shut up, Jack!" Brandon growled. "The lady isn't dead."

Miranda coughed, then groaned, then coughed out more water. Brandon continued to pound her on the back.

"Stop!" she finally gasped. "Please don't beat me to death."

"Sweet coz!" Kat knelt beside Miranda, wrapping the picnic blanket around her. "You gave us such a fright!"

"Amen to that!" Jack whispered, not daring to touch her.

Miranda must have become frightened when he kissed her. Nay, he cringed to admit. 'Twas not his kiss that had alarmed her. He distinctly remembered putting his hand over her breast and gently squeezing it. She had whimpered in the back of her throat. The devil take him for a

villain! He thought Miranda had enjoyed what he was doing. Instead, he must have unhinged her, so that she had
jumped in the river to save herself from further ravishment.
Now he could scarcely look at her, for fear of seeing the
loathing in her eyes. Jack hung his head in shame.

"We must get her back to the castle at once," Kat told
Brandon. "Lest she take a chill."

"Please take me home," Miranda mumbled. She didn't
look at Jack. "I want to die."

Jack groaned at her words; each one stung him like a
whiplash.

"My lord?" Kat put her arm around his shaking shoulders. "Are you all right?"

"Nay," he mumbled. "I am damned."

"Not yet!" Brandon scooped up Miranda into his arms,
then started across the field toward the silver gray walls
of Bodiam. "But you will be, if you sit there all night."

Kat pulled Jack by the arm. "Come, my lord. Let me
help you. Put your arm around my shoulder." She smiled
at him by way of encouragement.

"I am not fit for you, lady," he apologized, struggling
to his feet. "I am wet, muddy, and I fear that I would
cover your pretty gown with my filth. Besides, I am no
good company for man nor beast—certainly not for any
ladies."

Standing on tiptoe, Kat plucked a strand of water weed
from his hair. "Pray, do not blame yourself, sir."

Shaking his head, Jack stepped away from her tender
concern. "But I do, mistress. You harbor a devil within
your home."

Kat cocked her head. "Methinks I spy a guilty conscience. Well, then, for your penance, you may help me
pack up the dishes, and carry the basket back to the
kitchen."

Jack could not smile back at her. He had no right to be

so well treated by the woman whose dear cousin he had almost killed.

"To be your pack animal is an honor," he mumbled. "Lead on."

Several hours later, Kat stretched out her feet before the fire in the hall. After giving her cousin a hot bath, a bowl of barley soup and a warm posset made of milk, spices and sack wine, she and Sondra had tucked Miranda into bed with a hot brick at her feet. Through it all, Miranda kept wailing that she was undone, that Jack would think her a simpleton, that he had ruined his good clothes on her account, that she could never look him in the face again for all the trouble she had caused him, and more drivel to that effect. No matter what Kat had said, Miranda wouldn't listen.

"Leave her be, my lady," Sondra had advised Kat as they closed the door of the darkened bedchamber. "Miranda will come to her senses in due time."

Kat sipped some of her own posset, allowing its spicy sweetness to roll down her throat. In the window seat, Columbine played a gentle ballad on the lute while the sun sent its farewell rays through the high arched glass panes. Kat tried to decide what course she should pursue on the morrow. Was she going to be Lady Katherine, or was she still Miranda?

She luxuriated in a wide yawn. After all the excitement of the day, and the two weeks beforehand, exhaustion overtook her. She didn't even have the energy to climb the stairs to her bed.

"A sixpence for your thoughts, sweet mistress," Brandon remarked as he entered from the corridor. "May I join you?" He pointed at the other chair.

"Aye." Kat waved him into the seat. "Care for a posset?"

Brandon lifted a golden brow. "A friend of mine recently hinted that I take too much wine," he reminded her.

Kat made a face. "A posset brings blessed sleep."

"In that case, I will have some, for I will need all the help I can get, if I am to have any sleep with my bedmate tonight."

Tilting her head, Kat asked, "Oh? Does Sir Brandon snore?"

A pensive shimmer stole into the shadow of Brandon's eyes. Then he replied, "My Lord Cavendish is wallowing in his misery with a jug of your ale for his only comfort. He blames himself for your cousin's misadventure."

"Ah, just so." Kat poured out the milky posset from the pitcher, then passed her goblet to him. "I fear we must share the cup. I do not have the strength to search you out your own."

Brandon toasted her. "Since your lips have touched this cup, 'twill make the brew all the sweeter."

Kat crinkled her nose. "How now? Compliments? Methinks that sounds like Sir Brandon speaking."

"Perchance he is," Brandon replied.

Uncomfortable with the fact that he had spoken the truth, Kat returned her attention to the fire. The flames danced with a mesmerizing grace. Brandon sipped his drink in companionable silence, but Kat could feel him watching her and not the fire. Was he waiting for her to admit her true identity? Should she? Had she played the game long enough? If so, what then? Would Brandon want to discuss marriage contracts, dower rights and other businesslike topics so tedious yet so necessary to a permanent relationship? Would he talk about the heirs he wanted to have? Kat sighed softly. No, she didn't want to discuss any of those things—at least, not tonight, when her lips still remembered the warmth of his afternoon kisses, and her body ached to be held again.

"A shilling, then," he said without preamble.

Kat blinked out of her reverie. "What?"

He chuckled. "A shilling for your thoughts, since you wouldn't tell me when I offered you a sixpence."

"Save your coin, my lord. My thoughts this night could not be bought with even a pound." Nay, they were priceless.

"You look tired, my sweet," he murmured, drawing his chair closer to hers.

"Aye," she replied. "'Twas a long day."

"But one that I am glad of." He held out his hand to her.

She met his smile with hers and accepted the hand that he offered. "Aye, and I am glad too, my lord."

The firelight gave a warm, ruddy cast to his features. His hair gleamed like dark gold, one stray lock falling across his forehead. Once again, Kat realized how devastatingly handsome he was. The knight of her secret fantasies now sat by her fireside, holding her hand. Something in his quiet manner soothed her spirit. She drank in the comfort of his nearness. It wrapped around her like a warm blanket. With her hand nestled within his, she felt protected and at peace for the first time in her life.

Brandon gave her a little tug. "Come sit on my lap, and rest your head on my shoulder," he suggested.

She caught her lower lip between her teeth. How tempting that invitation sounded! Yet she feared what his offer might lead to. If he should press his advantage, she had no strength to resist.

As if he could read her thoughts, Brandon continued, "I fear I must disappoint you, for I am too tired to ravish you tonight."

Glancing at him, she saw a smile hovering about his lips.

"Methought you were inspired by rabbit stew and peaches," she remarked as casually as she could manage.

"Ah, that!" Amusement flicked in the blue eyes that

met hers. ''Methinks the rabbits grew tired, and have gone to sleep for the night. As you should do anon.''

''Aye.'' A yawn caught her by surprise. ''Oh! Your pardon!''

He tugged on her hand again. ''Come into my lap, and I will tell you a bedtime story.''

This time she could not resist his smile, nor his invitation. ''I fear I may be too heavy for you.''

''I think not.''

She allowed him to pull her out of her chair, then settled herself in his welcoming arms. Curling into the curve of his body, she laid her head on his broad shoulder.

''There now. What story would you like me to tell?'' he murmured tenderly in her ear.

''I know not, for no one has ever told me a story before,'' she replied. Sleep hovered about her heavy eyelids.

''Since you are so fond of rabbits, I will tell you the story of how the hare jumped over the moon on Midsummer's Eve.'' His voice lowered to a husky whisper. ''Once upon a time…''

Kat did not hear whatever else he said. She drifted on a golden cloud of drowsiness. From there, a deeper sleep was only a heartbeat away.

When she awoke next morning, Kat found herself still fully clothed, and rolled up in a blanket in one of the empty bedchambers. A freshly plucked rose, its pink petals studded with rain droplets, lay on the pillow beside her.

''By our larkin, my lady! You have slept a long time.'' Laurel looked up from the fire that she had been tending. '''Tis after ten.''

Kat rubbed the sleep from her eyes, then looked around the chamber. ''How did you know I was in here?''

Laurel's eyes twinkled. ''Montjoy told Sondra, who told me.'' Laurel warmed Kat's dressing robe before the fire. ''Every once in a while that old man surprises us all.''

Kat sniffed the rose. Its perfume filled her nostrils. "How so?"

Laurel brought the robe to the bed, then began to untie the lacing of Kat's yellow gown. "My lord sat up most of the night in the hall with you a-sleeping in his arms. He thanked Columbine for her music, and asked her to bank the fire afore she left. She told me 'twas a winsome sight to see you curled up, like a kitten, in that big man's arms. Lord help me, Lady Kat! The knots on your laces are monstrous hard to untie. Shows what sleeping in your good clothes does to them."

"And what of Montjoy?" Kat prodded.

"Oh, aye. He sat in the alcove and kept his eye on my lord, in case the gentleman had some mischief on his mind. But all that my lord did was to hold you, and sleep a bit himself, or so Montjoy said."

Kat stared at Laurel. "Montjoy stayed awake all night?"

"Aye, till near dawn. Then Mark, the squire, came in and woke him. The fire had gone cold, Montjoy said, because his bones were chilled. That's when my lord finally rose, with you still fast asleep. Montjoy directed him to lay you in here, so as not to disturb Miranda."

"And this?" Kat held out the pink blossom.

Laurel's lips curved in a smile. "My lord sent his squire running to the garden for it. He told him to pick your best one. Mark came back soaking wet, but with that rose. Montjoy said that my lord placed it on your pillow himself."

Kat smiled as she traced the line of her cheek with its soft petals. Then she recalled her ancient, faithful steward. "Poor Montjoy! I hope he took himself off to his own bed straightway."

"Aye, he did. Sondra made him a hot drink of daisies and gillyflowers to help banish the chill from his joints." Laurel loosened the laces, allowing Kat to draw a deep breath.

"Please tell everyone to let Montjoy sleep as long as he wishes."

"Aye, my lady. Now if you warm yourself by the fire, I will turn down the covers and—"

Kat blinked with surprise. "Whatever for?"

"You must be tired after last night. Methought—"

Kat laughed away Laurel's suggestion. "Nay! I am as fit as a new-tuned lute. In fact, I cannot think of a time when I have ever slept a better night. I am more than ready to face this new day."

The maid quirked her eyebrow. "Then I will fetch water to wash, and a bite to eat. Pray, what gown will you wear today? This one needs a good brushing and pressing afore 'tis fit for company again." She eyed the mound of yellow cambric and white petticoats.

Kat stretched, reveling in the sense of well-being that permeated her every fiber. "The light blue with the silver sleeves, methinks." She brushed the velvety petals of the rose across her lips. "Blue—the color of his eyes," she whispered to herself.

"Aye, my lady, but a word of advice. 'Tis raining sheets and torrents outside today. If you wear the blue silk, best stay indoors."

"Aye, Laurel. I shall heed your good advice." Kat sniffed the rose again. "I have no mind to wander far this day."

A knowing glint flashed into Laurel's eye. "Aye, my lady? Is it because a certain knight sleeps in the north tower?"

Kat twirled the stem in her fingers. She noticed that the thorns had been plucked off. How thoughtful of him! "Perchance. Now get you gone, Laurel!" Kat followed up her command with a laugh.

The maid answered with a giggle as she went out the door.

Wrapping the robe tighter around her, Kat strolled over

to the narrow lancet window, which looked out over the southern fields. Rain poured down the cloudy glass, turning the landscape into a watery world. Kat leaned her head against the stone frame.

Another day closer to the wedding, and then what? Last night had been such a new experience for her. Never had she been so comfortable in any man's company before. The last thing Kat had wanted was another man to run her life. Yet Brandon seemed so different. For one thing, he smiled at her as if he found her attractive, even though she knew that she was past her youth. Kat pressed the rose to her lips again and inhaled its sweet reminder of his affection. No one had ever given her so much as a bruised daisy before.

Brandon Cavendish. Could he possibly be as wonderful as he appeared? Or was that veneer as false as the name he affected—John Stafford? For two and a half weeks, they had bantered, played innumerable games of cards and chess, ridden horses around the home park and discussed crops, sheep, cattle, hunting dogs, servants, the king, court gossip—and the green-slimed moat. Only yesterday she had been brave enough to broach the subject she most wanted to learn about—Sir Brandon Cavendish himself.

Kat smiled as she remembered the sweet thrill of his touch and the exciting promise that lay behind Brandon's passionate kisses. Last night they had shared a different kind of tenderness, one that bespoke of growing older together by the fireside of their home, surrounded by their children. Kat bit her lip. Could she possibly have a child at the ripe old age of thirty? She knew women in the village who did, but they had been bearing children since their teens.

Kat swallowed the hard knot in her throat. Would Brandon repudiate her if she could not conceive? He had never mentioned children. She knew she should discuss the subject with him before they exchanged marriage vows. Brandon might appeal to the king, and call off the marriage because she was not a breeder. Kat could return to her life of quiet widowhood. The thought made her grow cold even though the room was warm.

Her mind kept returning to last night by the fire, and Brandon's comforting embrace. Kat inhaled the heady scent of the flower in her hand and wondered how her ordered life had suddenly become so complicated. The man had muddled her wits, and she did not know what she wanted.

Laurel reappeared bearing a tray of ale, a bowl of strawberries in cream, fresh-baked bread, butter and honey. "I knocked on Miranda's door, my lady, but she swears she will never come out again."

Kat puffed out her cheeks with exasperation. "I had hoped she would sleep off her experience."

"She pleads a headache," Laurel added.

Kat considered her cousin's cowardice. "We shall let her stay shut away, if that is her choice. The day is foul, and she should probably rest. I will look in on her after dinner." Coloring her voice in a neutral shade, she asked, "Has my Lord Stafford had breakfast?"

Laurel's eyes glinted with mischief. "Which gentleman do you mean, my lady?"

I shall wring Violet's little neck anon! Aloud, Kat replied, "Why, the gentleman who carried me up here, of course."

Laurel smirked. "Oh, that one! Mark said his lord went directly to his chamber and fell into bed. Said he was asleep afore his head hit the pillow."

"And the other lord?" Kat inquired. She sat down at the table and drew the tray of food closer.

Laurel remade the bed. "He called for a remedy for taking too much wine. Mistress Owens sent him up a syrup of primroses for his pounding head."

"It seems this morning will be a very quiet one," Kat remarked, savoring a plump, ripe strawberry. "I shall look over the accounts. Please bring the ledgers up here, Laurel, since Miranda has turned my chamber into a nunnery."

Chapter Thirteen

Pulling the bedcovers away from his face, Brandon squinted at the narrow window across the chamber. The sky looked gray and wet. Jack sat on the other side of the bed, with his head down between his knees.

Brandon stretched. "Good morrow, bag of misery," he greeted his boon companion. "Have you the time of the clock?"

Jack groaned. "If you must speak, speak softly. My head pounds like a drum on a battlefield."

Chuckling, Brandon swung out of bed. The motion of the mattress elicited another groan, followed by a curse from Jack.

"If I were a few hours younger, I would beat you for that! A plague on you, Brandon. Let me die!"

Brandon poured water into the basin, then splashed his face several times. "What ails you, Jack? Too overblown by drink?"

"Go away and be hanged!" was Jack's reply.

Brandon wiped the water from his face with a clean piece of huck toweling. He approved of Kat's attention to her guests' comfort.

Except that he wasn't exactly a guest, but the prospective master of a clean but drafty castle full of nubile maidservants, an old fox of a steward, a white witch for a housekeeper, a touchy French cook, an unmarried spinster cousin given to romantic fantasies, a moat that smelled to high heaven—and the most bewitching mistress he had ever met. He grinned as he regarded his face in his travel mirror.

"I look like a bristled boar," he remarked, stroking his jaw.

"That is God's truth," Jack croaked from the bed.

"And what is your pleasure this fine rainy day?" Brandon asked, working up a thick soapy lather over his dark blond beard.

Jack groaned again. "To die, and be done with it."

"A pity. I will wait upon my lady, in hopes to continue where we left off yesterday, before you tossed Miranda into the Rother."

Jack's red-rimmed eyes glowered over the top of the coverlet. "I never did, you smiling knave! She threw herself in rather than submit to my attentions. I am Cupid's jackass!" He flung the covers over his head.

Brandon applied his attention to his razor. For a few minutes, the only sound in the chamber was the rasp of steel against his whiskers. "So you plied her with your most insidious seduction, and the maid chose death before dishonor?" He rinsed his blade.

"Aye! 'Tis no wonder she did not even look at me when you revived her. To her, I am nothing but a shadow man."

Brandon suppressed his grin. "Methinks shadows do not suffer the pangs of a hangover."

"You would have done the same, if your lady had so disdained you," Jack retorted, his face reddening.

Would I? Brandon wondered as he continued to shave. Would Kat reject him? A dull rainy day presented a good opportunity to discover Kat's true feelings toward him as a husband. 'Twas time to introduce a new twist to his wooing. Why not? In the eyes of the church, Kat was his in all but words and witnesses. Brandon stroked his smooth cheek with satisfaction.

He hummed one of the king's compositions, "Pastime in Good Company," as he rummaged through his bag for clean hose and shirt.

"The devil take you and your croaking," Jack muttered, his voice muffled by the sheet.

"Nay, Jackanapes, 'tis my prayer that the Lady Kat will take me, croak and all." Brandon tied up the silver laces of his black velvet sleeves. Black suited him, or so the ladies of the court had often told him. Brandon hoped Kat would agree.

"So, the froggie goes a-courting?" Jack made a feeble attempt to sing but lapsed into another groan.

"Aye, wish me well in my quest." Brandon paused with his hand on the door latch. "Are you coming down to dinner?"

Groaning, Jack buried his head under a bolster.

"Should I send up a fair maid with some roasted meat for you?" Brandon continued, enjoying his friend's discomfort. Jack seldom displayed ill effects from drink. This occasion was a rare sight.

"Send for a priest to give me the last rites," Jack mumbled.

"And, I take it, you will stay abed all day?" 'Twould be easier to conduct his seduction of Katherine with Jack out of the way.

"All year!" Jack moaned. "Out! Let a man die in peace!"

Brandon grinned at the pathetic mound in the middle of the bed. "Peace be with you, my friend," he said in a softer tone.

Jack's heavy breathing was his only reply.

Kat looked up from her trencher with surprise as Brandon took his seat next to her. The chatter and clatter in the hall stilled as the castle's retainers regarded the couple at the head table. Kat colored most becomingly.

"Good day, my lord," she said softly. "I trust you slept well?"

"Well enough for the time being, sweetheart. A growling drunkard makes a poor bedfellow." Brandon helped himself from the dish of poached sole in mustard sauce that Mark offered him.

"Oh, Sir *Brandon* is unwell?" Kat chewed her lower lip and stole a sideways glance at him.

He winked at her. "Sir Brandon is...much overcome, I fear."

"With...with drink, my lord?" she stammered.

"Well, my lady, you did remark yesterday that the knave imbibed too much." He signaled Mark to fill his goblet to the brim with red wine. He lifted it to her.

She wrinkled her nose. For the first time, Brandon noticed that a few faint freckles frolicked there. He wondered if she sported freckles on any other part of her delightful body.

"Aye, I do recall that conversation, my lord. I still say so." She speared a piece of the dripping fish with her eating knife, then popped the morsel in her mouth.

Brandon found himself watching the motion of her rosy lips as she chewed. He marked how the corners of her mouth turned naturally upward.

"Your fish is getting cold, my lord," she observed after she had swallowed.

Brandon's mouth twitched with amusement as he applied himself to his food. "My apologies to the sole, sweet mistress. I will do it full justice."

His French sister-in-law, Celeste, would certainly approve of Kat's cook, he thought, savoring the taste and texture of the fish. A roasted pheasant in herbed jelly with pickled beets on the side followed. Poor Jack! What a meal he was missing!

"How fares your lady cousin?" Brandon asked, between mouthfuls of a salad made up of the blossoms of violets, marigolds and dandelions sprinkled with oil, vinegar and brown sugar. "I trust she has suffered no ill effects from her…swim?"

Kat gave an unladylike snort. "The only thing that is affected is her hard head. She thinks that…Sir Brandon is much put out with her for her foolishness."

Brandon furrowed his brow. "What foolishness of hers? 'Twas Jac…that jackanapes's fault for lunging at her."

Kat's eyes widened with astonishment. "How now? She said she slipped on the bank and fell in. She said nothing about him pushing her."

Brandon stared at Kat, then burst out laughing. "'Tis too rich! He thinks he frightened her, and she jumped into the river. *She* says she slipped by mistake!"

A flash of good humor crossed Kat's face. "Aye, and now my cousin has shut herself up in our chamber, and swears she is so mortified by her clumsiness that she will never show her face again!"

"Never is a long time," Brandon remarked in a lower tone.

"Aye, for at least the rest of the day," Kat replied.

Brandon sopped up the last of the sweet juice from his pear tart, then pushed the plate away with a sigh of satisfaction. He wiped his lips on his napkin, then gazed at his dinner partner with amusement. "Since we must entertain ourselves, mistress, how have you devised for us to while away the long afternoon?"

Kat shifted uneasily in her seat. Her emerald eyes widened when she realized that all the servants had vanished. Brandon hid his grin behind his hand. She had no idea he had instructed Mark and Christopher to engage everyone's attention in the kitchen. The squires had accepted their task with a good deal of chortling and sly winks to each other. Brandon preferred not to think what entertainment those two rogues would initiate before an audience of adoring maids and young potboys, whose sense of mischief was equal to that of the squires. He prayed nothing would get broken—at least, nothing that Kat valued.

Brandon drew out an exaggerated sigh. "It seems that we are alone."

Kat arched one red-gold brow. "Aye, so it appears. And by that smile I spy on your lips, you have already thought of a diversion. Very well, my lord. What entertainment do you suggest?"

Brandon had been waiting—praying—for just this question. Drawing a pair of dice from the pouch that hung from his belt, he held out the little wooden cubes to her. "I challenge you to a game of hazard, mistress mine."

Kat stared at the cubes. "I have never cast dice before."

Even better! Brandon cleared his throat. "The rules are simple enough, and you will learn as we go along. The object is to throw the dice so that the total number of dots facing up equals five, six, seven, eight or nine."

Kat plucked the dice out of his palm, then rolled them around between her fingers. "Methinks there is more to this sport than merely throwing numbers. I gather wagers are made upon the outcome?"

Brandon chuckled. "Thereby hangs the tale, sweetheart."

"Ah, just so." She cast a practice throw on the table. A one and a two landed facing up. "And what do you suggest that we wager?"

"For each loss, the caster must shed an article of clothing," he replied, inspecting his fingernails.

Kat stared at him in shocked amazement. "What a scandalous suggestion, my lord!"

Brandon nodded with mock seriousness. "I quite agree."

"'Tis most unseemly...for a maid, that is."

"Aye, 'tis true...for a maid." He challenged her with a steady gaze. "Afraid?"

Kat tossed her head. "Certainly not."

Brandon almost laughed aloud in triumph. "You accept my terms?"

"Aye, but on two conditions."

"Name them."

"Such a game would scandalize my servants, should they happen to come into the hall."

Brandon assumed a pious look. "'Twould indeed."

"Therefore, we must play this...game in the privacy of one of the chambers above." She floundered, not looking at his face.

I could not have said it better myself, sweet Kat. "I agree wholeheartedly, for the sake of your young maids. But I fear my room is unavailable. My Lord...Cavendish is still abed, nursing his woes."

She nodded. "And my chamber is likewise occupied by my sulking cousin."

Brandon struck his forehead, as if he had just been inspired by a bolt of wisdom. "What about the chamber you lay in last night? I know the way to its door," he added with warmth in his voice.

She flushed at his insinuation. "I am sure that you do," she replied. "There is naught in it but a bed, a chair and a small table."

Brandon flashed his teeth. "'Tis all that is required."

Kat's flush deepened into a crimson. "Just so."

Moving to her side, Brandon put his hand under her chin, turning her toward him. "And your other condition?" he murmured.

She lifted her eyes to him. A faintly eager look flashed in their green depths. "That you must call me by my given name."

You little minx!

Brandon paused, lightly stroking the petal softness of

her cheek. 'Twas the moment of reckoning, he admitted to himself. He was not a seducer of spinster cousins, but a man who had fallen in love with his betrothed. She watched his expressions like the cat she was called.

Slipping his arm around her waist, he drew her to him. "'Tis a pleasure to make your acquaintance at last, my Lady Katherine."

"God shield me! Where did you learn this goodly game?" Kat asked an hour later. The corner of her mouth twisted with exasperation as she glared at the two single dots she had just thrown. Not another crab! She was down to her shift, and one stocking.

Brandon rocked back in his chair, his grin widening. "At court. 'Tis a great favorite of the king's." His gaze roved over her and beamed approval.

By the book! Methinks he is taking off the rest of my clothing in his imagination! Her heart jolted and her pulse pounded.

"Oh, aye? Under the tutelage of Mistress Anne Boleyn?" she asked with deceptive calm.

Her companion regarded her with warm amusement. "Nay, sweet Kat, under the tutelage of Cupid."

Her mouth went dry. The man was too handsome by half. His powerful, well-muscled body was barely concealed by his remaining clothing: a pair of black-and-white-striped hose, a loose white shirt, open wide at the neck, and his codpiece. Kat tried to ignore this last article, but found it difficult. His overall appeal was devastating.

She moistened her lips. "Cupid? Are you in love?" She held her breath for his answer.

"Aye, my lady," he replied, his low voice dripping with seductive invitation. "'Tis the fashion to be in love these days."

His words sent Kat's spirit soaring. Patience! He had yet to confess that he was Lord Cavendish. They played a greater game than hazard, if her heart was to be the prize. "Do you think that…Sir Brandon is in love?"

His bold gaze softened to a caress. "Aye, you have snared his heart in your golden net."

Her body quivered with excitement like the jingling tambourine of a jester. Lowering her gaze, she studied the treacherous dice on the table. 'Twas too easy to forget herself, considering the way he looked at her. She pulled the collar of her shift a little tighter.

"Do you think that I love Sir Brandon in return?" she asked playfully, glancing at him through her lashes.

He set the chair back on its four legs, then rose with a graceful motion. He came round the table in two strides and stood behind her. The heat from his body surrounded her. A shiver thrilled through her veins.

"You bear all the marks of a woman in love," he replied, his voice grown suddenly husky.

Kat's heart thudded down to her toes. Her knees felt weak. *By the book! Get a hold of yourself.* Looking over her shoulder, she boldly met his smoldering gaze. "Ha! How do *you* know what a woman in love looks like?"

He wrapped his arms around her waist. "Give me a looking glass, and I will show you one," he whispered in her ear.

Her body tingled from the contact. His breath was warm and moist against her cheek as he drew her back against his chest.

She tried to laugh, but only a nervous titter emerged from her lips. "Do you mean me?"

"Well aimed and true." Lifting her hair aside, he pressed his warm lips to the nape of her neck.

She gasped at the contact, then closed her eyes to savor the heady sensation. "I?" she whispered.

"Aye, mad in love." Brandon's mouth grazed her earlobe.

A tremor began to build inside Kat, heating her thighs

and the secret place between them. Her limbs trembling, she settled back against him, surrendering to the pleasure of his arms around her.

"'Tis the season, methinks," she murmured. "They say that midsummer brings on a certain madness, and that there is little difference between a lover and a lunatic at this time of year."

He turned her in the circle of his embrace. The light of desire danced in his blue eyes. "Then you must seek remedy for this sweet malady." His deep baritone simmered with barely checked passion.

She reveled in his open admiration of her. "What remedy have you in mind?" she asked in a fragile whisper, though her heart knew the answer already.

Brandon traced his fingertip across her lower lip. "It begins with a kiss," he answered as his lips slowly descended to meet hers.

His gentle touch sent a shock wave through her entire body. The last shred of her defenses crumbled. Reaching her arms around his neck, she clung to him, arching her body against his. It was a kiss for her tired soul to melt into, sweetly draining away all the doubts and fears of her past experiences. Under his persuasive touch, Kat was drawn toward a height of passion she had never experienced.

His kiss deepened as he parted her lips with his tongue and entered. Moaning, she clutched him for support. Her mouth burned for more.

With laughter that mixed triumph and joy, he swept her into his arms as if she weighed nothing. Gently he eased her down onto the bed.

"Methinks I have won the wager of your last throw," he whispered as he untied the ribbons around the neck of her shift.

"Aye." She sighed as he drew the filmy garment over

her head. Though his fingers were cool, his gentle touch burned her skin.

His gaze drank her in like cold springwater on a summer's day. "You are beautiful, sweet Katherine."

Her name on his tongue sang in her ear.

After he pulled off his shirt, he lay down beside her. She purred at the sleek caress of his strong, hard body. With infinite tenderness, his finger outlined the firm mounds of her breasts. In response, the soft flesh surged at the intimacy of his touch. Bending his head, his lips stroked her nipples with a tantalizing possessiveness. She gasped as the pink tips firmed instantly under his persuasion. He kissed each taut bud in turn, enkindling a melting sweetness within her.

Thoroughly aroused by a desire she had never known before, Kat drew herself closer to Brandon. Embracing him, she trailed a tickling finger up and down the long, smooth planes of his back. Slipping under the waistband of his hose, she swirled her finger in the dimpled hollow at the base of his spine. He groaned.

"I am much too confined, methinks," he whispered hoarsely as he fumbled to untie the laces of his codpiece.

Kat experienced a giddy sense of pleasure as her fingers covered his. "Let me be your handmaiden, my lord."

His lips touched her forehead as he whispered, "Quickly then, for I am in agony."

With laughter rippling in the back of her throat, she released his manhood, then peeled off his hose, sliding her palms down his taut, muscled thighs. The sight of his arousal thrilled her.

Kat gasped as he lowered his body over hers, tucking her curves neatly into his own contours. His heat coursed the entire length of her. Her breasts tingled against his hair-roughed chest.

"You are intoxicating, like summer wine." Between

each word, Brandon planted kisses on her shoulders, neck and face.

His hands explored the soft lines of her back, her waist and her hips. Shivers of delight followed the path of his touch. She could not contain her outcries of pleasure. Aching for more of him, she buried her hands in his thick blond hair.

A golden wave of new-awakened passion and love flowed between them, shattering the protective shell that Kat had erected during the torturous years with Fitzhugh. Brandon freed her in a bursting rainbow of sensations. Passion radiated from the soft core of her body, surrendering her completely to him, as he hurled them both beyond the point of no return. As gold and silver star bursts welled up within her, Kat experienced the flowing of uncontrollable joy for the first time. Together, she and Brandon soared to the lofty heights of an unutterable, shimmering ecstasy.

Afterward, lying in his arms, their bodies still moist from lovemaking, Kat felt a comfortable peace and satisfaction. Never had she been so blissfully happy with a man. Never had she felt so fully alive within herself. Tears of joy pricked her eyelids. A cry of relief broke from her lips.

"Did I hurt you, my sweet?" he asked, stroking a lock of her hair that trailed over her breast.

"Nay." She smiled into his eyes with supreme satisfaction. "'Tis pleasure, not pain, dear heart."

He exhaled a long sigh of contentment. "Good, for I had hoped you might consider another roll anon."

She traced her finger along the muscled contour of his chest. "Do you speak of the dice or in bed?"

He grinned. "Both, for I desire to win *all* the wager." He fingered the single cream-colored stocking she still wore.

"On one condition, my lord."

He pretended to groan in pain. "You drive a hard bargain, sweet Kat. Name it."

Her finger curled around his ear. "Since we have now lain together, I greatly desire to know your given name, my lord."

"'Twill be yours in a week, dearest Kat."

"Pronounce it now," she whispered. "I long to hear it from your lips."

"Brandon," he answered, as his mouth closed over hers.

Chapter Fourteen

The rain had finally stopped by the time Jack crawled out of bed. The late afternoon sun made valiant efforts to break through the clouds. Jack's stomach rumbled, demanding food. After washing, shaving and putting on clean clothing, he stumbled across the courtyard to the hall.

Oddly, no one was there, except the dogs, who greeted him with wet affection. No one tarried in the alcove or hurried down the passageways. In the kitchen, Jack discovered the entire gaggle of giggling maids, as well as some of the off-duty men-at-arms, enjoying the impromptu antics of the two squires. Mark and Christopher had decked themselves with cast-off bits of women's clothing. Using mop heads for their hair and beets plumping their bosoms, the two pranced around the chopping table, exchanging bawdy quips and ribald pleasantries in high falsetto voices.

Rather than disturb the merrymaking, Jack helped himself to some bread and slices of cold beef. No doubt Brandon had succeeded in his conquest, and he was occupied with his own brand of pleasant sport. Thinking of Miranda, Jack envied their joy. Slipping out the side door with his food, he wended his leisurely way to the stables.

The sun had banished the last of the clouds and now

shone brightly. Jack swallowed the rest of his impromptu meal. He drew in a deep breath of the clean, fresh air. What he needed was some exercise to clear the alcoholic cobwebs from his brain. A good ride would do the trick. It had been several days since Thunder had had a proper run.

A half hour later, Jack, astride his charger, rode through the forest that bordered the western fields. The leaves decking the oaks, elms and ashes looked new washed and bright green. Unseen birds sang amid their branches, while impudent rooks cawed to each other from the treetops. Occasionally Jack heard a scurrying sound in the underbrush to the side of his trail, as a rabbit, hedgehog or badger sought cover from the horse and rider's intrusion. All in all, 'twas a fine afternoon for a gallop.

Coming out on the far side of the wood, Jack slowed Thunder to a walk and let the horse pick his own course. Meanwhile, Jack turned his thoughts once again to Miranda, and to his present quandary. If Brandon had succeeded in his plan to seduce the lady of the manor, had their game of disguising now come to an end? Could Jack present himself—as he truly was—to the innocent Miranda, and beg her forgiveness for his unmannerly action? He thought back over the past few weeks. While he had been so pleasantly occupied playing Brandon, what sort of portrayal had Brandon made of roguish Jack Stafford?

Had Brandon mentioned Jack's activities with the ladies of the court? Jack winced inwardly. Too true, all too true. While both men enjoyed their reputations as heartbreakers, it was Jack who actually lived up to the gossip. Sudden fatherhood had made Brandon grow more wary of romantic entanglements, and he had settled down to an occasional night with a discreet married lady. Not Jack. Any woman was fair game, and a number of the noblemen at court wore the horns of a cuckold thanks to him.

And what had ten years of wenching done for him?

Nothing, but jaded his opinion of women in general. Then he had met Miranda, whom he had thought was Lady Katherine. Even as he had wooed her in Brandon's name, Jack himself had fallen hopelessly in love with the sweet lady. And who was Miranda Paige? No doubt the oldest living virgin in England outside a convent. What a rare jest! The Jack of Hearts of Great Harry's court had been caught by a simple country spinster, without one conniving, conceited bone in her body.

What was he to do now? Brandon may not want to become a loving husband to a good woman, but, by God, the prospect looked better and better to Jack with each passing day. If he could ever coax Miranda out of her sanctuary, he would go down on his knees and beg her to marry him as soon as the banns could be proclaimed. Jack grinned at the idea. By Christmas, there could be a new little Stafford on the way. Fatherhood! The idea quickened his blood. It had made Brandon a better man; why not Jack Stafford?

Thunder whinnied and pranced sideways, nearly tossing Jack out of his saddle. Bringing the horse to a stop, he dismounted. A man huddled facedown on the side of the path. Beside him, a bundle of firewood lay scattered.

Jack knelt by the body. "God save us, are you killed?"

A shiver ran through the prostrated form, then the youth raised his head. "Scared the living wits out of me, sir," he sputtered, as he spat out some dirt.

Jack's eyes widened when he recognized the youth. "Wormsley! What in the devil's name are you doing here? Methought you and your scurvy master had returned to court."

Sitting up, Wormsley groaned. "Nothing, my lord." He would not meet Jack's gaze.

"Are you hurt?"

"Nay, my lord." Wormsley began to gather up his sticks.

Jack planted one foot on the largest just as Wormsley reached for it. "Not yet, you worm's namesake! First, explain what you are doing on Bodiam's property."

Licking his lips, Wormsley looked over his shoulder into the woods. "I dare not say, my lord," he replied hoarsely.

Jack grabbed him. "Methinks you would answer very well to a whipping," he threatened, though he had no intention of doing so.

The boy blanched but held his ground. "'Tis no more than what I get now, my lord," he muttered.

Jack relaxed his hold on the servant. "How now? Does Scantling beat you?"

Wormsley hung his head. "Aye, sir." He licked his lips again.

Stepping back, Jack observed the boy closely. He detected a light greenish tint under one eye, the mark of a bruise almost healed. "Is this abuse your master's custom?"

Wormsley scanned the deep-shadowed forest again. "Not until this past week, my lord. Ever since he discovered his aunt's perfidy."

Jack nodded. "You mean her trick with the nettles and pepper?"

Wormsley sighed. "Aye, my lord. Sir Fenton was much vexed by that, and flew into a rage."

"And you became his convenient whipping post," Jack added. "Why do you stay in his employ?"

The youth shrugged. "I've no place else to go, sir. And this new behavior of my master's has come upon him like a sudden fit." He lowered his voice. "Now there is more deviltry afoot."

Jack drew closer. "What do you mean?"

Wormsley glanced around, then gulped. "Sir Fenton is much besieged by his creditors."

Jack shrugged his shoulders. "This is old news, and twice told."

"My master tried to dissuade both his aunt and my Lord Cavendish from their marriage."

"Aye, and he made a dog's breakfast of that, as well. Sir Brandon and the lady have become most loving friends." Jack allowed a small grin. *Even as we speak.*

"When my master came to Bodiam, 'twas to persuade his aunt to give him the guardianship of the estate before the marriage could take place. He even had a paper for her to sign."

Jack uttered a curse under his breath. "Shrewd knave! For a tuppence, I'd toss him into that reeking moat."

Wormsley gripped Jack's arm. "But now Sir Fenton grows worse and worse. Since Lady Katherine played that waggish trick upon us, his mind has become unhinged."

Jack lifted an eyebrow. "Tell me all, and spare no details."

Wormsley's voice sank even lower. "He thinks upon nothing but murder, my lord."

"God's death!"

Wormsley crossed himself. "Amen to that, my lord. After we recovered from the nettles, he rode us hard back here. We now live in beggarly circumstances in a small abandoned woodcutter's hut over yonder. My master says little, except to curse me. At night I hear him whisper 'murder' as he sits staring into the fire. 'Tis enough to make my blood run cold. Every day, he takes to the wood with his crossbow. And, my lord, he is a fair shot with it. Last night, I overheard him mumble something about Sir Brandon meeting with a hunting accident."

"Jesu!" Jack stared at Wormsley. The servant's eyes gave no lie to his words.

"I have not known what do, my lord," the youth continued. "Indeed, I am afeard for my own skin. My master is much changed."

Jack thought quickly. Fenton lurking in the woods with a crossbow was threat enough, but his evil intention would bear no weight in a court of law unless he acted upon it. Nor did Jack even know where he could find the vermin. Bodiam's forest was Fenton's home ground. He must know every nook and cranny of it. Jack scanned the silent trees as Wormsley had done earlier. The madman could be sitting on a limb within bow shot this minute. No wonder Wormsley looked like a frightened coney rabbit!

Jack patted him on the shoulder. Under his shirt and jerkin, the youth trembled. "Take heart, Wormsley, for you have found a friend in me. Keep a good eye on your master, and send me word at Bodiam if you learn more of his plans. I know 'twill require much courage, but, I swear, all will come out right in the end."

Wormsley exhaled a sigh of relief. "I am your man, my lord."

"Aye, and so will you be in truth, when this adventure is over. My word on it."

The lad nodded. "Thank you, my lord."

"I would shake your hand, but we may be watched. Keep a good eye—and, Wormsley, sleep lightly with a knife under your pillow."

He nodded. "I already do so, my lord."

Jack gathered up Thunder's reins, then swung himself into the saddle. "God be with you, lad," he said quietly.

"Aye, my lord. And you." Wormsley glanced again at the trees.

Jack urged Thunder into a trot, going in the same direction as before. If Scantling had observed the encounter, Jack didn't want him to think that his servant had betrayed his evil intent. Best that he believe they had merely exchanged a few words on Wormsley's health, and nothing more. A half mile later, Jack turned his horse into the wood where he spurred Thunder into a brisk canter back to the castle.

* * *

"'Tis harder to put you back together, than undoing you in the first place, Kat," Brandon remarked as he fumbled with the laces of her bodice.

"Aye, my love," she replied, still basking in the afterglow of his more intimate touch. "But 'twould shock my maids should I come down to supper with the back of my gown hanging open."

"Aye, those sweet, innocent maids of yours." He pulled the laces tighter, then tied them together. "Methinks we must see them married soon, so that we need not go tiptoeing around our own home."

A warm smile danced on Kat's lips. How she liked to hear him talk of "we" and "our home." Aloud she changed the subject. "There is one thing that we must speak of before we leave this room."

Placing his hands on her shoulders, Brandon turned her around to face him. "And what is that, pray tell?" He kissed her on the nose. "Are you afraid that I have compromised your virtue? That my intentions are not honorable?"

"Nay," she replied. She smoothed out the creases of his doublet over his shoulders. Such magnificent shoulders! she thought. "I trust your intentions to be the soul of honor." *Even though you have not said you loved me.* She pushed that niggling thought away.

He took her hand in his. "My intentions are most honorable, and always have been."

She tilted her head. "Even when you swore you were Sir John Stafford?"

The lines around his eyes crinkled with a smile. "I never *swore* to that, sweetheart. I merely introduced myself by that name." He kissed her fingers. "Besides, Jack is an honorable man under all his posturing."

"'Tis Jack, I speak of," Kat continued, enjoying the attention his lips paid to her hand. "And Miranda."

"Ah, the hidden lady. What of them?"

"When we leave this room, who are we, my lord? Kat and Brandon, or Sir John and Miranda?"

Brandon nodded. "I see your point. Jack knows that your cousin is Miranda."

"She is in love with him, I fear."

Brandon gave her a wry smile. "So is half of Henry's court."

"Does Sir John merely dally with her affections in your name, or is there something deeper?" Brandon kissed her other hand. He made this serious conversation most difficult to continue.

"Methinks that Jack has met his match at long last. He swears he will wed the lady, if she'll have him."

Standing on tiptoe, Kat kissed his chin. "Do you think he speaks the truth? She has no dowry of her own, but what I will give her. No lands, no titles."

Brandon grinned. "Jack is rich enough in everything but love. In that area, he has been sorely lacking ever since I have known him. He has played the lover well, but with a false face. Never, in fifteen years, have I seen him as he is with your gentle cousin. Aye, he speaks the truth this time."

"Thank the sweet angels for that!" Kat rewarded Brandon with another kiss on his chin. "Then this is what I think we must do. Let us continue our sham before the household. If we do not, and Miranda learns the truth, I fear she will indeed enter a nunnery to hide her mortification. If I tell her that she *must* continue as me, she will do it, for she is a most loyal and loving kinswoman."

"And Jack will have his chance to repair any damage he may have done to her. I like this plan, sweet Kat. To seal the bargain, give me a kiss."

"Aye, my lord," she said, and sighed with pleasure. "I was waiting for your invitation."

"Miranda! Open this door! I am fast running out of patience, and clean clothes." Kat rattled the latch. From the top of the stairs, Brandon waved at her before he descended to the hall. She heard his whistling echo down the stairwell.

The stout oak door opened a crack. Miranda's pale face peeked out. "You are alone?" she asked, looking up and down the corridor.

"Aye, coz." Kat pushed her way past Miranda.

The bedclothes looked as if her cousin had fought off a dozen demons in the middle of the night. Kat knelt by the cold fireplace. "The evening draws near. You will catch a chill," she observed as she laid a few logs on the iron grate.

Miranda sank into the window seat. "I care not," she replied listlessly.

This mooning about has gone on long enough. 'Tis time I shake Miranda up a bit—for her own good.

While she considered what she should say, Kat struck a flint to the kindling under the logs, then blew on the smoking twist of straw until it burst into flame. Standing, she brushed the soot from her hands.

Kat took a deep breath. "Fie upon you, Miranda! I am most amazed, and do not know what to say!"

Miranda blinked. Intense astonishment touched her pale face. "How now, coz? Why do you speak so sharply to me?"

Kat summoned a withering glare. She put her hands on her hips. "And so I should! You have sat here the whole day, sighing and weeping for love—*over my betrothed husband!*"

"Oh!" Miranda covered her mouth with her hand. Two bright red patches spotted her white cheeks.

Kat continued as she paced the floor with long strides. "Aye, you should blush for shame! 'Tis six days and a bit until my wedding, yet you have acted as if 'twas you who had been wronged by Sir Brandon, and not me! What care will he have for you come Midsummer's Day?"

Miranda's face crumpled as she burst into tears. She buried her face in her hands.

"Sweet Kat, I had forgot! Forgive me, I beg you. 'Twas a wicked madness that overtook me yesterday. Truly, I meant no harm."

Kat sat down beside her and drew her weeping cousin into her arms. "There, there, dear Miranda. No harm is done, save to your pride. Sir...Brandon has been at sixes and sevens all day, thinking that he has offended you—meaning me, of course."

Miranda lifted her tearstained face. "Truly?" she whispered.

Kat pulled her handkerchief from her sleeve and handed it to her cousin. "As true as fire burns. Here, blow! Indeed, Sir...John only just told me that his friend felt so badly over you—meaning me—that he punished himself by drinking himself into a dead stupor. Now his head is paying the price."

"Poor Brandon!" Miranda murmured. "He should bathe it with witch hazel."

"I believe he went for a ride." Kat bit the insides of her cheeks to keep from laughing. Sweet, gentle Miranda! "But he will return for supper, and there he hopes that you—meaning me—will forgive him, and make him merry again."

Miranda shook her head. "Nay, Kat, I cannot."

"Why?" What foolish idea had Miranda taken now, Kat wondered.

"'Tis time to confess ourselves, Kat. Indeed, methinks 'tis past time and a half. We should have done it weeks ago."

Kat brushed back Miranda's hair from her face. "Before you fell in love with my Lord Cavendish?" she asked gently.

Miranda's lip quivered. "Aye. I cannot help it, Kat. He

has spoken so sweetly to me, and paid me more attention than I have ever dreamed possible.''

Kat hugged her again. "'Tis all my fault, I agree. I should have sought a husband for you years ago. Yet I selfishly craved the comfort of your company.''

"And willingly I gave it, Kat.'' Miranda blew her nose again.

"Aye, and I was so at peace, that I thought you were, too. Since marriage was so hateful to me, I forgot how much you wanted that blessed state. Forgive my blindness.''

Miranda sighed. "Nay, you gave me your friendship and a good home. I have been content.''

Kat arched an eyebrow. "Until two handsome blond knights rode through our gateway?''

Miranda nodded. "Aye,'' she replied mournfully. A fresh storm of tears threatened.

Kat wiped Miranda's face. "Be of good cheer, coz. Have I not promised you a husband yet?''

"Aye, but…but, Kat, I want yours!'' she wailed.

Kat rolled her eyes to the ceiling. Should she tell Miranda the truth now, or—?

The pounding of hooves over the causeway bridge stopped further conversation. Miranda raised her eyes to meet Kat's. Both women leaned out of the window. Below, Jack dismounted before his huge horse had come to a complete halt. After tossing the reins to a startled stable boy, he bounded up the stairway toward the hall.

"'Tis my Lord Cavendish,'' Miranda gasped. "Look at his stern expression!''

"God shield us! There must be something amiss!'' Kat jumped up, pulling Miranda along with her. "Quickly! Let us get you washed and dressed. As mistress of the house, 'tis your duty to find out.''

"But, Kat,'' Miranda pleaded as her cousin pulled off her dressing robe. "Shouldn't we—?''

"Nay!" Kat pushed her toward the washstand. "'Tis not the right time. Later, perchance. Stars, Miranda! Start dressing!"

With that, Kat raced out of the door. *Sweet angels! Have the French invaded the country? They can't! Not when I finally want to get married!*

"I thought you took a ride to clear your mind, not to lose it," Brandon bantered as Jack grabbed him by the elbow and pulled him into the alcove. "Speak plain."

"Aye," Jack panted, out of breath. "Listen to me, and you'll see what happened to my wits. There is a mad dog lurking in yon forest, armed with a crossbow, who seeks your blood. His name is Scantling, and he has murder in his heart. Is that plain enough?"

Jack's words wiped the smile from Brandon's face. "Is this God's truth?" he rasped, his fingers closing over the small dagger he wore on his belt.

Jack nodded. "Aye, I all but ran down his servant in the wood. The boy is half out of his wits with fear of his master. Scantling wants Kat's estates, and he is past caring how he gets them. He plans a hunting accident, and waits in hiding for you to ride past. Wormsley swears the knave is a good marksman. Hear me, Brandon? How can there be a wedding if there is no bridegroom?"

Brandon released his friend, then he leaned back against the wall. Only an hour before, he had held Katherine next to his heart and dreamed of sharing many happy years with her.

"We must protect the ladies, and all in this household, for the dog is rabid and may strike at anyone." As Brandon spoke, his anger bubbled over into a scalding fury. "Give word to our men that we will saddle our horses at first light and hound the cur into the earth."

Jack shook him. "'Tis *you* he seeks. You will ride straight into his snare."

"Nay, I will be the bait to spring the trap," Brandon replied sharply.

"You will be a dead man before you hit the ground," Jack growled. "Be warned, my friend. If I have to tie you to the bedpost until your wedding day, I will do so."

Brandon knotted his fist. "Make no light threats, Jack, unless you have the strength to carry them out."

Before Jack could retort, Kat appeared in the doorway to the alcove. "How now, my lords? What's amiss?"

"Nothing!" Brandon snapped, shooting a warning glance at Stafford. "Save that Jack saw a wild boar near the village. Tomorrow we will hunt him down and serve him with an apple in his mouth at our wedding feast."

"Come rack and ruin!" Jack muttered.

"My lords, my lady!" Montjoy's mournful voice echoed in the hall. "There is news!"

Kat threw up her hands. "Has all the world gone giddy before supper? Here, Montjoy." She stepped into the larger chamber. "What is all the new fuss?"

Gripping Jack's shoulder, Brandon whispered in his ear. "Your oath that you will say nothing to the ladies."

Jack returned him a glowering look. "Do as you please, and go to the devil."

"Good," Brandon muttered, "I am glad we understand each other." Then, in a louder voice he asked, "What is this news, Montjoy?"

The old steward looked at each of them in turn, then, staring at a spot above the chimney piece, he intoned, "There is a messenger come from the king. 'Tis for Sir Brandon Cavendish and Lady Katherine Fitzhugh." Pausing, he lowered his voice. "When you have decided among yourselves who will receive him, let me know. I await in the corridor."

So saying, Montjoy turned smartly on his heel and stalked out of the hall.

"Saints in heaven!" Kat sent Brandon a stricken look. "The king has changed his mind!"

Chapter Fifteen

Brandon's face wore an impassive expression. "Let us see what the king has to say."

His words, spoken in a cool, impersonal voice, drove an icy dagger into Kat's heart. Brandon was happy for this last-minute reprieve. At least, he was thoughtful enough to mask his pleasure from her.

Three weeks ago, Kat would have welcomed the king's mercurial change of heart. Now, 'twas her own heart that had changed. She recalled that Sondra had once said something about not appreciating a thing until you had lost it. Looking at Brandon's stiff posture and compressed lips, she could almost feel him withdrawing from her. Jack sent for the messenger.

Neither of them spoke, nor even glanced at each other. Brandon's fingers clenched into a tight fist. Kat saw his knuckles stand out white against his skin. She lifted her chin. She was no moonstruck girl, but a mature woman. She had faced adversity before, and she could do so again. At least she could be thankful to Brandon for one thing. He had taught her the meaning of love.

Montjoy escorted a young, mud-stained messenger into the hall just as Miranda descended the stairs. "My lords and my ladies," the king's servant began after his bow.

"I have a letter from Sir Thomas More." Pausing, he looked at the four people before him. "Who is the Lady Katherine Fitzhugh?"

Kat glanced over her shoulder at Miranda. Miranda appeared to have gone into a trance as she stared across the hall at Jack. Ignoring the messenger, Jack crossed to her side and took her hand in his.

Kat shook herself. "Give the letter to me. I speak for Lady Katherine." She held out her hand.

The messenger pulled a small vellum packet from his leather pouch. With another bow, he presented it to Kat.

She managed to return his smile. "You must be tired and near famished from your ride. Montjoy will take you to the kitchen, where you may eat as much as you desire. After that, he will show you where you may rest."

The messenger touched his forelock. "My thanks, lady."

After Montjoy took the boy out, Kat looked down at the letter in her hand. The end to her happy idyll lay under its fat wax seal.

"Open it, sweetheart," Brandon murmured.

Startled, Kat looked up into his ice blue eyes. She had not heard him move to her side. "My...my hands shake," she whispered.

"Let me come to your aid." Brandon took the packet. Slitting open the seal, he scanned the contents. A grin spread over his face, followed by his deep, rolling laughter. "A jest too rich and rare to be believed!"

Kat gritted her teeth. Their betrothal a rich jest? How happy and relieved he looked! The churl! How dare he take her heart, then grind it into the mud! She itched to slap him, just to stop his shameless laughter that grated upon her nerves like a rusted hinge creaking in a wayward wind.

"What is the news?" Jack asked, leading Miranda to the center of the hall.

Brandon managed to stop laughing long enough to answer. "The Lord Chancellor, Sir Thomas More, informs us to expect Robin Hood, Maid Marian and the whole band of Sherwood Forest outlaws at our wedding next Saturday morn! He further states that Robin will expect right royal treatment in every detail. He suggests that Lady Katherine lay in a goodly store of provender to feed the royal company."

A wave of light-headedness washed over Kat. She clasped the golden brooch on her bodice.

"Hoy-day, look to the lady!" Jack called a warning.

Brandon caught Kat as her knees gave way. "Think you were going to escape being wedded to me that easily, my sweet?" he whispered as he carried her over to the window seat.

Kat clung to him as he settled her in his lap. "Methought, for the briefest of moments, that you...that the king...that you were glad..." She reached for the cup of wine that Miranda handed to her, and drank the contents greedily.

Brandon chuckled near her ear. "Glad to escape wedlock? Nay, my lady. I have grown too fond of...playing hazard with you."

Kat drew in a deep breath of relief. She reveled in the warmth of his hands around her, and the aroma of mint, leather and musk that accompanied him.

Miranda gasped. "Then you know!"

Brandon groaned in mock surrender. "I fear we have been discovered, sweet Kat."

"Aye." She sighed, though, at this blissful moment, she didn't care who had discovered what. She was still betrothed to Brandon, and no one, not even the king, was going to stop her wedding now.

Miranda glanced from Brandon to Kat. "Have you no shame, sir? You know that she is Lady Katherine, and yet, you still dare to pay court to her, while my Lord Cavendish stands by. Fie upon you, Sir John! How could you encourage him, Kat?''

Brandon raised one eyebrow in amusement. "She's a pretty little vixen when she's angry, eh, Jack? 'Tis something you will have to watch out for in the future."

"Aye," he replied, gazing at Miranda with a soft, adoring look. "If the lady will have me."

Miranda merely stared at the grinning trio, tongue-tied. Her eyes grew larger. She opened her mouth, but no sound came forth.

Poor Miranda! This shock may send her back to our chamber for a month! Kat smiled at Miranda. "'Tis true, cousin. We have been outfoxed by these grinning rogues. I promise you, I *have* kept my pledge to Sir Brandon, for 'tis he who holds me in his arms."

Miranda raised her eyes to Jack. "And you are...?"

He kissed her hand, "Sir John Anthony Joseph Stafford of Fenderwick, but my friends call me Jack—and I pray that you will be the foremost of my friends." He gathered her into an embrace. Miranda swayed.

"Help me, I feel faint," she murmured.

Brandon rolled his eyes. "It must be something in the air, Jack, that makes our ladies swoon."

"Aye," he replied, sitting down next to Brandon, with Miranda in his arms. "Methinks the malady is marriage."

Kat sat up straighter. "Marriage! Alack, I almost forgot! Who does Sir Thomas mean by Robin Hood coming to our wedding?"

Brandon began laughing again, until Kat rapped him on the back of his hand. "'Tis none other but the king himself, my sweet," he told her when he had caught his breath. "'Tis a great trick of his to disguise himself in some outlandish costume, then surprise his unwary subjects."

"The king is coming to Bodiam in less than a week? God save us!" Kat gasped. How many of his court would attend him? Was she expected to provide sleeping accommodations for them all? What room would be good enough for the king, who she knew liked rich appointments? "Why is he Robin Hood?" she asked.

Brandon shrugged. "Why not? Great Harry has played bold Robin's part before."

"Maid Marian will be Lady Anne Boleyn, no doubt," Jack added. "Who the others will portray is anyone's guess."

Brandon kissed away the furrow between Kat's brows. "Fret not, sweet. The letter says that the company will reside at Lady Anne's home in Hever, not here. Furthermore, the king is a generous man. He knows that his court creates havoc upon a household, especially when he surprises the hosts. He will bring provisions, and a good cask of his favorite wine, methinks."

Jack nodded. "Aye, I remember a time when old Wolsey was still in power. My lord cardinal had a great feast at the palace of Hampton Court, which he once owned, you know. Just as the sugar subtleties were being served, there was a knock at the door. Who should it be but a dozen hooded men of dangerous mien, who said they had heard of the cardinal's feast and had come to be entertained."

Kat blinked. "Did Cardinal Wolsey call his guard?"

Brandon took up the tale. "Nay, for he knew 'twas the king and some of his henchmen. He invited us in, then set out another feast, which had already been prepared in the kitchen. 'Twas even more lavish than the first. Afterward the 'guests' asked permission to dance with the ladies present. Of course, the cardinal granted it. At midnight, the king took off his disguise, and everyone pretended to be amazed."

Kat's lips twitched. "You sound as if you were there."

Brandon gave her a mock leer. "Aye, Jack and I were two of the wickedest cutthroats you would ever meet. As

I recall, the ladies were quite taken to dance with such dangerous rogues.''

"Aye?" Kat inquired. "*How* well taken, my lord?''

Brandon colored slightly. "In honest amusement, Kat.''

"And you, my lord?" Miranda asked, having recaptured her composure. "How did you take the ladies?''

Jack cleared his throat. "I cannot remember any lady save yourself, sweet Miranda. All others are but shadows to me.''

"Jack always had a silver tongue," Brandon whispered in Kat's ear.

She giggled, then she remembered the message. "The king! Here! I must see to the pantry and buttery at once. Philippe will be in a frenzy over this! 'Twill make his day a red-letter one, or else he will jump into the moat. I am not sure which.''

Brandon grimaced. "Pray, for the sake of our dinner, that your good cook will not choose the moat.''

Giving Brandon a quick kiss, Kat rose. "Come, Miranda, we have much work to do. The king arrives in six days. Montjoy!" she called. "I have news that will make you weep whole onions!''

Miranda slowly drew herself away from Jack's embrace. "Till supper time, my lord?" she asked shyly.

"'Twill be a century till then.'' Jack kissed her fervently.

Standing at the doorway, Kat observed the tender scene with amusement. Miranda looked like she was in a dream world. No doubt she would keep Kat up all night with her chatter, if Kat did not share a bed elsewhere. She hugged herself at the delicious thought. Best to bring her cousin back to earth before Jack led her away to a convenient trysting place. "Miranda!" she called. "I have much need of you in the kitchen! Now!''

Jack released her with another kiss. "Go with Lady Kat, my love. We will talk anon. I have much to say to you.''

"And I will drink up your every word," Miranda replied.

"By our larkin, Miranda! You'd think you had just met Jack Stafford!"

Brandon watched Kat seize her cousin by the hand and drag her down the stairs. Once the women were out of sight, the lightness of his heart dropped away. "Wipe that ridiculous grin off your face, Jack," he snapped. "You look like the court jester's monkey."

Jack arched an eyebrow. "How now? What's amiss? What crab apple has stuck in your craw? Are you not pleased that we can shed our borrowed clothes and be ourselves again?"

Brandon nodded. "Aye, but think with your head, and not with your heart, my friend. The king comes in a few days. Meanwhile, Scantling roams the home park with murder his intent. We must find him quickly."

Jack put his hand on Brandon's shoulder. "Aye, I had forgotten for a moment. You are right."

"Let us gather our men in the stables, and plan our search for the morrow. Ask some of Kat's guard to join us, since they know the countryside, but we must swear everyone to the greatest secrecy. I do not want the ladies to know what we are about, until after we have done it. 'Twill only distress them more."

Jack's face clouded. "There is another that will distress your bride, if she accompanies the king. Have you given thought to that?"

Brandon flared his nostrils. "You speak of my Lady Bardolph? Aye, she crossed my mind at Sir Thomas's news. If she comes, what of it? What passed between us was over ten years ago."

"To spoil your happy day, she would tell Kat."

"Leave Kat to me," he snapped, cursing Francis's promiscuous mother. "Let Lady Bardolph go to the devil."

Jack shook his head. "Every man goes to the devil in his own way." He grabbed Brandon by the shoulder. "If you persist in coming with me on the morrow, you could be killed."

Brandon nodded. "Aye, that thought is uppermost in my mind at present. I pray God to let me live till Midsummer's Day. After that, I care not a whit what Lady Bardolph might say."

That night, Brandon's fierce lovemaking took Kat by surprise. When he kissed her, he could not taste enough of her, leaving her lips bruised by his ardor. He clasped her tightly against him, as if he could meld their bodies into one being. When they came together, the turbulence of their passion swirled around them, carrying them to greater heights than before. A hot tide of possession raged through Brandon. Afterward, he cradled Kat against him, whispering soothing endearments.

"Is something amiss?" she asked softly.

He answered in a ragged voice. "Now that I have found you, I fear to lose you."

She snuggled against him. "Never, my love. Till death do we part."

A small tremor shivered through him. "Let us not speak of death tonight, sweet Katherine. His grisly visage has no place in our bed." He smothered his last words on her lips, as he took her mouth again with the hunger of a starving man.

The pewter gray light of early morning had barely broken when Brandon slid quietly out of bed. Moving with deliberate stealth, he pulled on his hose, shirt, doublet and soft leather boots. Before he left the chamber, he took a long moment to gaze at Kat while she slept. Her glorious hair flowed across the pillow like a river of copper. Her lush moist lips still showed signs of his passion.

He went down on one knee beside her. "Remember me always, my love," he whispered in her ear. "I carry your love in my heart. You are my life."

With infinite tenderness, he brushed his lips across her love-swollen ones. She stirred in her sleep. Wrenching himself away from her side, Brandon stole out the door.

Returning to his own chamber in the north tower, he found Christopher dressing Jack in a light hauberk of chain mail, over which he fastened a thick leather jerkin. Holding Brandon's battle gear, Mark stood waiting.

"Methought I would have to ferret you out of Miranda's arms this morning," Brandon jested as he doused his face in cold water.

Jack snorted. "I have turned a new leaf, Cavendish. The lady is an innocent in the ways of the world. As a honest gentleman, I will wait until our wedding night before I sleep with her."

Brandon winked at the squires. "'Tis a good thing we have witnesses to your words, Jack of Hearts, for I shall hold you to them. This is a day to remember, when you did not take advantage of a lady's charms."

Jack glowered. "Miranda has agreed to be my wife, and I will honor her with all due respect. I charge you to do the same."

Brandon thought of Kat as Mark buckled on his leather thigh protectors. Since they were legally betrothed, and the lady not a virgin, 'twas no dishonor to lie with her before the wedding day. Though he admired Jack's restraint, Brandon carried no guilt for his time with Kat. If, by chance, Scantling killed him, he had, at least, savored a few moments of supreme happiness with her. A man could not ask for more. The next few hours were in God's hands.

Jack adjusted his mail cowl over his shoulders. "Ready to go a-hunting, Brandon?"

Brandon tightened his sword belt. "Aye," he answered

brusquely. *Kat, I love thee.* "To the stables, Jack. We burn daylight."

The sun's warm yellow rays peeked over the tops of the forest, promising another fine summer's day. In a few terse sentences, Brandon outlined the search plan to the dozen men-at-arms. They would move in a wide swath through the wood, the men keeping each other in sight. As the bait, Brandon would ride foremost in the center of the line. 'Twas like a boar hunt, he thought as he swung himself into Windchaser's saddle. Nothing more. His heart thudded in a cadence with the charger's hoofs as they trotted across the causeway.

On the far side of the tilled fields, Jack and Brandon deployed the men into a single wide line. The two squires took their positions in the rear where they could keep an eye on their masters, in case one of them was unhorsed or injured. Brandon pulled his mailed hood over his head. Then, standing in his stirrups, he saluted Jack. In like manner, Jack returned Brandon's salute. Brandon signaled Jess to sound the hunting horn, in hopes that Scantling would hear it and think that Brandon was stalking a deer.

Unexpectedly, another horn answered from over the rise.

Wheeling his charger, Brandon held up his hand to halt the advance of the line. Who dared to hunt on Kat's lands without her permission—unless the king had come early? Jack pulled Thunder to a stop beside Brandon.

"Who the devil is that?" he asked.

Standing in his stirrups, Brandon shaded his eyes. "I cannot see them. They are on the other side of the ridge." He whistled to Mark.

"Aye, my lord?" The youth's brown eyes blazed with excitement.

Leaning across his saddle, Brandon gripped his squire by the shoulder. "Take Jess, and ride to the top of yon hill—to the top, only. If you disappear over that rise, I will flay you within an inch of your life this evening. Do you hear?''

Mark grinned with enthusiasm. ''Aye, my lord.''

Brandon wished he had spent more time teaching Mark the value of patience and discretion. ''See if you can determine who answered our call. Report back to me at once.''

Mark pulled on his reins. ''I'll race the wind, my lord.''

Brandon held him back for a moment. ''If you cannot identify them, return immediately, and we will proceed as a group. Do not, under any circumstances, go over the rise.''

Mark nodded, then spurred his horse into a gallop. The chestnut gelding's long tail streamed out behind him as they flew over the turf. Mark circled Jess, then the two sped up the ridge. Brandon watched them with a growing sense of unease.

The distant riders stopped on the crest of the low hill. Brandon held his breath. His hand closed around his sword's hilt. Then Jess lifted his horn to his lips and blew the Cavendish call to arms. Mark rose up in his saddle, waved to Brandon then kicked his mount into action. Both riders disappeared over the crest and out of sight.

''God's teeth! I'll have both their hides!'' Goading Windchaser into his mile-eating gallop, Brandon tore down the line of men after his squire and huntsman.

Jack fell in behind him. The rest of the company thundered after the knights. As they dashed over the ridge, Brandon summoned the Cavendish war cry from the depths of his throat.

Halfway down the other side of the hill, he jerked Windchaser's reins. The warhorse reared, pawing the air. Brandon stayed astride. Below him on the road, a large group of horsemen surrounded several wagons. A red banner, bearing the likeness of a snarling wolf's head, snapped in the morning breeze. Jack turned Thunder in a wide arc, until he drew abreast of the prancing, snorting Windchaser.

"What ho, Cavendish?" he panted, wiping the sweat out of his eyes.

A shadow of annoyance crossed Brandon's features. "Sheathe your sword, Jack. 'Tis my parents who have arrived."

Chapter Sixteen

A tall, blond horseman broke away from the visitors and charged up the hill. Despite his ambivalent feelings at seeing his family come to Bodiam, a grin crossed Brandon's face as his younger brother rode toward him.

"Good morrow, Brandon!" Guy Cavendish shouted. "We have come to see a great rarity—you as a bridegroom!"

As the huge charcoal gray horse drew alongside Brandon's, Guy reached out and clasped his sibling's arm with affection. "How did you know we were here? Mother wanted it to be a surprise."

Brandon's lips twitched with a rueful smile. "Believe me when I tell you, I have never been more surprised in my life than now, little brother. How long have you been on the road?"

"Ever since the king's letter arrived telling of your betrothal. We began packing that very day, and here we are in good time."

Jack joined the brothers, slapping Guy on the back. "Well met, Archangel! Welcome to midsummer madness!"

Guy curled his lip at the nickname. Brandon laughed at his brother's discomfort. Guy, younger by eleven months, had a face so finely featured that he was often called "beautiful," an adjective Guy particularly detested.

"I see that madness has already touched your knavish countenance, Jackanapes," Guy retorted, delivering Jack a light blow to the shoulder. "You look more wicked than when we last met."

Brandon quirked an eyebrow at Stafford. "And well he should. Jack has stolen a lady's heart."

Guy snorted. "What else is new?"

"Nay, Guy. 'Tis for real this time. Our Jack of Hearts intends to bind himself in lawful matrimony."

"'Tis true?" Guy asked the grinning lover. When Jack nodded, he threw back his head, laughing loudly. "You speak aright, Brandon. There must be some madness in this southern air. I long to see Stafford's wedding almost as much as yours."

Turning their horses, the three rode down toward the wagons.

Guy tapped Brandon with his crop. "Be warned. Mother brought the children," he said in an undertone.

Brandon's heart slammed against his chest. Not having seen LaBelle and Francis in the three months since Easter, Brandon longed to hold them again. On the other hand, he had not told Kat of his offspring. Things were going to be very ticklish this afternoon at Bodiam Castle.

"Papa!" A bright blond sprite with flying braids stood up in one of the wagons and held out her arms to him. "Let me ride with you! Poor Windy! He looks full out of breath! Papa, here!"

Brandon's face spread into a broad smile as he reined in his horse by the wagon's side. Leaning over, he gathered his nine-year-old daughter into his arms. Her butterfly kisses covered his cheeks. She smelled of sunshine and lavender. "You've grown some more, Belle!" he said, swallowing down the lump in his throat. "Soon you will be too heavy for me to pick up!"

"Ha!" she replied, snapping her fingers under his nose. She draped her legs on either side of Brandon's saddle. "Hello, Windy! Are you glad to see me?" She leaned over the pommel to pat the charger's sleek neck. The horse perked up his ears at the familiar sound of her voice.

Brandon looked over his daughter's head into his mother's blue eyes. "Welcome, Mother," he said softly. "I see you've come to do me in."

Lady Alicia Cavendish dimpled in return. "You look fit, Brandon, but methinks a little discomfited. I gather you have not yet told your lady about the children?"

Leaning down into the wagon, he kissed his mother's smooth brow. Lady Alicia may be near fifty in age, but she was twenty in her spirits. "Things have been…complicated of late," he murmured.

"Bonjour, mon beau-frère!" Lady Celeste Cavendish, Guy's irrepressible French wife, tilted her face up to him. "Do I not get a kiss, as well. Eh? Or have I grown too fat for your notice?"

Brandon's eyes sparkled as he regarded his petite sister-in-law. "Your girth promises more good fortune for my brother. But I am not sure I should be kissing a married woman, and a pregnant one at that!"

"Ma foi!" she replied, grinning with a mischievous twinkle. "Methinks you have done such a scandalous thing before, Brandon, *non?*"

"You know me too well," he replied, kissing her. "I am surprised that Guy would let you travel so far. When is the baby due?"

Celeste shrugged one shoulder, then smiled at him. "Ha! Guy could not keep me away, and I am not due until the autumn—again. Besides, I intend to dance the night into dawn at your wedding, *beau-frère*. Petit Francis has agreed to partner me, eh, *mon cher?*" she asked, putting her arm around a serious boy of nine, who was also blond and blue eyed.

"*Oui,*" he replied, bowing as formally as the space in the wagon allowed. "*Avec plaisir.* 'Twill be my pleasure," he added.

Brandon nodded. "Your French accent has much improved, Francis. I am well pleased."

The boy smiled, basking in Brandon's approval. "I am glad to see you again, sir," he said quietly.

"And I am likewise glad to see you, Francis," Brandon gravely replied.

Brandon desperately wanted to call Francis "my son," but the boy had no idea of the kinship, despite his obvious Cavendish looks. As far as Francis knew, he had been sent by his parents to Brandon to be fostered as a page. Later, when the boy was older, he would learn the duties of a knight by serving as Brandon's squire. Brandon sighed inwardly. Perchance Kat could do what Lady Alicia and Celeste had been unable to accomplish in the past fifteen months—make Francis feel at home.

"Would you like to ride on Windchaser, as well?" he asked his son.

Belle wrinkled her nose. "Francis is the one who is getting too heavy. Windy won't like it at all." Belle had not taken well to Francis's arrival at Wolf Hall. Since then, she had baffled the shy lad by alternately adoring him, then plaguing him to death.

Brandon gave her a little squeeze around her middle where he held her in place. "Windchaser has a strong, broad back. He could carry Francis easily. Of course, if you were truly concerned for my poor horse, you could get back into the wagon."

Belle sighed dramatically, so that her shoulders went up and down. "Very well," she conceded with a grand air. "You may join us, Francis. But watch that you don't kick Windy."

Extending a hand to the boy, Brandon pulled Francis up behind him. "I see you *have* grown much, Francis."

Lady Alicia chuckled. "He has kept our village cobbler busy this spring."

Sticking out one foot, Francis waggled it. "New shoes for your wedding, my lord," he boasted with pride of ownership.

Belle flipped her braids over her shoulders. "Ha! His feet look like shovels. That is why Grandmama must cover them quickly. I have got a new dress."

Brandon hugged her again. "And what color is this dress?" he asked. Lord! It was good to have them close by him again.

"Blue, to match my eyes!" Belle regarded him over her shoulder. "Still, I don't understand why you must marry, Papa. What are you ever going to do with a wife?"

Guy and Jack, as well some of the Cavendish men-at-arms, roared with laughter at her innocent question. Brandon sent Guy a withering look. "Lady Katherine will be a mother to you, sweetling," he answered.

Belle snapped her fingers in the air. "Ha! What do I need with a mother? I already have Grandmama and Aunt Celeste telling me what to do. I don't need one more lady to order me about!"

Sir Thomas Cavendish edged his horse beside Windchaser. "Your papa is getting married because I want him to," he rumbled to his granddaughter.

"Oh." The child thought for a moment, then remarked, "Well if *you* say so, Grandpapa, then I suppose it must be so."

"You look well, Brandon," Sir Thomas continued, eyeing his son from helm to boot. "How goes the courtship? Or is that why you are dressed for combat?"

"Good morrow, Father." Brandon inclined his head to his sire. Sir Thomas looked as hearty as ever, despite his advancing age. Lady Alicia had always said that her husband would not die happy, unless he keeled over in his saddle while chasing some four-footed beast through a forest. Perhaps she was right, Brandon thought. "We were about to go hunting when we heard your horn."

Sir Thomas's bushy gray brows went up. "A-hunting, is it? Nothing like a good hunt first thing in the morning. Stirs up the blood. What is it you hunt that you need to wear chain mail?"

"A mad dog," Jack said quickly.

"A wild boar," Brandon answered at the same time.

Sir Thomas glanced from one to the other. "Methinks you are hoping to find both. Now if 'twas a bear, that would be good sport, indeed." He scanned the woods on the side of the road. "You don't suppose there would be a bear hereabouts?" he asked hopefully.

"Thomas!" Lady Alicia fixed him with a stern glare. "Let us meet your son's intended bride first, before you take the boys off to the forest for half the day."

Sir Thomas pulled one end of his gray mustache, then nodded. "Of course, my dear." He turned in the saddle and called to the men who milled about the wagons. "Don't sit there a-gawking all morning. To Bodiam!"

"Hold tight, Francis," Brandon spoke over his shoulder.

"Aye, sir," the boy replied, gripping Brandon's waist.

Wheeling Windchaser, Brandon urged him up the hill, instead of following the road. Best to take the shortcut back to the castle, to give Kat some warning—and to introduce the children to her.

As they trotted over the crest, an arrow sang from the trees. With a sharp cry of pain, Francis toppled off the horse.

For Brandon, everything seemed to freeze on the spot. Then events sped up as if happening within a flash of lightning. Brandon brought the charger to a halt. Dismounting, and pulling Belle with him, he threw them both to the ground.

"Papa! You're hurting—" Belle protested, trying to push him off her.

"Quiet!" he growled, "Someone in the wood is firing arrows at us."

A second arrow whizzed less than a foot over Brandon's head. Francis lay just out of his reach. The boy's face was ashen and his eyes shut.

'Twas Scantling's doing! Seeing his injured son sent a red tidal wave of anger surging through Brandon. That villain was a walking dead man. Brandon vowed to kill him with his bare hands, wringing the last drop of life out of the vermin. For now, he had to protect his children from the viper.

Lifting his head, Brandon shouted the family war cry, "A Cavendish! To me!" Then to his daughter, he whispered, "We must try to get to Francis. When I move, you must move under me. Can you do that?"

"A-aye, Papa," the little girl stammered. "Is Francis dead?"

Brandon gritted his teeth. "I don't know, Belle, but we must get to him. Ready? Now!"

With one arm still firmly around Belle, he lifted himself, then scuttled, crab-fashion, over the turf to Francis's side. Belle did her part by moving as quick as a cat. A third arrow embedded itself in the spot Brandon had just left. God rot the cursed knave! His aim was too good. Shielding the children with his body, Brandon called again for help.

His summons was answered by a deeper, thundering call to arms. Brandon could not remember the last time he had heard his father lift his voice in the battle cry, but the Earl of Thornbury's shout heartened him. Guy and Jack galloped past Brandon's prostrate form.

Raising himself up, Brandon shouted, "In the woods to the right." He pointed. "Take a care. The whoreson is damnably good with that crossbow."

The two plunged into the thicket of the trees, followed by Sir Thomas, still bellowing, and the combined forces of the men-at-arms.

Brandon knelt beside his son. The bolt had gone through the child's arm; its wicked steel barb protruded on the other side. When Brandon touched the shaft, Francis moaned, then opened his eyes.

"Lie still, Francis," Brandon murmured. "Are you in much pain?"

The lad licked his lips. "Aye, but I can bear it, sir."

"I am going to break the shaft, then draw it out." Brandon pulled off his leather gloves. He put the fingers of one between Francis's teeth. "Bite down on this. 'Twill help you stand the pain. Belle, close your eyes. 'Tis a bloody business."

"Nay, Papa." Belle took Francis's good hand in hers. "If he can bear it in his arm, I can bear watching it. Hold my hand, Francis, and squeeze," she told him. "I don't mind if you squeeze hard."

Brandon took a firm grip on the arrow. "Ready?" he asked his children.

"Aye," Belle answered for both of them.

Gritting his teeth, Brandon broke the shaft, then pulled out the arrow. Without prompting from her father, Belle covered the bleeding wound with a handful of her dress.

"Cut up my petticoat, Papa! Quick!" she commanded. "The blood is soaking my fingers. Francis, don't you dare die! You still owe me a sixpence, and I mean to collect it—later, that is."

The sun glinted off Brandon's dagger as he ripped several large patches out of her underskirts. His hands shook as he tied the cloth around his son's arm, then fashioned a sling. Mark rode up with Windchaser in tow. The youth dismounted while his horse was still in motion.

"Jesu! Is he badly hurt?" Mark asked, kneeling beside Francis. He brushed his hand across the boy's forehead.

Opening his eyes, Francis gave his older friend a weak smile. "'Tis but a scratch, Mark," he said weakly. Then he fainted.

Belle's lower lip trembled. "Is he...?" She looked up at her father.

Brandon expelled a long sigh. "Nay, Belle. He has lost a lot of blood, and has swooned." Gently he gathered up his son in his arms. "Let us get him into the wagon with your grandmother. Mark, put Belle on Windchaser, and lead them down the hill. She's been a very brave girl this day."

Belle flashed him a quick smile as Mark lifted her into the huge saddle. Cradling Francis, Brandon strode back to the waiting wagons. *'Tis my fault. Forgive me, my son. That arrow was meant for me.* Brandon's legs trembled at the thought of how close he had come to losing his children.

"What happened?" Lady Alicia asked, as Brandon laid Francis on the floor mattress stuffed with straw and wadding. Celeste tucked a woolen blanket around the boy, whispering French endearments in his ear. Mark lifted Belle from Windchaser's saddle, then handed her over to her aunt.

"Who has done this terrible thing?" Brandon's mother continued.

"A man who has sworn my death, Mother," Brandon replied, his throat dry and raw. "And now, I have vowed his!" He reached for Windchaser's reins.

Lady Alicia laid her hand on Brandon's arm. "The woods are full of our men. You will be needed when we get Francis to Bodiam. Is it far?"

Brandon shook his head. "Nay. Around the side of the hill and into the valley. Less than half a mile."

Lady Alicia gave him a firm squeeze. "Climb into the wagon, Brandon, and hold your daughter. By my troth, both of you are as pale as sheets."

Brandon tried to pull away. "Mother, I must go—"

She shook him. "So that the villain can shoot at you again? Nay, once a day is enough. Get into the wagon, and let us be off. Do not act the hardheaded pig just now, Brandon!''

Brandon started to protest, but the glare in his mother's eye stopped his words. Glancing over to Belle, he saw that the little girl was indeed very pale and shaken, though she sat up straight beside Francis. With a heartfelt sigh, Brandon climbed into the wagon next to Celeste, then held out his arms to Belle.

''Come to your papa, sweetling. You must help us take Francis to safety.'' Brandon settled the child against his chest, then spoke to his squire. ''Ride like the devil to Lady Katherine—you know which lady I mean?''

Mark nodded, then hurled himself onto his horse without the help of his stirrups.

''Tell the lady exactly what has happened. We shall follow presently.''

Mark spurred his horse. ''Aye, my lord!'' he shouted as he dashed up the hill. The horse's hooves kicked up clods of turf in his wake.

Leaning back against the side of the wagon, Brandon gave his mother a weak smile. ''You should be proud of the children, Mother,'' he said softly as he stroked Belle's sleek blond hair. ''I have never seen braver ones in my life.''

Lady Alicia patted her son's hand. ''I have always been proud of *all* my children,'' she replied.

The morning had started out pleasantly enough: making potpourri to scent the castle chambers for the king's visit, conferring with Philippe over the wedding feast, then the wedding gown fittings for Miranda and herself. The lazy peace was shattered when Mark practically rode his gelding into the hall, and panted out the terrifying news that Brandon had been attacked by some stranger in the home park. Then the squire announced that Brandon's entire family had come for the wedding, and was en route with an injured member of the party.

"Who?" Kat clutched the golden rose on her bodice. "Pray not Brandon?"

Mark shook his head. "Nay, my lady. 'Tis his page, Francis Bardolph, who was traveling with the earl and countess."

Sondra put down her needle. "How badly is the boy hurt?"

"'Tis an arrow through his arm." Mark swept back a hank of brown hair that had fallen into his eyes. "My lord removed it, but there was a great deal of bleeding. Francis is only nine, Mistress Sondra," the squire added.

"Oh, the poor poppet!" Miranda clasped her hands at the tale.

Kat's mind whirled like a waterwheel in a flood. "Sondra, mix the child a poultice to draw the vile humors from the wound. We'll put him in the chamber next to mine."

Sondra closed her sewing basket. "Aye, I will have all ready in a tick of the clock." She hurried out of the hall.

Kat tried to think of sleeping arrangements for her unexpected visitors. "Miranda, tell Montjoy as gently as possible that we have more guests. I don't want him to have a sudden attack of the miseries just now."

Nodding, her cousin lifted her skirts and dashed into the corridor, calling for the steward and the maids.

Kat wrung her hands. "How long do you think 'twill take them to come? Oh, Mark, you spoke the truth? My lord is safe, isn't he?"

Mark again ran his hand through his long locks. "They will be here directly, my lady. They come by the road, while I went over the hill and across the meadow. And my master is sound of limb, though he is angered by the injury done to Francis. He swears vengeance, my lady. I have never seen him look so black."

Kat clasped her hands tighter. "Oh, poor Brandon!"

Mark shuffled his feet. "My lady, there is something else you should know, but I don't know how to tell you."

The evasive tone in the squire's voice set off a warning bell inside Kat's head. From the look on his face, she guessed the news would be distressing.

She placed her hand on his shoulder. "Come, Mark, what is it?"

He chewed his lower lip before speaking. "I know my lord intended to tell you himself, but the time passed so quickly since we came and—"

Kat thought she would jump out of her skin if he kept up his preamble much longer. "By the book, Mark! For the sake of my nerves, tell me!"

The squire took a deep breath. "There is a little girl among the party. Her name is LaBelle Cavendish, my lady. She is also nine years old, and...and she is Sir Brandon's natural daughter."

"Oh!" Kat sat down on the window seat with a thump. Brandon had a child!

Mark knelt on the floor beside her. "My lady?"

Kat gave herself a shake, then swallowed. "I am glad you told me of this, Mark."

He searched her face. "Truly, my lady? I know 'tis not my place, but when you meet her, you will see the resemblance immediately. I thought to give you fair warning."

Kat willed her heart to beat slower. "You did well, Mark. I am grateful."

"Sir Brandon had both children on his horse with him, when he was attacked. Francis took the arrow meant for him."

Oh, Brandon! "Thank you for telling me, Mark. 'Twill help me understand...later. Methinks—"

A shout from the courtyard interrupted her. Looking out the window, she saw two wagons roll over the causeway and through the gate.

Picking up her skirts, Kat ran out of the hall and down

the entry staircase. Mark followed close at her heels. No doubt Brandon had his reasons for not telling her about his child, but that could wait. The most important thing was to tend to the young page and to try to ease some of the anguish that she knew must be eating away in the innermost part of Brandon's soul. Kat would sort out her own gnawing feelings in due time. Then the reckoning would be demanded and paid.

By the time Kat arrived in the courtyard, Brandon had lifted Francis out of the wagon. The child lay still as death in his arms as Brandon carried him toward the stairs. His bleak expression frightened Kat. It reminded her of a chalky mask.

"Mark told you?" he asked hoarsely.

Kat touched his sleeve. "Aye, he told me much. Take the boy upstairs to the chamber next to mine. Sondra has everything prepared. I will be with you as soon as I have greeted your lady mother."

Brandon's eyelids blinked once. "Kat, I—"

Kat did not want to hear his explanation at the moment. She needed time to gather her scattered wits. "We shall speak later, Brandon. For now, we must see to your page."

He cradled the child closer to him, then whispered, "Francis is also my son."

Kat came to a standstill. Brandon did not look back to her but continued up the stairway into the castle.

How many more children was that man hiding?

Chapter Seventeen

Half an hour later, the guests had dispersed to their rooms. Since Kat had not seen Brandon, she presumed he was still with Francis. Meanwhile, Mark and one of the Cavendish maids whisked the little girl away to the garden before Kat had the chance to meet her. In good time, she told herself. She did not think she was quite ready for motherhood this minute.

After welcoming Brandon's mother, and making sure nothing was wanting in her chamber, Kat put her hand on the door. Gripping the wood, she willed the oak to give her strength. "I pray you excuse me, Lady Alicia," she apologized. "I must see how your...the boy fares. Our Sondra is a wondrous healer. He will soon be well again."

With an understanding smile in her eyes, Lady Alicia beckoned to Kat. "Aye, I am sure that Francis is in good hands. 'Tis you who needs some healing, methinks."

Kat blinked. "I, my lady? I am quite well."

Her lips twitched. "When any woman is presented with several unexpected children, methinks she might feel faint."

Kat's shoulders relaxed. "You are very wise, my lady."

Brandon's mother chuckled in reply. "I have had thirty-three years of second-guessing my husband and our two headstrong sons, Lady Katherine. I have grown skilled with practice. Come, sit down and rest for a moment. Will you share a cup of wine with me?'' Before Kat could demur, Lady Alicia filled two goblets. ''We have had quite a morning, you and I.'' She handed Kat one of them. ''Please, do not think too harshly of Brandon. Things are not quite what they seem.''

Kat's cold fingers closed around the pewter cup. Sitting down on the window seat, Lady Alicia patted the cushion beside her. With a smile, Kat joined her. ''Things have not been what they seemed for the past month, my lady.'' She sipped the cool wine.

''Brandon told you that Francis is his son, but that is not quite the case,'' his mother began in her quiet voice.

Kat experienced a mix of confusing emotions. ''Then whose is he?''

''Ah! That is a question Solomon might have been able to answer, but not us lesser mortals. I shall make the best of the tale for you. Have you ever heard of Lady Olivia Bardolph?''

Kat recalled the name from some of Fitzhugh's ramblings about court life, but she had forgotten what he had said about her. ''She is a lady of the court?''

Lady Alicia quirked her brow. ''A lady? Aye, she calls herself that. Others do not. But certainly she inhabits the court. She is the wife of the long-suffering Sir Richard Bardolph. Oh, I have often felt such pity for that poor man!'' Lady Alicia shook her head. ''To speak plainly— Lady Olivia collects men as you or I might gather flowers on a summer's day.''

''Sweet angels!'' Kat gasped. Idly she wondered if Fitzhugh had been part of the woman's bouquet. Probably.

''Just so,'' Lady Alicia continued. ''After producing three healthy sons for her husband, Olivia grew bored with country life and begged Sir Richard to take her to court. Simple man,'' she said, and sighed. ''He did. Our good

Queen Catherine was pregnant yet again—poor woman. My heart grieves for her so. The king, who never did have an ounce of patience, cast his eye among the ladies for some diversion.''

"And he picked Lady Olivia," Kat supplied. The wine began to loosen the knotted muscles in the back of her neck.

Lady Alicia nodded. "Aye. 'Twas a brief fling, with no child as a remembrance. But after that, the lady's charms became very popular with the gentlemen of the court. Poor Sir Richard could do nothing, but smile and smile.''

"He should have sent her back home to the country.''

"Aye," Lady Alicia agreed. "I don't know why he didn't. The fact of the matter is that Lady Bardolph continued to present her cuckold husband with a child a year—all by different fathers. Not even the lady claimed to know which child was whose.''

"Good heavens!" Kat whispered.

"Then came the visit to France in the summer of 1520," Brandon's mother continued, warming to her tale. "You must have heard of the Field of Cloth of Gold?''

Kat bit the inside of her lip. She had wanted desperately to attend. The king had even sent a letter inviting her along with Edward. But Fitzhugh had forbidden her to go, though he went himself and had talked of nothing else for six months afterward. He had known how much she had longed to enjoy the sights and pleasures that he did. He took a cruel delight in describing the music, the food, the jousts and the dancing to spite her. After a while, Kat had shut her ears to his tales. It didn't hurt as much that way.

"Aye," she replied shortly. "I did hear some talk of it.''

Lady Alicia cast her a shrewd look, then continued. "I attended, together with my husband and both sons." Her eyes took on a soft sheen. "The boys were in their first flush of manhood then, and as handsome as any mother could wish. Brandon was twenty-one, and Guy was twenty. And they were as prideful as an entire flock of peacocks. Aye, all the ladies of the court made a great fuss over my sons.''

Though she had yet to meet Guy, whom Brandon had told her had the face of an angel in a church window, Kat could well imagine just how handsome the Cavendish brothers must have looked. Brandon at thirty-one was very attractive. Ten years earlier, he must have been—

"Cocky as roosters," Lady Alicia chortled. "And not a grain of wit between them. Lady Olivia couldn't keep her hands off either one of them—and in full view of their mother, no less!"

"Shameless!" Kat murmured, wondering what magic Lady Olivia used to charm so many men.

Lady Alicia tossed her head. "I told her that once, but she only laughed and reminded me that Brandon and Guy were of age, as indeed they were."

"And so she conceived Francis then in France?" Kat asked, doing some quick arithmetic in her head.

"Just so, but the lady had also lain with King Francis of France on at least one occasion, or so she claimed. When she began to show her belly at the Christmas festivities that year, she announced that she carried a French royal bastard. When a boy was born the next spring, she named him for the king of France. However, as Francis grew older, it became obvious—even to Olivia—that the child had not inherited the French king's swarthy looks, but rather, he resembled a Cavendish. Our family has a remarkable ability to reproduce exactly alike, except for darling Celeste. Her daughter, Tonia, is dark haired like her mother. But the child does have the Cavendish nose and mouth.''

Kat mulled over this information for a moment, and found that she was still confused. "So one of your sons fathered Francis, but how do you know 'twas Brandon?"

"We don't." Lady Alicia shrugged. "No one does, least of all Lady Olivia Bardolph. We had no idea the child existed until about eighteen months ago, when Sir Richard wrote my husband asking if we would foster one of his cuckoos—not that Sir Richard ever referred to his wife's offspring as cuckoos, but you see my point."

"Aye," replied Kat, recalling how the cuckoo bird laid its eggs in other bird's nests, thereby avoiding the tedium of hatching and feeding its own offspring.

"When Francis arrived—like a waif in a storm, he was, my dear—we could see immediately that he was one of ours. Guy had just entered the Franciscan order—"

Kat choked on her wine. "Your pardon, my lady," she said when she could speak again. "I did not know Sir Guy was a priest." *And what is he doing married and a father now?*

Lady Alicia laughed. "Didn't Brandon tell you that story?"

Kat hid her own smile behind the goblet. "We have been at sixes and sevens here of late, my lady. Ours is another goodly tale to tell by a fireside. But, nay, we have not had much time to learn about each other. You have spotted that truth already."

Lady Alicia swirled her wine in the cup. "Guy was not really cut out for the life of a monk, though he insisted upon it at the time. I thank the good Lord daily that Celeste came along before he had taken his final vows. But to continue my story. Guy was gone, and as far as we knew, 'twould be forever. Brandon claimed the boy as his and took him as his page. The lad adores Brandon."

Kat shifted the pieces of the tale around in her head. "But the child—he doesn't suspect that he is a Cavendish, does he?"

"Ah! You have hit the nut and core of it!" Lady Alicia smiled. "I am glad to see that Brandon is marrying an intelligent woman. Good for King Henry! But to answer your question. Nay, he does not. Sir Richard Bardolph may be a fool, but he is an honorable one. He has given his name to all of Olivia's children, and so Francis thinks he is a Bardolph.''

"Will Brandon ever tell him the truth?"

Lady Alicia tilted her head. "Francis is uncommonly wise for one so young—and in spite of such a disordered upbringing. Methinks he will suspect his parentage by the time he begins to shave, when he looks into the mirror at his face. I know that Brandon itches to claim him. Time will tell.''

Kat finished her wine in thoughtful silence. Lady Alicia's story settled one set of fears but raised another anxiety. "The little girl—is she Francis's sister?"

Lady Alicia regarded her future daughter-in-law with lively blue eyes full of unquenchable warmth. "Nay, she's his half sister, at most, cousin, at the very least. However, LaBelle *is* Brandon's child for certain.''

A small dart of jealousy pricked Kat. She tried to shake it off. Of course, Brandon must have had ladyloves in his past life. Fenton's poisonous words came back to her. "He beds anything in a skirt between the ages of seven and seventy. Half the men at court are made cuckolds by him." Kat's cheeks grew hot with the image of Brandon in bed with other women.

"LaBelle is a pretty name," Kat observed, fighting to keep her voice steady.

"Her mother was French." Lady Alicia reached out and took Kat's icy hand in hers. "Both children were conceived during the fortnight of King Henry's visit with the French king. Indeed, methinks there is an entire generation of nine-year-olds who can claim that place of origin as theirs. My sons were lusty young men, and new to the temptations of court. But that was ten years ago, and Brandon has matured. He is a most loving father.''

Kat blinked back a tear that threatened to fall. Why

should she be distraught? Fitzhugh had been unfaithful to her, even under his own roof. 'Twas well-known that men had certain appetites. What difference could Brandon's past life make to Kat now? *I love him. But what am I to him? One more woman to bed?*

"Tell me about LaBelle's mother, Lady Alicia."

The older woman smiled, then shook her head. "As Belle is Brandon's, I leave it to Brandon to tell you. But put your heart at ease. He has never seen the mother since."

Since when? Kat wondered. *Silly goose! Take what you have, and look for nothing more. Brandon will be yours on Midsummer's Day. That should be enough.* But the prickling sensation would not go away.

Kat rose. "I must see to Francis. We serve dinner near the noon hour. I will look for you then. And, Lady Alicia, my thanks for your good words."

Brandon's mother searched Kat's face with an astute look. She seemed to plumb Kat's very thoughts. "I can see that you love my son. I am glad. Follow your heart, and let the rest go. All will be well anon."

"I pray that is true," Kat whispered as she took her leave.

Kat encountered Sondra in the passageway. The house-keeper held a covered cup in her hand. "The lad rests easy, Lady Kat. The bleeding has stopped, and he bore my stitches very bravely. I gave him a cordial of poppy juice to help him sleep. Sir Brandon is with him now."

Kat eyed the cup. "Who is that for?"

Sondra gave her a knowing wink. "'Tis a soothing cup of spiced wine and milk for Sir Brandon. He would not say so, but I could see he is still much shaken by the injury to his page." Sondra thrust the warm cup into Kat's hands. "He will drink it down, if you give it to him, my lady."

"Aye, if he takes anything from me," she murmured. "My thanks, Sondra."

Clutching the posset, Kat walked slowly toward the sickroom. What should she say to Brandon? What would he say to her? Could she bear his stammered excuses?

Putting her hand to the latch, she paused as she heard voices inside, speaking in low tones. Francis's childish treble, not yet begun to turn, murmured in counterpoint to Brandon's mellow baritone. Unashamedly Kat eavesdropped.

"Mistress Owens says that I will have a scar," Francis told his father.

"Aye, my boy. Take pride in it. 'Tis an honorable wound. When you are older, you will learn that ladies consider such scars most intriguing."

Kat gripped the cup harder. Did Brandon speak from personal experience?

"Does Lady Katherine find your scars intriguing?" the boy asked.

Brandon chuckled softly. "I do not believe she has noticed them as yet."

What scars? Where? Kat resolved to investigate him closely the next time, if there was to be a next time.

"What is Lady Katherine like, my lord?" Francis yawned.

"She is kindness and goodness itself. She has a pretty face, and the greenest eyes you can imagine." Brandon's voice grew softer.

Kat leaned closer to catch his next words.

"And she has a heart that warms the world."

"Do you think she will like me?" Francis's voice quivered.

Lifting the latch, Kat entered the room. Father and son turned to look at her with eyes of equal hue and expressions that mirrored each other. *By the rood! I am glad that Lady Alicia told me the boy's story, or I might have swooned at this sight.* Brandon held her in his gaze. The glow of his welcoming smile warmed her across the room.

"Kat, this is Francis Bardolph, my page." His simple words held a wealth of feeling in them. "Francis, I have the honor to present to you Lady Katherine—my wife." A look of pleading entered into his expression.

Her slow, secret smile told him that she understood.

Francis struggled to sit up. "My...my lady, I am your obedient servant," he gasped with effort.

Kat knelt at his bedside. "I am delighted to meet you, Francis," she said, smoothing his blond hair across his forehead. How like Brandon's! "'Tis an honor to have a hero at Bodiam Castle."

Francis blinked, then glanced up at Brandon.

"I believe the lady means you, Francis, for you did indeed save my life." Brandon coughed to clear the huskiness from his voice. "I am in your eternal debt."

Kat kissed Francis on his pale cheek. "And I already like you very much, Francis. You must promise me that you will get well quickly. I would deem it an honor for you to escort me to my wedding to your...your lord." Kat glanced up at Brandon. His eyes glistened.

"'Tis my honor, Lady Katherine," the boy murmured. His eyelids fluttered. The next moment he lapsed into a healing sleep.

Brandon helped Kat to her feet. "I fear you came too late for Francis to drink that," he remarked, indicating the cup still in her hand.

With a sly smile, Kat shook her head. "Sondra made this for you, and she made me promise to see that you drink every drop."

Lifting the cover, Brandon sniffed its spicy scent. "Will this potion induce forgetfulness, Kat? I wish I could blot out what happened this morning." He looked down at the sleeping boy. "When I saw him lying on the ground, with that arrow sticking out of him, the arrow meant for me..."

Lacing her fingers within his, she offered him the cup. "Drink, my love. 'Twill ease your soul for a time."

Closing his eyes, he quaffed the posset in one long swallow. His tongue sought out a stray drop on his lip. When he looked at her again, a timorous smile ruffled the lines of his mouth. "They say that confession is good for the soul, and will ease it better than any drink." Putting the cup down on the side table, he offered her his arm. "Will you walk with me, sweet Katherine?"

She threaded her arm through his. "Aye."

Brandon and Kat made their way through the corridors and past the hall, where milling servants wrestled with a great many chests, bags, boxes and baskets. Kat wondered how long the Cavendish clan planned to stay. From the look of it, Lady Celeste would be giving birth to her babe at Bodiam five months hence.

Leading Kat out of the bustling castle, Brandon found a private spot in the rose garden. On the archery range on the far side of the hedge, they heard a child laughing. Kat drank in the unusual sound. How odd! In all her years there, first as Lewknor's wife, then Fitzhugh's, she could never remember hearing a child's laughter echo on the walls of Bodiam Castle! Fenton had never laughed.

"'Tis my daughter, Belle," Brandon's voice broke into Kat's thoughts. "I know I owe you an explanation." He seated her on the stone bench.

Kat folded her hands to keep them from shaking. She forced her lips to part in a small stiff smile. "Were you planning to tell me about your children before or after the honeymoon?"

Brandon studied her face with an enigmatic gaze for a moment before answering. "I hadn't decided when to tell you about Belle and Francis. At first, when I pretended to be Stafford, just remembering who I was supposed to be took all my thought. Then, when we discovered each other, I fear I turned coward. I didn't want to spoil our time together by telling you about my children. I was afraid that you would not take the news kindly. I still have that fear."

Kat clenched her hands tightly within the folds of her skirt. "Because that would bring your other...women into our life?"

Brandon's gaze never left her face. "Aye. I make no apologies, except to say that I was young. Flattery turned my head, and shut out my better sense."

"Your mother told me about Francis." As Brandon sat down next to her, Kat heard him release his breath. She continued, "He is charming, like his father—either of them. I am glad to welcome the boy into my house."

Lifting her hand, Brandon pressed it to his lips.

Kat continued. "Your mother also said that *you* must tell me about Belle." She regarded him with a speculative look.

He sighed. "Belle's mother was a girl from Calais. Her father provided wine to the tent village where our Henry and King Francis strove to outglitter each other. Yvette accompanied her father on his daily rounds. Within days, she became a common gamester to the whole camp." Brandon arched one brow. "Do you understand?"

An unwelcome blush crept into Kat's cheeks. "Aye, she was a whore," she said quietly.

"Not exactly." He gave a bitter laugh. "Yvette did not charge for her favors. She gave them away. And I took them often. I think back on it now, and wonder how I could have been so foolish."

"Oh?" It cheered Kat to think he felt contrition.

"I could have caught the pox," he responded.

"Oh." She sighed.

Catching her chin between his thumb and forefinger, he turned her face to look at him. "I loved Yvette with my body, but not with my heart. Do you believe me?"

His blue gaze clung to her, watching for her reaction. Kat's lower lip quivered. She wanted to trust him. "How did you find out about Belle?" she asked.

He stroked her lip with his thumb, sending little flames

licking through her. "At the end of two weeks of revelry, we returned to England, and I promptly forgot all about Yvette. You see, there was Lady Olivia Bardolph—my mother told you about her?"

"Aye." So there was more to that story. Kat's heart grew heavy.

"She made fools out of Guy and me—aye, and Jack Stafford, too. If you will forgive me for saying so, that woman was an easy glove, and she didn't care who tried her on, so long as he was young, handsome and amusing."

The blood began to pound in Kat's temples, but she refused to acknowledge how much Brandon's words had shocked her.

"Olivia was finished with me long before she started to show with Francis. A year and a half later, two nuns arrived at Henry's court. We were at Greenwich at the time. 'Tis a day I will never forget."

Kat thought she detected a hint of embarrassment in his tone.

"The nuns carried a little girl with them, and they asked for me. You can imagine the jests and quips that bounced off the walls of Greenwich. A bastard had come seeking its father in the arms of the church—literally! Ha! It seems that, when Yvette's family discovered she was with child, they sent her to a convent near Rheims, where she bore the little girl. As soon as Yvette had recovered from childbirth, she left."

Brandon's eyes darkened into a wintry blue at the remembrance. "She abandoned her daughter without a backward glance. She had told the nuns my name as the father, and that I was one of King Henry's courtiers. The nuns kept the child. They named her LaBelle, the beautiful one. When some of their order chanced to make a journey to London, the mother superior sent Belle with them to find me. After all, I was the son of a wealthy man and could care for her."

Kat cleared her tight throat. "You knew the child was yours?"

Brandon nodded. "From the moment I first beheld her. You have just met my family, but I am sure you have already noticed how alike we are in face and feature."

"Aye," Kat replied, remembering how much Francis looked like Brandon.

"And the strangest thing was, when I saw Belle, I loved her immediately." He shook his head with amazement. "I had not expected fatherhood would so ensnare me. I took Belle home to Wolf Hall. 'Twas a bit difficult to explain things to my mother." He paused, then smiled at Kat. "But I think that was nothing compared to explaining it all over again to you. In truth, I feel like a schoolboy caught with a wench and his hose around his ankles." He gave her a wobbly grin.

Kat squeezed his hand. "Go on, my love."

Brandon relaxed at her touch. "Mother was delighted to take Belle under her wing. She said she had nothing but men and boys to bring up, and she was glad of a little girl to spoil. And spoil her, she has. My daughter rides rough-shod over us all. I fear you will have your hands full, if you will accept her."

Kat nodded. "She is yours. Of course, I accept her."

Brandon smothered her last words with his kiss, his lips warm and sweet on hers. Though they had loved the night before, the events of the morning made the time seem like forever ago. When he drew away, her lips savored the imprint of his tenderness.

"Thank you, Kat, though I warn you'll be taking on a little hellion." He pressed another kiss into the palm of her hand.

A shiver of pleasure rippled through her. "I am glad of your children, Brandon." She looked down at his hand holding hers. How large and strong it was, yet how gentle! She took a deep breath. Now was the time to tell him that she may not be able to give him a child of their own. She gazed into his dark blue eyes.

"Brandon, I—"

Stopping further talk, he kissed her with a fierceness that took her breath away. When their lips met, Kat felt buffeted by the tempest of their passion for each other. She clung to Brandon as if, in letting go, she would be separated from him forever. Drinking in his fever, she returned it in full measure. The time and the place spun out of her consciousness. Only Brandon mattered now.

"Papa!" A little girl's voice shattered the moment, bringing the world to a standstill. "Papa, what are you doing to that woman?"

Chapter Eighteen

Breaking off his kiss, Brandon spun around. Belle, her hands planted firmly on her little hips, glared at the pair. Kat covered her mouth with her hand, while her green eyes twinkled with amusement. A rush of heat suffused Brandon's face.

"Papa?" Belle caught his displeasure. Nevertheless she jutted out her little chin and stared back at him.

Mark and the nursemaid appeared around the corner of the high yew hedge.

"My lord, my lady, forgive us!" Mark's words tumbled out like a spring torrent. "One minute she was with us, and the next—"

Belle wheeled on the flustered squire. "Ha!" She snapped her fingers. "You were too busy telling Polly all manner of lies. 'Tis *you* who should seek my forgiveness, Mark. I could have shot you both with an arrow before you realized that something was amiss!"

Brandon managed to find his voice. "Belle! Enough! First, there will be no more talk of shooting arrows at people. There has been enough of that today for a year of Sundays."

Belle's eyes, blue as cornflowers, wavered a little. "Aye, Papa. I didn't really mean that I would shoot Mark and Polly, only that they weren't paying any attention to me.'' She stuck out her lower lip.

Brandon swallowed his discomfort. Belle's behavior was a very poor introduction to her new mother. What would Kat think of his child's bad manners? ''Belle, you know you should not have run off from Polly. At the moment, you are a guest here. Please remember that.'' Turning to Kat, Brandon took her hand in his. She squeezed his fingers, which gave him a little reassurance. At least, Kat hadn't stomped off at the first taste of Belle's sour words. ''Katherine, may I present my daughter, LaBelle Maria Cavendish?''

Kat bestowed a warm smile on the child. ''What a beautiful name! I am very pleased to meet you, Belle.''

Belle stared at Kat as if the lady were an exotic creature come from the Americas. Brandon had the urge to shake his daughter. How could Belle embarrass him in this manner? Usually she was such a charming, loving child.

He plunged on with the ritual of introductions. ''Belle, this is Lady Katherine Fitzhugh.''

Belle wrinkled her button nose. Catching her father's eye, she bobbed a small curtsy. Brandon relaxed a little.

''I am honored,'' Belle mumbled, looking at her shoes.

Brandon decided to ignore her misbehavior for the moment. First impressions were so important. He really wanted Kat and Belle to become friends. Kat squeezed his hand again before she let go. When he glanced at her, he saw a glimmer of understanding in her eyes.

Kat bent down to the little girl. ''Welcome to Bodiam Castle, Belle. I hope you like it here.''

Belle rubbed the side of her nose, then shot her father a quick glance. ''The moat stinks. It smells like something died in it,'' she remarked. A spark of challenge lit up her eye.

Brandon curled his fingers into a fist. By the rood, what had gotten into her? ''Belle!'' he growled.

Kat touched his sleeve, then returned her attention to his daughter. The little minx looked extremely pleased with herself.

"Aye, you have cleverly discovered our problem," Kat remarked smoothly. "And, I wonder, can you suggest a solution?"

Belle rubbed her nose again. Brandon's mouth twitched. Clearly Belle had not expected Kat to take her insult so calmly. He could only imagine how some of the other ladies of the court might have reacted when faced with his offspring. Thank the Fates King Henry had betrothed him to Kat!

"My papa can take care of it," Belle replied, fixing him with a pointed look. "Papa knows everything."

Brandon groaned inwardly.

Kat's copper brows swept up. "Does he? I am very glad you told me of that, Belle. Brandon, I leave the moat, and its odors, in your capable hands."

Brandon glared at both of them. At the moment, he had a lot more on his mind than Kat's green-slimed cesspool. Now, thanks to the prattling of a nine-year-old vixen, he faced a very unpleasant task in the near future.

He bared his teeth in a semblance of a smile. "'Twill be a pleasure, ladies. Kat, I beg your leave to speak to my daughter in private?"

The twinkle in her eyes increased in merriment, though she inclined her head gravely. "I must attend to our dinner. 'Twill be served soon. I look forward to seeing you again, Belle." With that, Kat retired from the garden.

Sweeping up Belle in his arms, Brandon carried her to the other side of the sundial, away from Mark and Polly. No matter. Polly had ears only for whatever drivel Mark told her, and his squire had eyes only for Polly, whom he had not seen in several months.

Once out of earshot, Brandon put Belle back on her feet, then he hunkered down to her level so that he could look her directly in the eye. "How now, Mistress Lack-manners? What is all this about?"

"What?" Belle retorted, attempting to play the innocent.

"Do not tread so lightly upon my patience. You know you were impolite to Lady Katherine, and she is to be your stepmother anon."

Belle made a face. "Oh, Papa, do you *have* to marry her?"

Brandon prayed for fortitude. "The king commands it. Your grandpapa desires it. And, understand this, Belle, *I wish it.*" He said the last three words very slowly, so that she could not misunderstand him.

Her lower lip quivered. "Will you go away with her, and I'll never see you again?"

He drew his child closer to him. "Nay, we will all live together."

Her light brows knotted together into a tight bump. "Here? In this stinky place?"

"You have offered my services to clean the moat. Once that is done, 'twill smell as sweet as May blossoms."

Belle put his arms around his neck. "Papa, the lady does not like me," she whispered, as if imparting a great secret.

Brandon set her on his knee. "Lady Katherine knows all about you, Belle, and she still said to me that she wants you to be a daughter to her." God in heaven, he hoped that was true!

"All?" gasped Belle. "Even about Grandpapa's spectacles down the well?"

Brandon made a mental note to speak to his mother concerning the whereabouts of Sir Thomas's hated reading glasses. "Everything." He gave her a very serious look. "Methinks that 'tis *you* who does not like my Lady Katherine."

Belle only shrugged, but Brandon knew he had hit the core of the problem.

"This day has been an eventful one for all of us, Belle. Francis suffers a grievous injury, and you have found yourself in a strange house." He smoothed her hair in the way he knew she loved. "I have much on my mind, including the moat, and I need your help and understanding."

"Aye," she replied, though she didn't look at him.

"Good. I shall hold you to your word of honor, Belle." He put her down, then stood. "One more thing, sweetling."

"Aye, Papa?" She looked up at him with the face of a cherub.

"There will be no toads, or any other foul creatures, put into Lady Katherine's bed. Remember this well, for I share her bed."

Belle sighed. "Oh, Papa. Not just one—for good sport?"

"Not even a tiny spider, or 'twill be no sport at all for you." He gave her his best imitation of his own father's stern look. "Mark my words, LaBelle."

She appeared to consider what he had said, then asked, "Does Lady Katherine serve tansy cake at dinner?"

"You will have to ask her," he replied, caught off guard by her shift of subject. "Now, away with you, and wash your hands. 'Tis time we eat. And, mind you, don't toss the dogs any bones until dinner is over."

As Belle skipped over the crushed shells of the path back to Mark and Polly, Brandon wondered if he was really cut out to be a father. How was he going to handle Belle after his mother and Celeste had returned to Northumberland?

The day wore on. Both dinner and supper came and went. Brandon grew more uneasy over the long absence of his father and the other men, who had spent the whole day searching for his attacker. Surely no harm had come to any of them, or he would have heard by now. Leaving

Kat to entertain his family, Brandon climbed to the northern battlements. He stared into the darkening woodlands as the long evening twilight turned the shadows into purple specters.

Pacing along the wall walk, he willed the host of riders to burst out from the covering of the trees. Brandon had never been the most patient member of his family. Unlike Guy, who thought things through, Brandon plunged into the unknown with a cheerful grin on his face. Action, not waiting, was his bent. Brandon smote the stone of the parapet with his fist.

Vengeance upon you, Scantling! Barbarous villain! I will have you in my tender mercies for seven days before you die.

Brandon cursed under his breath. What was he but a sluggard, skulking behind a curtain wall, while his family thrust themselves into danger on his behalf? He possessed no more valor than a tamed duck, waddling toward the roasting spit. He had half a mind to saddle Windchaser and go looking for them. The more Brandon paced, the better he liked that idea. As the moon made her first appearance in the pale evening sky, he could stand it no longer. He dashed down the spiral stairs to the courtyard.

Just as he reached the stables, he heard the clatter of many hooves over the causeway bridge. Guy, then Jack, drew up by the stable door.

"What news?" Brandon held Moonglow's head while Guy dismounted. "Did you find the cur?"

"Nay!" Guy threw his gloves onto the cobbled stones. "The knave is as slippery as an eel. There was not a briar nor bramble, that we did not look under or trod down."

Jack patted Thunder's nose before leading him back to his stall. "We thought we had him several times, but the trail proved false. We found his lair—empty. Methinks he has taken poor Wormsley and gone into deeper hiding."

"Or left the shire altogether," Guy suggested. He pulled

off his heavy saddle from the large gray horse's steaming back. One of the grooms relieved him of the load.

Brandon shook his head. "Methinks not. Scantling has no other resources to fall back upon. He has cast his dice upon this board. Methinks he will hazard his very life as the stakes. Nay, he lurks around Bodiam still."

Guy stretched, cracking his joints. "I am for a hot bath and food, brother. Tomorrow, we will—"

Sir Thomas rode up. He swung his leg over the pommel by way of dismounting, then he tossed his reins to one of the men-at-arms who accompanied him.

"No villain, my boy, but good hunting all the same." Brandon's father beamed with pride. "Shot a buck for your lady on the way back. Caught him in the gloaming, when the creature thought 'twas dark enough to come out and take a drink. Two arrows—straight and true. Fine hunting!" He slapped Brandon on the back. "Good woods here. Full of game." He grew more serious. "We'll find that villainous knave in good time, my son. I swear it. How does the boy?"

"Well enough. He sleeps." Brandon bit back his disappointment. Tomorrow, he vowed, he would take to the forest and find the snake himself.

"Good! Good!" Sir Thomas pulled Brandon along as he walked toward the entry stairs. "Now introduce me to this new lady of yours. How does she look? A good breeder?"

Brandon cast a quick glance to heaven, begging for another pound of patience. "You will like my Lady Katherine, Father. She is everything I have ever wanted in a wife."

Sir Thomas gave him a hard stare. "When did you ever want a wife, much less her qualities? Come, show me this wonder-worker! Do you think she'll like the buck?"

Brandon hid his grin. "She will be most grateful for it, methinks. The king comes to the wedding—or so we have been told—and brings some of the court. Lady Katherine loses sleep over the prospect of feeding them.''

His father's brows shot up. ''The king, you say?''

''Disguised.''

Sir Thomas nodded. ''Naturally. Who does Great Harry portray this time?''

Brandon smiled even more, despite himself. ''Robin Hood, with all the merry men of his band.''

''Zounds! 'Twill be a fine excuse for a hunt. A real hunt in proper style!'' Sir Thomas's eyes snapped at the prospect.

''Not until we can rid the forest of its man-killing beast, Father,'' Brandon said.

''And we shall! We shall! My word upon it! Now, my boy, what sort of table does this wench of yours set? I'm near famished!'' So saying, Sir Thomas pushed Brandon up the stairs ahead of him.

In the late evening, Francis's temperature began to climb. Sondra applied another poultice of herb twopence, Solomon's seal and narcissus root to the wound, then gave the boy an infusion of willow bark in hot water for the fever. Despite her medications, the boy's sleep grew more fitful during the darkest hours of the night.

For propriety's sake, now that Brandon's family was under her roof, Kat returned to the bed she shared with Miranda. Her cousin accepted her return without question or even the raise of an eyebrow. Kat lay wide awake, missing the warmth she had found in Brandon's arms. As the hours advanced and no sleep came to her, Kat got up and pulled on her dressing robe. If she couldn't sleep, she may as well make herself useful by sitting with Francis. Poor Sondra must be exhausted.

Slipping out of the room, Kat moved like a ghostly spirit down the hall. As she put her hand to the latch of the sickroom door, she heard voices across the way, where

Brandon's parents were lodged. While Lady Alicia spoke in muffled tones, Sir Thomas's voice came clearly through the thick panels of the oaken door.

"Aye, the lady is pleasant enough, I warrant you, my love," he said. "But look at her! She must be near eight and twenty! Too old for childbearing. Two husbands in a dozen years, and not one chick to count? What could the king have been thinking when he matched Brandon to her? I made my desire for an heir plain enough."

A deep shudder of humiliation ran through Kat as she listened to her own fears spoken aloud. Her face grew hot with embarrassment.

Lady Alicia murmured something, then Sir Thomas continued. "Bah! With Brandon, all women are the same. He's never cared for one more than any other. I could buy him a wife at the fair and 'twould be all the same to him. When the king comes, I will speak with him before our son is tied to Lady Katherine. Henry is of the same mind as I am. He will understand my concern for a grandson to inherit Wolf Hall after I'm gone."

Kat bit back a sob of pure misery. Bad enough that Sir Thomas considered her too old to wed his son, but the thought that Brandon considered her no different than his past light-o'-loves cut to her heart.

Lady Alicia said something else. Sir Thomas replied, "Oh, he'll get over her soon enough. As soon as he is back at court, there will be another woman in his life the next week. And she had better be younger, and a breeder."

Kat's embarrassment melted into a simmering anger. What did Brandon's father think she was—a broodmare? How dare he discuss her in such a casual fashion! Even if it was in private with his wife. Kat tossed her head. She would not give Sir Thomas, or anyone else, the satisfaction of seeing her humiliation. This was what came of listening at keyholes! Lifting the latch, she slid into Francis's chamber.

By the flickering light of the low-burning candle, Kat saw Brandon sitting by his son's bed. The yellow glow made both of their faces look pale and otherworldly. Dark shadows gathered under Brandon's eyes. At the sound of her step, he turned.

"He is very warm," Brandon said, his voice cracked with emotion.

Kat moved to the bedside and put her hand on Francis's forehead. His skin felt dry and hot to the touch. "Sondra told me this often happens with a wound such as his," she murmured, not daring to look directly into Brandon's tortured eyes. He may not harbor deep affection for her or any other woman, but he certainly loved his children. "Have you ever suffered an injury such as this?"

"Aye." His answer came out like a sigh. "I fought alongside the king against the French some years back. The campaigns came to naught, but I received several badges of honor. An arrow wound in the thigh, a sword cut here and there."

"And did you ever have a fever?" she asked, finally looking directly at him.

"Of course, but I was a full-grown man and could shake it off," he growled. "Francis is a sturdy little fellow, but he is so very young." This last came out as almost a sob.

Kat laid her hand lightly on his shoulder. "He has your strength, my lord. He will get better soon."

Brandon drew in a deep, rasping breath. "Are you a soothsayer, who can look into the future?"

"Nay," Kat said, though she wished at this moment that she could. "Go to bed, Brandon. You need your rest. I heard you say you plan to search on the morrow for the villain who did this deed."

He flashed her a look that she could not fathom. "Aye," he answered shortly. "I am the one that whoreson wants. I will flush him from his bolt-hole."

The venom in Brandon's voice chilled her blood. "Take

care of yourself, my lord," she whispered. "I would not have you brought home with an arrow through your heart."

His expression turned grim. "I do not intend for anything to pierce my heart." With that, he rose from the stool. Planting a kiss on her forehead, he left the room.

Pulling her robe closer around her, Kat took Brandon's place by the bed. A basin and a pitcher of water sat on the table near at hand. Kat wrung out a cloth in the cool liquid, then applied it to Francis's forehead. The boy moaned in his sleep.

Kat did not know how long she sat with the child, bathing his fevered brow again and again. Time stood still in the darkness. The click of the latch startled her. Looking around, she saw Belle creep into the room. Dressed only in her long shift and with her bright blond hair unbound, the little girl looked like the spirit of an angel with a golden halo around her head.

"Belle," Kat whispered. "'Tis late. You should be abed."

Belle knelt down beside the boy. She touched his hand. "He's very hot," she whispered.

"Aye," Kat replied, watching the child intently.

"What medicine has he taken?" Belle asked in a remarkably grown-up manner.

"A tisane of holly leaves for fever and a poultice made of yarrow mixed with hog's grease, olive oil and wax for the wound."

The girl nodded as if those had been her prescriptions, as well.

Kat wanted to gather Belle in her arms but restrained herself. The child had shown her a marked coolness this morning in the garden. Kat understood Belle's concerns, but she didn't quite know how to address them. She knew how to care for a sick old man, but not what to do for a heartsick young girl. Having never been around children for any length of time, Kat felt herself at a loss.

"Would you like to stay with me and help me keep Francis cool?" she asked quietly. Belle could sleep late in the morning.

"Aye," the girl answered gravely. On her own initiative, Belle took the cloth off her brother's forehead and dipped it back into the basin. With quick, deft movements, she wrung out the excess water, then reapplied it to Francis's hot skin.

"Your father told me how very brave you were this morning, Belle," Kat told her in soft tones. "He is very proud of you."

"We couldn't let Francis die," she answered, never taking her eyes off his face.

"You must love Francis very much," Kat continued, watching for Belle's reaction.

The child didn't answer immediately, but instead dipped another cloth into the water, wrung it out and put it on Francis's wrist. "My grandmama says it helps if you keep the pulse points cool."

"Aye." Kat wet a third cloth and applied it to Francis's other wrist. "Are you and Francis close?" she asked again.

Belle shrugged one shoulder in a perfect imitation of her Aunt Celeste. "He helps to pass the time at Wolf Hall." Her lower lip trembled. "He is awfully hot, isn't he?"

Kat slipped her arm around Belle. She was gratified that the child did not pull away. "But he is very strong," Kat soothed her. "Just like your father is strong."

A lone tear rolled down Belle's cheek. She dashed it away with the back of her hand. "If he dies, I—I..." She looked up at Kat for the first time. "I have been a torment to him in the past."

Kat brushed a stray lock of hair off Belle's forehead. "Are you sorry for that?"

Belle sniffed. "Aye. He is my best friend." Her blue eyes narrowed. "But don't you dare tell him I said so."

Kat repressed a smile. "Cross my heart and hope to spit," she intoned.

They sat for a while in silence. Belle climbed into Kat's lap as the chill of the wooden floor seeped into her bare feet. Kat hoped this little chink in Belle's defensive armor would widen enough to permit Kat an entry.

Just when Kat thought Belle had drifted to sleep, the child murmured, "My father loved my mother, you know."

Kat's heart turned over, though she managed to maintain an outward calm. "I'm sure he did," she mumbled in reply.

"She died giving birth to me," Belle continued. "Papa loved her so much that he's never wanted to marry again."

Till now. Belle's unspoken thought hung in the still air.

Kat cleared her voice. "Did your papa tell you about your mother?" she asked lightly.

"He cannot bear to speak of her, because he misses her so much. Grandmama told me so."

"Ah, I understand." *In more ways than one.* Of course, Belle would have asked about her mother at some point in her life. What else could a loving grandmother have told her? Yet that persistent little voice in Kat's mind suggested that maybe Brandon had really loved Yvette, since he loved her daughter so very much. By the book! What difference could that make now? 'Twas ten years ago!

In the cold gray of dawn Brandon tiptoed into the sickroom to check on his son, before he rode out to seek Fenton Scantling. He raised his brows with surprise to find Kat with Belle cradled in her arms—and both fast asleep. Taking a blanket from the chest, he gently draped it over his two beloved girls. He wasn't sure how Kat had wrought this miracle, but it cheered him. Touching Francis's brow, he discovered the boy's skin was cool, and he slept curled on his side, a position Brandon knew his son favored. Kissing all three, he left them in the care of the angels and saints.

Count this morning as your last, Scantling.

Chapter Nineteen

Wormsley shivered as he dozed fitfully inside the hollow trunk of a great oak that had died long ago. The dank air reeked of decayed wood and the unwashed bodies of his master and himself. Curling into a tighter ball, Tod cursed his ambition for the thousandth time in the past two weeks, and wished he was back on his father's pig farm. Even pigs had a cozier sty than this hole.

Giving up on sleep, Tod slowly opened his eyes. Through the leafy branches overhead, the sky turned pale in anticipation of the dawn. Another day to be hunted down like an animal.

Finding himself alone, Tod struggled into a standing position and stretched as much as the hollow diameter of the giant oak allowed. His stomach rumbled with hunger.

They had not eaten a real meal since yesterday morning in their tumbledown hut. Afterward, Sir Fenton had gone off with his crossbow. Tod had thought his master only meant to practice at targets. The servant had cleaned up their sparse dwelling, then hauled fresh water from the stream.

Suddenly Tod had heard a hunting horn on the far side of the forest. The sound of it had made his heart almost stop beating. Only two men in the neighborhood would be going a-hunting on this fair morning: Sir John or Sir Brandon. Shutting his eyes, Tod had sent a prayer winging to heaven that 'twas Sir John who chased the deer, and not his master's sworn enemy, Sir Brandon. When the second horn had answered the first, Tod knew that his prayer had been for naught. His quandary lay in what he should do next.

Escape! Sir Fenton may owe him six pounds in back wages, but 'twas a trifle to being apprehended and hung as an accessory to murder. Pulling out his small canvas poke, Tod had stuffed it with his few belongings. He hesitated for a moment. Should he take one of Sir Fenton's gold chains in lieu of payment? What if his master did no harm and returned to the hut to find his servant gone, along with his jewelry? Tod gulped. He knew Lord Scantling would waste no time issuing a hue and cry throughout the shire to catch a thief. Wormsley would be hung for thievery instead of murder. What difference did that make to the hangman's rope? It stretched just as far.

While Tod was pondering these unpleasant alternatives, Fenton had bounded back to the hut.

Catching sight of his servant's bulging pack, Scantling panted, "Good thinking, for once, you slug! Follow me, if you value your hide!"

With that, Fenton had snatched up the poke, then dashed out the door. Panicked, Tod had left a large loaf of day-old bread on the table and had followed his master into the woods again. In the distance, he heard the crashing of underbrush and the shouting of dozens of men.

God in heaven! He's killed Sir Brandon! I am doomed!

With a growing despair in his heart, Tod had realized that his only slim hope of escaping with his life now lay within the twisted mind of his master. Without asking what had happened or where they were going, Tod had followed blindly after Fenton. Like a weasel, Scantling wove in and out through the tangles of the woodland floor. Thorns and sharp branches tore Tod's clothing and gashed many scratches in his face and hands. On they plunged, until Fenton came to a huge grandfather oak. From the base to top, it rose well over a hundred feet, with a trunk between four and five feet wide. The oak had been a youngster when William the Conqueror came to claim England for his own.

"Up!" Scantling had barked.

Like one of the monkeys that entertained the king with their antics, Scantling had hoisted himself into a smaller tree that grew next to the venerable giant.

He has gone stark, staring mad! They will find us in no time, sitting in a tree like a pair of brainless squirrels. Regretting the day he had ever taken employment with Sir Fenton Scantling, Tod hitched the pack more securely around his shoulder, then frantically climbed after his master.

When Scantling had reached a branch of the oak that was level with the smaller one he stood upon, he leaped to the larger tree. Turning, he signaled to Wormsley. *I hate heights!* Gritting his teeth, Tod crossed from one branch to the other. When he looked up, Scantling had completely vanished.

"My…my lord?" Tod called softly. The sounds of the hunting party had drawn closer.

"Down here, you worm!"

From the center crotch of the great tree, Tod saw Fenton wave his hand. Slipping over the branch to that point, Tod found himself staring down into a yawning cavity. The entire center of the oak was completely hollow.

"Get in, you dolt-head, or they will spy you and find me!" Grabbing Tod by the ankle, Scantling had pulled him down. The descent was both terrifying and painful.

A thick pile of dead leaves lined the bottom of the hole. Even though both men were spare in form, it was a tight squeeze. Neither could sit at the same time. Scantling had chuckled as Tod looked around their wooden prison.

"A clever badger hole, eh?" he whispered.

Tod pinched his nose to hold back the sneeze he felt building up from the dust that swirled around them. "How did you know of this place?" he asked.

Scantling chuckled again. "'Tis been my secret hidey-hole since I was a lad. My Uncle Edward liked to beat me for no reason at all. I would escape to the forest as often as I could." Scantling stroked the walls of the hollow tree with tender pride. "'Twas once a bear's nest, methinks. Over the years I improved upon its size and appoint-ments." He pointed to a small hole at eye level through which the dappled sun shone. "There's a lookout on each side." He yawned, then snapped his teeth like a cornered dog. "Now we wait."

The wait had terrified Wormsley to near-hysteria. Out-side, they had heard the men and horses pass by, then double back again. At one point, a shout almost directly outside nearly caused Tod to wet his hose. One of the men had found a strip of cloth snagged on a branch. A foot away from Tod's face, Scantling had glowered at him, then pointed to a tear in Tod's sleeve. Tod didn't dare to men-tion the many rents and tears in Scantling's own fine cloth-ing.

All through the interminable afternoon and long evening twilight, Tod and his master waited inside the trunk of the tree, as the search party crashed hither and yon around them. Though numb with terror, Tod admired the tenacity of the hunters. At one point, Scantling had whispered, "I don't see why they are making such a fuss. I missed Cav-endish altogether and hit only a boy."

Tod didn't dare ask for clarification. His teeth chattered.

Blessed darkness finally descended. The horsemen rode away, and night sounds filled the forest. Finally Scantling had allowed them to climb out and relieve themselves. Tod could barely move his cramped limbs and had nearly fallen from the branches on the way to the ground.

The forest was pitch-dark. Putting his lips very close to Tod's ear, Scantling had whispered, "Do not think of running away. The night creatures are about and would tear you to pieces in a minute." At close quarters, Scantling's grin had been feral. "And if Cavendish has posted a guard, you would swing from a rope before daybreak." He gripped Tod by the collar. "You are as deep in blood as I. Do not forget it."

Those had been the last words Scantling had spoken to Tod. After a short interval outside in the clean, cool air, his master had pushed him back up into the branches, then down into the hole. Now another morning had dawned, cold, gray and heavy with rain. Another morning in hell.

As Scantling had predicted, the men returned, this time with dogs. Every so often one of the beasts sniffed and whined around their tree. One even made water practically next to Tod's ear. The strong scent of urine filled his nostrils.

"Scantling!" The forest echoed with Brandon Cavendish's bellow. "I know you are still here. I will find you, pernicious bloodsucker of children! I swear it upon my sword. Say your paternosters now, for when I see you, 'twill be your last moment on this earth. Hear me, Scantling? Hell's mouth gapes wide, waiting for me to cram you into its maw! A plague upon you!"

Tod shivered at the cold fury in Sir Brandon's voice. Scantling only smiled, then made a rude gesture. They heard Cavendish's great horse move farther away.

Later it began to rain. At first, 'twas only a pitter-patter through the thick leafy roof above them. Tod welcomed the wetness and held his mouth open to catch its soothing drops on his parched tongue. Then the rain increased, sending a steady torrent down into their miserable hole. Even then, over the wind in the branches and the lash of the raindrops, Tod still heard the men and dogs out hunting for them. *Go home, my lord, and warm yourself by your fire, and take comfort that we have none.*

What manner of injury had his master done that kept Lord Cavendish out in this miserable weather? Tod dared not ask. The gleam in Scantling's eyes had taken on a frenzied fire.

The gray of the afternoon changed into the gloom of the evening as the downpour continued. Wet, chilled to the bone, starving and utterly miserable, Tod decided that he would willingly cast himself upon Cavendish's mercy if he were given half the chance.

"How…how long will we stay here, my lord?" he ventured to ask as the sky turned blacker. They were the first words he had spoken in hours.

"Until I say so." Scantling's answer slithered back.

Moistening his lips, Tod summoned up as much courage as he could. "They have gone for the night, my lord. We could leave now, and be well out of the shire by first light."

"Nay!"

"But, my lord, we shall die in here anon."

"*You* have that distinct possibility." Scantling caressed his threat in a singsong tone. "But I will have what I came for. Come day after tomorrow, I will kill the bridegroom in his wedding clothes. And none will be the wiser."

Icy fear gripped Tod. God's teeth! He was caged with a madman—one who had already prophesied his death! Leaning his head against the rough wall of the tree, Tod tried to think. He recognized the first fingers of panic clawing at his soul. Gritting his teeth, he prayed as he had never done inside a church.

Something was amiss with Kat, Brandon surmised, but what it might be, only she and the good Lord knew. She had presided over the supper table in her usual charming way, but they had barely exchanged words, even though they had shared their cup and trencher. After the board had been cleared and the trestles put away, he planned to speak with her alone. Instead, his father demanded a private conference. Once they had withdrawn into the alcove, Sir Thomas lost no time saying what was on his mind.

"When the king comes day after tomorrow, I will ask him to dissolve your betrothal," he announced.

Brandon's stomach tightened as if a fist had been jabbed in his gut. "But why, Father? 'Twas *you* who desired me to marry, and now, so do I. Has the Lady Katherine shown you any discourtesies?"

His father waved away the question. "Nay, she is warmly hospitable. The fact of the matter is that she is too old for you."

Brandon could barely believe his ears. He took a deep breath to steady his voice. "Kat is a perfect age for me. She is no giggling girl, fresh out from behind her mother's petticoats. She has wit, charm and an intelligence that I find most refreshing."

Hearing himself say these words, Brandon realized how true they were. For the first time in his life, he wanted to get married and he wanted Kat to be his wife. He loved her with all his heart.

Sir Thomas shook his head. "She is too old to bear you an heir! I will seek to dissolve this match, then ask for a younger wench instead. You will see. By this time next year, you could be well on your way to becoming a father." He beamed at the idea.

Brandon gritted his teeth. "By this time next year, I could be dead of the plague. And, lest it has slipped your memory, I am already a father—twice over, in fact."

The older man set his face into a stubborn mask. Brandon had often seen this expression during his formative years. He knew that once his father had gotten an idea in his head, nothing short of a direct bolt of lightning could change it. "As much as I love them, both Belle and Francis were born on the wrong side of the blanket. They do not carry our family name.''

Brandon gripped his hands behind his back. He felt like a stripling again. ''When Francis is old enough to understand, I intend to recognize him as my son and heir. He will carry my name then.''

Sir Thomas knotted his eyebrows. ''The boy is still a bastard.''

Anger licked at Brandon's self-control. ''If any man, other than you, Father, called Francis a bastard to my face, he would be lying cold on the floor now. I love the boy as my life. He is my heir. It does not matter to me if Kat cannot give me another.''

''It matters to me—and to a court of law,'' his father growled.

''Then leave Wolf Hall to Guy's children. He and Celeste seem most adept at producing offspring. Wolf Hall will be overrun with little Cavendishes for the next decade.'' Brandon's voice sank into a whisper. ''But understand this, Father, I will have Katherine as my wife, and I will marry her in two days, as God as my witness.''

Sir Thomas returned his son's glower. ''And, in two days, I will speak to the king.''

Afraid he might do something regrettably rash, Brandon turned on his heel and strode out of the alcove. He encountered Kat just outside. Her face had gone quite pale. When he started to speak to her, she lowered her eyes and fled up the stairs. God's nightshirt! She must have overheard his father's words, though Brandon had striven to keep their voices low. Had Sir Thomas already said something to her earlier today? Was that why she had hardly glanced at him during dinner?

Brandon started up the stairs, but he heard her slam the door to her chamber. She drove the bolt home. Perdition take the woman! He must talk with her before the canker of his father's threat festered within her. He bounded up the rest of the stairs, then knocked on her door.

"Kat? I pray you, open up. I must speak with you." He had to tell her how much he loved her.

"Not tonight, Brandon," she answered quietly, just on the other side of the latch. "I am tired, and have a headache."

"Nay, Kat, you enjoy uncommonly good health. Open to me."

She gasped softly, then asked, "Will you break the door down as my second husband sometimes did, Brandon? Is this what I have to look forward to? Another loveless marriage?"

Brandon pounded the door. "Kat! Open this door so that we may discuss this matter like two reasonable adults. Please?"

She did not answer him. Brandon pressed his ear against the wood and thought he detected a quiet sob or two. "Kat?" He spoke in a gentler tone. "My father is as set in his ways as I am set in mine. I fear I inherited his stubborn streak. Understand this, my lady. Come Midsummer's Day, I *will* marry you!"

Her answering laugh held a bitter note. "To defy your father? To prove you are a man of your word? I do not care to be a pawn in your family disputes. I bid you a good-night, my lord."

He heard her move away from the door. He considered hurling himself through it, but her earlier accusation stopped him. He would rather be racked in two than be the bully Fitzhugh had been to her.

From down the corridor, Francis called to him. Curbing his frustration, Brandon answered his son. He found the boy propped up in bed, surrounded by pots of flowers and platters of half-eaten sweetmeats. When his father appeared in the doorway, Francis laid aside a cup-and-ball game.

"How now, my boy. What's amiss?" Brandon seated himself on the stool. "And are you supposed to be eating such rich food so soon?" Picking up a sugar comfit, he popped it into his mouth. Delicious!

Francis eyed the bounty of sweets around him. "Some of the maids have been bringing them to me, my lord. First, Pansy came with a plate of marchpane. Then Rose brought the candied fruit. This evening, Violet presented me with the comfits. How can I say nay to them? They are all very sweet."

Brandon regarded his son. "The girls or the food?"

Francis grinned. Jesu, the boy looked a lot like Guy when he did that! It occurred to Brandon that he had not seen Francis smile very often in the past. His page always seemed so earnest. Bodiam obviously agreed with him.

"Both, my lord," he replied.

Brandon had difficulty swallowing his second comfit. Zounds! The boy was only nine! Too young for the sap to rise just yet, wasn't it? On the other hand, perhaps the time had come for a certain man-to-man talk with the lad, before the boy got himself into real trouble.

"Are you having a fight with Lady Kat?" Francis asked.

"Not exactly. She has overheard my father's opinions of our marriage, and it has distressed her." Brandon pursed his lips at the idea of Kat crying herself to sleep.

"Sir Thomas does not want you to get married, my lord?" The boy stared at him openmouthed. "'Twas all he spoke of, for over a month. He couldn't wait to get here. He does not find Lady Kat pleasing?"

Brandon drew in a breath. How could he explain the desire for an heir to his own unknowing heir, without jeopardizing the boy's later opinion of the Cavendish family? How did such a simple thing as a country wedding get so complicated?

"No one could know the lady and not love her," Brandon told him. "My father feels that the lady is far too good for me."

"Is she?" Francis asked with alarming frankness.

Brandon thought about it for a minute. "Aye, methinks she is."

"Then you must do something to prove yourself worthy of her, my lord," Francis advised in a very matter-of-fact tone.

Since when had the boy become so skilled at understanding women? Brandon was several decades older and years more experienced than his son, and he had yet to fathom the workings of a woman's mind—Kat's, least of all.

"Aye," Brandon agreed, reaching for a third comfit.

But what? For two days, he had been unsuccessfully hunting for Scantling. Perchance Jack and Guy were right, and the knave had fled the environs. What else could Brandon do between now and his wedding day to prove his love and devotion to Kat, and to erase the sting of his father's heedless tongue?

Kat lay awake half the night, pondering what she should do. In the end, she fell into a dreamless sleep. The sun was halfway up in the sky when Laurel awakened her the next morning. Outside, whoops and shouts rang in the clear summer air.

"What's amiss?" Kat asked, pulling on her robe. "Pray, do not tell me that the king has come a day early?" Only half the meats had been prepared, and today was to be given over to baking. She was nowhere near ready to feed the renowned royal appetite.

Laurel rolled her eyes merrily. "Oh, no, my lady! You will never guess in two months of Sundays! 'Tis a wonder!"

More yelling outside drew Kat's attention. Just then, Miranda burst through the door. A becoming flush set off her complexion. "Leaping trout, Kat! You are a slugabed! Hurry! Get dressed! You must come and see!"

"What is it?" Kat splashed water into her face from the basin.

Laurel dropped several petticoats at once over her mistress's head. "All the household is abuzz. Even Montjoy looks—happy. Young Master Francis insisted that he be carried out to watch. Master Jess carried him down, Lady Kat, so there is no fear that the boy has overexerted himself. He's set up on a rug under the willow by the causeway, and holding court with six or seven of the girls." The maid tied all the petticoat laces together into one bow.

Miranda pushed Kat into a chair, than knelt and drew on her stockings while Laurel brushed her mistress's hair. "They've been walking around since daybreak and looking ever so serious. You would think they were planning the conquest of France!

"*What* are they doing, and *who* is doing it? By all the saints! What is happening in my own house?"

Both women giggled at once. Then Miranda answered. "Sir Brandon has organized his brother, my Jack, and the three squires. They are going to clean the moat."

"Have they lost their minds?"

Chapter Twenty

A festival air enveloped Bodiam Castle. Colorful banners already flew at the four corner towers in preparation for the wedding on the following day. Mouthwatering smells of fresh-baked breads and pastries wafted from the kitchens. Under the trees on the far side of the causeway, Montjoy directed the placement of trestle tables for the wedding feast. By the time Kat arrived on the scene, practically every living soul in the castle had gathered on the greensward, as if waiting for a masque to begin. Only the cooks and maids in the kitchens, and Sir Thomas, who had gone off hunting at first light, were missing.

Under a spreading oak tree, Lady Celeste and Lady Alicia sat amid a bevy of cushions. Both ladies worked on their embroidery hoops while they surveyed the noisy, lively scene. Maids, stable boys, grooms, potboys, men-at-arms, all the knights' retinues and most of the castle dogs ran up and down along the banks of the stinking green moat, shouting, laughing, barking and generally tumbling about. Polly, Belle's nursemaid, shadowed the little girl, who frolicked with her skirts hiked up to her knees. Montjoy appeared to be thriving amid the happy chaos. His step had a certain spring to it; his voice rang with a firmer tone as he ordered about every servant within range.

"Hey ho, Kat!" Celeste waved, beckoning to the mistress of the house. "Pray join us and enjoy the spectacle of your lord and mine getting foully wet." Her dark eyes flashed pure merriment.

Kat sank down onto one of the cushions. Columbine handed her a mug of morning ale and a cold piece of pigeon pie left over from last night's supper.

"Why didn't someone tell me what they were going to do? They can't seriously consider jumping into that water! 'Tis unhealthy. Even Sondra says so."

Lady Alicia threaded her needle. "Aye, but Brandon has set his mind to it. And 'tis a beautiful day for a swim."

Kat could only gape at her betrothed's mother. Just then, Brandon, Guy, Jack and their three squires came around the far corner of the moat. All of them were dressed in their shabbiest clothing. Brandon waved at Kat. Gathering her skirts, she ran to stop them. 'Twas madness!

She grasped Brandon's arm. "I pray you, my lord, you cannot be serious! The water is foul."

"Aye, so we have noticed, Lady Kat," Guy agreed in good humor.

"After due consideration, we think the problem is a blocked sluice gate." Brandon grinned at her like a schoolboy. "Jack thinks 'tis a dead sheep, but I personally favor a horse carcass."

The rest laughed at his observation.

Kat looked from one to the other of them. "Brandon! You can't send one of the squires down to clear it!" She wrung her hands. "The boy will perish from the vapors alone."

Brandon nodded, though his eyes twinkled. "I agree. 'Tis why I am going down myself."

Kat clasped the rose brooch that had become so much a part of her attire. "Brandon, you can't! 'Twill kill you!"

He stroked her cheek with his knuckle. "I have given

you so little since I came here to woo you, consider this a wedding present."

"Lackwit! I don't *need* an unblocked moat." *Lord help me, but I do need you!* Brandon's eyes turned a dark, fathomless blue.

Jack cleared his throat. "Your pardon, my lady, but you do."

Brandon leaned closer; his breath fanned her cheek. "A kiss for luck?" he whispered.

"I...I, oh, Brandon!" Throwing her arms around his neck, she sought his lips.

He pressed her to him, caressing her mouth more than kissing it. His touch was a delicious sensation that sent swirls of liquid fire down to her toes. How long had it been since she had last savored his kiss? She returned his salute with a fervor that took her by surprise. She tingled to the tips of her fingers.

Guy chuckled behind Brandon. "We burn daylight, big brother. And you should see the surprised look on Mother's face."

Brandon gently withdrew, leaving Kat's mouth burning.

"Remember where we left off, my sweet," Brandon murmured. "Methinks I will be in need of much remedy later today."

"Aye," she gasped, trying to catch her breath. "One boon, I beg of you, Brandon."

He cocked his head.

"Do not drink the water."

"I have no intention of drinking it, sweetheart. But I thank you for your concern. You must give me something sweeter to taste anon." Brandon winked at her, then turned to his companions. "On for England, Great Harry and Saint George, my friends. Into the dreaded moat!"

Whistling, the six strode off with a jaunty swing to their steps. Not content to sit under a tree and watch from a distance, Kat followed them as they made their way along the bank to the near end of the moat, where the fetid water was supposed to flow back into the Rother River. Many of the household crowded after Kat, eager to see the most unusual spectacle of three great knights bathing in their odoriferous moat.

Upon reaching the source of the blockage, Brandon began stripping off his doublet, then his shirt. The other five followed suit. In no time, all six stood bare to the waist. Only their high-waisted hose and codpieces kept them from complete exposure. Around her, Kat heard the squeals and giggles of her entire flock of young, impressionable maids.

"Ooh! Look at his shoulders!"

"Stars! I've never beheld such men as them!"

"I've never seen a man with so little on!"

"Look at his...oh, my!"

Kat glanced over her shoulder at the entranced girls. Appreciation and longing shone in their collective eyes. *By the book, Brandon! You will corrupt all my girls with such a wanton display.* Kat sighed as she admired him. Such a manly display! Though Guy and Jack both possessed fine sets of shoulders and rippling chest muscles, it was Brandon on whom she gazed with a hunger that she could barely mask. How fine he looked as he flexed and stretched! What powerful arms! And how good they felt around her in the dark of the night! She colored at the thought.

Brandon saw Kat watching him. He flashed her another wink, and then jumped into the brackish water. The small flock of swans, who ruled the moat, ruffled their feathers, arched their necks and swam away with an air of outraged dignity.

Belle dashed up and down the bank. "Is the water cold, Papa? Can you touch bottom?"

The slime rolled down Brandon's shoulders as he stood

up. The water level was as high as his chest. "Aye, precious, but 'tis slipperier than an oyster to stand upon."

Making a face at the smell, he worked his way over to the blocked sluice gate. The stench grew worse as he stirred up the water. Most of the assemblage backed farther up the bank. Kat held her nose but stayed where she was.

At the point of the trouble, Brandon paused as he felt around the bottom with his foot. Taking a deep breath, he disappeared under the surface. Kat found herself holding her breath, as well. He seemed to stay under for an awfully long time. Longer than Kat could manage. Perchance he had been overcome by the filthy muck.

"Jack!" She implored, never taking her eyes off the spot where the water thrashed against the sluice.

Jack's splash answered her plea. Miranda materialized at Kat's side. She too held her nose. "I have never seen the like!" she murmured, watching her love with adoration.

Kat gave her a sidelong glance. "They are the greatest fools in England, and if Brandon dies, I will never forgive him for this day!"

Miranda blinked. "'Tis not Jack's fault!"

"I was not speaking of Jack, but Brandon. What is keeping him down there?"

Just as Jack prepared to dive under, Brandon's head, then his shoulders broke the surface. Gray mud slithered off his arms. His beautiful gold hair was plastered with gray mud.

He whooped as he shook the water out of his eyes. "We are both wrong, Jackanapes! 'Tis an ancient cow down there!" He tossed a muddy skull up onto the bank.

The maids squealed louder but did not retreat. Belle squatted down beside the filthy thing to inspect it at closer range.

"Belle! Don't touch that!" Kat called to her.

The child merely regarded her with mild surprise. "'Tis

a great marvel. Francis will be so envious, because I saw it first!'' She sat down next to the loathsome object, though Kat noticed that the child minded her warning.

Brandon slicked back his hair. ''Mark! Pip! Get some ropes, and buckets. There is a lot down here that needs to be cleared.'' Glancing at Kat, Brandon grinned. ''My compliments, Lady Kat! You have provided us with excellent sport this day!''

Before she could tell him to leave the rest of the cow's skeleton alone, Brandon dived again. Jack followed after. With a tremendous shout, Guy jumped into the muck, practically on top of the other two.

'''Tis too bad we cannot lower the water level, so they could work better,'' Miranda observed.

Kat hugged her startled cousin. ''You have hit upon the very idea, Miranda! Oh, what a clever one you are!''

Miranda gave her a lopsided grin. ''I did?''

''Aye! Quickly, we must hurry! Columbine, Laurel, you others, come with me!'' Lifting up her skirts, Kat dashed around to the corner of the moat where Montjoy commanded his small army of potboys.

''Montjoy! We must take the water out of the moat!''

Montjoy slowly raised his thinning brows. ''Of course, my lady,'' he intoned. ''My very thought, indeed. Do you have a magic spell?''

''Buckets!'' Kat gasped, arriving at his side. ''Tubs! Pitchers! Basins! Bowls! Anything that will hold water. We will form two lines of people—one at the sluice where Sir Brandon is working and one at the other end where the river gate is.''

''Very good, my lady,'' replied Montjoy with a puzzled frown.

''Oh, don't you see, Montjoy? 'Twill be a line of brimming buckets from the moat to the river, and then empty ones back again. I should have thought of this a year ago when the problem first became noticeable.''

A beatific smiled wreathed Montjoy's lined face. Kat could not remember when the old man had looked so over-joyed. "An excellent device, my lady!"

With that, Montjoy moved faster than Kat had thought possible. The old steward literally shocked the troops of men, boys and maids into action. With more shouts and yells, everyone dashed off at once—some to fetch the items needed, others to form the lines under Montjoy's direction. Belle, seeing the increased activity around her, left the decayed skull on the grass and promptly joined the bucket line by the sluice.

Kat approached Francis and his little band of young ad-mirers under his willow. "How are you?" she asked.

Rolling his eyes, he answered with a wide grin. "Feel-ing much better, Lady Katherine, though I wish I could help my lord. I am a dull sluggard lying here."

How the boy reminded her of Brandon! Kat resisted the urge to swoop down and give him a big hug and kiss. 'Twould not be proper to shower such familiar attentions upon a mere page, especially not in front of his impres-sionable audience.

Instead, Kat asked, "I wonder if you could organize your company here to bring out food and casks of ale for everyone? 'Twill be a long day's toil, but the sun is shining in a friendly sky, and merry hearts make the work lighter."

Francis inclined his head gravely. "'Twill be an honor to serve you, my lady," he replied.

Kat's lips twitched. "Good, Francis! With Montjoy oth-erwise engaged, you are in charge of our picnic."

"Aye, my lady." He turned his bright blue gaze upon his three admirers. "Now, Pansy, you and Rose here..."

With a grin, Kat left him. It made her heart swell with love to watch him. No wonder Brandon was so proud of the boy! A small dart of pain struck her heart. How she wished she could give Brandon another son like Francis! Or any child for that matter! She pushed away the idea.

She did not care what the king might say tomorrow, when Sir Thomas voiced his displeasure at the match. For today, Brandon was still hers, and she would savor that possession to the fullest, even if her lord currently was covered in slime.

"Oh, la, la, Kat! You are a wonder-worker!" Celeste complimented her, when Kat rejoined the ladies in the comparative quiet under their tree. "I do not think I have seen Guy in such a motley state in all my life! *Quel amusement!*"

Lady Alicia smiled with maternal satisfaction. "My boys have always enjoyed playing in the mud. Indeed, as children, they were happiest when dirtiest."

"Ah! But 'tis the bathing afterward that I think I like better!" Celeste gave a wicked grin. "Oh, la, la! Guy will be in *my* power then!"

Interesting idea! Kat made a mental note to start kettles heating bathwater after the noon dinner break.

Lady Alicia tapped Celeste with her fan. "You are a shameless creature, my dear!" she teased. "And you, a dignified mother!"

"Oui!" Celeste agreed, not looking the least bit ashamed. "How do you think I became a mother in the first place?"

Kat joined in their laughter, but it had a bitter taste in her mouth. More than ever she wanted to become a member of this loving family—a far cry from anything she had ever known. If only Sir Thomas weren't so fixated on an heir! If only Brandon could love her for herself!

Quit sighing for the moon! Make merry today and let tomorrow take care of itself. You still have this night.

Fenton observed Wormsley through slitted eyelids. The slug had become a millstone around his neck. No one knew they were back on Bodiam's lands, unless Wormsley escaped from Fenton and babbled his master's intent.

The churl must disappear permanently. His usefulness was long over. Fenton wrinkled his nose. The boy stank in his foul clothing, and he positively reeked of fear. Fenton had grown quite weary of his whining company. He cast another malevolent glare at the youth, who dozed fitfully within arm's reach. No witnesses to point an accusing finger at Sir Fenton Scantling, Lady Katherine's most loving nephew, when Sir Brandon Cavendish was mysteriously cut down on his wedding day.

Marriage! The very word conjured up a reddish haze before Fenton's eyes. A month ago it had seemed entirely possible to nip this impending disaster in the bud. A poisonous word here and there, a suggestion of foul character whispered in the right ears, and the match would be annulled by the parties involved. Except the biggest party involved in this match was the king, and he was a very determined one. A pox on that tub of royal lard! Fenton ground his teeth.

Tomorrow was the wedding day, and Cavendish's last upon this earth. Fenton idly wondered how the man was passing his few remaining hours. He snickered to himself.

Wormsley yawned. "My lord? You spoke?"

Why not do it now and be done with it?

Wormsley rubbed the sleep from his eyes. "Is it day?" He squinted up toward the hole above them. "Are they out again to look for us? My lord? Are you well?"

Fenton stood. "Aye, Tod, my friend, I have never felt fitter."

The youth pulled himself up to his feet. His knees knocked against Fenton as he did so. Fenton recoiled. 'Twas bad luck to touch a condemned man.

"Can we leave now, my lord? I perish with hunger and thirst."

Fenton slipped the strap of his crossbow over his shoulder. "My very thought indeed."

So saying, he pulled himself out of their hiding place.

Once in the open air, Fenton inhaled deeply, enjoying the freshness of the morning.

"My lord?" Standing at the bottom of the hollow, Wormsley extended his hand to Fenton.

How disgusting the boy looked! Fenton unstrapped his crossbow. From his quiver, he selected a bolt. Taking his time, he slid the arrow into the shaft of the weapon.

Wormsley's eyes grew rounder. "My...my lord? Do you see an enemy?" Tod asked in a strangled voice.

A smile curled Fenton's lips. "Aye, Tod, I do."

The youth swallowed. "Is it Cavendish?" he whispered.

Fenton's smile widened. "Nay, Tod. I am looking at him even as we speak."

Wormsley backed up against the side of the trunk. "But...but you look at m-me, sir," he stammered.

Fenton nodded. "How observant, my lad!" He drew back the bowstring and notched it into place. Lifting the weapon, he sighted it down into the hiding place. "You have my complete attention."

Wormsley dropped to his knees. "M-mean you me, my lord? I...I have d-done you no wrong. You cannot mean to k-kill me, sir!"

A thrilling sensation of supreme power washed over Fenton. 'Twas much better than drinking the best cask of Canary wine. His finger touched the trigger. Wormsley's shaking body filled his sight.

Wormsley buried his face in his arms. "Sweet Jesu, save me."

The idiot presented his entire back to Fenton's arrow.

"I shall see you in hell, Tod!" Fenton squeezed the trigger. The bolt barely had time to sing its death song before it struck home.

Without a whimper, Wormsley crumpled to the ground. A dark stain immediately spread across his back. The dry leaves soaked up the blood. At this close distance, the bolt had probably shot straight through the vermin's body.

Fenton shouldered his bow, then swung to the opposite tree and from there to the ground. Great Jove, it felt good to be able to stand up and move unfettered again. A lovely morning! Humming a little tune to himself, he made his way through the tangled briars. The great oak and its grisly secret were quickly out of sight and mind.

"'Tis clear, my lord!" From his position at the closed river gate, Mark called to Brandon.

Brandon's mud-caked face literally split with his grin. He swept his gaze around the busy scene. For the first time in several hundred years, the silted bottom of the moat lay exposed to the waning rays of the late afternoon sun. The dispossessed swans had been forced to seek comfort on the bank. There, most of them had gone to sleep, tucking their heads under their wings, leaving one cantankerous male on guard. He hissed every time Belle crept close to the flock.

The household servants lay in tired heaps on the greensward, exhausted by their successful labors to drain the watercourse. Several wagons drew up next to the pile of debris: bones, pieces of rusted plate armor, oddments of kitchen pots and utensils, a rotten heap of mud-preserved leaves, broken crockery and lumps of indistinguishable metal. Within the hour, the debris would be trundled away to the castle's refuse pit.

Brandon's grin widened as he spied Kat running toward him. Her hair, like a burnished copper cloud, billowed unbound and free about her face. The hem of her plain green gown was soaked with the muck. Her feet were bare like his. Mud splotches decorated her bodice, her sleeves, and speckled her fair face. All in all, Brandon didn't think he had ever seen her looking more beautiful than she was this minute.

"'Tis done?" she asked breathlessly.

"Give the word, and Mark will open the gate. Then we

shall see if the river will do its part." He chuckled. "On such a grand occasion, there should be music and fireworks."

Kat tossed her head. Her eyes sparkled. "I do not care for the trappings, so long as our labors have not been in vain."

Lifting his head, and cupping his hand around his mouth, Brandon shouted across the moat to Guy. "Is the sluice clear?"

"All clear," his brother shouted back.

The servants stirred and sat up. His mother and sister-in-law got up from the haven of their shade tree and drew closer to watch. Out of the corner of his eye, Brandon saw Jess lift Francis and carry the boy down to the bank.

Behind his back, Brandon crossed his fingers. A childish thing to do perhaps, but he desperately prayed that the thing would work. There was no way of knowing, but to do it.

"Give the word, sweetheart," he said in a low voice to Kat.

"Now?" She clasped her hand over his brooch. Her simple gesture swelled his heart.

"Aye, unless you want to wait for the king to do the honors."

Kat wrinkled her nose. "Nay, 'tis my home, my office." She took out her wrinkled handkerchief, and waved to Mark. "Let the river flow!" she cried with a touch of drama.

Mark put one foot on the top of the wooden frame and planted the other firmly on the bank. Polly had to restrain Belle from rushing to help the muddy squire. Mark took hold of the top of the gate and pulled. At first nothing happened, save that Mark grew very red in the face. Then, with a loud sucking sound, the ooze on the bottom released the embedded timbers. As the gate slowly rose in its frame, the brown waters of the Rother gurgled through.

Brandon expelled the breath he had been holding. By the stars, the thing worked! At his side, Kat laughed and clapped her hands like a young girl.

"Saints be praised, Brandon! 'Tis a miracle!"

The in-rushing waters gathered more speed as they poured through the fully opened gate. The torrent sloshed against the banks as it rushed around the first corner of the castle. From the other side, Brandon heard Guy's victory whoop. The people on that bank cheered and waved their hands.

Kat turned her lovely green eyes fully upon his face. "*You* are the miracle," she whispered. A few tears streaked a clean path through the dirt on her cheeks.

He bent down and kissed her nose. "So are you, my lady."

She blushed under the mud.

Jack joined them, shouting, "A race, Cavendish!" With that, he plunged into the cleanest water of the day.

Mark and Christopher grabbed Pip, Guy's young squire, and tossed him into the moat. They followed with loud splashes and geysers of water.

Guy dashed around the corner. "By my troth, Jack just swam past me!" His eyes grew larger when he saw the squires splashing each other. A broad grin lit his face. Without checking his speed, he lunged for Brandon.

"Your pardon, Lady Katherine," he shouted as he grabbed hold of his older brother.

Brandon put up his hands to protest, but Guy outweighed him. In the next instant, both Cavendishes were once again floundering in the moat, only this time looking a good deal cleaner.

Stable boys, potboys, serving men, guards and one or two of the hapless maids joined in the watery melee.

"Papa, Papa!" Belle's shrill voice sang out over the general noise. "Papa, please! Catch me!" Belle tore away from Polly's grasp. Lifting high her skirts, she flung herself at him.

Brandon caught her in the air, then ducked them both. They surfaced at the bank beside Kat.

"Can she swim?" Kat gasped.

"Like a blessed fish." Francis, still in Jess's arms, gave his sister a wry look. "She looks the very picture of a drowned rat."

Brandon smiled up at his son and Kat beside him. What a beautiful sight they made! What a wonderful day this had been!

Wriggling in his arms, Belle stuck out her tongue at Francis. "Ha! You are just jealous because you have to stay quiet!" Then she squirmed and pointed at the wagons. "Oh, Papa! Stop them! They are taking my cow skull away! You promised I could keep it!"

"I'll get it for you, poppet!" With that, Kat hoisted up her hems and raced across the grass toward the laden wagon.

Watching her run, Brandon expanded his chest with satisfaction. Standing chest deep in a castle moat with his dripping daughter in his arms, his son nearby, and watching the love of his life dash fleet as a deer, Brandon knew he had, at last, found his corner of paradise. He couldn't wait for tomorrow to come.

Montjoy picked his way over the wet bank to the edge of the moat. "My lords," he intoned to the cavorting knights. "Your bathwater is ready in your chambers. I pray you take advantage of it before it turns cold. And, my young Lady Belle, Mistress Polly awaits you with a scrubbing brush. Supper will be served in an hour."

Without waiting for a reply, Montjoy bowed and retired with his dignity intact.

Belle shook the water out of her eyes. "Great Jove!" she fumed. "Just who does he think he is?"

Brandon kissed her on the cheek. "Don't tell anyone, Belle, but Montjoy is the *true* ruler of Bodiam Castle."

Tod's fingers dug into the leaves and rotten wood. He gripped them tightly as he lay facedown, breathing in the mold and dirt. No perfume of Arabia could have smelled as sweet. He still lived!

Taking a deep breath, he pushed himself into a sitting position. The spent arrow fell beside him. His left shoulder felt numb, though he knew it was only a matter of time before the pain would set in.

He closed his eyes and murmured a heartfelt prayer of thanksgiving for his life. Then he looked up.

The sun still lit the sky, though Tod saw by its angle that it was late in the afternoon. Using the side of the trunk to steady himself, he inched his way to a standing position. The opening yawned a few inches above him.

Shaking his head to clear the ringing noise in his ears, Tod reached up to grab the rim of the cavity with his right hand. A wash of fiery pain rolled over him. He leaned against the side for support until the pain subsided.

If I stay in this trap until darkness, I will never see another dawn.

Gritting his teeth, Tod sprang up, grabbed the rim and hauled himself out of his intended grave. He inched along a thick limb, where he rested. The ground shifted and swirled under him. 'Twas a long way down. Tod closed his eyes again.

God in heaven, I hate heights!

"You there!" an imperious voice shouted directly under him. "What the devil do you think you are doing up there?"

Tod gripped the branch, then opened his eyes again.

A horseman shielded his eyes as he looked up at Tod. His steel gray mustache fairly bristled. In one hand, the man held a bow with an arrow notched against the string.

"Did you think you were going to attack me, eh?" The rider took aim.

Tod gulped. "Nay, sir! I pray you, do not shoot!" He raised his good hand, lost his grip and fell out of the tree.

Tod hit the forest floor with a stunning thud. Pain engulfed him. He saw colored stars dancing before his eyes, and a rushing wind filled his ears.

"The devil take it!" The rider bellowed somewhere in the distance. "You've been shot already!"

"Aye," Tod murmured.

Then a sweet, blessed blackness claimed him.

Chapter Twenty-One

"Mmm." Brandon sighed with pleasure as Kat washed the clotted muck out of his hair. Lying back against the side of the wooden tub, he closed his eyes while she massaged his scalp. "By my troth, sweetheart, if I had known how good this felt, I would have rolled in the mud long before this."

Behind him, Kat smiled. The back of his neck lay bare, tempting her to kiss it. Later, she told herself. There was little time for a dalliance. Montjoy would be announcing supper any moment.

"I am glad you are so pleased with the bath, my lord. I wish the same could be said for Belle. It took both Polly and me to get her—and that wretched cow skull—presentable. I am not sure what we would have done if Celeste hadn't intervened." She picked up a nearby pitcher filled with clean hot water. "Bend far over, so I may rinse you."

After the dousing, Brandon squeezed the water out of his hair. "My lady mother assures me 'tis merely a stage. By the time Belle takes to bathing in a civilized manner, she will give me something else to worry about. 'Tis the problems of child-rearing."

Kat wrung out the cloth she had used to clean his back. "I do not know the first thing about children, Brandon," she said softly, looking down at her fingers. "I have never been around them, except for Fenton. He never seemed to be young."

Brandon shifted in the tub so that he could look at her. Cupping her chin between his thumb and forefinger, he lifted her face to his. "You will make a most excellent mother." He kissed her tenderly on the lips.

Kat tried to stifle her sob, but he heard it. Drawing back, he searched her face. She kept her eyes downcast. She couldn't bear to see his disappointment when she told him the truth. 'Twas time he knew. Tomorrow was the wedding day—or maybe not.

"How now, sweet? What ails you?" he cajoled. Taking her hand, he kissed it. "Do not tell me you are a nervous bride."

Kat gazed fondly at his hand holding hers in such a natural way. How large and strong it was, yet how gentle! She had to tell him. Time had run out.

"I...I must confess something to you, Brandon, and I pray you will not think ill of me."

He nuzzled her cheek. "What could I possibly think, but good of you? Mmm, sweet," he whispered in her hair.

Ignoring the tingling ripples of delight coursing up and down her spine, Kat girded herself with resolve. Now or never. She could not pronounce her wedding vows with a lie in her heart.

"I am glad you have Belle and Francis, because I...I do not think I will be able to bear you a child."

Stopping his love play, he regarded her seriously.

God shield me! I was afraid of this! Never mind, say the rest, and be done with it. "In all the years of my marriage to Fitzhugh, I could never conceive, though he came often enough to my bed. I fear I may be barren." She chewed her lower lip.

Brandon's eyes turned a darker hue, though he said nothing. At least, he still held her hand.

Kat plunged ahead with a rush of words. "I overheard your father say that you wanted an heir, and I—"

Grasping the back of her head, Brandon pulled her toward him. He smothered the rest of her words with his lips over her mouth. She caught her breath at the flaming passion of his kiss. When he looked at her again, she saw a blue fire dance in his eyes.

"'Tis my father who craves an heir. Though he loves both his grandchildren by me, they are bastards." Brandon spat out the word, as if it burned him to hold it in his mouth. "My father desires a Cavendish male to carry on the family name and titles. Two nine-year-olds are more than a match for me." Reaching across to her, he traced his finger down Kat's cheek. "Forget whatever my father has said."

Kat's lips trembled. *I cannot weep now. I cannot show him how much I fear Sir Thomas's threat to stop the marriage.* "But the king comes tomorrow, and your lord father means to—"

Brandon placed his finger over her lips. "Shush! Let us not speak of the getting of children now, sweetheart. I much prefer the *making* of them."

He rose out of the tub, water cascading down his magnificent physique. His manhood stood boldly erect. Before Kat had a chance to say anything else, he swept her into his wet embrace. Her knees weakened as his mouth descended. He took her lips with a savage intensity. Her consciousness seemed to ebb and then flame more distinctly than before. Let supper wait! Let tomorrow wait!

Still kissing her, he carried her across the chamber to the bed, the same bed where they had first made love. His lips blazed a trail of hot kisses down her neck. The caress of his mouth across the tops of her breasts set her on fire. His hands slipped down into the gown's neckline, searching for her pleasure points. Kat whimpered and arched her back to meet him. His other hand moved under her skirts and explored her thighs. His fingers inched up, with deliberate slowness, to her center. His teasing touch sent currents of desire bolting through her. Her bodice grew too tight.

"Undo my laces," she panted as she cast her head back on the pillow. "I cannot breathe."

He continued his sweet, torturous stroking. "Is this gown a valued one?" he asked, nibbling her earlobe.

"Nay!" she gasped. She knew she would burst at any moment.

"Good," he murmured. Grasping a firm hold of the green lawn material, he ripped her dress down the middle. He untied the ribbons of her shift, then he pulled the neckline out to its widest extent, baring her breasts to him.

Lowering his head, his tongue tantalized the dusky pink buds of her nipples, which had swollen to their fullest. Under his stroking fingers and his tongue, her body ignited with liquid fire. A fury of passion and desire shook her. She abandoned herself to the sweeping whirl of unutterable sensations. A moan of ecstasy slipped through her lips.

"Now! Please!" she gasped, pulling him to her.

He moved over her, than lowered himself. She welcomed him joyously into her body. They seemed to melt together. Her world was filled with Brandon—only him. They moved together with exquisite harmony, soaring higher until they reached the peak of ultimate delight. She shattered into a million glowing stars. Groaning her name, Brandon found his release. His love flowed into her like warm honey. Holding to each other tightly, a cloak of contentment and peace enfolded them. Kat sighed with pleasant exhaustion.

Brandon caressed a lock of her hair, which tumbled over his arm in a copper cascade. "You are a wonder," he murmured.

Kat smiled, waiting for him to say the words she had so longed to hear. *Say it now! Tell me that you love me.*

"Kat, I—"

The door shook with a tremendous pounding. "My lord!" Mark called from the hall. "You must come quickly!"

Brandon dropped his head to her shoulder; his clean golden hair brushed against her cheek. "I will skin the knave alive, I vow it!" he growled softly in her ear. Then he sat up and shouted, "What the devil do you want?"

"Your lord father, with Sir Guy, and Sir John, request your presence most urgently, my lord."

Kat relaxed against the pillows and sighed. "You must go, my heart. I will delay supper." She kissed the back of his hand. "Your squire's voice is full of urgency."

Brandon blew an errant curl out of his eyes. "That whipster of mine has the devil for a timekeeper." He got off the bed, then pulled on the clean set of hose that Kat had placed on the stool by the tub.

Mark knocked again. "My lord?"

"Anon!" Brandon roared at his unseen squire. "And you'd best pray that the matter is a serious one." He donned his shirt.

"Aye, my lord," the youth replied. "Your father brought home Tod Wormsley from the forest. He's been wounded and near death."

Kat's eyes flew open. "Tod! Angels in heaven preserve him!" Clutching her ruined bodice, she got out of the bed.

"Amen to that!" Brandon thrust his feet into his leather boots, then tossed his doublet over one shoulder. He crossed to Kat's side and planted a gentle kiss on her forehead. "Take this mark as my pledge for a new gown." His eyes shone with a soft look when he smiled down at her. "You are the balm of my soul, sweetheart," he murmured. Then he was gone.

Kat fell back among the tumbled bedclothes. *What a shameless wanton that man has made of me! Aye! And I'd do all it again in a heartbeat.*

She placed her hand on the spot where he had lain beside her. The coverlet was damp and warm from his heat. She sighed deeply. *Katherine, you are the biggest fool God ever created.*

Mark led Brandon downstairs to the small alcove, then the squire withdrew to join the rest of the castle's inhabitants at a noisy supper in the adjoining hall. Sir Thomas, still attired in his hunting cloak and boots, drank deeply from a tankard. Guy and Jack, their hair damp from their baths, had serious expressions on their faces. They greeted Brandon in subdued tones.

Sir Thomas eyed his older son over his mug. "About time."

Brandon thrust his arms into his jacket sleeves. "How is the lad?" he asked, his fingers fumbling with his buttons.

"Lives," his father answered simply. He slammed his tankard onto the small table. "But he has lost a great deal of blood. That healer is with him now. She says tonight will tell his fate."

Brandon made the sign of the cross. "Pray God for his recovery."

The others followed suit.

"Amen to that!" Sir Thomas bristled as he looked at each of the younger men in turn. "He's a brave lad! Said that he swore to tell you, Stafford, that his master has lost his wits. Said that he is coming to the wedding and he hungers for your blood, Brandon." The eldest Cavendish glared at his son. "Does this drivel make any sense to you?"

Brandon curled back his lip. "Aye. 'Tis Fenton Scantling, Lady Katherine's nephew."

Sir Thomas's eyebrows shot up. "The same who shot Francis?"

Brandon made a fist behind his back. "Aye."

"Methought he had fled the district," his father barked. "Truly the man is a lackwit to stay."

"How the devil did he escape our search?" Jack asked.

The Earl of Thornbury snorted. "I found the boy hanging onto a tree limb. My squire took a look around. That poxy tree had a hollow center. William saw an arrow at the bottom of it, and a wealth of blood. 'Twas a miracle the boy could pull himself out of that hellhole!"

Guy whistled through his teeth. "No wonder we never found them!"

Sir Thomas waved the subject away. "'Tis tomorrow that burdens my mind. We must call the wedding off."

Brandon felt as if he had been slapped in the face. With his body still aglow from Kat's lovemaking, the last thing he intended to do was to let her go now, especially at his father's whim. "Nay," he replied steadily, staring directly at his father.

Sir Thomas's blue eyes glowered. "Listen to me, boy. We do not speak of the lady, 'tis your king you must now consider. His chamberlain sent word an hour ago that the royal party lodges at Hever, and will be here by ten o'clock tomorrow morning. We are not to begin the ceremony without the royal Robin Hood!"

"I will marry Kat, father, come hellfire and brimstone!"

Sir Thomas slammed his fist on the tabletop. "You will go to the devil soon enough, I warrant. You haven't heard two words that I've said, Brandon! This Scantling means to kill you in your wedding finery, and in full sight of the king. We cannot allow a madman with a crossbow near His Grace. Or you, for that matter."

Putting sweet Katherine aside, Brandon's mind considered the problem from a different point of view. "This bloody-mouthed cur will come in a disguise, methinks. One that will not draw attention."

Sir Thomas threw up his hands. "God's teeth! More masques! First, we have Robin Hood and Maid Marian, and Lord knows who else. Now we have a murderer dressed up as...what?''

Jack snapped his fingers. "As one of the villagers or farmers. Lady Kat wants to be married in the little church on the other side of the meadow, so that all her people can witness it. The chapel here is too small."

"But the chapel inside the castle is safer," Guy mused. "'Twould be better to move the ceremony there."

Sir Thomas looked pointedly at Brandon. "'Twould be better to dispense with it altogether. You know my thoughts on this matter."

Brandon gritted his teeth. "All too well, Father, but my mind is made up." He leaned across the table. "And I am much like you, sir. I have a very stubborn streak."

"Bah!" Sir Thomas strode out of the alcove.

Guy sank onto the bench. "One day you will try his patience too far, big brother."

"Aye, but that day has not yet come." Brandon straddled the stool and regarded his sibling. "Mark me, my friends! I have just been gifted with a most marvelous plan."

"I knew it!" Jack crowed. "When did you not have one or two plots up your sleeve, Brandon? What is our little game this time?"

"'Twill involve more disguising," he replied with a wicked gleam in his eyes.

Guy groaned. "As long as I do not have to dress up as a woman, I am ready for anything!"

Brandon chuckled. 'Twas one of his best ideas yet, if only Kat and the hapless squires would agree.

"Tonight, after the household is abed..."

A hand closed over Kat's mouth, startling her into wakefulness. Fenton! she thought, as she struggled to free herself from the bedclothes.

"Kat!" Brandon whispered in her ear. "'Tis I, sweetheart. You must be still."

Kat blinked as the last vestiges of sleep cleared from her eyes. Brandon smiled down at her, then kissed her nose. Was it morning already? It had taken Kat hours to fall asleep. And what was Brandon doing in her chamber? 'Twas very unlucky for the bridegroom to see his bride before the ceremony.

"Brandon! You should not be here!" she whispered.

He chuckled. "Aye, but events outpace us. We must be up and about early."

Beside her, Miranda jumped. Glancing at her bedmate, Kat saw Jack leaning over her. By the glow of the firelight, she made out the figure of Guy at the foot of the bed. All three men had the most devilish grins on their faces.

Kat pulled herself to a sitting position, then crossed her arms over her breasts. "What's amiss? Is this some sort of mischievous trick to play upon a bride before her wedding day? Truly, gentlemen, I am a bit too old for such games."

Brandon sat down on the bed beside her. "You are as youthful as eternal springtime, sweetheart, but there is more to this midnight visit than jests and tricks."

"'Tis midnight?" Miranda gasped, rubbing sleep from her eyes. "Crickets!"

"Shush, my love." Jack stopped her mouth with a kiss.

"'Tis the first hour of Midsummer's Day," Brandon crooned, running his hands along Kat's arms. "The dawn comes earliest this morn, so we must be about our business quickly."

Kat shivered under his touch but refused to give in to its suggestion. "So? Good morrow and goodbye, until we meet at the church door."

"My very words," Brandon continued in his soft, seductive voice. "I wish I could spend an hour or two discoursing with you, fair Katherine—you look passing sweet at this moment—''

Guy snapped his fingers several times. "Get on with it, Brandon! The cock will crow too soon."

"Then to the heart of the matter. You know that your nephew has taken a hearty dislike to me?"

Kat nodded. Brandon stroked her cheek, making it very difficult to concentrate on anything but his tempting presence.

"Wormsley has told us that Scantling means to kill me at the church door."

"Nay!" Kat put her hand to her mouth. "'Tis too wicked!"

"He must have lost his wits," Miranda gasped.

"My thoughts exactly, ladies." Brandon grew more serious. "I promise you, this will not happen. I will not put you into any kind of danger, sweet Katherine."

The devil take him! Brandon and his craven friends were going to run away, leaving her at the church door. "Was this your idea or your father's?" she asked coldly.

Brandon knotted his brows together. "My father has nothing to do with this, Kat. He wishes to call the wedding off."

"And isn't that what you are doing this minute—slipping out of a marriage you do not want? At least, you have the decency to say goodbye before you sneak out of here like a thief in the night."

Leaning over, Brandon whispered in her ear. "If we were alone, and not in such a hurry, I would prove to you how much I want to slip *into* this marriage, my sweet."

Kat's skin tingled all over.

"About it, man!" Jack snorted impatiently. "The long and the short of it is this, Kat. Your elderly priest stands waiting now in your chapel to bind you and my silver-tongued friend here in holy matrimony."

She must be dreaming, Kat thought.

Brandon chuckled. "Ah, Jack of Hearts, you have such a way with women. But he speaks the truth, Kat. 'Tis Midsummer's Day, and by royal command—and by my heart—I will wed you in holy mother church."

"But what of later this morning?" Kat glanced at Jack and Guy. She wasn't dreaming. "What of the king?"

"My first thought is to make you well and truly my wife," Brandon continued, his gaze speaking volumes in blue. "Later?" He chuckled under his breath. "The king is not the only one to play a part. We have devised a mummery that will catch out the villain. Afterward, if you want to be married again, we can do that, too."

Kat tried to read past his laughing expression but couldn't. "You are marrying me to defy your father?"

Guy groaned. "Was there ever such a cautious woman? You offer her honorable marriage, and she questions you like a judge! Let's do this the old-fashioned way. Just pick her up, Brandon, throw her over your shoulder, and carry her to the chapel as is! Jack can bring the maid of honor."

"Coz! They have gone stark, staring mad—or else drunk too much wine!" Miranda tried to pull the sheet up to her chin, but Jack refused to let her.

"Nay, my love," Jack whispered. "We are stone sober, and in serious earnest." He pulled back the covers from both women.

Brandon stood, then held out his hand to Kat. "Will you marry me, sweet Katherine?"

He means it! Now! And I still do not know what is in his heart. I will not go into yet another marriage without love. I'd rather die!

She pulled her hand out of his. "Nay, I cannot," she whispered, blinking back her tears.

Chapter Twenty-Two

Brandon looked as if he had been struck. "'Tis my father. What bribe did he offer to you to reject me?"

Kat stuck out her chin. "None. 'Tis my own choice."

Brandon drew himself up to his full height. The light from the fire made him look even taller. The only sound heard in the chamber was the pop and hiss of the logs in the grate.

"Very well, Lady Katherine." He drew out his words slowly. "I thank you very much for your...hospitality, and I wish you a pleasant good-night. But, before I leave Bodiam, will you please tell me what it is about me that so revolts you?"

Kat gasped. She could sense, rather than see, the barely controlled power that was coiled in his body. She wanted to touch him, but he had moved out of range. *One wrong word, and you will lose him forever. Is this what you truly want?*

She leveled her gaze at him. "I cannot marry a man who does not love me."

"Doesn't love...?" Brandon seemed to collapse within himself. "Of course, I love you, you little idiot!" he roared when he recovered the full command of his voice. He plucked her out of the bed and shook her. "What makes you think I don't? Haven't I shown you my love time and again? What of this afternoon before supper? What about the moat?''

Kat gaped at him. "The moat?" she echoed.

"Aye, that foul, stinking, puking, green-slimed moat! Do you think I'd ever consider cleaning it out if I didn't love you?''

Kat gazed at him, hardly daring to believe her ears. "You love me?" she asked softly. "For me alone? Not my lands? Not my estate? Not for childbearing? Not to spite your father? Just me?''

He crushed her against his chest. Under his doublet, she felt the rapid beating of his heart, as if he had been running very hard. Then he set her on her feet on the cold floor. He went down on one knee before her.

"Before God, and before these grinning witnesses, I, Brandon Thomas Cavendish, do swear upon my sword that I love you, Lady Katherine Fitzhugh, with all my heart and soul until my dying breath. Furthermore, I will cherish you, protect you and be faithful to you alone all my life. Will you please marry me now, before the priest in the chapel falls asleep?''

Kat could not keep her tears from spilling down her cheeks. "Aye, Brandon, I will." She looked around for her robe, but it had disappeared among the bedclothes. "Give us a few moments. Miranda and I must dress first.''

With a growl, Brandon grabbed her and threw her over his shoulder. "Why bother? 'Twill take only a few minutes, then I'll have you back between the sheets in no time.''

Guy opened the door. "That's the spirit! I like to see the old customs kept up.''

Kat thumped Brandon on the back as he carried her down the corridor. "Put me down!" she whispered just as they passed the senior Cavendish's door.

Brandon patted her bottom as he bounded down the stairs. ''In due time, my love!''

Behind them, Kat saw that Jack cradled Miranda in his arms. Not fair! *She* was wrapped in his woolen cloak, and her cousin didn't seem to mind this midnight abduction in the least.

Within five minutes, Kat found herself standing barefoot and in her shift in front of old Father Robert. Her only ornaments were the blue ribbons that tied the neck and sleeves of her flimsy garment. Beside her, Brandon blazed brightly in his blue satin doublet with gold trim, white satin slashing on his sleeves, and his black-and-white-striped hose. Her unbound hair hung about her shoulders, without even a veil to cover her head in the house of the Lord. Kat stared at her toes in shame.

Brandon lifted her chin with a gentle touch. ''I love you so much, sweet Kat, that I will marry you in your smock, and I will still assume your debts, if you have any.''

Startled, she looked up at him, He winked at her. Married in her shift! 'Twas an ancient but still honorable way for a maiden to be wedded. Still, poor Sondra had worked so hard on her gown—two of them, in fact.

Just then Father Robert began the marriage ceremony. Brandon took her cold hand in his and squeezed it. She relaxed against him. When the moment came to pledge him her troth, she did so with all her heart. His hand shook a little when he placed his thick golden band around her left ring finger. His kiss was long and lingering.

After the brief ceremony, Brandon wrapped his blue velvet cloak around her, then swept her into his arms with much more tenderness than before. The three witnesses signed the marriage register, Guy paid a golden angel to the yawning priest, then everyone stole back upstairs. Less than ten minutes had elapsed.

Instead of returning Kat to her room, Brandon went farther down the hall to the chamber Kat had come to regard as "theirs." A single candle burned on the table beside the bed, and a pitcher of wine with two goblets stood with it. The fresh sheets were turned back invitingly.

"I see that Jack arranged things well," Brandon murmured in her ear. "He is ever the romantic."

After another kiss, much more lingering than the one they had shared before Father Robert, Brandon quickly shed his finery. Then he lifted the white lawn shift from Kat.

"Sweetheart, my *love*, you are a feast for my eyes, and my soul!" So saying, he swept her up into his arms. Together they fell back on the bed.

"By the book!" A dozen thorns pricked Kat's backside.

Uttering a string of oaths, the like of which Kat had rarely heard, Brandon hopped out of the bed, then pulled off the covers. The bottom sheet was strewn with several dozen roses from the garden, all with their thorns intact. A small note lay among them. Snatching it up, Brandon held it under the candle.

> "Joy upon your wedding night, Papa and Kat!
> Your loving daughter,
> LaBelle Maria Cavendish"

Sitting on the edge of the bed, Kat laughed until her sides ached, while Brandon swept the sheets clear of Belle's gifts.

"How did she know your intent?" Kat asked much, much later as she lay next to her most loving husband.

Brandon chuckled low in the back of his throat. "I did warn you, my Lady Cavendish. Sometimes methinks our beloved daughter is a faerie changeling!"

Midsummer's Day dawned in brilliant sunshine. "King's weather," Sondra called it. High up in the north tower, where they had hidden themselves in Jack's room,

Kat and Miranda watched the wedding feast being laid out by Montjoy, Philippe and the kitchen servants.

"Do you think we shall get to eat any of that?" Miranda asked with longing. She and Kat had had only some bread and cheese brought up to them by Jess.

Kat didn't care. She still wafted on the cloud of her wedding night with Brandon. Only an hour ago, she had slipped back into her room, hurriedly dressed in her plain gray wool gown, while Brandon again donned his blue satin clothing. After a soft knock, Jess had entered, followed by Mark, Christopher and Sondra. The squires looked far from happy. Sondra, on the other hand, had positively glowed with suppressed excitement.

"'Twill be the talk of the shire for a decade," the housekeeper had chortled, arranging the two identical wedding gowns over the bed. "Hurry now, Lady Kat."

Brandon gave her another kiss, followed by a wink.

"Take care, my love," Kat whispered. The seriousness of his undertaking had hit her with full force, when she saw the gowns that she and Miranda would never wear.

"Aye," he said as he kissed her again. "I have not finished with you yet, my *love*."

Jess had spread out an old gray cloak on the floor. Brandon helped her lie down on one end. Just before he rolled her up in it, he whispered, "I love you, my lady wife."

The cloak muffled Kat's answer. The next minute, Jess had thrown her over his shoulder like a grain sack, and had carried her out of the chamber. Though she couldn't see his progress, she knew that the huntsman took her to the north tower. There she and Miranda were to remain until Fenton had been apprehended.

Jess hummed to himself as he made ready to leave.

"Joy on *your* wedding day, Jess," Kat remembered to tell him. "And mind that you tell Sondra that you love her."

"Aye, my Lady Cavendish." He grinned widely. "She

hasn't let me forget it.'' With a jaunty whistle, Jess departed.

Lady Cavendish! The mere name gave Kat goose bumps of delight. Miranda, cloaked and hooded, joined her ten minutes later.

'''Tis very strange to be an observer at one's own wedding,'' Kat murmured, watching as the villagers gathered on the greensward beyond the freshly flowing moat.

''And mine, I hope,'' Miranda murmured. Kat hugged her.

Scanning the crowd, Kat wondered if Fenton was really down there. It had cut her to the quick to learn he had been Brandon's attacker, and was also the one who had left Tod for dead. Thank God, the youth had survived the night. Sondra assured her that the boy would recover in due time. It relieved her to see so many of the men-at-arms dressed as commoners and standing among the people.

A hunting horn sounded beyond the wood. Miranda dug her nails into Kat's arm.

''Do you think 'tis the king?'' she asked with a thrill in her voice. ''I have never seen him before.''

''Nor I,'' Kat replied. She watched the crest of the rise.

The horn sounded again, then over the hill the most splendid company of outlaws rode down toward Bodiam.

Kat clasped the brooch pinned to her simple bodice. '''Tis he in the flesh!''

A large man astride a gleaming chestnut warhorse came to a halt before the causeway. He was dressed in the traditional Lincoln green from feather to boot, and wore a black mask over his eyes. Even so, his reddish gold beard and his regal bearing were unmistakable. The many rings on his fingers flashed in the sunlight.

Lady Alicia, acting on behalf of Kat, came forward and greeted the king and his company of a dozen or so courtiers.

"That must be the Lady Anne Boleyn." Kat pointed to the only woman in the company. She was dressed in a simple gown made up in shades of brown, orange and gold. The materials appeared to be satin, damask and velvet. A flower wreath circled her head and her dark brown hair fell unbound almost to her waist.

Miranda made the sign against the evil eye. "They say she is a witch," she whispered.

"Be still, Miranda! You've been listening to too many of Sondra's tales. Oh, no! There goes Sir Thomas straight to the king. I'll wager he hopes to put aside the match."

Miranda giggled. "He is too late!"

Kat sighed, remembering the past few hours. "Aye, I am now properly wedded and bedded. But I hate to begin my marriage incurring the wrath of that old man. I liked him in the beginning, and his wife, Lady Alicia, is delightful."

Tapping her on the shoulder, Miranda pointed. "Speaking of the lady, look! She is pulling Sir Thomas back, and the king is laughing."

Both women jumped as a fanfare of horns sounded from the parapet just outside their door. The crowd set up a roar as two tall figures, both clad completely in jousting armor, walked in step with each other over the causeway toward the king.

"Who?" Miranda looked at Kat.

A slow smile flitted across Kat's lips. "Unless I am gravely mistaken, yonder are our knights. Few men are as tall as they, and I spy Guy Cavendish over there next to his wife."

Miranda wrinkled her brows. "But why armor without horses, and with their visors lowered? None can tell which from which!"

"Clever, clever!" Kat leaned farther out the window. "That is the whole point, good coz. Fenton will not know whom to shoot! And their armor will protect them, if he does.''

"He wouldn't dare! Not with the king at hand!"

Kat grew more serious. "Aye, methinks Fenton's mind has gone so far over the brink that he has become quite mad, and does not know a hawk from a handsaw."

Another fanfare blared from the castle wall.

"Now who?" Miranda asked, craning her neck. "Leaping trout, Kat! Look! They are wearing our gowns."

Two veiled figures, one on each side of Montjoy, glided over the causeway. Sondra's masterpieces elicited cries of pleasure and applause from the gathered crowd. The king roared with laughter, his deep voice carrying up to the tower window. As the figures turned toward the king, Kat saw their backs. She giggled.

"No wonder Mark and Christopher looked much out of sorts this morning! Methinks they are the blushing bride and her handmaiden. See? The bodices are not laced up all the way. The squires' shoulders are much broader than ours."

The veiled squires both executed deep, though wobbly, curtsies to the king, and another one to the mysterious knights. Montjoy, stiff with decorum, managed to support the youths. Then one of the knights stepped forward, bowed from the waist as much as his armor permitted, and offered his arm to one of the "ladies." The second knight followed suit with the other "lady." Thus paired, the couples began to proceed toward the little country church that nestled beyond the meadow.

"Oh!" Miranda began. "They will be out of sight soon, and then we will not see—"

Suddenly everything happened at once. A shout from the crowd on the left drew their attention. At the same time, one of the knights stumbled, then fell forward. The two "ladies" dropped to the ground much quicker than a normal lady could. The remaining knight drew his sword and advanced toward the disturbance among the spectators. Just then, the king's hat, festooned with fine pheasant's feathers, flew off his head and landed far beyond the outer ring of the gathering. Many women screamed at once.

Kat, watching with rising horror, fixed her eyes on the fallen knight. Ice enveloped her heart. Not Brandon!

"What has happened!" Miranda gasped, watching the scene below erupt into a seething, boiling mass of people.

Dashing across the room, Kat yanked open the chamber door. "I know only one thing, Miranda. 'Tis your lord or mine that is down, and I will be at his side come rack or ruin."

She ran down the spiral stairs, her skirts billowing out as she went. Miranda clattered behind her. With each step, Kat stormed heaven with her prayers. *I love him! I love him! Dear God, please do not make me a widow, before my wedding day is done!*

The day started well enough for Sir Fenton Scantling. He had enjoyed a good night's sleep in a tenant farmer's cottage. The murders of the peasant and his family did not weigh upon his conscience any more than did that of Wormsley. What were they, but expendable clods? By the time their bodies were discovered under a pile of hay, Fenton would be master of Bodiam. 'Twould be an ironic jest to initiate an investigation of their foul end!

The farmer's clothing, stale and stinking, fit well enough, and a plain brown cloak covered the crossbow. After a good breakfast, Fenton loaded up his double bow with two arrows. Two shots—one for Cavendish, and one for Aunt Kat. Why not? Why wait years for her to die before he could inherit the estate?

After that, while the jabbering villagers clustered around the fallen bridal pair—united in death; how tragic!—he would slip into the castle through the garden gate, where a change of clothing in his chamber would turn him into

Sir Fenton Scantling, the grieving nephew. As the new master of Bodiam Castle, he would demand full justice for this unhappy affair. Fenton snickered as he cut through the forest. The plan was too perfect!

Rounding the huge oak, Fenton slapped the trunk. "Sleeping well, Wormsley?" He chortled at his own joke, then hurried on.

As he had anticipated, the villagers and folk from miles around had already gathered on the greensward. Banners hung from the castle and waved in the light summer's breeze. Under a cluster of oaks, long trestle tables waited for the wedding feast. Minions from the castle ran back and forth with covered dishes and platters. Fenton sniffed the mouthwatering aromas. A pity that all that food would go to waste! Nay! When he took command of the tragic scene, he would offer the cooked meats and pastries to the crowd. That would keep everyone occupied, while the bodies were carried away.

Fenton chose a spot with the sun behind him. Good view for him, and poor for anyone else seeking the origin of his arrows. Holding his bow under his cloak, Fenton relaxed and waited.

The arrival of the king proved to be the first nick in his well-laid plan. What the devil was Great Harry doing here, in the middle of nowhere? And why were he and his closest friends dressed up like foresters of an earlier age?

"Greetings, good people!" The king acknowledged the crowd. "I am Robin Hood, and have heard of your festivities this day. Fair Maid Marian and I, and many of my men, have traveled far from Sherwood Forest to bring the happy couple good luck upon their wedding day!"

The gabbling mob cheered. *Geese!* Fenton curled his lip.

A woman whom he did not recognize, but dressed very richly in cloth of gold and green satin, curtsied and welcomed the royal arrivals. Fenton took a deep breath to steady his nerves. No matter if the king was here. 'Twould make a better diversion for him. No one would cast a second glance at a lowly farmer on the edge of the crowd.

Then an older knight stepped forward. A pox on it! 'Twas the Earl of Thornbury, Brandon's father! Fenton recognized the snarling wolf's head the man wore on his surcoat.

"Good Robin Hood!" the old man called, raising his voice above the din. "A word with you, I pray!"

The king laughed heartily, and his courtiers joined in his mirth. "How now, my lord? Methinks I spy the father of the bridegroom!"

The crowd cheered again. Fenton curled his lip again with disgust.

"Good Robin," the old man continued. "My son entertains second thoughts about this marriage."

The king waved away the idea. "All bridegrooms have second thoughts on their wedding morning. 'Tis natural, eh?" he asked the crowd.

The people cheered and applauded. Then the lady dragged Sir Thomas back to the side, speaking rapidly in his ear. Cavendish's wife, Fenton surmised. They will have much on their minds anon.

The second nick in his plan happened just then, when the trumpets from the castle announced the entrance of the bridegroom. Fenton started, when he saw two knights in brilliant armor cross the causeway. What scurvy, shag-eared, knavish trick was this? With their visors lowered, how could he tell which one was which? Could he reload and fire a second set of bolts? No time.

While Fenton mulled over this problem, the third nick appeared. The horns sounded again, and two veiled ladies made their entrance, escorted by that crow in satin hose, Montjoy. The crowd, always eager for a new sport, shouted their approval.

Which one! Whom should he shoot first? When? This was not what he had planned. 'Twas not fair!

Fenton slipped his finger to the first trigger pin. He must make his decision in the next few seconds, or all would be for naught! One of the knights stepped forward and took the first lady's hand. It had to be Aunt Kat and Cavendish, though Fenton did not recall his aunt being as tall as the lady who now grasped the knight's arm. Perchance she wore a pair of those high-heeled pantofles, so that her slippers would not get muddy when she walked across the meadow to the church.

Do it now! Now! Now! Something inside his head buzzed, as if an angry bee had flown into his ear. Must do it now!

In one swift move, Fenton lifted the crossbow and fired the first bolt. The knight crumpled. Next to Fenton, a woman screamed. For a split second, he was tempted to send the second bolt through her. No time! No time! Shoot!

Someone pushed against him as he pulled the second trigger. Fenton had no idea where the arrow flew. At that moment, someone wrenched the weapon out of his hands. He felt a blow from behind, and his knees gave way under him.

Nay! This can't be happening! 'Tis not supposed to be this way! Fenton fell to the ground. The buzzing grew louder in his ears. Then it stopped.

King Henry heard the whine of the first arrow. Horrified, he saw one of the knights collapse. Flee! his brain prompted him. *A traitor is in the crowd!* The king fought to control his horse, which pranced to the side as the people suddenly surged forward. A second arrow sang through the air. For one long, terrible moment Henry saw it aimed squarely at his head. It came on and on, its razor-sharp barb pointed directly between his eyes, like the finger of an avenging god. As a terrified rabbit cornered by a fox, the king of England discovered that he could not move, nor utter a sound. Then the bolt skimmed over his head, taking his green velvet cap with it in its flight.

The sights and sounds of the moment swirled back into focus. The king's voice worked again. "Arrest that man!" he bellowed. "He is the wickedest varlet that ever chewed with a tooth!" Henry wheeled his horse, then reined in the frightened animal.

The crowd parted, as one of the knights dragged a half-conscious man into the clearing. He dropped the felon on the ground before the king, then raised his visor and saluted his monarch. A wave of relief washed over Henry when he recognized Brandon Cavendish.

"The traitor, your grace." Brandon poked the villain with his steel-clad foot.

"God's death, 'tis Lord Scantling!" The king eyed the shaking man. "A pox upon you! You are not worthy to have your name repeated."

The miserable cur, dressed in common garb, attempted to pull himself into a kneeling position. Blood ran from a cut on his head, and his face showed the marks of many blows.

"Mercy, your grace," the wretch burbled. "My arm was jostled. I did not mean to aim at you, but—"

"Rogue!" the king roared. "You have lived too long! Away with him!" he ordered his shaken bodyguards. "This vermin offends my sight. We shall meet again, Scantling—in the Tower of London."

At this pronouncement, the traitor fell forward into a gibbering heap. The guards hauled him away, the miserable wretch's heels scoring two furrows through the grass as he went.

"Lock him in the dankest cell you can find," the king called after the departing men. Let him drink sewage until doomsday! Henry thought to himself, as he waited for his heart to stop pounding. Sir Brandon bowed, then turned into the pressing crowd.

Lady Anne rode to the king's side. "Your grace? Are you well?" she asked, her large dark eyes made even wider by her fear.

Henry smiled fondly at her. "Aye, my love, I am. God has preserved me from such a miserable end."

Leaning over her saddle, she took his hand in hers. "England would be lost without you, sire, and so would I."

Henry regarded her, then nodded. "You speak the truth, my dear."

Kat pushed her way through the crowd to the fallen knight. The feathered end of the arrow protruded between his breastplate and the shoulder guard. Both squires had thrown off their veils and were attempting to crawl toward the injured man, but the long skirts of the gowns impeded their movements. The other knight had plunged into the crowd, seeking the source of the attack.

Kat dropped to her knees beside the knight. "My lord, my love! Dearest Brandon, are you in much pain?"

A deep chuckle welled up from inside the knight's helm. "I thank you for your sweet words, Kat, but you shower them on the wrong man. As for me, 'tis but a scratch. Where is that rascal squire of mine? A plague on this armor! I cannot get up!"

Kat didn't know whether to laugh or cry at Jack's assurances. She glanced at the struggling squires. Truly 'twas comical to see them flailing about in volumes of skirts and petticoats. "Miranda, 'tis Jack who is in need of your assistance. He'll prefer your healing touch to mine. I'll help Mark and Christopher, before they rip up Sondra's handiwork."

Miranda descended upon Jack like an anxious butterfly. Stifling her laughter, Kat untied Mark's laces, then she turned to help Christopher.

"Methinks you should keep them in their skirts, sweetheart. They make very pretty girls, indeed!"

Kat whirled around to find a large knight in armor towering over her. She resisted her impulse to throw herself into his arms, at least, until after he had shed his gleaming scales.

"You are looking well, my lord," she remarked demurely, as Mark unbuckled Brandon's helm, then lifted it off his master.

Brandon shook his hair out of his eyes. He inhaled a deep breath. "'Tis a fine morning for a marriage, my lady, and we have a goodly number of friends and family who have come to see us wedded—including Robin Hood and his court. Do you suppose you would mind marrying me again?" He grinned down at her.

Kat curtsied, spreading the skirts of her plain gray gown. "'Twould be a pleasure, my lord, considering that Robin Hood looks a little impatient."

Brandon lowered his head to whisper in her ear. "After such a fright, our royal lord is impatient to *eat*. He keeps eyeing the wedding feast." Brandon cocked his head. "By my troth, Kat, your lips look as if they are waiting for a kiss."

She stood on tiptoe. "They are, my love."

Kat felt his lips feather-touch hers like a whisper. She quivered at his sweet tenderness.

"Sweet Saint Anne, Papa! Say your vows again, and be done with it!" Belle stood a few feet away from the happy couple, her blue eyes sparkling with excitement. "Let us marry everyone off, so that we may start the feasting and games!"

Brandon sighed against Kat's lips before he drew away. He regarded his daughter with a stern expression. "Aye, but before we do, Mistress Long-ears, let us discuss the matter of a bed of roses with the sharpest thorns in England."

Belle stared right back at her imposing father, then rubbed her nose. "Philippe has made a mountain of tansy cakes, with mint cream," she replied, wisely choosing to ignore the question. "And Francis says he will eat them all!"

Brandon shook his head with defeat. "Then by all means, we shall hasten to the church, so that you may get your share of the tansy cakes."

"Good!" Belle whirled away with a flurry of blue skirts, yelling as she went. "Francis Bardolph, stop eating those at once! Papa says they are mine! Francis, do you hear me? I hope you puke!"

Brandon chuckled as he took Kat's hand in his. "Welcome to the Cavendish family, lady wife."

Kat hugged him, armor and all. "You do not know how glad I am to be a part of it, my husband!"

Epilogue

Wolf Hall, Northumberland
November 1530

"What's this?" Sir Thomas Cavendish stared down at the dish his page had just set before him.

Lady Alicia covered her smile behind her napkin. "Roasted crow, I believe," she replied with a straight face.

Sir Thomas's gray brows rose up his forehead. "How now? Crow? Has our larder sunk so low that we must dine upon crow?" He poked at the bird with the tip of his eating knife.

Lady Alicia maintained a bland exterior though inside she quaked with mirth. "Nay, my good lord. 'Tis a fowl I especially ordered for you today. You'll like it. 'Tis stuffed with sage, onion and rosemary—for remembrance," she added pointedly.

He sawed at one of the legs with a distasteful expression on his face. "Explain, please. What have I forgotten this time?"

"Your manners, for one thing." Lady Alicia pulled out a packet from her deep sleeve. "I received a long letter from Bodiam Castle this morning."

"Humph!" Sir Thomas chewed the morsel thoughtfully.

"Brandon is pleased to announce that Kat is with child."

Sir Thomas swallowed loudly, slurped a large mouthful of wine and then stared at his smiling wife.

"A child? When?"

Lady Alicia's smile broadened. 'Twas such a pleasure to tease her husband, and this time he certainly deserved it. "In March, at the coming of spring."

Sir Thomas regarded her solemnly. "Pass the mustard, my love," he requested in a softer tone. He took another mouthful of the burnt crow. "I acted badly with Katherine, didn't I?" he mumbled through the mustard and meat.

"Aye, you did," Lady Alicia agreed.

"Never even gave her a wedding present, did I?"

"I don't believe so, my sweet."

Sir Thomas gnawed on a scrawny wing. "I suppose she would not mind it too much if I sent her a little something now, do you think?"

Lady Alicia patted the letter. "I should think a rather large something might be more appropriate, like a service in silver and gold, perchance?"

Sir Thomas slathered more mustard on the crow. "My thoughts exactly! A large something, indeed." He munched some more, then asked, "And I suppose that a letter of apology is in order, as well?"

Lady Alicia smiled, then nodded. "A very long letter."

"I shall write it immediately after dinner," he proclaimed. Then he added, "You know, this crow isn't half bad with a lot of mustard—and seasoned with contrition."

Leaning toward him, Lady Alicia whispered in his ear. "And I have ordered your favorite for the sweet course—tansy cake."

Sir Thomas's face broke into a boyish grin. "With mint cream?" he asked hopefully.

"Is it served any other way, my love?" Lady Alicia replied.

* * * * *

Author Note

Bodiam Castle in East Sussex is owned and operated by the National Trust of Great Britain. Built in the fourteenth century, Bodiam today is a hollow but romantic shell of its former glory. Despite its ruined condition, visitors can still sit on the window seat of the great hall, climb the curved stairs to the battlements and peer out the window of Kat's second-floor bedroom, located in the southern square tower. The moat, now filled with water lilies, still laps against the outer walls of the castle.

I am deeply indebted to Francie Owens, a docent at the Folger Shakespeare Library, for her expertise in Tudor herbs and remedies.

I hope you have enjoyed Brandon and Kat's story. Please write, I love to hear from my readers. My address is: PO Box 10703, Burke, VA 22015-0703.

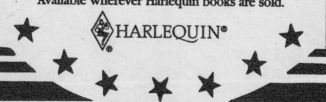

Welcome to *Love Inspired*™

A brand-new series of contemporary inspirational love stories.

Join men and women as they learn valuable lessons about facing the challenges of today's world and about life, love and faith.

**Look for the following June 1998
Love Inspired™ titles:**

SUDDENLY DADDY
by Loree Lough

IN GOD'S OWN TIME
by Ruth Scofield

NEVER ALONE
by Lyn Cote

Available in retail outlets in May 1998.

LIFT YOUR SPIRITS AND GLADDEN YOUR HEART
with *Love Inspired!*™

**Steeple
Hill**™

1698

From the high seas to the
Scottish Highlands,
when a man of action
meets a woman of spirit
a battle of wills—
and love—ensues!

Ransomed Brides

This June, bestselling authors Patricia Potter and
Ruth Langan will captivate your imagination with this
swashbuckling collection. Find out how two men of action
are ultimately tamed by two feisty women who prove
to be *more* than their match in love and war!

SAMARA by Patricia Potter

HIGHLAND BARBARIAN
by Ruth Langan

Available wherever Harlequin and Silhouette
books are sold.

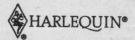 

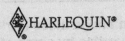

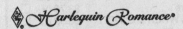

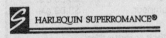

Don't miss these Harlequin favorites by some of our bestselling authors!